LAST ONE HOME

BOOKS BY JOHN EHLE

Fiction

Last One Home
The Winter People
The Changing of the Guard
The Journey of August King
Time of Drums
The Road
The Land Breakers
Lion on the Hearth
Kingstree Island
Move Over, Mountain

Nonfiction

The Cheeses and Wines of England and France,
with Notes on Irish Whiskey
The Free Men
Shepherd of the Street
The Survivor

Last One Home

John Ehle

1817

HARPER & ROW, PUBLISHERS, New York
Cambridge, Philadelphia, San Francisco, London
Mexico City, São Paulo, Sydney

To Lil Meredith
and Frank Forsyth

FIRST EDITION

Designer: Jane Weinberger

Library of Congress Cataloging in Publication Data

Ehle, John, date
  Last one home.

  I. Title.
PS3555.H5L3   1984   813'.54   84-47567
ISBN 0-06-015337-7

---

84 85 86 87 88 10 9 8 7 6 5 4 3 2 1

47019

CONTENTS

Last one home sleeps in the broken bed.
                    —Mountain saying

I am all the daughters of my father's house, and
all the brothers too—and yet I know not.
                    —Shakespeare, *Twelfth Night*

PART ONE
Youth

One

He was named after a prominent Virginia family. His mother had read about the Pinkneys in a copy of the Asheville *Gazette*. The name, she explained, was as if sent by God, but his father contended at the time that it was unlikely for God to be found using the Asheville newspaper, or anything else in Asheville, for that matter.

Of course, the boy came to be called Pink. His birth date was December 10, 1881, so he was under Sagittarius. He survived the usual childhood diseases, attended school each spring and fall, sat in the drafty building, the church, which served the school needs, on a hard wooden bench listening to the pastor, Mr. Murdock, ramble on about God's mercies, which he had labeled in groups of seven, that being, he said, God's number. One of the Ruffins, a neighbor, claimed that the pastor could count only to seven: "That was as far as he ever could go, and he went there ever' week."

This little Pinkney, here on the second bench, a delightful face, a pretty child, indeed, with something like a rosebud of a mouth when he squints at his books. "Little Pink, tell us the first batch of God's gifts to us. What did you say? What did Pink say? Say it louder. Yes, yes indeed, the world around us. That's the answer, Pink. The world around us, and its round beauty, generosity, its sweetness, so that your father can break open the surface of his land in the spring and plant seed, and they will push sprouts up here directly, will grow according to their kind, so that he will have a field of corn, or a field or rye or wheat or a garden space full of sweet potatoes, just as he pleases, or he can put a male and female pig in a pen and they will produce pork, given a few months' time, or he can take his long rifle and go into the mountains all about, rising like the walls of castles, and on the far reaches he can shoot himself a grouse or deer, a turkey or bear, a coon or rabbit, and bring it home for the stew pot. Put a piece of venison in the pot with a few carrots and onions, children, add a speck of salt, then put the best pod of red pepper and a clove of garlic, if you have one, then let it stew in cider, good apple cider taken from a fresh keg, and let it stew for three hours before tasting it. You need no flour to thicken it. Nobody loves a potato more than I do, but don't add potatoes to a venison stew. Just cook the dish as I told you." He paused to consider the startled faces of his trusts, children of ages six to sixteen, all dressed in homemade clothes turned out of cloth woven by the women of the family from flax and wool, their hands scrubbed clean with creek water and home-made lye soap, their eyes bright even in this dark church. That was the way he taught, his mind drifting from one item to another, never wandering far away from food. He was a talking cookbook, as the boy Pink came to realize, with a religious flavor. The living Christ was as dear as any dish on the table, the best cook and the best Christian overlapped in his own mind and lectures. "Now Pink here, he is his father's son. We all know his father from our visits to his store, and seeing him on the road and in church. Pink is a little boy, but he will become like his father and older brothers, Harry and Wurth, and his sisters. He will look like them, talk the same way, use the same words and expressions, write the same. Pink, are you listening? You seem to be staring out the window. Something out there attracts you, does it?" Even his criticisms were soft and gently formed, without sharpness anywhere. He knitted together all problems in his life into a ball.

Pink defended him at home. His father was the storekeeper and principal landowner in this valley, and he had a first vote in matters of the church and school. Perhaps he would have sent Mr. Murdock on his way years ago, except that his sons were friends of the pastor—Wurth, then Harry, and now Pink.

Pink measured up to every test, those in school for reading, writing, and arithmetic, and the seriously considered tests required for acceptance as a man, which had to do with riding a horse, hoeing rows of corn, rows that were almost endless there in the bottoms that the Wrights planted along the river; plowing, using the type of horses that the Wrights had brought into the mountains generations earlier; repairing wagons; making liquor; smoking hams; fishing for the brown trout in the river and the speckled and brook trout in the streams; hunting, and this had to do with such simple affairs as shooting rabbits on Thanksgiving morning, or shooting a few doves or quail or grouse or pheasant, enough for a meal, or shooting coons in the chicken yard, or shooting foxes or trapping them in the trap set by the creek—one could sometimes lure a gray fox but never a red one, which was smarter than a man, the preacher, Mr. Murdock, claimed—and included deer hunting whenever the deer came down as far as the road, which was often enough, and then, too, there were the bear, to be hunted whenever a boy felt that he was old enough. No woman ever shot a bear, no girl was ever expected to shoot one, but a boy ought to decide to shoot a bear.

Pink was equipped for a hunt when he was sixteen. He was given a rifle of his own. Not every boy had that, but not every boy's family was as wealthy as the Wrights. He was taken up to the ridge that separated North Carolina and Tennessee; there he camped out with the men for the first half of a night, then without sleep was led through black forests, dark as a coal hopper, bumping into trunks of trees, slipping off rocks, listening to the growls and barks of dogs, the curses of the older men, until at last the finder dog let out a call. Once the bear was treed, Pink was led through the woods to the spot and lanterns were lit, were held up as the men waded in among the howling dogs. High in the tree an animal's eyes reflected back the lights, and on order Pink fired, his new rifle jarring his shoulder, almost knocking him to the ground. He steadied himself as the dogs, silent now, stood guard, and then high in the tree he heard the sound of limbs breaking, the cracks and groans of the tree as the bear descended: he saw the dogs pull back a ways and heard limbs break just above his head, and the bear fell with a plop on the ground, dead. It was a young bear, a small one. Soon Pink went off to himself—this was when dawn was breaking—found a quiet place and allowed tears to roll down his face. The preacher came along, said he was looking for water to drink. He paused for a moment, put his hand on the boy's, the first time he had ever touched him, then put his arm around him and held him for a little while, without uttering criticism, either of the boy or of the hunt, or of the family or the local rites.

As Pink grew up, he became less and less like either of his brothers—Harry, who was four years older, or Wurth, who was six years older. Harry was the more adventuresome; he was an avid hunter and explorer, and also, even at an early age, was enamored of women. Being of the valley's wealthy family, he could afford to court daughters of the poorer families, among whom fathers were ambitious and dowries were skimpy, courted girls in several mountain families, and there were those who contended that his first long trip away from home was required for his safety. He went as far as St. Louis, and when he returned eight months later, he was "older by a decade," according to his father; he was a man grown out of the place of his birth, grown strange to it. He even looked odd sitting at the dinner table, his father said. He became a stranger in his own home and began arguing forever and a day with Wurth, the oldest son, who was solid, steady, loyal, who was interested in the affairs of the store. According to his mother, Wurth was like a house cat, always following his father around, sitting for hours in the store near his father, contentedly tolerating the foraging talk, watching the trades, while Harry hunted, or rode horses up and down across the thousands of acres the family owned, or climbed high into the rock-ribbed mountains all about, or swam in the river to Tennessee, then swam home. Wurth remained contentedly near his father and dutifully carried out every order, each assignment, even doing his school-work at the store.

"Well, I have Wurth always at hand, you have the girls," the father told his wife. It was true, there were two girls, both older, as well as the three boys.

From the house window in the loft where he had his bed, merely a pallet, Pink could see out over the farmyard and the vast fields, with mountains rising steeply from their edges, all of it part his; he could see the wealth of this place basking in the moonlight, with clouds often playing across the face of the moon, the moonlight sweeping, advancing, and receding over the land, clouds dancing. One night when he was seventeen, a year after the bear hunt, he waited by the window until the moon was hid pretty well, so that the light didn't fall on the house, and then he climbed from the window and groped his way slowly to the edge of the roof, where he dropped a cloth bag to the ground, then dropped into the yard. There he huddled in a ball, waiting breathlessly, for fear the dogs would bark, awakening someone.

Not a sound, except of the little river flowing past, stroking the bushes and tree roots along the bank. He got hold of his pack and, with one eye on his father's bedroom window, made his way to the fence. A dog began to growl warnings. He shushed her and crept to the side of the barn.

The yard had many sheds, and there was a large crib just over near the spring, and there were two old wagons that his brother Harry had traded for. He reached the side of the barn and paused. Not a sound, not even of the dogs. He crept forward toward the barn and was almost to the doors when he heard the scrape of leather, then a buckle being fastened on a saddle. He crouched near the water trough. He saw little or nothing but could hear one of the horses move in her stall, then he heard the sound of a man breathing. Somebody, a thief, was in the barn taking one of the horses.

The horse moved again. Pink heard the thief speak to it, murmuring soothingly. He saw the horse as it was led toward the barn doors, near where Pink crouched. The thief passed close, within reach; the horse's big rump passed close to the boy's head. "Now just a minute," he heard himself say as he sprang forward, landing on the back of the thief, forcing him to the muddy ground, seeking his neck with his hands, the thief growling surprises and curses.

A mellow shaft of moonlight swept over them, and Pink found himself looking down into his brother's face. "Ah, Lord 'a mercy," Harry murmured between his teeth. "I mighta known you'd be on to me." He smiled laconically. "I'm on my way, Pink."

"They'll die if you go," Pink said.

A weary frown came over Harry's face. "I'll die if I don't."

Pink looked off toward the house, where a single lantern was lit now. "He's up," he said. "Or mama is."

"Going to the privy, that's all," Harry said.

"Might have heard you."

"Get off my arm, Pink, afore I knock you silly."

Pink relaxed his grip, pushed himself to his knees.

"What you doing out here?" Harry asked, staring at him. Then he saw the pack in the gutter. "You leaving, too?"

"No," Pink said at once.

Harry crept to the pack and felt inside it. When he pulled out a shirt and a pair of underwear, a chuckle came into his throat. "Both of us on the same night?" he whispered.

"I can't go now, can I?" Pink asked anxiously.

Harry stuffed the goods inside the pack, leaned his head against the barn side. He waited patiently while the lantern marked a path from the back porch to the outhouse. The lantern was left on a rock outside the outhouse door for a few minutes, then his father returned to the house. "He never heard a thing," Harry said.

"He'll hear that horse, once you leave," Pink warned him.

"Not if I walk him slow, far as the ford," Harry said. "You want to come with me?"

Pink bit his lip, trying desperately not to say yes. "No thank you," he whispered. "Not both of us."

"You're too young, anyway," Harry said.

"I'm old enough," Pink said, miserable in his soul now that all his plans were disrupted.

"You going toward Asheville or Tennessee?" Harry asked.

"I was going to Asheville, get a job there at the tannery."

"Stinks in that place."

"Well, I know that," Pink admitted. "Work there till I get something else."

"Papa come find you, yank you out by the hair of your head. You're not of age."

"No," Pink admitted. "I'm seventeen."

"What about your girl?"

"I don't have a girl," Pink said firmly.

"Yeah? You can have mine."

Pink belched. He was nervous; his stomach was upset. "Tend to your business," he whispered abruptly.

"She's not been used," Harry said easily, a grim smile appearing. "They have girls for hire in St. Louis, if you want to come with me."

"No, no," Pink said.

"I can tell you how to do with them."

"No thank you," Pink whispered.

Harry chuckled, wiped the back of his hand across his mouth. "I can even stake you for a time or two, then you'll know how."

Pink's belly groaned again. "Harry, how long will you be on the road?"

"Oh—" Harry looked off toward the top of the ridge. "I think all my life."

"You never mean to settle down anywhere?"

"Oh, yeah," Harry said. "Here, take my hand." He pressed Pink's hand hard enough to hurt, though probably he didn't mean to hurt him. "You tell them I hated to leave, but I can't breathe so well here, Pink. You tell Papa."

"Yes," Pink whispered.

"And mama." Harry pressed Pink's hand once more. "Both of us can't go on the one night," he said. "You understand. You stay here. I'll give you Amanda. She's about your age."

"For a year you've courted her," Pink said, somewhat accusingly. He had always liked her, wanted her for himself.

"I felt her breasts, not even through the dress either, but then she cried and said she'd tell her papa about it. That's all."

"Oh, Lord," Pink moaned. "Tell her papa, and he come after you with a bull whip, would he?"

Harry snickered, then laughed quietly. "Too many parents around here." He rumpled Pink's hair. "Someday I'll be as old as papa, be fifty, and I'll remember tonight, Pink, you and me out here crouching near the barn wall, waiting to see how our lives will get started. My life is going to begin tonight, Pink."

"I know it is," Pink whispered, awed by the thought.

"I'll think back on you with that there bag, wanting to go work in the tannery." He chuckled deep in his throat. "I'll send you a hundred dollars, Pink. But just now you better go on into the house. Maybe you should go first to the outhouse, then make your way to the house. You can hide that pack in the barn."

Pink nodded, consenting.

"Papa might wonder how you got to the outhouse without his hearing you go out, that's all."

"He was asleep," Pink said.

"You tell him that." Harry, groaning, got to his feet, stretched. The moon was well exposed just now, and he stood there staring at it, waiting for clouds to cover it. "I leave all that's here, I know it. I'm leaving you and Wurth my fortune tonight, Pink."

"I'll leave, too—later, that's all," Pink said miserably.

"Hope Amanda will be more accommodating," Harry said. "You tell her your big brother told her to take care of you. Get her out on the creek bridge. What say to that?"

Pink snickered nervously. "She's been your girl, Harry."

"She'll fall off, if she don't mind you," Harry said, and began to laugh contentedly. "I meant to try that." He had to hold his hand over his mouth to hide his snickering. "Oh, well," he sighed finally. "Leave it all to you, boy," he said, his gaze scanning the wide valley, the store, the church just beyond, the rows of houses along the valley road, homes of lesser families, all English and Scotch-Irish and German stock, his eyes pausing for a moment on Amanda King's house, which he could see set up a cove, moonlight playing across its tin roof. He led his horse to the gate, which he opened enough for the horse to move through. He left it open and walked down the middle of the road, not once pausing or even looking back.

Pink had to cram a fist against his mouth to keep from calling out. I'm the one being left, he told himself, caught between two brothers, one grasping to hold all at home, the other tasting the world outside.

"First of all," he assured Amanda King, "I wouldn't dream just now of leaving here. You can see what Harry's leaving has done to people, to you, to mama, to several people around here." As they both knew, for days his father had sent out messengers to Asheville, Morganton, Boone, Burnsville, Newport, asking about Harry and where he might be found.

"Your papa doesn't appear to mind so much about daughters leaving," Amanda said ruefully, pausing at the edge of the church lot. They were approaching the main valley road; this was after Sunday-evening service. "You're not in a hurry, are you?" she asked, turning toward him.

"What say about daughters?" Pink asked. "You raise girls knowing they'll go off with their husbands."

"Well, I know," she said softly, acknowledging that. She was a pretty girl, all right, about seventeen, well-filled-out, and she wore a clean white dress with bits of lace around the neck and hem. The dress was fashioned close at the waist and had a wide belt. The bodice had blue buttons, though here at night as darkness settled they shone as black. She wore old shoes, that was the only incongruous note, probably a pair her older sisters had worn, and they were torn and bruised and splotched. Of course, her father was a cobbler, as well as farmer, but he rarely did anything except tend his livestock.

"I might leave someday," Pink said, watching carefully to discover what annoyance that held for her. She did appear to cloud over at once, which pleased him. "Go to Asheville, take the train from there, like Harry did."

"Harry did?"

"At least I know he started out toward the Asheville road."

She stared at him searchingly. "How do you know?"

"He took the ford when he left the house."

"You saw him?"

"Just happened to," Pink said, not wanting to claim credit for anything more. He walked on as far as the bridge, stood looking down at the flow of water. He turned to her suddenly. "I thought about leaving, too."

"Oh, my," she whispered, following him onto the bridge.

"I mean, it was that close to my going." He turned abruptly and caught her in his arms.

"No, no," she exclaimed, surprised.

In a rush he was embracing her, kissing her neck, her face. He filled his arms with her and felt of her warm body through her dress, then dug his hand into her bodice and felt her naked breast, even as Harry had. She held to him, trembling, kissing his lips, his forehead, his cheek. He felt himself being drawn into the fold, into her warmth, into the circle that her sweet arms made around him, holding him.

People approached along the road. At once he withdrew from the closeness, separated himself from her, and they sat on the edge of the bridge, their legs dangling.

"Evening, Amanda, evening, Pink," her sisters said as they passed. "Better come on home soon now, Amanda."

He awoke next morning thinking of her, his body attuned to the need of her, and he couldn't stop thinking of the moments of intimacy he had stolen with her. He found himself that very next evening, even on a Monday, crossing the Wright fields, going along the road to the King land and up the cove road to the main house, humbly to sit in her parents' parlor. On subsequent nights, she waited for him near the branch, always in view of her father's house. They would sometimes fish the stream, or maybe weave a trap for rabbits or squirrels, or they would see which one could name the most trees or flowers or shrubs, but all that was incidental to his, to their mission of discovering one another. He told her what he thought about every night in his tortured bed.

Even so, even talking boldly, he must hold back from her; her family and the other citizens of the community were always close by. At times he was grateful for such guards and shackles; something inside him would not consent to any bondage that snuffed out the hope of leaving here, perhaps joining Harry, and he realized a slip, one slip with her, and she would prove to be shackles enough.

Joshua Wright, who was Pink's father, and Enid King met from time to time in the course of life in the community. They both planted much the same crops and had the same schedule, with need for extra workers at the same season, so that the Wrights might arrange to help the Kings one day, provided King's sons and nephews would help the Wrights the next. The chief meeting place, where most arrangements were made, was the store, where Joshua Wright presided, making trades, selling merchandise, buying furs and ginseng and other herbs, which he would in time ship to Asheville. "Well, it seems to be progressing," Wright would say, referring to the romance between the two young people.

"Yes, it goes along," King would say.

"One of these days, soon now, you'll need to decide on a dowry," Wright would say.

"Not much a poor man can do," King would tell him. Of course, he wasn't poor, as everybody knew. The Kings were one of the best-established families out this way, had snaked their wagon back into this country in 1800, or thereabouts, quite soon after the Wrights had arrived, had hacked and burned and grubbed big fields, fencing and guarding some of the fields reaching high on the sides of the mountain.

"Oh, you have land enough to cut off a hundred fifty acres," Wright told him.

"Pshaw, listen to that, would you?" King said. "I'm about ruined."

"Write your boy James, ask him for the return of what you gave him."

"Never thought he would leave. Up he went, took his wife and baby and a bed."

"Stands idle, house is empty," Wright said. "Maybe he'll give it back to you."

"He claims he'll sell it."

Wright grumbled about that, but remained cautious; it was not the custom here to advise another man without request, or to criticize.

"Where is Harry now?" King asked, allowing no show of concern to creep into his voice.

"He wrote me from St. Louis."

"Well, he's gone then," King said.

"Took him out of my will this past week, there being no advantage to me in a son that travels so much."

"You never did give him anything?" King asked.

"No, no. I was careful."

"As to my daughter Amanda," King said, "she'll not get any land."

Wright allowed the words to settle before mentioning the Crawford girl, Victoria, who also was of courting age. "She's blossomed out, is blooming. Girls will sure surprise you, emerge might-nigh overnight. She's to have land bestowed on her."

King shook his head irritably. "I'm surprised land matters to you, when you have more land than anybody else."

"I hope each woman my sons marry brings with her enough ground to work and stand on, for her own family."

"You can easily parcel out your place, while I'm down to a nubbin," King told him. "I've cleared the mountainside all the way up."

King went away to worry about what Wright had said. He liked his daughter and wanted the best for her, and the best was clearly Pink Wright, a handsome boy with civil ways, who would come to inherit a fortune. Also, Pink appeared to like Amanda well enough to start a family with her. He listened one night as his wife recited about all the names of boys in the valley, and not a one, to hear her talk about it, would compare with Pink.

No boy could be judged better than another, King told her, until he was working on his own land, proving himself, and making trades to feed his own wife and children, when he's shaping the earth around about to better their lot, when he's acquiring, storing, fencing, girdling, burning, adding to and building again, digging out a place for his family. "Whether any boy of seventeen is a winner can't be told until he's well away from his papa's fires. How that boy's been pampered all his life," King hinted, enjoying the terror this would stir in his wife's face. "I never saw proof he would work."

Most every night, Adeline, the mother, was heavy with anxiety, and often Amanda wept. One night King, relenting, said he might be able to give her ten acres of his hilly land adjoining the Wright property to the east, if that would satisfy her. This stirred his other daughters to wrath, so that all the women in his household wept most of the night.

Next week the Wrights invited the Kings to Sunday dinner, and after the feast the two fathers walked together up to the King pasture and measured off the land that was to be included, Wright moving the line farther into the King holdings, taking in a little poplar woods. "Now, as for the cattle to be offered?" Wright said casually, peering approvingly at the herd of beef cattle grazing nearby.

"Cows?" King said, awakening to the new danger.

"The boy will also need a plow horse," Wright said, "but I can loan him one."

"My Lord help me," King prayed, trying to keep control of his temper.

Arriving at a site ideal for the house, Wright paused. "Now then, what we'll need to do is get together and cut the logs first, then hire McNaughty to notch them properly. We'll set the cabin here, and the barn there, and over there the crib."

King began to stammer objection; he had not meant to build anything. "A few quilts," he managed to say, "a few quilts was all her oldest sister had to offer."

"Now, as to furniture, I suppose you have more'n enough in your house, and so do I."

King sank down on a stump of a hickory and wiped his forehead dry, using the sleeve of his shirt, and smiled down at the dirt at his feet. He had known, he had known full well not to engage the Wrights in bargaining. They were predictable winners every time. "Lord God," he whispered to his dear maker, pleading for relief. "Could get a prince of Egypt, with any such dowry," he said, grinning. "God knows," he whispered, "could get the Duke's second son."

"She'll need a table, two chairs, a dipper," Wright said, recalling his own bride's arrival at the family house. "Will need bed clothing, two or three pans and pots, at minimum four dishes."

King decided the Wrights didn't marry into a family; they took over all its holdings and left the parents to scrounge.

Pink, aware of much of the bargaining, was powerless to influence it. He knew he was not by nature a farmer, and all this talk about pastures and fields troubled him. He was not a hunter or explorer either. He was more a storekeeper by type, but his brother Wurth had the store in his grasp and didn't appear to be ready to relinquish any part of it.

Pink supposed he could try to farm; for Amanda he supposed he would farm. Lord knows, he could hoe as well as anybody, and her working in the row beside his would make even that tedium a celebration. He could gather in his crops and make them safe, for Amanda's and their children's sake. And he would grease his wagon wheels and oil his saddle, and live the life of a farmer, for Amanda, for those warm nights near her, in the bed with her, in return for her warm body, all this he could see himself doing so that never would she need to kneel before the changes of her own life. What would be her payment in return for his life? he wondered. Child-woman, sweet woman. What could he require of her?

As for Amanda, she longed for marriage with all her thoughts and dreams. She was of an age to start a family of her own; she was ripe to begin. By now she had learned the crafts required of a young woman. Of equal consequences, she longed for babies to bear, to hold, to nurse, to love, to teach, to rear. Her body strained toward birth. After all, birth and death were the two exclusive provinces of the woman. The men could go out to bargain and barter, to borrow and exchange, but the women held most of the life-caring duties, were from birth preparing for them, and Amanda was of an age to begin giving her life to others, and accepting nourishment from them. Furthermore, she could card, spin, weave, sew, quilt; bake breads, cakes, pies, cook chicken, pork, venison; churn butter; make soft cheeses; grow abundant crops of potatoes, carrots, onions, beans, peas, spinach, parsnips, turnips, lettuce, basil, thyme, apple mint, bay leaves, sage; could help harvest maple syrup from trees and steal honey from the wild. All these challenges awaited her and made her eager to be underway.

The wedding was to be in spring. The Wrights' logs for the new house were delivered all on a single day, were brought by hired workmen. There was an abundance of logs for a one-room-and-loft dwelling. There was an argument over the privy, which had to be dug, the Wrights waiting for the Kings to do it. King had two sons living up this way and they claimed they would not dig a sister's privy. There was a limit to what a brother could be asked to do, they said. The Wrights went ahead and built the privy themselves. Almost every detail of the homestead had to be arranged to suit Joshua Wright, and it was true that adequate furniture had to be provided. All this was for one daughter's wedding. But, just as summer follows spring, there the homestead stood finally, as pretty as any Pink had ever seen, even with fencing in place. He proudly moved about the house and into the yard to see the view, which was expansive. He could see the sun set into Tennessee of an evening. His life swayed as he walked about his own place. And when was it to be his? Why, whenever his mother and Amanda's mother agreed on a day, one affording time for cakes to be baked, the linens finished, the preacher to be scheduled. Look even now at the gifts. See there, a cow in the pasture, a work horse, the barn all finished, new and straight and sturdy. The doors shut tightly. All is done now, except for taking the woman into the house.

Her grandmother, who was sixty-four, sought to advise her. "Mandy, you'll need something firm to lie on, something more'n feathers, maybe boards under the mattress, when you have to return the pushing. Best I ever found was a laurel bough."

Amanda choked, coughed. "Ma'am?" she said humbly.

"When you're out of doors, pick you a bough with an inch and half stem, one hanging low, about a foot above the ground. Rest on that, and it'll give you the nicest spring upward you ever found."

Boards or boughs, just what the delicate night would be like Amanda couldn't even imagine. It would be spent with her lover—a precious word, lover—and she trusted that it would not be unkind. Admittedly there were dark warnings from some of the dour women. She would find it painful, the first times, they warned. There were hints of demands she might not like. There was conflicting advice. One aunt allowed only one position: the woman on her side with one leg raised. She was dead set against any others, for instance claiming that lying flat on the back with both legs spread would lead to ruptures. Amanda's mother disagreed, but did agree that a woman ought not to ride atop a man, or allow herself to be entered from the rear. Amanda, a novice to it all, was prepared to assume whatever position seemed comfortable, that would allow love to move through her body and a baby be formed inside her. That was the dearest thought she had, not the entering of her body by her husband, as delightful as that promise was, but the growing inside her body of the baby. Her own bed of linen and muslin was nothing when compared with the warm, soft, moist bed within her body in which her babies would grow.

And the baby with its tiny hands, its little eyes, its button nose, its pink bottom would solve a world of dissent in the family, it would weld together the parts, it would slobber love onto the hands of the father, it would enrich the milk of the mother, it would lie between them on their bed, wetting them and warming them, and would complete the union. There was no other way, as she saw life, for a woman to complete the family, or complete herself as a woman.

They were mere visitors at their house. Not yet married, they weren't supposed to go inside it yet, but he ducked inside anyway, she following. They were in the one room, a bed in one corner, a stove in another, and a fireplace in the north wall. Steps of a ladder crept up the south wall to the loft. Everything was new and glistening; even the logs had been skinned and hewn recently and were damp. He built a small early-May fire in the fireplace and the smoke curled up the chimney. She crouched beside him, staring at the blaze as his hands worked over it, encouraging it with chips of wood, feeding it carefully. "Outdoors the wind is howling," he told her.

"There's nothing more important than a fireplace in a cabin," she said. It was a trembling moment, here in their own place, and being beside him.

He put his arm around her. They crowded the fire, holding to one another, two frightened children. Even then, alone with her, he didn't dare commit himself to her, or take her.

That night Pink went home the back way to the road. He crossed at the cemetery. "Life and death, life and death," he murmured. He paused at the church. Laura Phillips was singing. Must be her husband pumping the organ during her rehearsal. Amanda's mother had chosen Laura to sing, she having the sweetest voice, even though her accent was Yankee; she hadn't lived in the mountains long. He listened to one song all the way through, then went on to the store. A lamp was lit inside there. He climbed the steps, peered in through the glass part of the front door, and saw his father bent over the ledger desk. He was sitting on a high stool, but was not writing; he was reading one of his many books and had come here to be away from the noise of the house and family.

Inside, Pink stoked the fire in the stove for him. The older man continued reading. Pink selected a rocker and fell to speculating silently about his own life, whether when he was as old as his father he would be as much a person, or less, or would be in any way different. Finally, his father brought the lantern over to the stove, put it near the boy's elbow, and sat down in his favorite chair, a ladder-backed rocker. He pulled a raggedy quilt over his legs. Three cats came after him, following like trained animals at a circus, and plopped down near his feet, quite close to the stove, purring. An old dog came closer, sniffed at Pink's shoes and legs.

"What I did," his father began quietly, "was to tell the women to do next to nothing for a wedding-night celebration. Usually there's too much excitement and whiskey, too much food. You'll want to sneak off, anyway, won't you?"

"Yes, I'd say so."

He smiled at Pink. "It's the finest part of a man's life, this loving business. I think some men are better at it than others, and some women, too, I'm told. Your brother Harry when he first went off to St. Louis came home talking about women as if he had taken on half a dozen different ones, and they were all different, as he told it. Same fittings, same fixtures, same odors, same compulsions, but all different. Now, that was Harry talking to Wurth, not to me."

"You ever have—have much experience, papa?"

"With women?"

"Oh, I don't know why I asked that," Pink said, embarrassed.

Wright rubbed his nose, gently massaged his neck. He cleared his throat and spit at the stove, the spittle steaming against the metal. "A man is a crazy damn fool," he whispered. He knitted his fingers, formed a single ball of his two hands. "Lord knows."

"You're not old yet, papa."

"Uh huh," he said breathily. "You know in the Bible, in First Kings, the first chapter, there's the story about King David, who late in life lacked warmth, and the doctors said to send for a beautiful virgin and let's see if she could get warmth into him. So somebody selected a pretty one, and she was assigned, and the Bible says she did her best, did well." He looked over at Pink, a crooked smile on his face, his watery eyes lighted by the lantern, alive with good feeling and humor.

"Did it help him, papa?" Pink asked.

"Why, you know it must have," Wright said. "What you reckon ever happened to that form of medicine?"

Pink laughed contentedly, pulled a spare quilt around himself. "Don't know."

"Not a doctor that I know offers such a cure. Medicine has gone out the window," Wright commented, closing his eyes and resting his head back against the chair.

The rhododendron near the church should have been blooming by this week in June, but chilly weather had delayed the buds' opening, so Wurth Wright and two other young men went into lower country and brought back a wagonload of purple boughs, enough to decorate the church. That same night, before the wedding day, a swarm of men took time to talk with Pink about what would be expected of him, how many times a week he should serve his wife, the conversation proving extremely confusing to him, the advice mingled with raucous laughter. At last the instruction was over and he was allowed to go to the loft bed, his last night in his father's house, he imagined, and from the loft window he could look out over the fields and the hills of home. A wave of nostalgia swept through him, followed by one of intense unrest. What on earth was he doing, marrying now? Rising from his bed, in a fit of passion he began to push spare clothing into a pillow case, but his energy withered finally, limply he concluded he would not leave here, leave her, leave all that had been planned for him.

He ate breakfast alone. Wurth had eaten and had gone to work. His mother fixed him pancakes, sausages, stewed apples. By noon he was dressed in his finest suit and was taken to the church in a wagon, so that he would not perspire. That was his mother's idea. He felt like a dunce riding the wagon, everybody in the churchyard turning to welcome him. His brother Wurth helped him down and stood nearby. Wurth's son, Fortner, age six, clung close as a shadow, the ring burning his pocket.

A wagon approached from the west, along the main valley road, a troop of children around it yelling. Into the churchyard came the wagon of the King family, with Amanda sitting high on the buckboard, beside her father. Her mother and two older sisters crouched near the tailgate. Her older brother, Sims, walked along in the dust behind, his own wife and two children trailing along.

Laura Phillips sang well. She was a beautiful woman, too, as Pink realized once more. She wore a fancy dress with many yards of lace on it.

When the pump organ struck up the melody to "Here Comes the Bride," everybody stood, and the bride entered from the outside, through the main door of the church, her father with her, he for the first time in years wearing a necktie and suit. The bride, dressed in dazzling white, was blushing. After the ceremony the couple escaped to the outdoors, rice flying through the air, falling on them, clinging to their hair. There was much laughter. There were no tears at all at this wedding. Not even Mrs. Wright or Mrs. King wept. Once the church became empty, long, wide planks were brought indoors and laid across the backs of the pews, up and down both sides of the main aisle, and food in covered dishes was placed on them. A barrel of apple brandy was unstoppered and a siphon was injected into it. Men filled their cups with that, talking louder now, pleased to be on holiday, free from field work, standing about with friends and members of their own family, everybody part of the success story of this valley. The children took their overflowing plates to the near edge of the cemetery, where Mrs. Crawford appointed herself to talk with them about the meaning of marriage, how two people became one, her explanation avoiding physical union, and out of the one came children, "such even as I was once," she told them.

A boy lit a string of firecrackers. When they were expended, a few men took pistols out of their pockets and blasted at tree targets, laughing at their failures as well as their successes. Pink was urged to try his hand. "Try your best shot now, boy, while you can still stand," one wag told him, handing him his Colt. Pink aimed at the target, which was a feather stuck in an old balm of Gilead tree: he split the feather. "Why, he'll do all right tonight," the wag said, laughing uproariously, staggering.

Darkness came; the couple sneaked away from the church and went along the dark road to their own place, Pink carrying a lantern. Pink admitted he had had a few drinks. He stumbled along, leaving the road just beyond the bridge. At the house, they found a fire glowing. Pink closed the door and locked it. He paused, stood humbly staring at her, feeling half sick to his stomach and unsure of himself. Amanda put a pot of water on for tea, then crouched before the fire to warm. Even then he watched her silently. My wife, he thought. Slowly he went to her and crouched down beside her, took her in his arms and kissed her, then rested her back onto the floor and began to untie the lacing of her dress.

CHAPTER
Two

Amanda had been certain she would conceive a child at once, and when no success occurred in the first several months she became baffled, and her need for sexual union became insatiable. The winter was spent in bed, she admitted, and even so was without the result she wanted.

Her mother often queried her about the delay; her sisters expressed their concern and suggested Pink must be at fault. Pink's mother also became involved. She asked Pink if everything was going all right at home, her own way to question whether the fittings and fixtures of the conjugal act were satisfactory. Every Sunday, or virtually every Sunday, Pink and Amanda sneaked to church and stayed as close together as the traditional seating would allow—the men on one side of the church during the service, the women and small children on the other. By arriving late, they warded off some of the more personal questions and stares.

Nine months passed, filled with affection, laden with bliss, ripe with desire, dripping with lushness and richness; there was no disappointment all that year, except her failure to conceive. Even though there was bland admission that the man might be the one deficient, might suffer some lack of substance in his sperm or lack of assertiveness in his manner, or perhaps had hesitated to possess the woman, all such admissions of Pink's possible failures were perfunctory compared to the possibilities attached to Amanda: that she was not fertile, or was not attracting him, or must not be fully giving herself to him, not suffering even pain gladly, not wanting the baby enough, not praying for it humbly. Apparently, Amanda concluded, a woman must use prayer, guile, imagination, subterfuge, scents, smiles, nakedness, pride, humility. She must learn to groan and, on occasions, to cry out.

Her own mother brought her what perfume she had. Her sister Martha, who had always shown more jealousy than the other one, brought a few drops of musky oil, which she had made herself; she would not say with what ingredients. These drops were to be rubbed by Amanda into her pubic hair just before mating, and also a judicious drop was to be inserted deep into her body. Amanda told Pink she might bear a porcupine instead of a baby, if she didn't take care. "There's simply no telling where that oil has come from," she said. It did have a nose-clearing, enveloping bouquet.

"Might make a boy," Pink said.

They laughed about it, but they did use the serum; they were approaching desperation.

Perhaps it all helped, the conversations, the musky oil, the questions, the experiments, for during the month of June she conceived. At once her own life seemed to open fully, she appeared to flower; all the other women at church noticed. She walked about beaming, full of pleasure, so rich with joy she could not, would not conceal it. She knew she was the envy of all the women who were not pregnant. She was a flower opening, a pleasure to see, even to meet on the road and talk with, though she only wanted to talk about her pregnancy. Sick of a morning, she liked even that; everything associated with her baby was rewarding. Sweet miracle, she had her own child deep inside her where she could care for it, protect it—most of all protect it. "You be careful how you lie on me," she told Pink each night. "No, no. I'm afraid, Pink. I'm really afraid now. No, you let me get on you, honey. No, I don't mean to go all the way down."

She wanted him so much. Her appetite for love and for making love was greater than ever before in her life, but she was forever restrained because of the baby inside her. She would not even jump a small puddle in the road for reason of the baby. She would not sit on a bench without a pillow. Some of the precautions were perhaps needless, she admitted, as her own mother had told her. "I've known women to work in the fields and bear the baby between the corn rows," Adeline King said. "I've known women to ride a horse to the midwife's house, dismount, and walk into the house." No argument made any difference; Amanda moved slowly, carefully, and whenever she bumped into a table, as often she did now that her belly was extended, she would at once lie down for a while, to allow the unborn child to recover. All the while her mind swam with wonder and happiness, with gladness and gratitude to God for the child.

Finally she excluded Pink entirely. He could touch her, hold her, kiss her, but could not enter her. She would even hold his hard penis in her hand and try to release his passion; she would writhe with passion, herself, and she would guide his fingers, to try to find release, but he must not enter her body where the baby lay. Hers was now the baby's body. For a month or so she went on that way. One evening Pink overcame her restraints, but as soon as the act was completed she crawled off the bed and made her way outdoors, and sat on the privy in the dark for an hour or more, waiting to see if the baby was lost or not, tears rolling down her cheeks all the while onto her naked breasts.

When she felt the baby move inside her, she crept back into the bed where Pink lay and begged him to listen at her belly to hear the baby, to put his hands on her to feel the baby, to confirm that it was still alive.

Much of this was beyond Pink. The blessing was a nuisance. He could not quite believe the importance she attached to the birth. He tried to live with her within the boundaries she set, but they were foreign to him. He was afraid for her more than for the baby. His love was for her; he felt no affection for the unborn child. He wanted the child to be born, but at the same time he did not know the child, which already was imposing changes on his habits, his sexual needs and desires, his wife's body and interests; the baby was tampering with his own control of his own family.

Unborn, unnamed, without features, the baby was already a person to Amanda, who even talked to it, sometimes for hours, told it stories about events yet to happen; there was not a biddy in the yard that she did not show the eyeless baby, and in turn not a bird on the sill. She would warble on about flowers and budding trees, and late on a warm day took the child swimming, talking to it as she waded into the creek at a deep place, and once the creek water reached her thighs, she told the unborn baby that in a few more steps it would begin to feel the effects, the cold, and the invigorating current of the water. Amanda then crouched slowly down into the water and admitted later she had feared the child might drown if left underwater for a long time.

There must be a midwife given notice, and Pink listened attentively to Amanda's and her mother's discussion of midwives of the valley, as to which one had the best score. Amanda discussed this issue until it was in tatters, all the while knowing that Adeline King herself would try to take charge, even should God send Gabriel down from Heaven to officiate. "She's my mother, she's not to tend to me," Amanda assured Pink.

"Well, we'll see about that," he told her. "Your mother—"

"A mother does not deliver her daughter's baby. It's not done."

Pink carried word to a midwife finally selected, told her he would be calling for her in due course. As instructed, he measured the trip to her house, made sure which of her doors to knock on, and at which window should she not hear the door; she told him she was deaf in one ear, and if she slept on her right side, she couldn't "hear thunder and hit in bed with me." He got straight about what conveyance she would be needing—a wagon, unless it's real bad weather, and then a horse will do, but with a man's saddle. "I'll need the horn to hold on to."

And he listened dutifully at the belly of his wife; with his own hands he felt the baby move inside her, and he reported its motion to estimate its vigor.

"But is it moving more than yesterday?" she wanted to know. "I think it's stronger, do you, Pink?"

He learned to agree. One morning he heard nothing, pressing his ear against Amanda's naked belly faithfully as he could. He admitted as much to her, and she was in despair. He wondered what she thought could have happened to the baby overnight, with her lying on a feather mattress, her husband forbidden to touch anything below her navel. Had a pillow fallen on the little intruder? Was this nine-month impostor, with its tiny heart, never to be born and release its father? Was Pink's life to remain a list of notes to himself as to what to do in this case or that, or where to be, or when to go for the King crib, the one being mended, or whether or not to take word of the birth first to the King house or to the Wright house—this latter instruction changing from day to day as Amanda mulled it over.

Finally the relief offered itself, the moment of birth came, the spasms in the womb of his lover began, and at once all details seemed to fly into confusion. He went for Mrs. King, then raced for the midwife, forsaking wagon, horse, and saddle, virtually dragged her from her bed by banging on her door until the locks sprung. He led her down the hill in the dark, even without a lantern to see by, trusting memory to show him the path, the woman alarmed and grudgingly amused, saying he was not the first young husband "to come to me unraveled."

Pink stood in the yard at dawn. Frederick Enid King himself came to join him, as did his brother Wurth, the three dutifully listening for sounds of the baby.

"Now, that there cow needs milking," Enid King commented, studiously studying Amanda's Guernsey, careful to avoid any gesture that would suggest he would himself milk her. "It'd be a damn shame to cause a good cow pain. Wurth, can't your wife come milk that cow for Amanda?"

There were five women present soon, counting Pink's mother and Amanda's two sisters, who began asking why the delay. Pink said he didn't know whether there was any delay.

"Oh, yes," one sister said darkly, "oh, yes."

Pitiful words, *Yes, oh, yes,* mean, stinging words to Pink that penetrated his flesh and lodged there, like Indian arrows that would not pull out. *Oh, yes.* Such nonchalant words, but lofty in meaning. Hear the double thud as they strike the flesh. *Oh, yes.* "Ah, Jesus," he moaned. Turning from the sisters' worried faces, again he approached King himself.

"You'll never split it now," King told him.

"What's that, papa?" Pink asked. "Split what?" he asked.

"You ought to know by now. Can't split hickory. Where'd you grow up?"

"I don't want it split. It's to be a cutting log."

King squirmed part way around so he could look down at it. "I tried to split hickory when I was a boy. My papa had a devil in him one December, and he knew I wanted an orange he had. Now listen, I'd never laid eyes on an orange before and had no idea what it tasted like, but he ate one before me, sat there in a rocker and ate it all, juice running down his beard, his eyes glittering, watching me, said I could have one if I split a fireplace log. First he gave my little sister Martha one to split, an oak log, although I didn't notice, didn't know the difference back then, and she split hers easy and got an orange. Then he gave me a hickory log to split."

No sound from the house. No cracked door. The east window still stood open, but not a sound came from it, and Pink dared not approach it. There went that musky sister to look inside, but not a word of hope came from her. Well, that was good news, for she was a quick bearer of calamity, that one.

"All I could think of was my orange. I was not much of an axman. My older brother, Jesse, who is now living in Oregon, was the best of the lot. Of course, I had watched it done for years, and now I swung and hit that damn log, which was dried-out hickory, prime hard-rock hickory, nothing else, and that ax bounced off. Well, papa put the orange a fine distance from me. Oh, man, I swung it again, let me tell you, I swung hard and that there ax bounced . . ."

Smoke curling up from the chimney was caught by gusts of wind and whipped about, but no sound of a baby came from that log room. Let the child be born, let it be born now; something is indeed wrong, Pink decided. Lord knows, he might himself survive a failure, but it would very likely destroy Amanda. There was his own father now approaching the yard gate, silent as a lord approaching an execution, staring at the house as if the house any minute might reveal a secret to him.

". . . Broke the ax handle. My father got to cussing about that, breaking the ax handle, said it wasn't supposed to split, and then he got to laughing about my trying to split a hickory log, and he went into the house to tell my mother about his joke on me, and I ate that there orange before he could come back out, ate it peel and all."

The door opened. Mrs. King stood there, alone. Weary, see how she leans on the door post, wiping her hands on her apron, Pink noticed. She motioned for Pink to come to her, and he approached slowly.

"It's a boy," she said. "Must be eight pounds."

"Is it? How is Amanda?" Pink broke into a grin.

"Well, now I want to tell you, that was a rough delivery. The baby was not positioned properly for birth. It was a rough delivery, Pink. Amanda's not—there's something wrong inside of her, I'd imagine, so we're going to have to discuss it before she bears another one."

"All right," he said willingly, scarcely hearing her warnings. "Oh, yes," he said, happiness sweeping upward, joy at the birth, at Amanda's success, at the triumph of today, never mind the future.

He broke past Mrs. King, burst into the room. The midwife, her hands bloody, looked up at him, her face contorted. Even that, even the sight of his wife's blood, did not discourage him. He moved to the bed, which had soppy red towels draped on the bedstead, threw himself on his knees, and began to utter praise. He could see the baby at Amanda's breast, sucking. Amanda was so weak she could scarcely see through her tears, she wasn't even sure who he was, so he took her hand and told her his name, told his wife his name, and kissed her hand, her wrist, and began to talk expansively about their lives together, the years ahead.

Pink rarely had his farm work done on time; he was forever and a day running behind with it. "You have three mouths to feed now, and a fourth soon on the way, I imagine," his mother told him, with typical sense of rising, ever-increasing calamity.

He preferred to stay near the trade lot, and most of all he enjoyed going to Asheville to deliver merchandise for his father, or to help a neighbor deliver his crops there. Everybody in the valley knew they could count on Pink to help them get their sheep or hogs or horses or geese to market. Sometimes he was paid precious little for such trips, and, as he knew, by now he had run up a debt at the store. He was not the only one in the same situation, of course, half the valley's families were, and the debt was less awkward for him since he was a Wright, was in a sense part owner, an inheritor of the store itself; even so, he was losing out in his day-to-day work. As yet he had not got a hold of his new life.

He wasted time. Even Amanda thought to mention this. He would go visit various craftsmen, even seek to apprentice himself. He helped the potter for several weeks without a cent to show for it. Potting was hard physical work, too. By nature Pink was a clever bargainer, a trader. He felt he could work the store very well, but his brother Wurth became nervous whenever he approached the place, even got an upset stomach, and the store's limited business never seemed to justify yet another hand, anyway.

His winter wheat needed harvesting; he hired it done. His spring plow was wanting; he hired it done. His lambs needed worming; he asked Mr. Terry Roberts to do it for him. Meanwhile, he bought a small herd of horses, drove them to Asheville, and made a profit. His next deal had to do with geese: he bought up spare geese until he had a yard full, then led them to market in Asheville, forty-seven miles over rutted, winding mountain roads. Another time, when he was exasperated with the farm's routine, he sought his father out one night at the store to ascertain which families had run up the biggest debts, and in the next weeks he sought them out, bargained with them, usually arranging to drive some of their animals into town. He did well with such transactions, at least to his own satisfaction; however, Amanda and her parents were skeptical, felt insecure with will-o'-the-wisp maneuvers.

As the time went by, this came to be the manner in which Pink lived: work, which he avoided, and trading, which he sought out. He was living on luck, his brother Wurth told him. "Come a depression, where will you be, Pink?" Wurth's resentment of everything Pink tried to do was apparent, and he did seem to gloat on Pink's failures: Pink's flock of sheep, admittedly bedraggled; a dog-scarred flock of ducks, now numbering only half as many as when the wedding took place; a milk cow and a calf, the calf as yet unbred, and therefore dry; a couple of goats that were getting into everybody's garden and were a nuisance; a horse that needed shoeing and apparently had some internal disorder that would require bought medicine; a wagon with a busted wheel. On and on Wurth could recite the litany of his brother's failures. However, he looked with suspicion on Pink's exploits as a trader, watched with envy each success he achieved.

Pink, who never argued and had no idea of causing pain to anyone, much less a brother, began avoiding Wurth as best he could, even missing some of the family business lunches his father arranged weekly. The decisions were not satisfying to him anyway; they were discussions of who wanted to borrow money and what security was offered, who wanted to sell land or buy timber or furs. The decisions were made by his father, and so were the profits.

Once the baby had a smile, he became a person to Pink and became Pink's pride and joy, a companion during long evening storytelling sessions and on ever so many hikes to the grandparents' houses. Interestingly enough, the child had been named after his Grandfather King. This had been Amanda's doing, surprising to Pink and flagrantly disappointing and sometimes amusing. During the pregnancy she was friendly to the idea of Pinkney being the name, if the baby was a boy, but at the moment she listed the name on the actual birth certificate, which she went out of her way to do herself, she inscribed Frederick Enid King Wright, even keeping the "Enid," which Pink contended was a woman's name.

Pink's own parents were resentful. Amanda's brothers and her sisters were peeved to have her assume the family title for her own child—her first-born brother had held it until pneumonia struck him down in the bitter winter twenty-four years ago. Mr. Enid King was ecstatic. Pink's own response vacillated; certainly he knew there were disadvantages to the name Pinkney, but he did resent Amanda's assuming such complete authority over the child.

However, soon Pink and everybody else thought of him as Frederick, dear cooing, smiling Frederick, a sweet, round-faced, dancing-eyed bundle of cries and slobbery laughter. His very first laugh came at six months, about the time Amanda announced to Pink, and to her mother, as well, her second pregnancy. Pink thought little about the pregnancy but was beside himself with pride about the laugh. He used every ruse he knew to make that little one laugh again for him, for his Grandmother Wright, for his Grandfather King. There had never been, Pink decided, a baby as loving and happy as this one. The child would grow up to be a lawyer, a judge, a governor, a senator, or he might be a doctor and drive out diseases, grapple with tuberculosis and diphtheria. He would be the builder of railroads, the designer of buildings, the preacher standing before four thousand Methodists at the camp meeting at Hot Springs, swaying with powerful thoughts the willows of Almighty God. This baby, this little child, would strike the biggest bell.

And be a lover, too, and a kind person, and be generous to a fault, and be strong enough to swim along the river to Tennessee. This baby. This little Frederick, soon to be a God-man, would assume the dreams and titles his father had some years ago imagined for himself.

See the pretty woman following him along the laurel-white-petaled paths to the pool of warm water that only they knew.

26

At first Pink was home most nights. Of course, it did take four to ten hours to reach Asheville, depending on the weather and the conveyance, and some of his trades were complicated in that he traded for stock or produce rather than money. A buyer might not appear until evening, or even until next day, maybe too late for Pink to start back home. In one case he stayed away from home three nights in a row, long enough for Amanda to become frantic. Then in early December, when she was getting large with the second baby, he was gone still longer. He traded for a riding horse and belatedly discovered its lameness. He was unable to trade it satisfactorily in Asheville, but heard of a possible buyer near Brevard, a horse breeder, and he led the horse to Brevard, sold it there at a loss, stayed two nights with the buyer, a man named Perkinson, a Northerner by birth. He returned to Asheville, arriving in mid-afternoon to find one of the Wilkinson boys trying to sell a load of apples. This Wilkinson needed to return home for a sister's wedding, so Pink bought the apples and waited in town overnight, selling them next day in bushel lots door to door, making back his horse losses. He missed a ride back home and had to walk most of the way, arriving at his own home on the fourth day.

Amanda argued fiercely that he was not to travel anymore. She had marked the nights on the floor with a piece of charcoal, had fixed supper each night, she told him.

He took the baby from the crib and nursed him on his lap, talking with him, telling him about Asheville, how there was always something doing in Asheville, a trade to be made there. The baby didn't understand a word he was saying but was pleased to be talked to, and cooed and laughed and tried to stroke his chin.

This was the sort of combat that ensued, as Pink viewed his life here, with Amanda anxious and demanding, and Wurth maneuvering carefully for his own gain, yet being a brother, being friendly, even considerate and loving. The duals were hard as steel, but were clothed in flesh, and Pink found himself eager to escape. He was born to avoid controversy. In August and September, during the apple market, he worked in Asheville for ten days, then went back for six more days later on, in spite of Amanda's hurt feelings, and in November, when the Christmas decorations had to be put up along Lexington Avenue in Asheville and everybody prepared for gift giving, he worked at the King store. The store was an assembly of stalls, with its main trading lot in the front of it, where farmers could unload their wagons. Hugh King, a cousin of Enid, had decided that his store would be open twenty-four hours a day, six days of the week. Of course, he couldn't stay awake for all that schedule, and here was Pink Wright, married to a relative, a friendly man anxious to help everybody, an excellent trader.

Soon after that, the rumor took form that Pink would leave, to move to Asheville. Up and down the valley people believed it and asked how they could expect to keep their own sons at home, if even the Wright sons were delinquent. There was the charge of subterfuge, of taking land from his parents and her parents and wasting it, and what of the house that had been built for him by the Kings and Wrights, with many other hands helping? What was the reward of the wedding that the community had arranged, now that this young prince and princess were going? Had they any legal right to leave here? Were there no laws protecting families? What right did parents have in this ever-changing world? Were the Wrights to have Wurth, nobody but Wurth, the least colorful and exciting of the Wright boys, was Wurth to be the sole son left for them?

All for what? For that store Hugh King was building in a mud slab at the foot of a street in Asheville? Was that the goal? And who was Hugh King but a poor man who had left his farm near Glory, North Carolina, five years ago and had bartered his way to a modest station, quite above anything he had known in Glory, where his own and his wife's people clung to the eroded soil like laurel sticks. Were Hugh King and his like, was his shanty store in the city to be the siren call that would drag even a Wright son from the arms of his parents?

Wurth was stunned by the reports. He sought to find the trick in it all. He would not accept at face value that Pink would be departing without conditions.

When the rumor persisted, Wright himself sent one of his daughters to Amanda, to find out what the problem was. She came back weeping, claiming there was, indeed, an offer made to Pink. Wright walked up to the King house, himself, and commiserated there with Enid, seeking understanding, and Enid said Hugh King was stealing his family and Pink was a willing victim. King said he would burn their house before he would see it deserted; he would take back his property too, if he could.

The Christmas season arrived, catching everyone in the valley in its net, the crest rising at Christmas Eve and Christmas Day with a happy round of visiting to do, house to house, room to warm room. The families sang the old carols. There was the smell of rich food cooking. These several days were clear, astonishingly clear even for the mountains; every tree stood out on the ridge crests, each trunk stood against the blue sky. Not a cloud was to be seen. Not a rude sound was heard to disturb the mellow gurgling of the creek, the more somber raspy voice of the river. No wind was in the sky these days.

The baby was born in May, on the eleventh day. This second birth was full of pain and complication, as much as the first; and in the hours of waiting Pink came to recognize the danger as reality. The midwife told Pink not to come for her again. "I'd cut that thing of your'n off first, if I was you," she advised him. "She might-nigh died, and I've never lost a mother. I'll not risk my life record on another 'un." Adeline King was also intense in her accusations, complaining to Pink about the scant attention he had given Amanda, about his travels, which she claimed were threats to break up their house, all of which contributed in her opinion to the baby's being bruised all over. "Just look at her little face."

Amanda lay unconscious for a day and night, breathing huskily through her open mouth, her own face blue where she had struck herself repeatedly on the bedposts. "Now, you'll need to make plans different from what's been," Adeline instructed Pink adamantly. "You'll need to reckon on her dying, if there's another'n."

He agreed, he consented.

CHAPTER
Three

A manda went with him to visit in town; under protest she packed up enough diapers and other clothes and rode their "wounded wagon," Hallie bouncing in the maple cradle that Pink had secured to the back of the wagon bed. Frederick tried to sit up all the way, but he nodded, lost balance on the downhill stretches when the wagon was moving almost fast as breathing, as Amanda said. And, when the family reached the outskirts of town, they found themselves in a procession of wagons, a mile-long string of mountain people trying to get inside the gates, where no less than Teddy Roosevelt was to speak.

Pink parked beside the road and unhitched; he led the two horses; Amanda carried Hallie on her hip and held Frederick's hand. "The boy's about whooped, Pink," she complained, but on he went striding forward, wanting not to miss a speck of entertainment. He tied the horses to the back wall of Hugh King's store, fed them a pail of corn, put a water bucket before them. "I chained the wagon and put a lock on the chain," he told Hugh, "but I suppose somebody could steal the wheels off of it."

"You know they can," Hugh admonished him. All these people coming to town annoyed Hugh, upset his routine. Anything that upset Hugh's routine was either an absurdity or a danger. "I had hopes of going to see him myself, but there's so many doing it, I think I'll stay here to the store." Hugh was only four or five years older than Pink, but he looked considerably older. He had always looked mature, even as a boy, and was sage and studied. Amanda rather liked him, was proud of his success in his store, even as she resented the appeal he and his store had for Pink, the appeal that his town had, for that matter.

Amanda couldn't get near enough to the town square even to see Mr. Roosevelt, much less hear a speech, so she went back to Hugh's, but Pink decided to move to the other side of the square, to try to get closer, and he hurried off with Frederick, riding him on his shoulders. Amanda at the store nursed Hallie, then washed out diapers in tubs of spring water, hanging them—little square flags of family life, she thought—on a hitching post alongside the store. She hadn't brought enough diapers after all, she decided. Hallie did seem to get nervous whenever she traveled, even if it was only a little way, as to Grandfather Wright's house, and this trip to town had about stripped the baby clean. She was easily excited.

Pink circled the crowd and came up the back side of a north building. He and a man from Hendersonville managed to jimmy open the back door of a building and climbed to the third floor, where Pink pried open a hatch onto the roof. With Frederick clasped in one arm, Pink edged his way to the ridge, where he perched, one leg to the north, the other to the south. Below him was a sea of human beings flooding the square, turning it into colors, flowing down the side streets for two or three blocks in every direction, with more people and horses moving about at the frayed ends of the crowd. Below him a speakers' platform had been erected and draped in flags and bunting, and on it a string band from Waynesville was strumming away. The platform flew the Stars and Stripes on the right, and the flag of the State of North Carolina in the left. "We be melted in a little while," he admitted to Frederick, and laughed. "Be tar babies, sure enough," he said. From that high perch they could see most everything going on, could see the carriage slowly move through the crowd, bringing the waving politicians close to the platform, could see Teddy himself mount the platform steps, his arrival terminating the work of the musicians, the beaming politicians waving to the crowd, hat in hand saluting them, while a groaning response came back, a song, a male welcome, the men's consent to honor him. When Teddy Roosevelt began talking, his voice appeared strangely high-pitched to Pink. From where Pink perched, he could make out some of the words, broken phrase here or there, but nothing had much continuity. On and on the broad-chested bantam rooster crowed. "He's a fighting cock," Pink told Frederick, "is a game rooster, I'd guess."

When Pink finally got back to the store, he told Hugh some of what he had seen. Frederick was asleep in his arms. Pink had tar stains on his pants, so he said he would go up to the used-clothing shop in a while and buy himself a pair of pants. "Where's Amanda?" he asked, intending to tell her what he had done.

"Nettie took her home to wash your baby's face," Hugh said disgruntledly.

Pink carried Frederick there, less than a block away. He sat on the front porch and studied the people passing on the sidewalk—a wooden sidewalk. The road itself had a layer of concrete on it, was one of the first streets to be paved. "It's a miracle, a town like this," Pink proclaimed to an unimpressed, unsmiling Amanda, who perched on the edge of the porch swing, Hallie in her lap, waiting for word that they were to start home. "You turn on a spigot and water squirts out. Have electricity coming to the houses now. Have a hundred street lights around the square."

"It's a miracle," Amanda admitted. "Pink—"

"Have John Philip Sousa here tomorrow," Pink said, smiling at her. "Twenty-piece band."

"Pink, we're going home," she told him.

"That's at the opera house. Never thought I'd get a chance to see him."

"Pink, you're not to delay these children and me from—"

"You—you want to go see him tomorrow afternoon, Amanda?" he asked hopefully, grinning at her.

"Pink, I'm so worn out hauling around this child and trying to keep her changed—"

Nettie King came out from the house, an ear of boiled corn in her hand, dripping butter. Chewing on it, she leaned against a porch post and stared critically at Pink. "Well, did you get your fill of politics?" she asked him.

Nothing could keep him from staying the night. The four slept on pallets on Nettie's floor, and next day he tried to get tickets, but finding there were no tickets to be bought at any price within his means, he hurried with the boy up the street to the town's theatre, where a play was scheduled with a touring company. There he was able to trade his hand-tooled leather belt for a ticket down front, one lone ticket. He took Frederick through the usher's station, saying the boy would sit on his lap, and for the entire four acts—an almost interminable presentation of a Dion Boucicault melodrama, he sat wide-eyed, holding the two-year-old. The boy, daring not a word, was subdued by study of his father, entranced, eyes blazing, concentrating on the score of actors moving across the brightly lighted stage.

Pink told the story of the play to Amanda. He tried to tell it to Hugh, as well, but Hugh interrupted after a while, said it sounded like damn foolishness. "When you come to work with me, Pink," he told him, "when you do arrive, now I hope you'll not go running off to waste your time like this, will you?"

After that outing, he stayed at the house with Amanda for some months, saying nothing more about moving to the city. In late March now and then he would go hunting, generally accompanied by Wurth or Enid King. He would come home to stare at the fire and talk to his boy and baby girl. He would lie in the bed beside Amanda without daring to touch her.

Then in April, he made a trip to town. Soon after that, one evening at dusk, he told Amanda they would be leaving here. It was his right to make such a decision, he informed her. "We will take all we own that can be moved," he said. She began to argue; however, that evening an hour after dark, three wagons came down the hill road from the ridge, crossed the river, made their way to the road that led to Pink and Amanda's house. Hugh King drove the lead wagon. He and the two other drivers came indoors and, without a word, began to move the furniture. The packing, such as it was, was all done in a matter of minutes. Amanda stared dry-eyed, astonished as the bed linens were crammed into the chests, as the dishes were wrapped in newspapers and put in a box, as even her box of soda and bags of spices were packed in pots, their lids tied shut. The pigs and chickens were caught, their feet were tied, and they were loaded in one of the wagons. The cow, the calf, and the horse were hitched to the back of the third wagon. The fires inside the house were doused with water and the spring bucket was then stacked on the wagon. Amanda watched with dismay as the last lamp was extinguished, then that lamp was packed away, and she with her baby, bundled in blankets, were shown to the third wagon, where a buckboard seat was reserved for them. Pink took Frederick with him in the second wagon. Without much noise, with a mere touch of the reins on the horses' backs, the beasts lurched forward into their harness, the wagons moved forward. The house door, left open, moved in the wind. "You want to stop and close it?" Hugh inquired of Pink.

"No, it'll close soon enough," Pink told him. "Let Wurth do it."

On the ridge road, Pink looked down at the village, the smoke curling up lazily from the chimneys of houses huddled in plowed fields, the river winding between rows of balm trees.

"Can you ever go home to visit?" Hugh King asked him.

"Don't know," Pink told him, a smile lingering. It was his life, after all, to risk, to gamble with. A man planted himself as surely as he planted any other crop, and the place turned him into itself, the land helped shape the man. He would not plant himself in soil he couldn't grow in. A place conspired in various ways to grow its own people, even as it grew its own pines and oaks and hickories and laurel. In the end, at death, it took unto itself the bodies, so that even they nourished the land from which they had come, had at least in some ways become. He meant to transplant himself and Amanda. The children wouldn't mind, Hallie and Frederick would not even remember this place, but leaving would tear at his and Amanda's hearts.

"You say goodbye to anybody?" Hugh King asked, staring down at the village.

"No," Pink said. "Papa must know I have to leave." At the ridge crest they met the Vances returning home, and Vance raised his cap off his head, as at a wake or other solemn ceremony. His women were dark as death, without smiles on their faces.

Pink walked along beside Hugh's wagon for a long way. The exercise helping relieve the pressure he felt. He and Hugh began to talk about the store, a few changes Pink suggested, and the house Hugh owned, which would be lent to Pink as part of his pay. And they talked about life, how it was in the city. Then Pink talked about the strangeness of tearing up his roots.

Four generations earlier, in the 1780s, all this land the wagons rolled through had been purchased and the holdings first registered. The early settlers had been a new breed for all times, in that they needed to accept no territorial claims on their land by any distant power, whether French or English or Spanish or Indian. They were themselves the conquerors, the flesh and blood and bone offspring of Jutes and Danes conquered by Saxons, conquered by Normans. Most had been workers of land owned by lords who took tithes, who governed it from pillowed chairs. None of that humiliation was to be tolerated now. These English and German and Scotch-Irish settlers had divided this great territory, which had never been owned by individuals. This plot is mine, from that there bent tree to the red rock in the middle of Bear Creek, then up the creek to the bold spring, then along to the bee tree my boy and me marked with three notches, then with the ridge to a forked spruce, then down the hill to the startingplace, two thousand acres in all, more or less. These Wrights and Kings and the other families—famished for land to own—these survivors of servitude, were hungry for their own pieces of earth and meant to live on them, and clear them, nurture them, and be nurtured by them. Those three wagons were moving through land that had been in that way parceled out. Those wagons were rolling away from land that over a hundred years ago had been so proudly parceled out to Pink's ancestors. The tall man walking along beside one of the wagons was leaving his inheritance. He was walking off the land his family had passed on from father to son. He was leaving the fences that had been built, the solid cribs, the cleared fields, the stone and chestnut rail fences, the stone chimneys, the smokehouses, the cattle and horse barns well dovetailed, the springhouses, apple houses, chickenhouses; he was leaving oxen and horses, cattle and sheep, pigs unnumbered, numberless; he was leaving forge and mill, hoe and saw and hammer and sledge and chain, yoke and harness. Leaving the roads that were in place. Leaving father, mother, brother.

The house in town they moved to had suffered from standing empty for some time now, while Hugh waited hopefully for Pink to reach a decision. Pink built fires in the three grates, in hopes a warm house would prove welcoming. There were four rooms. It was a square house with running water in the kitchen, and a privy in the backyard. Also outdoors were a woodshed and a small chickenhouse. Just now Amanda's milk cow and calf stood in the grassless backyard, near the chickenhouse; there was no pasture nearby or in sight, and no shed at all except the woodshed.

The entire family crawled into one bed, once it was made, and Pink slept till midday. Amanda had need to be up, to feed the babies and to arrange the furniture. When Pink appeared she said nothing to him. Hugh King arrived, and he and Pink took the stock on to sell it on Lexington Avenue—a straggly, pitiful procession, the cow walking in the lead, the calf and horse following, the pigs in a cart, two neighborhood dogs barking at them.

By the time evening arrived, Amanda had supper ready. That is, she had a chicken roasted and milk-and-flour gravy made, had a few potatoes and hot biscuits. She had the furniture arranged well enough for use and a table laid in a corner of the kitchen. Pink, who had been at the store working, had a jar of whiskey, from which he sipped repeatedly. After supper, they took the two chairs from the table to the parlor, where a coal hearthfire was warm on their hands and faces, and Amanda told about the locks, which ones worked, which key worked or was missing. This she told without emphasis, out of a daze, Pink now and again sniffing his jar of whiskey, tasting it. They were like strangers thrown together in a family, neither sure of the other. On the walls firelight cast shadows of their tilting bodies as they sought and avoided one another. The shadows are just about as real as we are, Amanda told herself.

Guests arrived, Hugh King with his wife, bringing gifts: a cake, a pint of butter churned that day, fresh milk, eggs just laid, a peck of apples, most of them Golden Sweets, a jug of molasses, several molds of cheese Nettie had made that morning, which she said could use further wheying. Taking over the chairs, the women chatted, discussed the need for a new crib, for a parlor table that could be used for dining, for another chair or so, for curtains, while Pink and Hugh worried about whether the windows were shutting tightly enough.

Finally the guests left, a porch light showing them the walk to the street, then the children had to be put to bed. After Amanda took a lantern to the privy, she reported that a possum had moved through bushes nearby. "Have to pick him up by his tail one evening, or he'll eat up my garden."

"We going to have a garden?" Pink asked her, surprised.

"Why, I'd say so," she said.

"Store has food enough, and the food's part of my pay," he told her.

Helplessly Amanda considered him, considered this new addition to their predicament. "Even so," she said.

After she went into their bedroom, he sat near the fire reading the Sears Roebuck catalogue, and only when she was almost asleep did he turn off the lights and crawl in beside her. Amanda mentioned that Nettie had a cow, even here in the city, and she wondered if she might have her cow back. He said Nettie had a pasture at her house. She mentioned wanting a bigger fenced yard for the chickens, too. He told her there were eggs at the store, eggs were virtually being given away on Lexington Avenue, everybody had more eggs than they wanted. He slept beside her, but they were still in two worlds; camped together, they were like foreigners in a foreign place.

She knew the Bible said that she was to leave her own people and go with him, that his people were to become her people, his ways her ways. However, she had known his people and their ways all her life, had been trained to take her place with them. He had changed his people and ways and was challenging her. Even so, there was no need to stretch her own patience about it. One life they had to live, and she knew it must be lived together. A person must respond at such times. She must be a weaver of lives, as well as threads. "I tell you, Pink, what I'm thinking," she mentioned to him. When he said nothing, she continued undaunted, "I think we're going to be all right here."

Pink had no set hours to work at Hugh's store. He would go up there first thing of a morning and do whatever was needed, haul goods off farmers' wagons and do swapping and selling until there came a slack time, then he would come home for an hour, play with his babies, do a few chores, such as bring in the coal. Then directly after the noon meal he would go back to the store, returning home for the evening meal and a quiet time listening to Amanda discuss the house, the way something was or wasn't working, or a pain she or a child had, and tell about her day, which often took up half an hour of time, Amanda meandering about among details that others, most anybody, would forget or dismiss. Then he would return to the store. If Hugh wasn't there, Pink was in charge. More often, both were there making trades, bargaining for different lots of merchandise.

The store, merely an assembly of stalls and sheds, grew or receded week by week to suit the need. It had a wooden floor over only part of the area, gravel on the remainder. There was a big wood stove set near the front door, with a stovepipe jutting upward through the tin roof; the stove heated the area around itself, hugged itself with heat, and often in that effort the stove and stovepipe turning a vibrant amber. A person standing nearby would soon be warm on one side, even though cold on the other. Pink avoided the stove, found it a nuisance to become warm only to have to hustle back out onto the street to meet with a visitor from up home, or a farmer from near Black Mountain who had a hog for sale, or was hawking a load of firewood, or a box of quilts his wife and daughters had made, or a bolt of cloth they had woven, or chairs locally made, or an old table his father had made from a wide board of walnut, or a box of Mason jars full of canned apples, or a few jars of whiskey or brandy, or a keg of cider, or two one-gallon cans of paint bought some months ago and not needed, and not returned until now, the farmer's next trip to town, or a farmer wanting to trade a load of cabbages or a dozen apple trees properly grafted.

Pink had to know the value of most everything, and this knowledge had to be in his head, not on a piece of paper. There was precious little paper around the store. Also, values changed hour by hour, as well as month by month. In the morning a bushel of peas might be worth more than the same bushel in the afternoon, owing to a tide of similar merchandise flowing in.

Pink's main assets included his memory for figures—he could add, subtract, or multiply in his head—and he was able to discusss a price on a man's products without angering him. Some of the other market men along Lexington Avenue would say: "Oh, not that, you're not trying to sell that, are you? Why, it's not worth anything at all, now is it?" That attitude annoyed farmers whose livelihood depended on the merchandise. Pink's inclination was to praise the person and the goods. His reason for not taking an offering was his lack of need just now for it, or space to store it, or money to buy it with. He was always the one admitting the fault. Of course a farmer would know, if he stayed near the store, that Pink did buy goods of similar type all through the day. If they accosted him about that, he would laugh and say the world changes, has to change. If a mistake was made, Pink admitted to it. If a fault existed, Pink admitted it was his own.

Hugh King would watch him, a pleased awed grin on his face. He told Nettie there had never been a single person complain about Pink, even though Pink had to turn down nine out of ten who came to him. "He'll stand there in the road talking for twenty minutes to a man about his ailments, or his wife's ailments, or where he's from, what size family he has, all the while knowing there's no gain in it, and when he sees the man again he'll ask about his ailment and his family, recalling the names of the children. He has a thousand friends all over the street, even though only a hundred ever sold him a dime's worth of anything, and he gets first offer from half the men in this territory. They'd rather be turned down by Pink Wright than bought by another."

Each year every stand on Lexington Avenue near about lost money in winter and early spring. These were the hard days, several months of tightening belts, trying to sell banjos, guitars, knives, or to trade silver and gold coins, or rifles, pistols, steel traps. Pink led Hugh King into the fur business, then into the ginseng trade, both of which Pink knew from home in Vancetown, from the family store.

The store was growing, that was the truth of it; the store was becoming a success. Already it was the largest store on the street.

Amanda was first to notice that, whenever she told a story to Frederick, Hallie was as likely as he to laugh at it. This was when the boy was about four years of age and Hallie three. And Hallie also knew that Frederick was supposed to clean his shoes before entering the front door of the house; whenever Frederick forgot, which was common, Hallie would remind him. Amanda noticed these and many another sign. It was not that Frederick was dense or dim, she assured herself, but only that the little girl was exceptional. And talk—well, Hallie could talk a blue streak, as her father termed it. At dinner he would ask each child what his or her day had been like, what had happened, and the boy, Frederick, would respond briefly, but that Hallie would talk for several minutes about a collection of incidents, and her recitations delighted her father, stamped a big grin on his face as he listened, asked him to stop eating his supper to consider the bouncy, pretty miracle next to him at the table. Her precociousness was disturbing to Frederick, however, and Amanda found herself now and then interrupting Hallie, trying to silence the child, because she could not bear to look at Frederick's surprised face as yet again she bested or corrected him.

Then, too, Amanda worried about Pink's attitude toward them, his shift of interest from Frederick to Hallie, which was all too apparent. After supper Pink would take both children to the porch swing, set one on each side, and would tell them about his trades at the store that day—perhaps he had made a sale to the new hotel, one of three that had recently opened—and it did appear that the girl understood what he was saying and followed with interest, while Frederick soon was playing with Pink's string necktie, or was trying to get his father's watch out of his pocket. Hallie likely as not asked her father quite intelligent questions.

Of course, other parents had similar problems. Boys develop slower, Nettie King told her. She had read that in a magazine. Nettie herself had three boys, only gave birth to boys, to hear her talk about it, and some were quicker than others, she had noticed, Brodie being brighter than Noah, according to her, but Noah had an asset in his dependability. Brodie had run away from home twice, and he only ten years old; both times Hugh had found him down at the railroad station looking at the trains and the tourists, and talking with the Negroes.

"I told him, You'll turn into a Negro, if you don't take care," Nettie reported to Amanda, adjusting her back to the pillows in Amanda's porch swing, staring about at the world in her characteristically forthright, direct manner. "Brodie would roll his sleeves up to see if it was happening yet."

"What was happening?" Amanda asked, one eye on Frederick and Hallie, who were playing in the front yard, a bit too close to the road to suit her. "You children come closer to this porch before I cut a switch," she called to them.

"Turning black on his skin." Nettie fanned herself with a Central Methodist Church fan that had been stuck in the swing slats. "I caught Brodie in the back of the hall, near the back window, taking down his pants and peering at himself, to catch the first sign of darkening."

Amanda laughed. "Why, you never."

Nettie studied her expression, to judge her sense of humor.

Amanda called sharply to her own children. Frederick was down on the sidewalk throwing dirt at a wagon that was rolling by. Amanda told him and Hallie to come to the porch steps and sit down. Slowly, reluctantly, they approached the steps, Frederick a ball of mud by now, his hands and clothes covered. "I'll have to dump you in a tub here directly," Amanda chided. "Hallie, how can you play in dirt and not get dirty?"

"Was playing an angel," Hallie told her.

Amanda considered that, winked at Nettie. "That's nice." The child did seem to have a unique imagination.

"I finally had to tell the boys they wouldn't turn into coloreds," Nettie confessed.

"What sort of angel were you?" Amanda asked Hallie.

"Blue-eyed," Hallie told her.

Amanda laughed. "Oh well." She did love her so much; often a wave of affection would pass through her, a current of pure love for her and, of course, for both her children. She simply wanted to squeeze them.

The two women walked out to the backyard. Even if they came together three afternoons a week, they would make a tour of the backyard. With the children trailing, the women paced the garden, which was only eight twenty-foot rows, a garden scarcely large enough to make a meal of anything, Amanda complained. "And no paddock, no place for a cow." That was a recurring criticism of the city, that she had no cow, and therefore no pet to care for, to move from feeding place to feeding place, and no schedule requiring her presence of a morning and evening. "I don't know where I am, since I don't need to be anywhere," she said to Nettie.

"Hugh says people try to buy our pasture," Nettie said, "now that houses are built all around."

Amanda stopped in the middle of the butterbean row. "What will he do?"

"Why, he'll trade anything he owns given time, saving the boys and me," she said. "Then I'll have to do without, that's all."

The hot southern sun beat down on the two women and the two children, an afternoon sun from a clear blue sky. The mountains were outlined starkly all about. "Pink says the mountains here are resting, while at home they loom up at you," Amanda said.

"No, they don't come on you unawares here," Nettie agreed. "They give warning."

"He says we have more gentle land in Asheville than other places have."

"Well, I don't know about that."

"Did you spank Brodie for running away, going to the station?"

"Twice found him down at the station. I worry about the boy sometimes, but when you have several . . ."

"I was about to say, does spanking do any good?"

"I can't spend all my time on any one, now can I?"

They walked back to the boxlike house, took chairs in the kitchen, leaving the door open to the little back porch, and Amanda made tea, which she served with cookies, the children sharing with them, except that their tea was weaker. The four people sat at the kitchen table, one to a side, letting the day lapse. "So much time in the city," Amanda said lethargically. "Sweep the house and try to dust, that takes thirty minutes."

Nettie frowned at Hallie, who had floated her cookie in her tea and was bobbing it up and down with a finger, softening it.

"Straighten the beds. How long does that take? Ten minutes at most. Then there's a spate of cooking the morning till Pink comes home. He's here the better part of an hour. There's nothing for all afternoon, except for that little garden and my chickens. And now Pink says two different neighbors told him the rooster wakes them up in the morning and we ought to get shut of it."

"Well, what else is a rooster for?" Nettie asked.

"No, don't get rid of Rainbow," Hallie cried, and Frederick at once took up the chant, imitating her.

"Imagine it's on Sundays neighbors like to sleep," Nettie said, nibbling at a cookie. "Well, I'll say this, it's pleasant not to have to grow all your own food, giving the devil his due, and it is the devil's life. We have more meat here, too, you'll have to admit that; we have more meat in the city than we ever had in the country, where we had to arrange for it and loiter out."

"Loiter out?" Amanda asked. "What does that mean?"

"You know yourself if you have a hog killed you've got to use only what you need, have so much lard and meat to last till next time."

"Next time what?" Amanda asked.

"Next time you kill a hog. That'll be the following winter. Can't go out and kill a hog in spring, now can you? nor summer, nor autumn. Have to have the cold weather."

"Loiter out?" Amanda asked, persisting.

"Have to loiter it," Nettie said, nibbling at her cookie, ignoring the criticism of her choice of words.

Amanda shrugged, turned to stare out the kitchen window at the garden place, where birds were circling now. "If I had a cow, I could be churning this evening."

"Well . . ." Nettie smiled bleakly, nodded. "That reminds me," she said, and took her bonnet from her apron string, where she had tied it, and put it on her head, making ready to go home.

"Hallie climbed up on the chickenhouse roof again," Amanda complained to Pink after supper. Hallie looked up from the table where she was writing out her name in floral lettering. "Sunday we can go to ride, can't we, Pink?" Amanda said.

The children set up a racket, urging him to say yes.

"Go out into the country," Amanda said. "Somewhere. I'll fix a picnic, like last time. Maybe we can find a church to stop at," she said. She preferred the country churches. There did seem to be more religion in them. The Methodist church here in town was stiff and proper; the choir did the singing and the minister talked about the need for pledges for the furnace repairs.

"What if it rains, papa?" Hallie asked, recalling the one complication that might well deter them. Whatever carriage Pink rented or borrowed, none would protect the driver, Pink himself, from rain.

"Oh, hush, Hallie. Tend to your own knitting," Amanda said to her.

The child pouted. "Ma'am?" she said, and suddenly stuck her tongue out at her.

"Did you see that? Did you see that, Pink? Did you?" She was breathless from surprise.

"Now, now," Pink said, scooping Hallie up in his arms, going away with her, telling her as he hurried away that she ought not to stick her tongue out at her mother, even in joking. The harm was done, however; tears welled up into Amanda's eyes. Frederick put his little arm around her, told her not to cry, called her mummy, mummy, and began crying himself while she cuddled him close. She kissed his forehead and his fat little cheek. Pretty boy, pretty little boy. Everybody said he could win a prize in any baby contest, if she would only enter him. There was one at the church coming up soon now. "Did you see what she did, Frederick?" Amanda asked him.

Sometimes she went to the cloth shop. The manager would let her take home cloth for dresses or shirts, or yarn for knitting, Pink later to pay the cost. Soon she had made enough clothes for the children for years to come, and had made Pink a dozen shirts. For other clothes usually she would go to the rag shop, which was operated by a church group to help poor mountain people. Wealthy patrons up north had sent clothes, those no longer needed, and the clothes were available for a few pennies. Pink had two wool suits from a shop in New York City, two pairs of leather gloves, and he had seventeen silk neckties, which he rarely wore, and pants enough; he had a hunting jacket, a pair of fisherman's hip boots, a pair of galoshes, and cleated shoes, which he wore to the chicken lot in muddy weather.

Amanda often went inside the shop, passing the time, but she didn't understand Winkler, the manager, a stoop-shouldered, half-blind fellow, a local amateur historian who insisted on knowing who she was, who her father was, and what people she had come from. He once had asked her to trace her ancestry back to English settlers, the Scotch-Irish, or the Germans, the immigrant groups who, as Winkler said, "bought all this land, once it was free of Indian ownership, bargaining among themselves for it, then bred and fussed and warred and became people strange as Asians," all that according to Mr. Winkler, who sometimes spoke at the new library. "But if indeed your grandmother was German," he had said to Amanda, "where is one word that's German in your vocabulary? You see, there are no German words remaining; the English ate them up," he claimed jubilantly, triumphantly.

"Ate up what?" Amanda had asked, a hot spell striking her. She had no idea what the old man was barking about.

"Ate up the German," he proclaimed. "The English eat up everything." He laughed, as if this were a fit story to be telling, with her little children hiding behind her skirt. Later Hallie came to her in the parlor while she was putting coal in the grate and asked if an Englishman had eaten her grandmother, and Amanda had to reassure her.

The cloth shop was more popular with Amanda. There were many new colors of cloths, now that factories were making them. "Law, I never would put that there color on my back, nor on them youngins neither," an old woman customer told Amanda, blushing. "Hit's a scarlet letter."

"Here's a bright green, mama," the shopkeeper told the old woman. "Look at this," he said, folding a piece over his forearm, holding it just below her neck. "There you are."

"Not fer me," the old woman croaked. "Hit's for Sal, though. Hit'd suit Sal."

"Wouldn't hurt, mama, to have a blouse or two for yourself. See this here yellow. Look how it shines." He took it to the window, where sunlight glistened on it. "That's valuable stuff. Comes from Greensboro, is shipped in by the railroad."

The old woman had not taken her eyes off that yellow cloth; she was mesmerized by the color. She would not be deprived of it, a piece of it, enough for a bonnet if not a dress. "Is it sumac?" she asked.

"What's that?" The storekeeper asked, curiously considering the question. "No, it's cotton cloth."

"Is the color made from sumac?" she asked, whispering as if she were venturing into secret territory.

"Why, they never told me."

"I've made a yellar out of sumac, and one out of goldenrods, but there's a natural dullness to them."

"Nothing natural about dullness. You ought to stop thinking that way."

"Used to use cochineal for a red, but we never got it that bright," the old woman admitted.

"No, you can't do it," he assured her. "It's not country dyes. It's made up—somehow or other. It's mixed."

"Well, we stirred our'n."

"Yes, I don't know just where it all comes from. It's done in beakers, somebody told me. It's a secret, I'm sure."

"From me?"

"From me, too. Every company has its secrets. Now this here lavender is for curtains, I'd say. Can you imagine your cabin with lavender curtains on the east window to catch the morning sun, brighten your day? And here, this here is a new color, can't recall the name, think it starts with a c. And this here is a bolt of wool, one hundred percent wool. . . . "

The old woman felt the fabric, frowning thoughtfully. "Won't hold up, wove that way," she said. "Too loose to last."

"Don't you worry about lasting. When it wears out, you come buy a new piece. Wear it out quick as you please and come buy another piece."

"My wool cloth will outlast a man's life," the old woman told him proudly.

The shopkeeper smiled kindly at her. "Don't want to sell anything like that around here, ma'am," he admitted.

Young people particularly were annoyed by the homemade cloths and their dull colors, and the symbolism of rural isolation attached to them. They wanted what was new and bright, never mind that it would wear out, rip and snag. One mother of a dozen children told Amanda she was reluctant to part with any more money for cloth. "My papa never bought a piece of cloth in his entire life." Roughly she pushed her two oldest daughters out of one shop, both dressed in factory-made dresses they had bought. "Look exactly like a rose garden," she called, storming after them. "Better run show off afore them dresses wears out."

There was a store for selling canning jars, but it was open only in the summertime. There was a shop for gifts, candy being the most popular item, stick peppermint candy particularly. "The chocolates are too bad to run," the storekeeper told Amanda one day, when she asked for a box of chocolates to take to Nettie on her birthday. There were cafés where a few set meals were provided: beef stew, beans, potatoes, strong coffee, fruit pies. Ben Raper made his beef stew himself, much as his mother had back in Wilkins Gap. He would cut the lean beef into chunks, brown them in bacon drippings along with a handful of chopped onion and carrots—"Enough to taste, but not quite taste"—then simmer them in water and beef stock for two or three hours, seasoned with salt and garlic. If he didn't have garlic, he would use a handsome supply of pepper, but usually there was garlic.

•   •   •

44

One January day Pink was cleaning up around the store when Clarence Crawford, one of Hugh's cousins, approached him about the matter of an insurance policy. Clarence had just begun selling insurance and was not familiar with the policy. Turned out, as Hugh commented later to Nettie, that it began to look as if Pink were selling the policy to Clarence. Quickly Pink would grasp the meaning of the various sections and would explain to Clarence what was being offered. "When you die you get a thousand dollars," Clarence kept telling Pink. That was what he cared about.

"I don't know what I'll do with it then," Pink told him.

"No, it's for your widow. What would she do today, if you passed on?"

"Marry better than she did the first time."

"Don't you have children to home? What about them?"

"Wait a minute," Pink said, unfolding the policy on a bin of feed corn. "It says either the policyholder or the company can cancel this policy on thirty days' notice."

"Either one," Clarence reiterated. You have the same right that the company has."

"But, if I get sick, the company can cancel."

Clarence pawed helplessly at the policy form. "Do you want to buy it or not, Pink?"

"Don't know," Pink said, scanning the other clauses, jabbing his finger at various exclusions.

Later in the week he visited an insurance office in town, where two different policies were offered, and of the three he decided Clarence's was the best, and he told him so and said he might buy a policy later on, if only to help Clarence out. Later that week he even sold a policy to a farmer, and had Clarence write it out. Yet again he sold a policy, the commission going to Clarence once more. The third time he made a sale, however, Clarence told him where to get a supply of policies for himself. Before the month was out Pink had sold half a dozen, making enough to pay for two new cushioned chairs to give Amanda, and a rubber ball for Hallie.

CHAPTER
Four

A family of Swiss living near Henderson-ville made a sterility cream for women to use. It would kill male sperm on contact, the inventors claimed. Pink arranged for delivery of a supply, expecting it to be a boon. The Swiss man, who brought it in canning jars to the store, sold it either by pint or quart. The recipe was secret, but there was a fair amount of turpentine in it, Pink could tell that, and there was maple flavoring. Anyway, Pink would get a whiff of maple now and again. "Bambuds in it," Pink told Amanda one night in bed. "You smell the bambuds?"

"Well, that won't hurt me, will it?" she said. She was not completely at ease with the medication, which did sting when first applied. She wanted to bear another baby, that was the truth, and disliked using the cream.

"You boil them in suet," Pink told her. "Make salve."

"I know how to make salve," Amanda told him, cuddling close to him. "Is that all it is, I wonder?"

"It's more'n that," Pink assured her, taking her in his arms. "Must be fifty percent alcohol at least." He loved Amanda deeply, loved her in the manner of a man who has never known another woman. This was not a matter of personality but of a deeper, life-rewarding functioning. She was the only person he had known intimately, touched intimately, been touched by, since leaving his mother's breasts; Amanda was his only companion, in the sense of body or emotions. He was renewing himself with her, moving deeper into life than he would be able to go alone, or, he supposed, with any other person.

What other young man would have presented himself to her, if Pink had not, he wondered. That Pearson boy? The Colemans' eldest? Maybe an older man would have stepped in and taken advantage of the opportunity, a widower with land and stock, with a few children in need of a mother. Pink had never asked Amanda about alternatives. He had never wanted to expose her to idle tortures.

When did he begin loving her? After Harry left, the commitment had grown, matured. Was it on the wedding night, and the subsequent nights when they found each other, experimenting, exploring? Was it a result of the birth of the children? Yes, that was much it, and the recovery from those ordeals. Was it in the evenings sitting about explaining, asking, recognizing himself in her, seeing his reflection softened in her, molded by her, or remolded, finding the reflection he had come to rely on and need, the knowledge of himself that she revealed?

On moving to town there had been unraveling of some family ties, and confusion caused by having new interests. It was far more difficult in town to be one family, except here at night in the dark she and he could come together and erase a fleet of doubts and hesitancies.

One evening after dinner, while they were alone, she confessed to him that she was pregnant. She said no, it was not an error, she had missed three periods in a row.

"Three?" he exclaimed. "Three?"

"I couldn't believe it, Pink, the times," she said quickly.

"My Lord, Amanda," he groaned. "Well, we must see what can be done about it, even so."

"Do what?" she said, frightened.

He stormed away from the kitchen, furious with her. Here she was three to four months along the way, a baby forming, and only now she had told him. He retreated to the porch swing and considered his predicament. Work at the store was going well. The ginseng trade particularly was a boon. His insurance sales were occupying too much of his time, perhaps, but gave rewards. Amanda had finally accepted town life. But now this— this catastrophe. He walked uptown to Clarence's, took his beer over to a corner table, pulled up a chair, got off to himself to think about his own problems, but two farmers from Burnsville came in, sat with him. They had brought in sixteen crates of chickens. "Have a fair load," one of them told him. "Went from farm to farm buying them up. Mostly old birds, but they'll stew."

"Dumplings," the other farmer said.

"Hotels don't need them, tuberculosis hospitals turned me down. What on earth can I do?"

Pink made an offer, which after two beers they accepted. He paid them and sent them to unload the crates at Hugh King's store.

It was late at night, several beers later, when he arrived at the porch and crept to the swing. It made a creaking noise, which annoyed him, because he didn't want to awaken Amanda. He moved to a rocker.

Well, after all, they were located in town now, with doctors nearby, he told himself. Let the doctors decide if the birth was dangerous. This wasn't going to be a midwife delivery. The doctors would operate, if need be, remove the baby. Was the child to be named Pink Wright, Jr.? The Junior was a nuisance, he supposed. Could use a middle name different from his own. That would allow him to spare the Junior. Could let Amanda do that much, choose a middle name from the Bible, anything except Job.

The chair made sharp noises on the porch floor, so he decided not to rock. He couldn't sit there rigidly, however, so a step at a time he made his way to the door. The screen door screeched as he opened it. He managed to open the front door, but only after pushing it sharply; it stuck at the bottom. He made his way into the parlor, stumbling once over a stool. He sat on the sofa for a few minutes, listening to determine if there were footsteps about, or cries of a child.

No sound from Amanda. She was sleeping, secure with her new baby forming.

Hugh was at the store when Pink, an hour later, arrived. "You back again?" Hugh said, a grin coming over his face.

Pink straddled a chair. Sleepily he considered Hugh. "Amanda will walk all over me, Hugh," he said, "if I don't take care."

Hugh suddenly laughed. "I hope so," he said.

He woke in early morning. He had slept on the sweet-potato bags. They were knobby and hard—not as poor a bed as apples made, but not as accommodating as grain, either. He made his way to the apple section and chose a Jonathan, the best apple grown here in the mountains, in his opinion, but this one was not sweet. He tossed it across the street at the gutter and picked out a Sheepnose, instead. He left a note on the desk for Hugh and made his way up the hill to his own house, anxious about Amanda, knowing she would have awakened by now. No telling what she would think of him, come into the house looking like he had slept all night on a bed of potatoes. Even as he first opened the door, he saw her. She was sitting at the back of the hall, Hallie in her arms, Frederick beside her, his head in her lap, asleep. They were there, watching the front door. "It doesn't matter about the baby," he announced.

She laid Hallie aside and awkwardly got to her feet and came forward a few steps. Tears were standing in her eyes, and they began rolling down her cheeks as she hurried to him. He moved into the dark hallway and took her in his arms, held her close, kissing her.

A month later her body naturally rejected the baby, and this sent her into a stupor of regret and fears, of blame of herself, of obstinacy in her depression, so that Pink and the children were powerless to affect her. In time, in several months, she appeared to be all right once more.

Five

The town itself in 1904, when Amanda and Pink arrived in it—tucking themselves under its skin, beginning to breathe its wood- and coal-scented air—had a web of streets, most of them dirt-surfaced, which entwined in helter-skelter fashion, skirting the hills, such as the Battery Porter Hill, where lounged the Battery Park Hotel, made of huge porches and shaded rooms. The mass of downtown streets lay between Battery Hill on the west and Beaucatcher and Sunset Mountain on the east, a distance of perhaps a mile. Another less-busy system of streets lay to the west of Battery Hill, with streetcar tracks down the middle of Patton Avenue and of Depot Street, which curled like a snake all the way to the river and the railroad station, the tannery, the stockyards, passing along the way some two-score unpaved roads serving workers' houses.

Then west of the river, across the concrete Smith bridge, which just now was weathering to a tan-gray, there was yet another settlement, mostly of white working families, mountain people who had pushed their way here from the steeper terrain and were hovering just beyond the river.

The city had a population of fifteen thousand souls and was the largest in the mountains. It had never had much of a plan for itself, except as a county seat, a chance occurrence otherwise, beginning with an inn and a drovers'-lot shed where a few thousand pigs and horses and cattle could be fed of a night. It had been a stagecoach hub, as well, with spokes going out in four directions, the teams being changed at lesser stations every nine miles. The town became a terminus of the railroad, and later a hub for the railroad. It grew. It flowed along its own valleys, like a broad, living river, shaped by the mountains all around, and by Battery Porter Hill near its center, and by roads following the easiest routes to save energy of walkers and riders.

Back about 1887 a few foreign dreamers had arrived, among them the wealthy son George of wealthier father William Henry Vanderbilt, who had been sitting on one of the porches of the Battery Park Hotel after dinner looking off toward the Pisgahs when the thought occurred to him to build a house here, in what seemed to him to be the prettiest scenery he had seen anywhere in the world, and to build a village, as well, a self-contained, planned community of his own, something a duke might make in England, or a noble lord of ancient France. He did as well as he could with his idea, hiring 1,000 workers, constructing in five years on a spot south of town a palace of 250 rooms and a village of perhaps 50 houses, with a church and shops. A decade later other wealthy visionaries arrived, among them Dr. Clove, a patent-medicine manufacturer, and some of these became more practical about even laying out subdivisions. All of them were outlanders, glorying in the mountain people and their simple preference, their peculiarities, their shy wives and pretty daughters, their lean, soft-spoken sons, their toothless grannies given to careful, silent scrutiny, their old men dipping snuff and watching out for dangers.

Two planing mills. An ice factory. Two meat packers. A cotton mill. A business college was now getting underway in a fleet of offices on Patton Avenue. Three auto dealers were hawking their shiny wares. A hospital had opened. Two new office buildings had just opened, along with other buildings. A hundred tourist houses, two banks—watch the unfolding as the town grows, the blossom opens, the husks fall to the sides.

· · ·

Leaning against the wagons or standing near the ever-running concrete drinking fountain men argued about politics. Almost all of them were republicans, result of anti-slavery attitudes. Also, they discussed religion. Jesus and his saving sacrifice were everywhere accepted, but ever so many adults could work up concerns about doctrine, types of baptism, ordination of pastors, and the wiles of church people. "Stood up afore us and said there the new widow sat, young and helpless, couldn't work for mourning, couldn't chop her firewood, couldn't shoot the foxes and other varmints that raided her place. Now who out there will volunteer to serve the Lord this way? The preacher would name off a need, then take a show of hands. Within a month, he got her fireplace wood cut for the year, her stove wood stacked near the kitchen, her fences mended, her garden hoed, her stock bred, her smokehouse stocked, and then he married . . ."

The men laughed and also pretended anguish at such stories; there were many scheming wiles attributed to pastors.

"If the woman dies in the midst of your baptism," a known Methodist asked a known Baptist, others listening, "is she to go to Heaven? I'm asking if she dies between the Father and the Holy Ghost? Let's say it's cold water and she dies while she's immersed the second time."

The Baptist spit a stream of tobacco juice at the gutter, carefully wiped his mouth with the back of his hand. "Would go two-thirds of the way to Heaven," he said.

"Why, ain't God enough? Or Jesus? You've already done the main two parts," the Methodist reminded him.

"Oh, yes," the Baptist admitted. "You're right. Go three-quarters of the way there," he conceded.

"Well, she's going to be lonely outside the gates, off in the woods, ain't she?"

"No, not so. She can camp with the Methodists," the Baptist said.

The whereabouts of children and babies who had not survived to the age of accountability was a bone of contention, and since scarcely a family did not have bitter memories involving such losses, either a brother or sister, or a son or daughter, the various doctrines came under scrutiny. "Air ye saying my little girl is not with Jesus?" a man petulantly shouted into the face of an ordained Presbyterian pastor. "Air ye saying it to my face?"

The preacher saw the glimmer of a knife as it opened. He swallowed, smiled as best he could under difficult circumstances. "I'd say the child's in Jesus' own arms."

In addition to politics and religion, the men and women were given to arguing about Indians. Most of the mountain people had lost family members to Indians in the early days of settlement and earlier during the Revolution, and there had been women raped and children kidnaped by them.

Tourists, who were likely to view Indians, a few of whom visit Lexington Avenue occasionally, as pleasant curiosities attuned mystically to nature, to be photographed and revered, were likely to be startled by views of those mountain people who had been reared in hostile surroundings.

Pink had lived in town three years before he even met a Negro. This man's name was Buxton, and he worked at the Battery Park Hotel, which advertised itself as being the finest hotel in the southern United States. Pink had never been inside the place, but had marveled at it from the foot of Battery Hill, where it perched like a great winged bird. The wings were porches that overlooked the rows of blue mountains to the south and west, and looked down at the town itself, with its wealth of small church steeples. Buxton worked there. He was handsome, big-bodied, had bright eyes and perfect teeth, which he showed off when he smiled. He would come to the market accompanying the chef of the hotel, a foreigner who spoke no English. Buxton, therefore, often did the bartering for the vegetables and fruit, hams and firewood, and whatever else they needed. Every day he and the chef arrived, and Pink advised Buxton and, as best he could, the chef, who was German. Pink also sold Buxton an insurance policy, one large enough to provide him the type of funeral he wanted. Buxton came to like Pink and persuaded a number of other blacks to take out insurance policies with him, so that Pink sold ten policies to blacks working at the hotel.

Negroes were still a novelty to Pink. He had seen none back home, not one. In the old days, people in that county didn't have slaves, didn't like slaveholders, and as a consequence such a person, should he have a slave with him, must be out of the county by nightfall. After the Civil War, after 1865, black people were rarely encountered up there anywhere, even in the daytime. Here in Asheville, however, many freed slaves and their children had taken refuge. They took jobs working for the railroad as porters and station attendants. Others worked for the hotels as porters and cleaners. Mountain whites were unwilling to do that sort of work; a mountain man would not do cleaning, and although a woman would clean up her own yard and house, she would not clean up anybody else's, except as a family member. Once the rich tourists discovered Asheville and settled there, building big houses, the blacks found jobs as house servants, yard men, chauffeurs and the like, and sent word back along the railroad to relatives, saying to come on up here, there was work. Asheville, as it developed, found itself with a growing Negro population. Their houses were made of planks, and all had small porches that perched on brick or wooden posts stuck in concrete sidewalks or in swept yards.

Inadvertently, Buxton and the other black policyholders created trouble for Pink quite soon. It was customary for each policyholder either to pay the agent or to take the payment to the district office on College Street.

The farmers always paid Pink. A mountain man would never seek out an office, exposing himself to officialdom; they would pay Pink or leave the money for him with Hugh or one of Hugh's boys at the store. The blacks, however, enjoyed officialdom and ceremony, and the black policyholders would go every time to the district office to pay.

The manager of the insurance company mentioned his annoyance to Pink, said it irritated white clients, many of them wealthy northerners, one of whom had asked directly if indeed the company insured "niggers." The manager, quick of mind, had replied this was done occasionally as a favor to white clients, in the case of the servant of a white policyholder. As Pink knew, that wasn't true; this manager would insure anybody on earth who could stand erect—he didn't require a physical examination or even an interview.

Pink worried about the problem but hesitated to speak to Buxton about it. He told Amanda, and Amanda, who was afraid of black people, was of little comfort. The problem coasted along for a few weeks, a few months. Christmas, Pink's busy season, came, and he allowed the matter to slide by. The insurance manager was becoming more perturbed. Also, Pink sold more policies to blacks, and the new policyholders also began to appear at the district office, taking their place in line with the white customers. Finally, the manager refused to accept payments at the office from blacks at all.

About this same time, in February, Pink was visited by a white farmer, who said his policy had been canceled by the company. This man said he judged the company had got word that he had been ill. Pink asked the district manager to reconsider, this man having been a policyholder for the year Pink had sold policies. The manager refused. The policyholder naturally felt Pink was involved, since Pink to him was the company.

One night at the dinner table, Amanda and Pink pulled their chairs close together and went over the wording of the policy he had been using for farmers and blacks, Pink marking the problems he had found with the policy, explaining to Amanda what was needed in the way of improvements. He penciled in the changes, marking out and revising. Next day he took the revised policy to the district manager, explaining his needs. Of course, the manager, who liked Pink, advised him against pursuing this nonsense. He referred to actuary tables, to degrees of risk. That same day, Pink took the corrected policy to Dunn printery, where Phil Dunn read it over carefully, clearing his throat from time to time and spitting tobacco or snuff juice into a tin can he carried on a string around his neck. "You need a hundred copies, Pink?"

"I have fifty policyholders, about that," Pink said. "I need fifty extra."

"Cost about as much to do two hundred as one, did you know that?"

"No, I didn't know anything in the world was like that."

"Once I'm set up, have the type set and locked on the press, it makes no difference to me. Now, what's the name of the company, Pink?"

"Amanda hasn't thought of one yet. She likes to name everything." He saw that the reams of paper on the shelf across the counter were in Monarch wrappers. "Thinking about Monarch."

"Monarch," Dunn said, penciling it in on the form. "What address you want?"

"Well, use Hugh's store," Pink said.

"Is this part of the store, Pink?"

"I don't know yet." He was anxious to know, certainly, and that evening sought out Hugh at his home. The two of them sat down in the parlor, with a coal fire to keep them company and a pint jar of liquor at hand. Pink said he had something to talk about, so Hugh prepared to listen; however, neither man wanted to proceed immediately to business. They talked about the liquor, examining the bead and wondering where its maker, Gus Stevens, had hid his still this year. "One year he put it inside his barn." Hugh removed his shoes one by one, stretched his legs out, twinkling his socked toes before the fire. "You remember his barn?"

Pink examined the fire through the jar. The liquor was properly made, in Pink's opinion. It was mellow. "I have this business problem, Hugh," he said, "need to talk with you about it."

"Gus has a pot-bellied still, hand-riveted, holds about fifty gallons of mash. Has three parts: the pot belly, the round head, and the condenser worm."

"You know I have been selling insurance for a while, since I arrived in town."

"All copper, ever damn bit of it."

"Make spare money out of it." Pink showed him the printer's proof of the policy. "Having these printed by Phil Dunn."

Hugh got his spectacles out of his vest and put them on. Warily he approached the writing, having developed early in life a fierce regard for the binding, burning quality of the printed word. He held the paper well away from his person. "I don't believe I'll take out any insurance," he told Pink, and offered him the policy.

"No, no, no," Pink said. "That's our company there."

Hugh looked over the paper once more. "Where is it?"

"We've been in on everything else together, and if you want a part of this, I would like that."

Hugh carefully folded the paper. He stared straight before him.

Pink said, "I mean to move my policyholders over to our company. I will sell to new ones, as well."

"What is it that you're selling?"

"Policies," Pink told him.

"What are the policies worth?" Hugh asked.

"Money when you die, for your funeral, or for your widow. You see, when the weekly payments come in, we put that money in the bank, and when somebody dies, we pay out of the hoard, according to whatever the policy is worth."

Hugh carefully laid the policy aside on a spare chair. He took a piece of tobacco out of his pocket and bit off some of it, moistened it under his lip. "Pink, you getting into it, are you?"

"Well, it's just like they all do it," Pink said. "It'll be risky at the first, until the weekly premiums build up, but once we have the money to meet the claims . . ."

Hugh reached out for the jar, wiped the lip with his thumb, then took a long swig of liquor. He handed the jar to Pink. "Now, when you come at me with the idea of the fur trade, that was something I could see. I could see furs. There's the money, there's the furs. Then you come at me with the ginseng, and there again the product was in sight. I mean it's right there on the counter, and it weighs so much and is dried so well or not, and money is paid for it. I can understand that. We do the same with other crops. I don't buy unseen; I buy what is seen before me, and I pay in cash money, not in promises. I peel off the money from the roll of money in my pocket. You know how I do. You do the same."

"I do the same," Pink agreed.

"Now, the store is doing well. It's a success. And I've given you ten percent of the store already and half the 'seng and fur profits, and all that's in writing."

"I don't have a copy of it, Hugh."

Hugh paused. "I thought I gave it to you."

"Not yet, Hugh."

"Well, I wrote it out. It's in the desk."

"I've not looked."

"It's in the desk. You can find it, Pink. It's signed and witnessed. Ted Peterson, the lawyer, wrote it out in longhand, said it was all right. He charged four dollars, and it took him four minutes. I thought to myself that he ought to have done it in gold." Hugh fretted about the bill, sat there worrying over the few dollars. "I wanted to make a copy first. I put it by to make a copy. You take it and copy it, Pink."

"All right."

"Then forget this other thing."

"Now, Hugh—"

"I mean, it's payment for a promise, for promise of something, but it's all in the air. You can't touch it. You don't pay the man for dying, do you?"

Pink had to laugh.

"You pay him because he paid you, but nothing else is exchanged?"

"Security, he has that," Pink told him.

Hugh gripped his hands together, as if seeking a station to hold to. "I don't know what's secure about the unknown."

"It's been done for years, Hugh. Up north they do it all the time. It's insurance, is all it is."

"Uh huh," Hugh said, unimpressed. "Well . . ." his voice trailed away. He shrugged helplessly.

"Now, it's a question of whether you want to be involved or not, in the company."

"In the Monarch? No, I don't need it."

Pink decided to try approaching the matter differently. He mentioned helping mountain people have a better policy. "Today, when a policy-holder gets sick, the company cancels him."

"Well, I hope you'll learn from them, if you go into this thing. I tell you, if you insure somebody and he dies, it'll strip you. Let's say a man's widow comes into the Monarch office and says she wants her husband's thousand dollars, or whatever it is. How you going to pay it?"

"Well, the company has to pay it."

"And quick, too, I'd imagine," Hugh offered. "I mean, if her husband's laid out in her parlor waiting for undertaking, for a proper suit of burial clothes and a casket, she can't wait around for you to sell your furniture."

"No. I realize that," Pink said. "You've come upon the worst of it, all right."

"Could be two widows a week arrive, the way men are dying these days. Amanda be afraid to answer the door."

"Not planning to use the house, Hugh. I couldn't very well run a company out of my house, because she would have trouble with it."

"I'd say so. Amanda would turn down every applicant. Make him run six miles to prove he was healthy."

"Well, there are other ways," Pink said. "The doctors have a blood-pressure machine and a heart—"

"Make him hang by his God-damned feet from a tree limb."

Pink took a drink of the liquor. "The danger only lasts until the premiums add up in the bank account, Hugh."

"The men bring you nickels, and the widows come for thousands of dollars, don't they?"

"Yes, but the nickels and dimes add up, Hugh."

Hugh said, "I'll pay you to stay out of this thing, Pink."

"Well, I'm going ahead with it."

"Monarch. You are Monarch, are you?"

"That's the truth of it," Pink admitted. "I'd like you in it, though."

"No, God no," Hugh said. "I'd pay money to be kept out of a thing like this."

"If I do have to borrow for the first claim or two, Hugh—"

"Hell, no, I'll die afore I take a live person's money for the dead." He was furious.

"I understand," Pink said. "Hugh, if I do come upon a claim soon . . ."

Hugh shook his head.

"I'll need to borrow a little bit for a short time, at interest."

Hugh glared at the fire, said nothing.

"I have three hundred dollars put by, that's all I have."

"Well, you have more'n your company has," Hugh told him. "Monarch don't have a damn dime."

"I have to take on one client my old company has canceled, and him sick."

Hugh froze in place; his chin stopped moving against the wad of tobacco. "How's that, Pink?"

"The company I've been with, they canceled on a client and him dying."

Hugh stared at the fire. "And what do you say?"

"I have to give him a policy."

"You intend to insure a dying man against his life?" He turned in order to stare squarely at him. He smiled, amusement overtaking him. "Well, sir, I'd say you're daft. Now maybe that'll save you in the long run. Maybe Amanda can plead for her baby's crib and spoons by declaring you are beside yourself."

Pink went by the store on his way home and in the desk found the legal paper Hugh had mentioned. The percentages were there, but Hugh had put in a provision that Pink could not sell his ten percent interest without selling to Hugh or one of his sons, nor could he will it to anybody other than them, either. Those stipulations had not been discussed ever, and they were disappointing to Pink now, even though he could see the point of them and even sympathized with Hugh's desire to keep strangers out of store ownership. Not much to do about this now he decided. He knew he could take away from Hugh most of the ginseng and fur trade, should he open his own store up the street, but he wouldn't do that.

"How did Hugh like the Monarch Company?" Amanda asked when Pink got home.

"He swore by it, Amanda," he told her.

Pink enjoyed having a beer in the afternoon at the tavern next to the printer's, at the corner of Lexington Avenue and College Street. There were at this time, 1907, fifteen bars in the city, serving whiskey as well as beer, and they were hangouts for all elements of the population, from the wealthy tourist to the itinerant bum. Pink came to know many people from every category, and since he admitted to being an insurance man, frequently one of them would ask about a policy and Pink would supply a copy for examination. Of each dollar he collected in premiums, his habit was to put in the bank seventy-five cents for payment of any claims that might arise. If a policyholder did not meet his premium, Pink would put the policy in escrow, a term that came to be well known among the blacks and mountain people. In other words, the policy would be set aside, its magic powers in abeyance, until back payments were made.

For four months not a single policyholder of the Monarch Insurance Company had a death claim. Then a one-thousand-dollar claim arrived, a policy of a mountain man who had lived near Burnsville. Pink took all the money out of the bank, eight hundred fifty dollars, every cent he had there, and borrowed the remainder from five different friends, then he traveled to the widow's house to deliver the money, paying in new ten-dollar bills, creating a sensation locally, which led to the sale of seven policies.

Pink sold several more policies during the week, as other people came to hear about the Burnsville payment. One young man, a Peterson, a fine person, came by the store to ask if he could have a stack of policies to sell around Brevard. He became a salesman of the Monarch Company, and he did well, too, with five sales the first week. Also, Pink sent him a hundred calendars, which he had ordered printed on mounting paper, with a picture of the Virgin Mary holding Jesus; these were to be given away. Of course, Monarch's name was prominent. They were the first calendars ever available to the mountain people. There had been a free calendar page printed every January in the newspaper, but few people subscribed. Normally, a person who needed to know the exact date was required to walk a ways, to a church or store or school, to refer to the newspaper page glued to the wall.

There were not enough hours in the day for Pink now. Hugh complained mildly, not to Pink but to others at the store. So Pink sought him out and told him he would give up the store, if Hugh wished. "I'll trade my ten percent for the house," Pink told him.

Hugh agreed, but asked Pink to continue working during the busy times in return for a salary.

Amanda followed all this with trepidation. There was no business Pink could have gone into that she would have felt more insecure about. So far as she could tell, the family was now stationed on the lip of disaster, was awaiting the imminent deaths of others, any one or two of which would plunge them into bankruptcy. One evening after Pink had finished his supper, Amanda put the children out of the room and discussed her concern with Pink, starting with a few comments about life in the country, about how she missed the country, the rise of spring, the burning of summer, the receding of autumn, the waiting season of winter. She talked a good deal about being near her own people, who would be helpful should anything occur to endanger the family. She talked about his father being a pillar of the community; they were cut off from him, would doubtless be denied help or even an inheritance from the Wrights. And in return for this world of security, she had come to this kitchen in a lumber-built, rickety house—all lumber houses were suspect to her—with a husband whose daily bread depended on a system of work that she had never heard of until he happened upon it, one which was deathly risky. Deny that, if he could.

Pink was annoyed by the criticism. He told her he had planted a new crop, that was all, one that was growing rapidly, seventeen policies sold the last five days. Admittedly that was not much in terms of weekly premiums, but the bank account was growing.

She felt that her family's existence was dependent on other people living for at least a few more years; every night in her sleep she imagined hearing the death rattle in the throats of people she did not know. "And how is today's new policyholders' health?" she inquired. "Do we even know?"

"I've not seen all of them, Amanda, but the reports are that they are forty or younger."

"Well, has a doctor seen them?"

"There's no doctor in Macon County, Amanda. I noticed that one woman applicant had borne a child a year for four years in succession, so she must be healthy."

Amanda ate a spoonful of food. "Her womb will fall to her knees pretty soon, if she doesn't take care."

"I wouldn't have to pay a cent for that," Pink told her.

"How old did her mother live?" That's the way most mountain people judged life expectancy, and indeed that was one of the questions asked on the application Pink had drawn up. He took out of his pocket the current applications, a stack of half a dozen that had come in since yesterday, and found the one for Florence Ylvisaker Johnson. He read her name out, stumbling on the middle part. "It's that Norwegian family," he explained. He traced along the form and announced that Florence's mother was still alive at seventy-four.

"And Florence is thirty?" Amanda inquired. She relaxed, nodded finally, so Pink put a check mark in the upper righthand corner of the form and sat there considering the miracle of business life.

Again, in 1907, Amanda became pregnant. She kept her secret, until in the third month the baby aborted naturally. Within six months, she was pregnant once more, and again nature imposed its penalty. She blamed herself and secretly blamed Pink for putting her into this form of bondage she could not escape, a bondage desperately wanted, loved with her life, feared as she feared pain, hated and longed for.

In most respects this was a happy time of life for Pink. He had no quarrels with anybody. His family was formed, enough family to suit him, anyway, and of ever-increasing interest to him he had his company. Monarch came to have a personality for him, to be his everyday companion, his hobby, his playful worry, the danger present every minute, the rich reward, one source of variety in his life. In 1907 he had over three hundred policyholders, some paying by mail, others paying at the print shop or paying him in person; not a few would come by the house every week and leave the money tucked in his screen door, or hand it to Amanda, or even to little Frederick. On occasions when he needed a sum of money, as for Christmas presents, he would take money from the Monarch account, a bonus for his work as president and owner.

A young banker, Theodore E. Wallerbee, watched over his account and made it a point to talk with him when he came by. Usually this was about half past four, when the bank employees were tallying. Most times Pink would need to get into his safe deposit box. Wallerbee had the keys to the vaults; the keys hung from a hook under his desk, near his right knee. He was careful about the vaults, as he was careful of everything. In age he was twenty-five, in stature he was a small person, with the prettiest, cleanest hands Pink had seen on a man. He had a squint to his eyes and was given to winking, perhaps involuntarily—Pink couldn't decide about that. Often Pink thought of people in terms of fruit and vegetables: there were apple people, pears, turnips, long slender bean people, curious cucumber people, there were field peas. Amanda was a ripe melon. He saw himself as being a pretty good eating apple. Hugh was a sweet potato, freshly dug, with some earthy smell still on it. Well, this man Wallerbee was a pear, a crisp, white pear, peering out of two eyes, winking, surveying the world before him as circumscribed by the walls of his office, the walls of the bank. Pink couldn't imagine him at home, or even having a home. Wallerbee could see most of his domain from his open doorway, from his desk. He could be counted on every evening about 4:30 to look up from his books and focus his eyes on Pink in his doorway, to wink at him. Then a smile would unfold. "Pink, Pink," he would say happily, "how is your insurance company this afternoon?"

Pink would show him the packet of new policies, or hold up a paper sack with his money in it—he always carried money that way, as did his father in Vancetown.

"You bring the money this time, or a sack of onions?" Wallerbee asked.

Pink peeked into his bag. "Don't know." He had himself started the joke about bringing onions to the bank by error.

"Too bad it's not apples," Wallerbee said, leaning back in his chair. "Time for a drink, Pink?"

"Always say yes to the first one."

He winked. A few quick steps to a cabinet. Swish of the arm as the office door closed. The bottle of clear liquid, two small glasses, each of them filled expertly, Pink sipping his, tasting it, letting the liquid flutter about in his mouth to sting and excite. Wallerbee downed his neatly, returned to his chair, rummaged though the sack of money, counting it, making notations. "New bill has been introduced at the legislature in Raleigh to require a hundred thousand dollars in hand, before an insurance company can be started, Pink." He was speaking nonchalantly, and was counting the coins as he said that.

"What bill you mean? One of my bills?"

"It's called the Harrison bill, named after a senator."

"I knew a Harrison or two."

"Are you chartered yet? Those papers I gave you to look over . . ." Wallerbee waited expectantly.

Pink nodded carefully. It was rare for another man to poke into his business. "Not sure."

"You still have them?" Wallerbee asked.

"They're in there, in the safe deposit box."

Wallerbee winked, nodded. "Better fill them out. You want me to take them with me to Raleigh, next time I go?"

"Maybe," Pink said, watching him warily, trying to figure out about his ways, why he would offer.

"I go to Raleigh once a month. I go on a Thursday, work Friday, spend Saturday with friends there." He nodded, winked. "Start home Sunday, arrive in here about midnight. "My sisters wait up for me."

"How much would I owe you?" Pink asked carefully.

Wallerbee nodded, accepting the question. "Not a cent. Glad to do it."

"I'm never quite sure what I ought to do in terms of banks and government," Pink admitted, launching himself on a subject that had annoyed

62

him since his company was begun. "I'm better at selling than keeping books."

"I see." Wallerbee wheezed, winked.

"I need something, but I don't know what, like the Catholic bishop said. I been thinking about putting the company on sounder footing."

"What measure will you take, Pink?"

"I been thinking about you," Pink told him. "You work for the bank, but must have time after work, and I was wondering if I might hire you."

Wallerbee leaned back in his chair and closed his eyes, seemed to be waiting.

"Do you know of any way I could persuade you to work with me?"

For a long while Wallerbee sat there stolid, his expression set as glass, even his breathing silent. He looked up suddenly. "Hand me that bottle, will you, Pink?" Pink set the bottle on his desk and watched as Wallerbee poured for them both. "I've watched your company grow," Wallerbee said. "It has certainly kept on. When we get it incorporated—what do you want, Pink? a partnership, a stock company, or a mutual company? You need one of them to get a license from the State—there is no federal law pertaining to insurance. With a state license, you will be legal."

"I wouldn't mind that," Pink said.

"Partnership, stock, or mutual company, which one?"

"Just like this bank is," Pink said.

"Very well, stock company. Let's assume one thousand shares at a dollar a share. You want your wife to own any?"

"She's scared to death of it," he said.

"Your children?"

"They're too little," Pink said.

"That man you work with. Is his name King?"

"He's not part of it."

"But you must have two others to incorporate, though they don't need to own much."

"You take some then."

"I will take fifty percent or nothing." There was no threat in his manner. He was merely announcing his fee. At the same time the words felt like blows to Pink. He sat down in a chair, searched about in his pockets for his watch, occupying himself that way while his mind raced along. It would be a load of worry off his mind to have his accounts kept, to have bills mailed out when due, to have claims evaluated, to have the government satisfied, and there was prestige in having a banker, even a young one, in his own company. "What do you plan to do for half my company, Wallerbee?"

"I would accept responsibility for the office matters. I would help arrange our loans, when we need them. I would advise you on investing the company funds. I will make reports to you as often as you like, accounting for every cent, every policy."

"Take you about half an hour each evening," Pink said.

"In return for very little profit at the moment."

"You have any children?"

"No." Wallerbee said. "Not maried as yet. My two sisters and I—"

"Fifteen percent," Pink said.

The eyes closed. That fellow has gone in hiding, Pink thought. The pear man wanted the stock, was anxious about it, all right. Pink had made enough trades in his life to be able to tell that.

"Thirty-five percent," Wallerbee said.

Pink said disarmingly, "Where you from, anyway, Wallerbee?"

"Pennsylvania." His eyes were still closed. "What do you say to thirty-five percent?" His voice was straining.

"That new law in Raleigh, will it affect companies that are already in business?" Pink asked.

It was several moments before Wallerbee replied. "No. They can be licensed anyway."

"In other words, my little company has an advantaged position."

Wallerbee hesitated, then nodded.

Pink studied the meticulous, careful man who had forgotten to tell him that. "Well, I need your help, Wallerbee. Twenty percent will please you well enough?" he asked, with the apologetic note in his voice that crept in whenever he made a firm offer. He seemed to be wishing the offer could be more. "Does it take more than two days to incorporate?"

"No," Wallerbee said.

He wanted into the company, Pink could tell. He was needed in it, in a way was an ideal man for it. "Put my wife, Amanda, down for the third person, at one percent, and you for twenty-four percent," Pink said.

Awake now, winking, moving, his clean hands seeking his pen, choosing papers, making notes, the 24 percent going near the top, followed by his initials, then Amanda's full name, with 1 percent after it, then Pink's full name with 75 percent after it.

"How much will it cost to incorporate?" Pink asked.

"I'll have my brother-in-law draw up the papers for free," Wallerbee said. "We'll only owe small filing fees."

"I'll need to take the papers home one night, so Amanda can sign them."

A laugh suddenly washed through Wallerbee, good feeling almost overcame him, and he marched around his desk and hugged Pink, then stood back, beaming up at him, his handsome head tilted to one side. "I believe we are about to make a fortune, sir," he said.

CHAPTER
Six

The economy of the mountain country was loosely hinged to the outside world, reflecting influences belatedly. In 1907, and again in 1908, panic arrived in tides and turnings. When one afternoon Pink went by the bank as usual, about half past four, to leave the new applications with Wallerbee, the bank was actually locked, shut down, with a sign declaring as reason the illness of the manager's mother, Mrs. Biggerstaff. Pink joined a group of worried depositors waiting outside, pouncing on hapless bank employees. At about three o'clock, Wallerbee came outdoors, clutching his jacket around his neck, the economic chill inside apparently having penetrated his clothing. The two men made their way to Patton Avenue, hurrying along, Pink asking about the company's account.

"It's going to be all right, if I succeed." Wallerbee stopped at a street corner. "There was a run on the bank. We got through till noon today." He stared worriedly, vacantly at the swarm of country people filling the sidewalks, workers trying to find access to streetcars, horses shying, two Ford cars bucking, backfiring. "We used all the money we could find." Pink stayed close to Wallerbee, insisting on details, even following him into Hatch Cole's hardware store, the two pausing just inside the door, letting their eyes adjust to the gloom. Pink knew Cole by reputation, as one of the most prosperous of the mountain people who had moved to the city. He was now in his fifties, was white-haired, big-bodied, towering several inches over six feet, his broad shoulders generally stooped, as if a weight rested on him. He appeared before them suddenly, his big head nodding above the frame of his rolltop desk. He nodded to Wallerbee, but his chief concentration was reserved for Pink, whom he had clearly not expected.

Pink stared at the bald spot on Hatch Cole's head, the spot reflecting the overhead small bulb, probably the smallest Cole could buy. Pink stood nearby, but out of the way as Cole and Wallerbee conferred, agreeing to transfer funds from one account to another, shifting Cole's own deposits, completing transfer of stock of the bank itself, apparently adding to the percent of ownership Cole held. Finally, once more the long body unfolded as Cole got up from his desk. He made his way slowly to the hat stand, put on his hat, again noticing Pink, who had retreated to wait near the front door. Sniffing the dusty air, Cole approached the door, reached a clawlike hand forward, clutching Pink's forearm, which he squeezed tightly. "You can sell me an insurance policy whenever you're ready."

Pink smiled. "I'll remember."

"A hundred thousand dollars."

The three men walked together up College Street, several of the farmers greeting Mr. Cole, this towering, almost majestic figure, he returning every salutation with courtly nod and murmured phrases. They turned at Pritchard Park, made their way to the bank's front door, opening it with a key Wallerbee took from his pocket. Around him half a dozen businessmen pressed, asking what the situation was. "Looks like Mrs. Biggerstaff will pull through all right," Wallerbee told them blandly.

Chilly in the bank, Pink noticed; the marble floor and columns exuded a tomblike coldness. He moved close to the vault doors, watched Wallerbee thumb through papers resting in a safe deposit box. Biggerstaff called out an order that more light be furnished. "I don't have the key to the switch," Wallerbee called to him. By now a dozen businessmen were huddled near the front windows, hearing the conversation but not understanding the words. Pink from where he stood could see Mr. Cole kneel on the bare floor, could see him dig his hands deep into a big safe deposit box, bringing out stock and bond certificates tied in bundles. From a second box he then took packets of money tied with string. He stacked these separately.

Biggerstaff came out; Cole was still inside on his knees, a big hulk, a black blob, a shadow, which Pink barely could make out. He heard the hulk cough, then heard a rattle of phlegm in his throat, then a hacking sound as Hatch Cole gathered his spit and splattered it against the wall of the vault. Cole stood. Turning, bending forward toward the big room, he launched his big body forward, holding to the bars near the door. "Wallerbee, you have the other papers to be signed?"

Wallerbee moved into his office, returned. Cole called for a lamp. Wallerbee played the light onto the papers as Cole went through them, sniffling now and again, coughing, finally folding the papers neatly, putting his copies into an inside jacket pocket, making his way to the office doorway, pushing himself into the main room, the bent body spinning slightly off course as it sought the open air and sunlight, his hands moving outward seeking support, one hand grasping Pink's forearm, the clawlike hand holding to Pink as the two moved powerfully forward, pausing only once they were in the coldness of the street, where Cole's big feet were suddenly solidly, securely placed, his legs spread. "Risky business," he murmured, and pushed himself and Pink farther along Patton Avenue, even as a four-horse carriage swung around the curve from Pritchard Park, the driver shouting warning at him, flashing his whip, two of the horses finally stopping on one side of a lamppost, two on the other, both drivers leaping off the carriage, running forward to secure them. Cole, uncaring, moved on.

He paused at the main door of his store, a physical weakness overtaking him, an odor of sourness exuding from him. The big man murmured, "I'm sorry I had to help. I shouldn't have required so much from them, but God knows I didn't ask for it, did I?" He fumbled in his pocket, brought out a pair of gloves, which he pulled on, then moved alone into the black hole of his store.

Pink returned to the bank and waited for Wallerbee to come outside. Biggerstaff came out first, alone, locked the door, said Wallerbee had gone home for the night, not to worry. He seemed to be on the verge of remembering Pink's name.

Pink stopped by Clarence's for a beer. Inside, the stove was throwing off heat, and the thirty or forty customers were boisterous, were celebrating their own lives and greeting one another. There was the odor of wood smoke, of sawdust on the oak floor. Pink stood at the bar, drank his beer. A bearded man four places down turned to stare at him, to focus on his face with some difficulty. "If I die tonight, you going to pay me my money, Pink?"

"I will," Pink said.

"You want me to go on living?"

"Yes," Pink told him.

"Then buy me another drink."

Pink did. Another man, a slight fellow with a leg limp, an injury from timbering, stopped beside him. "Had a job promised in Richmond, but my brother tells me not to go up there now, said it's all over for jobs everywhere, has dried up." He took a bandana handkerchief out of his pants pocket, unfolded it carefully, wiped his mouth, then his nose. "I had two eight-ox teams, had chains enough, had pots and pans for feeding ever'body, and I lost it all in the last depression. Just not a damn thing left, nothing left was worth a damn thing." He poked the handkerchief away in his pocket. "Course, it makes life more interesting, every change. Now this here piss-pot is on us."

Next morning Pink asked Hugh King about the store's bank account. Hugh said he had most of his money safely hid.

"I don't let on about any losses to Amanda," Pink said.

"How is she?" Hugh asked. "She pregnant again?"

"No. I'm trying not to," Pink told him.

"Yeh?" Hugh said, watching him closely. "How?"

"The little rubber things," Pink said.

Hugh laughed, marveling at the thought. "Put your pecker in an envelope, do you? I saw one on the ground here around the place," Hugh said. "Do you poke it in, or do you pull it on?"

"It's most any way you can."

That morning Pink took the company money out of the bank, every cent. At first he hid it under the parlor bed, then decided that wouldn't do. He ended up with the money in the attic, but instead of making him feel more secure, having the money made him feel more at risk.

This depression was similar to others in that it began elsewhere and moved slowly, like a leisurely, casual, deadly giant, toward the mountains, not with any intention of going to mountains or plains or hills; it was meandering about the country devastating whatever it encountered, squashing down business, closing jobs, tightening belts of hunger around the bellies of people, indiscriminately selecting them. "Why, it's going to take the clothes off my wife's back, looks like," one man on King Street complained. People were out of work; men who had had jobs for years, who had felt secure enough, were idle and angry. When the various factories, such as the blanket mill, started laying off workers, the storekeepers had to lay off, too.

Amanda knew within reason that there were hungry people in perhaps a third of the houses in her neighborhood. In one house lived two old people, Craig Arnold and his wife, and they never came out these days. Amanda would go to their door twice a week to deliver a cake she had baked.

The depression couldn't be fought, anymore than could tuberculosis or diphtheria or pneumonia or any other death-touching disease. A depression was not an animal to be hunted down with dogs either, or a substance to be seen, was not even as mist-bodied as fog. It would not clutch the throat, but it suffocated a man, anyway. In Starnes Cove a man hanged himself when he lost his farm; all he and his family had remaining was a wagon and harness, so he secured the harness around his own neck and dropped off the wagon bed and was found, neck broken, ʹdangling over his barn's number-three horse stall.

Up and down the land, men were failing, and everybody was frightened.

All the same it was the best time for trading for those with money, Pink noticed, even as Hatch Cole was demonstrating. Land and stock were selling for a pittance, if one only had money to buy with, ever so many men would work for very little, and choice office space could be leased for a song. Pink's Monarch had an opportunity to move against the tide, he decided, if he could get more cash money. He invited Hugh to come to Ben's Café with him, for coffee, to talk about this.

Ben Raper's café was a one-room affair on the west side of Lexington Avenue, next door to the cloth shop. When the two men arrived, Raper was explaining to his counter customers, all of them farmers, about conditions at his competitors' restaurants. Pink and Hugh listened as Raper berated the café across the street for cooking practices. "I know times are hard, but that's no excuse to take one handful of beef and two handfuls of potatoes. I mean that place right over there, I mean that Harold's Eatery is a-doing it. And that Mitford place up the street, they's putting peas in their'n." He went on and on about that pea place, as he called it. Pink took a table near the window and asked Maggie for two cups of coffee. He often stopped by here, but Hugh came in seldom. Hugh had two places he frequented, his shop and his house; he had no time for idleness, nor had he much patience with it. To sit down at a table and spend half an hour drinking coffee and listening to nonsense was not his idea of a sensible occupation. There was work needing doing, and if there wasn't, there ought to be.

The two men sat near the window, Hugh with his back to the glass so nobody would recognize him, come inside, and annoy him. "Now, what is it, Pink?" he said impatiently, looking about anxiously, as if he feared the wood stove or its hot pipe could connive to strike him. He was wary of most all contrivances arranged by mountain people. "You went up to your home, Nettie told me."

"Last week I went by, saw papa, ate with him and Wurth, listening mostly. I ate a squirrel stew."

"I ain't been home in a coon's age." Hugh took a sip of coffee, at once spit it back into the cup. He stared belligerently at the liquid.

"Ben keeps it on the stove all the time," Pink explained, "and he uses the same grounds over and over."

"They worry about the depression?" Hugh asked.

"They don't have much money up home for it to be depressed, but there are loans outstanding. They are eating well," Pink said. "Several talked to me about taking out policies, or adding to what they have." He waited for Hugh to comment, but was disappointed. "This can be a time of expansion for the company if I can get going soon, open a home office, Hugh."

Hugh frowned at the stovepipe. He tried the coffee once more, again to his complete disappointment.

"People are thinking of family's security now," Pink said, leaning across the table.

Hugh cleared his throat. "I don't know. It has no handle nor tail either, this depression. How do you grab hold?"

"If I can borrow on my policies, I can be ten times as big a year from now."

Hugh frowned at him. "Borrow on them?"

"The policies have loan provisions, and some have been borrowed against. If I can get somebody to buy up my loans to policyholders—"

"It'll take a while to convince any sane person to buy loans," Hugh said.

"The bank won't want to, but Hatch Cole invests in most everything else."

Hugh leaned back comfortably in his chair, tried to fit his long arm over the back of it, gave up on that, leaned forward, his elbows propped on the table. "I don't think Hatch Cole is a fool yet, either."

"I thought you might help me," Pink said, watching him hopefully.

"How much is it?"

"Twenty thousand dollars of loans," Pink said.

Hugh's expression froze. He was motionless all in a moment. He whispered suddenly, "Where'd you get that much?"

"Insurance accumulates that way," Pink said. "It beats anything you ever saw."

A big grin came over Hugh's face. "Well, I'm damned if it ain't robbery."

"I could expand tenfold, if I had that much cash money now. I could go into Hendersonville, Burnsville . . ."

"Now this is the time to hole up, Pink."

"Go into Marshall, Waynesville, Murphy . . ."

"We'll be sending you fare to get home."

"Now is the time to commission the best men. I can get the leaders in each community. There's now unemployed men in every town in the mountains. Get an office open here in Asheville on the square, put a sign in the window, get salesmen on the march."

Hugh laughed, shaking his head in wonder. "My experience with gambling is that a man loses at least one time in three, and if you gamble everything each time, then you will surely lose everything fairly soon."

"The opportunity will be lost to me if I wait," Pink told him.

"I don't buy apples until apple season, Pink. There's a season for everything." He waited for Pink to accept what he said, to confirm his acceptance of it, but Pink only gave him the Pink Wright winkle, as Hugh called his smile. Hugh spit into his coffee cup. "I want you to batten down the hatches, Pink. I'll not loan you on those policies, in order that you can dig a grave."

Outside on the sidewalk Hugh lingered, appeared to be dissatisfied. "Amanda's such a steady, dependable person, Pink," he said, "she certainly deserves what she has, a home with children about the place, a cat or two, a garden. A hard worker, not given to flights like birds. She knows the Bible—"

"She's perfect in every way," Pink admitted.

"She's steady, while you're off hearing songs, seeing visions. If you flip off the far side, you'll doubtless come to me for help, and I'm damned if I'll help you."

"I know what you're saying, Hugh," Pink said coldly, without encouragement.

"You're getting too old to be a delivery boy at the store," Hugh said, the words falling bluntly.

Pink, smiling grimly, unwilling to reveal his hurt, walked with him toward the store. Together they moved through the crowd of farmers and their wives, their sons and daughters, pet dogs and hunting dogs, chickens in coops, the two men walking down the middle of the street together as friends, but Pink's thoughts were disturbed. Too old to be a delivery boy. The words had stung him deeply.

Pink was driven to find money to prove his point, and the thought occurred to him to ask his father for it. He traveled alone to the mountain community, where he asked the Kings for overnight use of the parlor room, then that same night he walked down the hill to the store, where he knew from past experience he was likely to find his father alone, reading. He sat down near his father's big rocker and outlined the prospects he had, the potential of his company, the need for investment funds just now, and his father was patient. "Pink, come on back here and live," he said finally, after the presentation. "No, I won't help you go off on your own."

Pink then asked him to purchase the property he and Amanda owned in this valley.

"No, we don't need to buy what's at our disposal," Wright told him. "Slip another oak log—get a split one, put it in the stove, Pink, so we'll not get bone-cold sitting here. No, I don't want your house."

"Then let me sell it to somebody else."

"No. It's always been Wright land, and it always will be. Can you hear that wind out there? It's roaring."

"Yes, I hear it, papa," Pink said, selecting a rocker, removing his father's orange-colored cat from it. "That was Amanda's family's land, papa, originally."

"The breaths of your ancestors. That heavy gust of wind is from one who buried his first wife up the cove near the creek."

"Papa, I tell you I can double the size of my company—"

"You have a cabin here, land waiting. I told Wurth not to rent it out for more'n a season at a time, in hopes you'd be back."

"Will you loan me money on that cabin and the land?"

"No, no. It's not yours to borrow on, not exactly."

"It's my property, under your own word—" Pink hesitated. Argument was useless. "Then loan me money on my house in town."

"Pink, the first settlers had a world of trees to get rid of. In summer the sunlight never touched the ground in most places. In fall the leaves would fill the air in spells of color, fill the air and the wind, the earth tilting, and the sunlight would be allowed in, a miracle, they termed it."

"Tilting?"

"The earth tilts in fall."

"Tilts?"

"I think so. At times."

"The earth is round, papa."

Wright reached forward and patted a dog that had been whining nearby, wanting attention from him. "Well, if you think so."

"Papa, the world is round. It's proved."

"It might be," Wright said. "And, as another matter of science, man came from monkeys, you realize."

"Well, yes," Pink said, struck by the intricacy and secrecy of his father's personality, which he was meeting tonight anew.

"I judge matters by my own senses," Wright said. "A man who can't do that is adrift."

"But science is a study of facts."

72

"The most joy I have in life is reading at night, over here in the store alone. The Bible, I read that, and such poets and storytellers as come to hand. And I write, passing the time."

"Write what?"

"My thoughts." He brought from a locked, metal tea chest a stack of paper, a hand-written manuscript, which he cuddled on his lap, his hands smoothing out its corners carefully. "This is the third part."

"Papa, I never realized you ever wrote a word."

"I read and write, and pet my animals, and try to feel the pulse of being alive, and listen to the spirits in the air, and feel the tilting of the earth."

"Has Wurth read it?" Pink asked, and wondered if the question revealed jealousy.

"No, he knows it's private matters. He has his own journal, about the weather and details of trades. If I loan on your house in town, then he'll put it down in his book, with a few thoughts."

"Angry ones, maybe."

"I don't know. How much is the house worth?"

"It has plumbing and electricity, has a kitchen, is made of lumber, painted, has two porches, has a quarter acre of land."

"Well, it sounds like a proper place, Pink. You propose to draw up a deed of trust?"

"Yes."

"And the survey, I always ask for a survey."

"I have one."

"I don't mind, Pink, loaning up to two-thirds of its value, and you can get it appraised, or get Hugh to do it."

"Or the bank," Pink suggested.

"Yes, that'd do," Wright said agreeably, pausing to consider his old dog. He rested back in his chair, looking about at the lantern-lit space near the stove, at the empty chairs drawn up for tomorrow's visitors, at the gleam of the new guns and rifles in their locked racks, at the furs stacked on the floor nearby, at the eyes of a stuffed mountain lion that was stationed high on the east wall of the room crouched on a platform Mr. Wright's own father had put there just before his death. "You make the payments directly to me, Pink. I usually work in ten-year increments at six percent."

"I know, papa."

"If you had rather pay quarterly or monthly—"

"By the year suits me."

"That's all right. A tenth of the loan every year, plus the interest due on money that is outstanding."

No concession extended, no lessening of the customary interest, no shading of the requirements, Pink realized.

"I prefer the Genesis story to the jungle one, Pink, I believe. I don't know that either one is accurate, but which is the better story? We have man created by God in God's image, which takes place in a garden, that's story one, and we have man coming out of apes in a jungle."

"But one is scientific, papa," Pink insisted.

"I like poetry, don't you, Pink? I prefer poetry to what I read in the way of facts. Story one is better poetry. I'd be disappointed for my people to choose a sorry story over a beautiful one."

The smile was there. The wry smile of the mountain tradesman. Pink saw that the glimmer was in his eyes, playful, watchful, waiting to see what break might come in his adversary's armor. Pink laughed, abandoned the matter that way, realizing he could not draw from his father any concessions.

The wind, gusting, shook the building suddenly, and the cat hunkered down on Pink's lap.

"That's one of my ancestors moving from place to place," Wright commented, "always in this one valley, Pink. He never leaves us. Just now I suspect he's looking for one of his wives."

Mr. Wright walked with Pink to the trade yard. "You come on back here and live, Pink. Your mother and I want that." The moon was out, shining down on the sleepy community. A hundred yards away a mountain man was going down the road, singing. He was drunk, most likely. "How far away is the moon, Pink?"

"Two hundred thirty-eight thousand miles, Hallie told me."

Wright cleared his throat, appeared to be discontented with the reply. "It's been measured."

"Been measured thousands of times by people all through the ages. It's just beyond the ridge crest, looks to me."

Pink laughed, then realized his father was watching him studiously. "Lord knows, it looks like it, but it's far off."

"It's where it looks like it is," his father said. "Why wouldn't it be? It's just beyond that stand of firs on the ridge. That's where I see it." He caught hold of Pink's arm just about the elbow, pressed his fingers into his flesh. "It's nicer to think of that way."

My father is a lonely thinker, Pink realized. And a sort of poem himself.

Inside the store, Wright drew out a yellow pad from near the arm of his chair and wrote out instructions to an attorney in Burnsville to make a proper loan on the property in Asheville, and to do so expeditiously. He signed the order, Pink noticed, with a flourish, using his full signature, and put the number 4137 under it, as was customary with him. A symbol attesting to the signature's authenticity. The number was his mother's maiden name, Leih, printed and turned upside down. Pink commented on the number. "Most crooks can't remember it," Wright said. "It weeds them out. There was a g in the name originally, I believe, but it got left behind, lost in the American rush."

The intense heat was giving crinkly voice to the tin stove chimney, and a red hue at its first elbow joint. "How often you burn out a pipe, papa?"

"Just whenever," the elderly man admitted. "I sell pipes, so it's wholesale cost. Oak and hickory burn out metal. My stove even came through the bottom once, fire fell out onto the floor. Somebody had cleaned too many of the ashes out of it. Some damn helpful stranger, didn't know better."

Pink had the letter for the attorney, and as he walked toward the King home he folded and unfolded it. He was half a mile toward the King house when he noticed a woods fire in an area near the store. As he retraced his steps, he made out a red tongue of fire on the roof of the store itself. He began running for all his might. He could smell the smoke of old cedar. The fire was noisy and boastful, once he arrived nearby. Already half a dozen men had gathered at the site, howling instructions. "The ghosts from the cemetery must be bellowing the damned flames," one man shouted to a son. "Where's papa?" Pink passed close by, brushing his arm, mounted the steps of the wooden building, heat pushing against him, trying in gusts to hurl him away. He grasped the door knob and it stung his fingers. Again he grasped it, turned it, pulled open the door as a cloud of smoke, thick as water, rolled over him, felling him. Lying on the porch floor, a hand outstretched toward him and he took hold of it, pulled his father from the furnace into the air. Crawling to the steps, he tumbled down them, his father bounding on the steps, both landing on the cold ground near Fortner's feet.

A rain barrel was close enough for boys to slosh water on both men, using a bucket and a big hat. They sloshed them both head to foot, and kept wetting down the old man until at last he began complaining about it. By then the fire was making a great noise, thundering in the bowels of the store, issuing warnings and folds of smoke—more smoke than flame—in fact, no sign of flame inside, only on the roof. Mr. Wright, on his feet, asked Wurth where his cat was. He moved out a ways from the fire, called back instructions that were gobbled up in the fire's mouth. Other men and children, newly arrived, began hurling themselves about, excited by the damage and commotion, the tide rising as the sound of breaking timbers crackled, the building creaked as it was twisted, tested. Now and again the fire would rest, much as might a great beast in fits of hunger, a ravishing hunger followed by resting, considering. Whiskey was passed about. The fire is out, somebody said. No, the fire is merely gathering strength. Now, see how it blazes up near the rear of the store. "There it comes, boys. . . ."

On the spot a calf was stuck, bled, butchered, the pieces rushed forward to be hung as near the fire as boys could bear to carry them. See how the heat of the fire pushes the meat away, bends the poles. "Metal pipe is what we need," one man said. Drugged minds, sleepy dispositions, red eyes, men moving from place to place, trying to stay upwind of the building.

The roof collapsed at 4 A.M., or thereabouts. The fire was beautiful, was ceremonial, celebrating. By dawn, fifty people, maybe more, were seeking coats to put on, the fire no longer warming them. It was over, except to explain how it had started. There were, for instance, footprints of three men distinctly visible in the field, men running away. Enemies of old Mr. Wright, perhaps. Or maybe the fire started in the stove or chimney. "Where's papa?" Pink asked Wurth, conscious suddenly that the old man was not about.

"Must have gone home. Fortner, send to see if papa's to home."

"No, I was there," a boy said. "They were asking about him."

"Papa," Wurth called in a great voice, silencing everyone. A search began and, as the fire died lower, the search reluctantly extended into the ashes itself, where at 5 A.M. Mr. Wright's remains were indeed found; he had been drawn back into the building. His fleshless, steaming bones embracing the brass chest in which he had always stored his journal. Stark white on the charcoal embers were the bones. Pink crouched nearby. Inside the brass box, the manuscript was ashes. The gun barrel and the big square safe remained intact. Maybe what lay inside the safe, the deeds, the records of loans made, the wills, the dates of birth and death, all that remained, but nothing of his father's journal, or the books he treasured. Pink wandered about aimlessly, heedless of his own tears. He saw on the ground two marbles. My birthright, he told himself, holding them. They were two eyes of the stuffed mountain lion, perhaps the last one shot here, the last of that vanished breed. As was his father.

The will was read on the day following the funeral. To the daughters, a few remembrances were left. To Harry, who was not present, there was a silver watch. To Pink, a silver bowl that had been his great grandfather's and the deed to the farm he and Amanda believed to be theirs all along, with the stipulation that it could be sold only to a Wright. All else was left to Wurth, with the admonition that an effort be made to pass the estate on as a single trust, a retreat for the family.

CHAPTER

Seven

W urth and the Burnsville lawyer admitted a mortgage had been authorized,
so the mortgage was made. The money proved to be a boon, allowing Pink
to open new offices in three mountain towns, to print additional policies
and calendars, and to pay salaries for the first several weeks of two experienced insurance men he hired from other companies. When that money
was gone, Pink sought a loan from Wallerbee, who after three days of
reflection said no, he could not do that. "Jesus rose from the dead in three
days," Pink reminded him, "but you didn't make it."

Fretting about missed opportunities, Pink one day after lunch bundled all
the policies that had been borrowed against, then stacked the three bundles in a flour sack. Wallerbee followed along, sensing danger, advising
Pink not to take any new risks. "No, I'll merely see what Hatch Cole

offers," Pink assured him. Then, at the very door of Cole's store, Pink did hesitate. For fully a minute he paused, then, shaking his head, he led the way into the store—or whatever it could be called, more a means of decoration for Hatch Cole himself, a place he hovered in, pestering the dust, taking in money, buying and selling property. Hatch greeted them mildly, modestly, appeared to be preoccupied, which Pink accepted as a tactic of a trader.

"Is Pink carrying his dinner with him?" Hatch Cole said, nodding toward the bag.

Pink placed the three stacks of policies on the corner of the rolltop desk, pulled up a chair, and proceeded for a quarter of an hour to trace the history of the company. He said now he had opportunities to expand and would put up the policies as security for a loan. He covered the full plan, then rested, waited for questions.

"If you take my money, then I have none," Hatch Cole replied. He appeared to forget about Pink for a minute or two. "When you two walked in here, I was well-to-do, but you mean to have it, do you? Paying interest is sorry return. I see this town ready to make big growth, it's going to flower once we shake off this national calamity, and I can own more of it now than later. I can take my money and buy buildings now. You ought to get into the hotel business yourself," he said to Pink. "You'd be a humdinger, wouldn't he, Wallerbee? Has the personality for it. Never met a stranger, have you, Pink?"

Pink was baffled by the twists of the conversation.

"When you have money, there are hands held out from every direction, and you have to choose," Hatch said. "That's what I do. You've been honest with me. You want my money. I'll be honest with you. So do I."

It had not occurred to Pink that, should he work up courage enough to approach Hatch, he would be turned down. The Monarch proposal was sound; there was security enough here.

Wallerbee said, "It's high interest, that's what Pink offers."

Hatch Cole waved that consideration aside. "You two have this company, you two men. You own it together, do you?"

"Seventy-five to twenty-four," Wallerbee said, "with one percent to his wife."

"And it's growing. It will be valuable property one day, and in that day, I'll be getting my loan money back, and you'll have the rich company all to yourselves. I'll be here in my store fiddling around with nuts and bolts, and you'll be wealthy." He peered over his long nose at them. He moved the desk lamp, so the light fell more directly on Pink's face. "What you offering," he asked, "besides interest?"

Pink stared into his eyes. "Ten percent of the company."

"Thirty percent of the company," Hatch replied quietly.

Pink noticed the sound of the wall clock for the first time. It's ticking for you, Pink, he thought; it's for you to say now. "Fifteen percent, Hatch," he said.

"You can increase the company's size, you tell me. Do you want to own half a big pie, or three-quarters of a little one?" Hatch asked.

"What percentage will you give up, Wallerbee?" Pink asked turning to him.

"Nothing," Wallerbee replied at once. "My God, Pink, this is no time to take risks."

Hatch Cole considered Wallerbee, then he turned his bleary gaze once more on Pink. "I think this is just the time. I'll take twenty-five percent."

"Very well," Pink said.

Hatch Cole nodded, a flicker of pride showing through. "You did right. Now I'll loan you what the company needs at six percent."

"How much money can I have?" Pink asked anxiously.

"All you can use," Hatch said.

Pink rented an office for the company in the best building on the north side of the square, upstairs over a candy shop. It was a three-room suite, with a window overlooking the square and the tombstone cutter's shop directly across. Pink took the printer, Dunn, to the other side of the square and had him do a pen-and-ink drawing of the building, the entire structure, with the square's fountain in the foreground. Over the picture he wanted the word "Monarch," and under, the words "On the Square."

To begin his next phase of expansion, he decided to travel to Hendersonville, a village south of Asheville, because a farmer named Fletcher was going home and Pink could ride with him in his car. The road was never more than a hog wallow, but just now the creeks were swollen and at side fords the car was swirled about by the tide, its traction lost on the slick rocks. Occasionally Pink had to push it to help hold it on course. He came out of the streams, his pants wet, his lungs full of exhaust fumes. It took them all morning to get to Hendersonville, only twenty miles.

On the way he sold Fletcher an insurance policy on his wife.

In Hendersonville there was a store run by the Silver family. He had met them at the Asheville farmers' market many times. For his insurance, he set up near the front door; he sold three policies that day and found an enthusiastic young Silver son, Arthur, who had, according to his father, a way with figures; Arthur sold a policy to his father and one to his uncle, who was the owner of the livery stable. Pink put Arthur on staff as a commission salesman.

To catch a ride back to Asheville, he waited at the store until a car came by for gasoline. On the way he sold a small insurance policy to the driver, while helping to change a tire near Arden.

Another trip took him southwest to Murphy. On another he went north to Burnsville. On another to Old Fort, located at the foot of the mountain wall, and there he found a young woman, alert, attractive wife of the storekeeper, to work for him. Owing to a wagon accident, she was paralyzed from the hips down and spent most of every day sitting in the store. That day Pink sat beside her as together they talked with first one then another of the store's customers, Pink asking about their families and where they were from, and telling them about insurance once they began asking him about himself. He left at the store a stack of envelopes addressed to the Monarch Company. "I've numbered these envelopes," he told the new saleswoman. "You're a twenty-envelope office," he said, showing her the penciled numbers. "Whenever you've used fifteen, I'll send you another batch. One envelope for each application—one to one. Don't hold an application, not even for a day. We want to issue the policy soon as we can, before the buyer passes on."

Pink had one measure of sales advice: Insurance ought to be a pleasure, not an irritant; let the people anticipate the pleasure of being insured.

At five o'clock at the Old Fort train station, he climbed aboard a passenger car that had come all the way down from New York City. It was full, or almost full, of passengers. He stood at the back door of the last car, where he could see the sights unfold behind him, could see far down along the track. Whenever the engine up ahead muffled its throat as it entered a tunnel, directly his windows would black out, the world becoming a dollop of light at the end of the tunnel, receding, the noise of the train wheels resounding against the stone walls, exploding inward as the car emerged from the western end of the tunnel, only in a minute or so to enter yet another one, smoke billowing from the chanting engine in gusts and gasps, coating the windows of the cars. Now and again Pink could look out over the outlands, the endless hill country, a tapestry reflecting red sunset, with here and there a spiral of smoke rising from a far-off farmhouse, and in one place silver reflected off a river. The train entered the Swannanoa Tunnel, the longest on this climb, and for a minute or two the train rumbled and struggled in darkness, but once it emerged the groaning ceased as it swept around into the high Swannanoa Valley. Now through the windows Pink could see the mountains all around, blue and tree-clothed, could see wagons on the road as mountain people went home, could see a man still plowing in a steep field a thousand feet above the track.

Amanda had supper ready. The children sat around the table while Amanda waited on everybody, and he told the family about his journey, recalling incidents along the way, trying to make them sense the pride he had in his successes and the magic and wonder of his work. In his own mind he had come to think of the company as a relative, a child growing every day, responding to signals of attention he showed it, just as they did.

There was never an encouragement given the company that the company did not at once repay. The company was a member of his family, as well as his companion. It was the fields he harvested, the timber he felled without oxen or chain; it was the baby he had given birth to, as Amanda had given birth to two. It was the baby he might yet lose, he realized, even as she had lost three, perhaps more.

Indeed, within a month, Amanda once more became pregnant, and this time, as the weeks passed, the baby appeared to have stamina enough. Pink was distressed and consenting alternately. At his insistence Amanda agreed to visit a doctor. He made the appointment and took her as far as the door of the office building. He said he would wait there for her.

She had heard that doctors were extremely personal in their examinations, and she told Pink that she would not under any circumstances strip off her clothes. Once she arrived at the office, she made this reservation known at once. The nurse accepted her reluctance with good humor, and Dr. Zethrick Watkins, once he came into the examination room, contented himself with a few questions about matters of temperature and weight and blood pressure. "Now, perhaps, Mrs. Wright, I will be allowed to feel the baby's positioning through the dress."

Amanda was alerted at once.

"If you'll lie down on that table—"

Amanda lay down, as directed, but when he touched her, she pushed his hands away.

"Very well," he said good-naturedly, and nodded to the nurse, who felt of Amanda, then wrote something out on a piece of paper, which the doctor studied.

"Now, Mrs. Wright, it seems to Mrs. Simpson here that the baby is out of position in the womb. Under the circumstances I will have to insist on making my own examination."

Amanda, jaw firmly shut, shook her head.

"Your husband can be present, if you like."

Amanda refused.

"Then surely you will at least allow the nurse to feel the baby without all these clothes." When she refused, in exasperation he retreated to his office, where he contented himself with writing on his desk blotter.

Amanda was not by any means the first country woman who had rejected the physical examination, but the event did disturb him. When Amanda sat down in the patient's chair next to his desk, he handed a printed slip to her. "This is a painless device called x-ray that penetrates the skin and gives us an outline of the bones of the child, as well as the outline of your backbone and pelvis. Go to College Street—"

"How does it do that?" Amanda asked.

"I don't know. It's a machine. You lie on a table and the instrument takes a picture."

Amanda shook her head.

"You've heard of it, perhaps. There was an article in the *Saturday Evening Post* the other day." His nurse brought in two x-rays taken of others, and these he used as evidence. "You can wear your own clothes."

Amanda remained uncooperative.

"I can't explain how it works," he told her. "It's an invention."

"I don't want it," Amanda said.

"Mrs. Wright, I must have some indication of the positioning; we need all the help science can provide." He tapped the top of his desk for emphasis. "You will need to have an x-ray taken, so we can be prepared at the time of birth for what Nature offers."

"What will you do, knowing all that? You can't do anything."

"I can do something, Mrs. Wright. I can take the baby out through incision if necessary. I can give you a series of massages and exercises—I don't mean I would administer them myself," he added. "I mean you could have them given to you. I can give you pain-killing injections."

Amanda smoothed her dress down over her protusion. "I've never heard such foolishness." She riffled through her change purse, removing a folded dollar bill, which she offered him for his services. She left the bill on the corner of the desk.

Later Amanda asked Hugh if he knew about x-ray pictures, and Hugh said he hadn't heard anything about them. "But I've been busy here at the store," he said, which made her laugh.

Even more amusement—everybody, including Amanda, laughed about her doctor's visit—came out of Pink's car. He bought—at least the company bought—a four-door Packard touring car, property of a Mr. Haskell, who had driven it only two hundred miles before deciding he preferred staying around the house. Cranked into a roar, the car was a creature of danger, but when it stood parked in the backyard, it was an invitation to adventure. Pink gloried in it. Now and then he would drive forward as far as the sheds, then roar backward, do a circle, advance once again on the sheds. First time he took it to the square, he became convinced he was not competitive enough to make a successful driver. There were trucks, carts, wagons, stallions, mares, donkeys, even herds of sheep in competition; Pink would come to a stop well away from any interference, and this resulted in a stymied, halting journey. So, by the hour, he hired a young man, one of scores willing to work as driver of such a vehicle. He bought the lad a soft cloth to polish the metal with, bought him goggles and a black hat, and a hand-drawn map of the roads in the North Carolina mountains.

As if commanded to do so by Pink's pride, Hugh bought a small truck, which he bragged about so much Pink had to play a trick on him. The game went this way: Pink had his driver sneak around back and add a few gallons of fuel to Hugh's truck's tank. A week or so later, Hugh began to boast of his mileage. The truck was getting up to thirty miles on a gallon of gasoline. Hugh told everybody, and he laughed at Pink's praise of the Packard's fourteen miles to a gallon.

Pink had his driver put less fuel in the truck, finally none at all, which brought its miles per gallon to twelve. From thirty to twelve. Hugh most every other day had it in one garage or another for inspection. "Something's gone wrong with the damn thing."

Pink went further, had his driver siphon out some of the fuel from Hugh's truck; this resulted in a basement figure of eight miles to the gallon, and led to further exasperation and one fiery letter to a Mr. Henry Ford, Detroit, Michigan.

Pink had his driver add gasoline to the tank, a little bit at first, then more and more, until Hugh was happy with thirty miles to the gallon, prelude to a fall to twelve, where Pink, weary of the sport, left it, and left Hugh to mull over the peculiarities of an instrument capable of such variation.

On days set aside for car journeys, Pink would crawl into the back seat of a morning, a Mason jar of coffee with him, and a paper poke in which he had his papers. As the car drove out of the yard, Amanda and the children would stand near the porch steps waving.

Usually on every trip a tire would blow out: an explosive noise, followed by several seconds of swerving and alarm while Red Murphy, the driver, brought the car to a stop, followed by an hour of wrestling with the flat tire. They traveled with two spares, one on the front bumper, the other at the rear of the car, but in a day's journey they might have to use patches as well.

They put up at inns. The one at Burnsville was a favorite. Then there was a fine one at Saluda, another at Barnardsville. Usually the inns would have interesting guests, and there were always magazines Pink hadn't read. Next day after a good breakfast, he and Red Murphy would be on their way again.

One night at Marshall he was robbed. It turned out to be a tourist who had robbed him, and Pink was called to be a witness against him. That took three wearying days.

On another occasion, on a Saturday night he was arrested in Franklin for disorderly conduct and spent the night in jail. Next morning he was released with apologies, as soon as the sheriff found out Pink was president of a company. "You were shooting too close for comfort, Mr. Wright," he told him.

"I wasn't shooting at all," Pink told him.

"Well, somebody was," the officer assured him. This was a rough country, and in the future Pink made certain he was not present in any of the mountain towns on a Saturday night, not towns where timbermen were expected to come out of the woods for their weekly rout.

Whenever he returned from one of these trips, he had a well-ordered routine he followed. He bathed first and put on clean clothes. He ate the dinner Amanda had cooked. He talked with his children for about an hour. Then he and Amanda went off to their room.

A death claim came in now and then. Wallerbee, who now worked a few hours every day at the company office, sent out the checks after a cursory study, which he and Pink would make. A claim came in from Franklin. A man named Lincoln had died in his bed. On Lexington Avenue Pink sought out somebody from the Franklin section, said he was sorry to learn of the death of Mr. Lincoln.

"How's that? Did he die?" the man asked. "He appeared to be in health day before yesterday."

The evening mail brought a second claim for the same neighborhood, from a Mr. Clive Porter. Once more the cause of death was natural. Two days later a third claim came in from nearby, so Pink arranged a southern trip. He arrived in Franklin without announcement early one morning and selected a big rocker on the inn's front porch. As men walked by on the sidewalk, Pink asked if they knew Clive Porter or either of the other two. He said he had money for them. Within an hour the claimant named Lincoln stopped by.

"I have the money for you," Pink admitted. "I have five hundred dollars. Are you Harold C. Lincoln?"

"Yes, that's the one."

"Born here in the country forty-nine years ago last June first?"

"Yes. You're talking to him, all right. Where's the money?"

Pink gave him a receipt to sign. Lincoln cautiously read the receipt, then backed away, left the pen on the banister rail. The other claimants arrived later and moved to the table to read the receipt. The third man read the receipt aloud, as requested by several people on the porch. "I hereby claim that I died in this country of natural causes, and I hereby acknowledge receipt of my insurance policy money in full from the Monarch Company." Of course, the story began its journey out over the countryside. "There's no other company with such personal service as you've seen this morning," Pink contended, returning the money to his pocket.

As the depression deepened, men turned up without funds in increasing numbers, men who would go to work for Pink on purely a commission basis. The remark was made on Lexington Avenue that here directly we'll all be working for Monarch and be selling insurance to one another.

Now and then Pink would write his mother a letter, one lavishing endearments and praises, and she would write him. He would not go to visit her, however, wishing to be free of memories of his leaving home and the animosities of the family. However, as Amanda progressed in her pregnancy, he agreed that she should have her own mother come to stay in town for a while, as well as a midwife, and further that he would go for them in the company car. He wrote his mother, and wrote Amanda's too, and said he would soon come to see them. One morning he sneaked away alone in the car; by noon, once done with a few business chores nearby, he drove over to the little house he and Amanda owned, found it occupied by a family of Germans, who said they rented from the Wrights. Pink went by the store, where Wurth at once made accounting for the house and land, every penny that had been brought in, both rents and crop shares, minus such expenses as had been paid, minus taxes, minus a commission of six percent for renting it out.

At the Wright house Pink talked for a while with his mother and invited her to go for a ride in his car, if she dared trust his driving. His mother readily agreed. Wurth argued with her, pointed out in staunch tones that she had never even been inside an automobile before. She said the novelty attracted her. Pink bundled her up in shawls, put a pillow at her back and another on her stomach, so that she would feel safe when they hit a hole or rock, and he spun the powerful motor. Wurth called out warnings. Pink turned the car, backing through a fence, and headed for the valley road.

He and his mother stopped from time to time to say hello to friends, his mother always remaining straight-backed, staring intently forward at the road, even when they were at a stop. On the way west toward Tennessee, he decided to risk taking a climb, and high on Grayback Ridge he skitted along a trail for a mile or so, showing her the view of the Black Mountains nearby, the tallest mountains in eastern America, he told her. He stopped the car, and from the windows they looked across a bald pasture at the great range, with white clouds for its evening hair, mist for its mighty breath. "They tell me when a person gets on top he sees the world, can see the Chinese tickling each other."

"Can you, Pink?" she asked earnestly.

"Yes," he told her. "Wurth says so."

"How would he know?" she said disparagingly. Back home, she confided in him, "It's easier to stay here to home and not get my mind confused by travel, but I do like it so."

Wurth was still unnerved by the incident, by her going off like that, especially since she left without him. "She's suffering memory loss, has mind trouble as it is," he told Pink.

It was late in the afternoon when Pink dared to go by the King house. Once there he found that they had been expecting him and were tired of waiting. A Mrs. Warren had agreed to come with them to town for the birthing, she being the best midwife around, and consequently having the stiffest terms. Among them, she was to have a bed of her own, with cotton sheets, no muslin or flour-sack material, and she was not to be required to cook or wash up.

Next morning on the way back to town, Mrs. Warren occupied half the back seat, her cloth bag of personal possessions on her lap. "I've delivered about two babies a month," she told Enid and Adeline King, speaking up suddenly. "How many does that work out to?"

"If it's forty years, that'd be eighty times twelve," Adeline said.

"Been slowed up by ghosts, or there'd been more. Wore me down many a time," she admitted. "Will ride you up and down."

"Did one ever lay a hand on you in anger?" Pink asked her.

"They whoop you, if you don't do."

Pink kept looking through the rear-view mirror at her, this common mortal, untutored, woman of witchcraft and faith in the unnatural, soon to be the one to oversee the complications of this birth.

On the third day of Mrs. Warren's visit, about 10 A.M., Amanda went into labor. There ensued an argument between Mrs. Warren and Mrs. King about which bed the baby should be delivered in, Adeline arguing for the parlor bed, Mrs. Warren preferring to use the bedroom itself, but she would not carry water to it, she said, not think of emptying a bed pan. Apparently these chores were to fall to Adeline, her assistant. Nor were the men allowed to stay inside the house. They must be outdoors, waiting where she could see them. They were not to sit on the porch, "Nor ary place under the house roof, or its elves." Of course, she meant eaves.

All this disturbed Pink, and before he left the house, he tried phoning Dr. Watkins to see what might be done about admitting Amanda to a hospital this afternoon. Watkins was on the golf course, his wife said, was expected back at his house before dressing for dinner that evening. Would Pink like to leave a phone number where he could be reached?

Pink had no number, except his home's own phone, which he was deprived of. He knew no other doctors in town.

At noon the labor became painful, earnest; Pink was told by Mrs. Warren to go into the backyard, to remain near the chickenhouse. He and Enid King upturned two bushel baskets for seats and a third, between them, served as a table for a Mason jar of peach brandy that Enid had brought for tasting. "She's nothing but a witch," Enid confided. He had to hold the Mason jar with both hands to steady it. "I love Amanda so much, did you know that?"

"I love her," Pink admitted.

"Away back up in Big Bear Cove, there's said to be a mother that's bore nineteen."

"Well, I don't know what's up there," Pink said, staring at the windows at the southwest corner of the house.

"I find it harder to breathe in town, don't you?" Enid commented. "Now, there's those who can breathe anywhere."

Pink occasionally saw Mrs. Warren pass the window.

"A man grows into whatever belts he's wearing," Enid said. "He breathes the best he can, wherever he is."

Amanda screamed and at once Frederick and Hallie began hollering, crying. This was about three o'clock, and Pink wanted to go find Dr. Watkins, but King reminded him that the yell might be the last pain of the birth. "What would you tell him? You can't move her now, anyway. And that witch won't let him inside the room. Now settle down here."

At four o'clock another cry went out, then quiet. Pink moved as close to the window as he dared and called out, asking what was happening, but nobody replied. About five he heard a baby crying, and he felt relief, rich and kind. He charged into the house and heard Amanda laughing and crying at the same time, and heard the baby crying, all these sounds mingled together, and pushed into the room, where he saw the naked boy seeking his mother's breasts and safety and comfort.

From the ranks of the weathered porches of the Battery Park Hotel, one could look out over the Pisgah Mountain Range, and scores of lesser peaks resting in the sun and clouds. Few of the mountain people ever ventured into the hotel's shaded interior, where wealthy tourists took their ease. Now and then a local doctor or lawyer or judge would go inside for a meal. The dining room of the Battery Park was said to be patterned along continental lines, and the waiters, all of them blacks, were trained by Europeans. No errors were made there, no sign of rush, no failure in providing all the dishes listed on the four-page menu, or the wines on the wine list.

Amanda decided she wanted to be taken there for dinner on her tenth wedding anniversary. She had read a story in one of Hallie's magazines about a man and woman venturing out of a patterned life, and their adventure had resulted well. She hired a young mountain girl, one of Nettie's nieces, to come sit with the children that special evening. She fed the baby, then used pads to keep any dribbles from marking the dress, which was her wedding dress. After bearing three children, she could still get into it. She was walking in a dream just now, unsure what she was getting into; she was dealing with foreign things, a new belt buckle, a new pair of shoes, a new shirt for Pink, which she had laundered to take the stiffness out. She was ready to launch them both on an experience neither was secure about.

Pink had the company car. With her beside him, nervously he drove up the winding drive to the top of Battery Hill, the car bucking and bolting. They arrived at seven, which she had heard was the earliest fashionable hour for dinner here. After some discussion, Pink allowed the liveryman to take his car to park for him—he had never heard of such a service. He and Amanda on the first porch paused to look out over the mountain world, blue-hazed, sleepily resting under fluffy clouds.

The doorman nodded to Pink, as if perhaps he remembered him from a previous visit. At the dining-room doorway, the headwaiter, who had a Monarch policy, started, then smiled, nodded to Pink. "A table by the window, Mr. Wright?" he asked, and led the way to a table situated so that they could look out over the city as the sunset warmed the buildings.

"How did he know you?" Amanda whispered to Pink.

"I delivered groceries here," Pink told her, and the two of them laughed.

There were no menus presented. Instead, from the kitchen a German wine was brought along with two tall glasses, and a while later the European chef presented himself at their table, bringing with him a black interpreter, another policyholder, to say he would select and prepare the dishes. "It is my best effort," he told them.

There they were, soon delightfully intoxicated with wine and notoriety, riding on a magic carpet, provided by Lexington Avenue and Monarch customers.

After dinner Pink decided to ignore the presence of the car. They walked into the district of shops, where they looked through glass windows at the fancy offerings of the world. Hand in hand, like teenage lovers, they walked past the jewelry stores, the new department stores, leisurely speculating. By the time they reached home, everybody was asleep, including the mountain girl, who was still sitting in a rocking chair in the parlor. Pink led Amanda into their own room and shut out the world.

Later, when he was asleep, she climbed out of bed, took a chair close to the window, and looked off toward Battery Hill. Tonight he had been the handsomest man in the dining room, she reminded herself, at the finest hotel in the South, and she, she must admit, had been the prettiest woman there, and they had love in their eyes, too, a rare sight she thought in a big hotel.

A rain began, surprising her. All evening the sky had been bright and clear. Maybe the mountains had poked holes in the clouds. The raindrops

tickled the tin roof, made popping noises, each drop having its own moment of life. Be careful, Amanda, she thought. God, do take care of us,
look with kindness on us. We are holding to our lives without much help
from others. Our own people are way off. We are a leaf on the tree of the
world. We are an even more fragile creation, a family, the most loving
creation, the one most full of jealousy, of affection, the one knowing the
highest wonder. God, help us. God, be kind to us. Give us special care, as
we risk ourselves.

The new baby was taken by Amanda and Pink to the store, one of his
first outings. Pink carried him proudly, introducing him as his namesake.
Trailing along behind were Frederick and Hallie. Pink didn't mean to offend either of them, but Amanda noticed they were hurt by his references
to the new child as the heir apparent.

"You never did like your own oldest brother," Amanda reminded him.
"You can imagine how it feels." They were lying in the bed late at night
talking, the new baby asleep nearby. "Frederick noticed it the most. He's
not as bright, not as quick as I would like," she admitted.

Pink was well aware that the boy had not taken to reading or arithmetic.
"Is he dumb? He's not, is he?"

"He's clever in some ways, but he's not quick. Now, you are quick, if
you want my opinion, you see all parts of a problem at one time, but Fred
can't seem to put a large number of pieces together."

"Of course, the new Pink might not be able to either."

"What are we going to call him?" she asked sleepily. "Not new Pink, are we?"
"Pink."

"But you're called that. How will we tell the difference?"
"I'll ask Wallerbee."

That made her laugh. He was now referring even the family's decisions
to his partner. He had asked Wallerbee about birth-control devices, as she
knew, and had been supplied with a new brand of condom. Pink had
stashed the packet under one corner of the mattress, and he turned on a
light now and showed the rolled-up tube to Amanda, admitting to her
what he had in mind. She was lying there in bed, the covers pulled up
under her chin, watching him. He unpeeled the wrapper and figured out
how the gadget could be unwound. It was slippery, had a gelatin on it like
Vaseline.

Amanda kept giggling. "You'll never get it on." She laughed as the contraption slithered about. Finally, he was left dejected, sitting in candlelight, the messy rubber in his hands. Amanda, snickering and giggling,
put her arms around him and pulled him back onto the bed.

* * *

There was much commotion about the baby's name. Each time Amanda announced that Pink had wet himself, there was tittering among Hallie and Frederick. "Well, I won't call him Junior," she said. Pink suggested they call him little Pink. "A little Pink is almost white," she told him.

"Call him Rose Pink," Hallie said.

"Could call him Light Pink," Pink said.

"Pink One and Two," Hallie said.

"It's such an unusual name, anyway," Amanda said worriedly.

"Pink Pink," Hallie said, which made Frederick convulse with laughter.

"Young Pink," Amanda said. "Have known the youngest son to be called Young."

"That'll not do," Pink said. "No stature to it. What say to Mark?"

"The grown Pink is papa," Hallie said.

"Mark?" Amanda exclaimed. "Where does that come from?"

"Wrote a gospel," Pink said.

"But where does it join with Pink?"

"Be likely to make a mark in the world," Pink explained.

"You wanted him named Pink, insisted on that, and you mean to call him Mark?" she asked.

"Mark Pink, Mark Young Pink," Hallie recited.

Pink asked Amanda, "You have a better idea?"

She hesitated, fought off her sense of disappointment. "You insisted on Pink, now want to call him something else."

Hallie began at once calling the child Young, and it was she who carried him about most often anyway, who frequently rocked him or swung with him on the porch or tossed him on one of the beds. "Young Pink," she would chorus.

The Wrights had a commode installed just as soon as the city finished laying the sewer line, and at the same time Pink put a tub in the bathroom, a room he partitioned at the end of the hall. Such improvements were among the first on the street. Hallie took a bath as often as she could get inside the bathroom. "She sneaks baths," Amanda claimed. "No child needs to be that clean." Amanda herself would relax for long stretches in the tub, causing Pink to complain about the bathroom being always occupied. "Ask Wallerbee what to do," Amanda called to him.

Within a year, Pink wanted her to stop nursing the baby. He had read in a magazine that a mother ought not to nurse her babies at all, a concept that amused Amanda. "Well, what are they for?" she asked, touching one of her own breasts. "Hallie was given to nursing me every hour, if she could."

"Mama, please," Hallie said, casting an embarrassed glance toward her father.

"It's hard on a woman to nurse," Pink insisted, "causes her breasts to droop, and the doctor said that cow's or goat's milk has—"

"Moo," Amanda told him.

"You're very old-fashioned, aren't you, Mama?" Hallie said to her.

Amanda stopped nursing Young when he was two, sneaking only a few more lingering, delicious weeks of touching, sucking, warming, caring. After that she sought him out two or three times a day, to hold him on her lap, his little body curled up like a baby in a mother's body, and stroked his little head, his firm shoulders, his curved back with the knobs of spine bones, which she would count. A handsome little boy, his legs and arms beginning to lose their baby softness, roundness. "Pretty blue eyes. Put them in their sleepy-time boxes, save them, are you?" she said, and kissed his forehead, hugged him, trying to get all of his body into her arms, loving him completely. A father could not do that, she knew; he was never the bodily home of any other person. A father might seek to govern, to direct, and even to cherish another person's body, but it was not his prospect to house, to feed, to nourish.

At the time of Young's birth, mention often appeared in Asheville of unrest in Europe. Germany and England denied the potential of war, while admitting differences of opinions having to do with trade and access to trade. These issues were assigned to diplomats who traveled between London and Berlin, with other journeys to France, Belgium, Austria-Hungary.

"Austria-Hungary," Hugh murmured, reading the Asheville newspaper, looking up to pin his oldest, most delinquent and handsome son, Brodie, with his gaze. "Where is that?"

Brodie, rummaging through a stack of apple bags to find one large enough to house four heads of cabbage, looked up long enough to say it was the same as Germany to him.

"It is gypsies?" Hugh asked him, tilting back in his new swivel chair, for which he had traded two twenty-pound salt-cured, hickory-smoked hams. "Saw gypsies the other day, come here for feed. Scared your brother Allen, almost made him wet his pants." Hugh was always joking with Brodie, his most daring son, about Allen. "There was a band of gypsies used to come through Asheville every summer; camped at the branch below the house, till it got turned over to developers. We would stand in our yard and lean on the fence and stare at them, whispering about them selling their own children, or kidnaping our women, not to mention painting their wagons. . . ."

"I doubt if they ever sold children, papa," Brodie told him.

"You don't know," Hugh told him. "You don't even know where they're from."

In July of 1914, when Young was only a year old, Austria delivered an ultimatum to Serbia. This was reported in the Asheville paper. Sir Edward Grey of Britain proposed a conference to determine a peaceful solution to European animosities, a proposal rejected by Germany. Hallie, age twelve, had looked up the countries at the library, which she often frequented, and said Archduke Francis Ferdinand had been assassinated and, of more outright concern to her, his wife had been slaughtered, a pretty woman, too, as judged by a picture the librarian, Mrs. Frazier, showed her. The Asheville newspaper said Britain meanwhile had called its fleet into Atlantic waters. On August 2 Germany sent an ultimatum to Belgium. This came as a surprise to those in Asheville who were noticing foreign events.

Next day the King of the Belgians appealed to King George of Britain, and the next day yet, to the further confusion of Hugh and others in Asheville, Britain declared war on Germany. This was reported in the Asheville newspaper alongside the item reporting that Germany had declared war on Russia. "Now, where in hell is Russia?" Hugh demanded of his sons and customers. "Those countries will need to fight until there's a United States of Europe," he declared, "and we're damn fools if we get mixed up in it."

That same day, August 3, Germany declared war on France. The next day, Germany declared war on Belgium. There followed over the course of the following weeks other declarations of war, which Hugh noted in pencil on his wall, Austria against Russia, Serbia against Germany, France against Austria, Britain against Austria, Japan against Germany, Austria against Japan, Austria against Belgium, Britain against Turkey.

Germany invaded Belgium, and drove forward to enter Brussels. The French army retreated from Alsace-Lorraine. The Germans moved on to Namur, took Tournan, Sedan, destroyed Louvais, took Soissons, all to Hugh's consternation. The French Government in September evacuated Paris. British and French troops met the Germans at the Battle of the Marne, the battle beginning September 6.

A preacher named Ellis, who had a Baptist church in a little community west of Canton, came down the street calling for repentance, saying the Battle of Armageddon had begun. Most everybody had heard of Armageddon, but not many, maybe not any, had a clear idea about it. Reverend Ellis declared that seven was central to the strategy, and there were seven in the war against Germany and Austria. When challenged, he named five, then faltered.

"The Battle of Armageddon is to be fought in Palestine," a woman named Babcock, a widow, called out to him from the sidewalk.

"Well, it'll go there soon," he assured her, waving her aside.

"It's not going thataway," she called out.

By the time Pink reached Clarence's, the newspaper had been divided among the three customers, and there was a lively discussion about whether the Marne was pronounced in two syllables or one. "It's French, ain't it?" one man demanded of the others. "Then it's Mar-nay."

"Marne is all I ever heard," another said. Of more consequence, the newspaper said that if the British and French did not halt the German army at the Marne, Europe would be overrun by Germans and Britain no longer would be the dominant power on earth. Virtually everybody present in Clarence's was predominantly English in background—that is, they were English, Welsh, Scotch-Irish—but there was some question about whether they wanted to admit to a love of England or not.

"My father's people is half German," one fellow commented, then fell silent when three or four men turned on their bar stools to frown at him.

Another man, an old fellow from Pensacola, said, "My grandfather married a German woman, went to the outlands for her, and she was a worker, my lord, she was a worker, and so clean you could eat off'n the floor. Now any of you want to eat off an English floor?"

"What's that got to do with the war?" Clarence asked him. "They're shooting at one another," he said worriedly, studying the offending newspaper. "We ought to go ourselves. How long does it take to get there?"

"You'd get there by Christmas, if you hurried," the old man told him.

"I can't go this month," Clarence said. "The eating apples is still ripening."

"But to save England," the old fellow commented dryly, chewing on one of Clarence's sassafras sticks, which were kept in a bowl on the bar. "To save bloody England, Clarence."

Clarence considered that, then noticed the smile on the fellow's face, and on other's faces. "I don't think you men understand the seriousness," he told them, "of the apple season."

Among the Lexington Avenue men who volunteered for the army were Noah and Brodie King. Brodie tried to get into the air corps but was found to be color blind, cause to reject him for flight.

CHAPTER
Eight

Young had more attention as a baby than most children, since he had his mother and an older sister to care for him. During his early years he rarely touched the floor, so anxious were the two to hold him, nurture him, dress him up for visits to houses in the neighborhood or to see his Uncle Hugh. Hallie was always and a day hauling him to Lexington Avenue, giving him plump ripe cherries, wild raspberries, plums that made his mouth pucker. Hugh would ride him around in a sling, calling him his papoose. Little spoonfuls of honey were suitable food for him, Hugh would tell Hallie and the others watching the baby eat. Biblical, he would say. "Waiting for that unleavened bread to fall from Heaven," he told them, snickering at the thought. "Might put us all out of business, if it falls heavy."

Once put down at night, Young would often bawl in a loud voice, reminiscent, Pink said, of a calf taken away from its mother. He could really yell, too, and would do so for hours on end, unless Hallie or Amanda went to him, or Pink, for that matter.

When he was three he was talking as well as any other child of five. At four he commenced a new spate of bawling, and Amanda, Hallie, Pink went running, racing one another to calm him. On the fourth night, however, Amanda announced house rules, restricting the others and restraining herself. The first hours of that night were full of challenge, but sometime during the night Young grew exasperated, and the family heard him call out, "Isn't anybody going to come and stop this awful noise?"

Young's hair on his left side would stand up in the morning, no matter how much Amanda brushed it. She came to love it that way. He was given to moods, more even than Hallie had been, to changes from smiling joy to thunder and scowling. He would hold a grudge longer than Hallie or Frederick. He was quick to learn to read, as quick as Hallie had been. And he still yielded willingly to Amanda's petting him, holding him, and on occasions when she was occupied and appeared to neglect him, he would seek her out and ask for her attention. "I need a hug, mama." She would lead him to a rocker and take him on her lap, the two giggling at the way his legs no longer would fold up quite right, and his arms would get in the way, and one evening he said to her, "Mama, why don't I fit any longer?"

Then one morning his life began to change. "I'll do it myself," he said to his mother. He was talking about tying his own shoes.

"I don't mind helping you, Young," she told him. "Here, you have the laces twisted." She could sense his attitude tensing as she straightened them. "You've never tied your shoes."

"I can." He did, too, showed her how well he could.

"Don't know what's coming to us," Amanda said. "Hallie taught you, did she?"

"We were in the swing," he said.

"Hallie, Hallie," Amanda said under her breath. "Take my baby from me." In the swing, in the swing, she thought, always in the swing with Hallie, climbing trees with Hallie; the two did seem to be in yoke. Hallie showing him how to strip the corn ears and feed the grains to the chickens. Hallie arguing that it was time for the boy to have a dog of his own to take care of. Hallie trying to teach him to read; put his eyes out reading so young, Amanda complained.

The boy and Hallie would sit in the shade of the backyard. They had a place on the grass where Pink had tied a big rope to a tree limb, so Young could swing out on it. Young for hours would listen to her tell him stories, his favorites being about horses. Hallie was at an age when she loved horses, too, more than any other animal, and more than people, for that matter. He would touch Hallie, holding her hand, or even resting his head on her leg. She was always talking about the whole, wide world, of which he was, as she told him, heir, prince, master, explorer. He and Hallie, and Hallie's horses, were part of the world.

Amanda would see them there. She might be working in the garden and would hear him laugh. On hearing him, she would straighten and stand like a person possessed of a single thought, staring off at the horizon, wondering, piecing together her own attitude. She never called to him while he was ensconced with Hallie. She would look off at the horizon, as if listening to voices instructing her, or as if she were catching bits of a tune long since gone.

Frederick proved to be a competent boy, steady, dependable, honest, clean, polite, civil, and he had a gentle sense of humor. It was when compared with Hallie that he appeared to be dull. Hallie could entertain the family for an hour a night merely talking about observations made that afternoon. She never forgot a date, a message. Why, send Hallie to the store, say, to get sugar, baking powder, a tin pie pan, two ham hocks, three pounds of green beans, a tomato for her father, enough peaches for dessert, and tell her to pick up the scissors that were being sharpened at Martin's shop, and to ask how much a combination lock would cost for the attic cover, yes and do get a pint of heavy cream from Mrs. Bradshaw's staff— take our jar with you—and the biggest bottle of cider vinegar. Yes, Hallie, and a head of cabbage.

Why, the child would march off to the markets without so much as a single note written and return an hour later, talking about all she had seen, whom she had met, what they had said, and she would have everything. Every single item. And to the penny she would recall the cost of each, having made judgments about cream and beans and tomatoes and scissors, all without fault.

Send Frederick to the market, what a difference. First of all, he would not come home in time for the beans to be cooked for supper, if he remembered them at all. He would become fascinated by some attraction or other, become attentive to somebody's story, and he was so utterly polite he would never think to interrupt anybody or walk away.

Frederick and Hallie were in the same young people's group at church. The group had tea parties and gatherings to study the Bible and church history, and they had a choir that practiced for Christmas services. There was not an abundance of religious fervor at Central Methodist. Back home the ministers were eager to communicate their souls' affections and convictions; at Central Methodist everything was under control, but the Sunday-evening services were most pleasant, were replete with hymn singing and prayers for people sick and infirm. The young people were encouraged to sit with one another at that service, boys and girls together, which was an additional attraction.

When Hallie was twelve, Frederick thirteen, a revivalist, a handsome young blond giant from Wales, arrived for a week of evening services. There had not been a revival at the church for four or five years, so there was much ground to plow, as the older people admitted, a glint in their eyes.

At the opening services, Amanda, full of apprehension and hopes, took both of the older children. The church was packed, the evangelist was persuasive. After the emotional appeal, Hallie was the first one out of the pews to go forward, which stunned Amanda. The child popped out into the aisle, as if she were a star attraction. Anything for excitement, that was Hallie, the child would do anything for an experience. Amanda felt it was one thing to be saved, but quite another to be saved first. After all, Hallie's sins were pretty much under control, anyway; she was not a gross sinner. It was true she would not hesitate to open any book or magazine, would venture into any story, exposing herself to the vagrant, foolish thought of others, but she herself was not a mean person, and there on the very first night, at the first call, went Hallie down the aisle, and there sat sweet Frederick, left at the docks, clutching his copy of the Bible, glancing up at Amanda for direction, his soul apparently flooding with confusion. Amanda grabbed his arm, held him to his seat. Law, don't tell Pink, she thought. Why had she done such a thing? With God calling, with the Holy Spirit exercising his powers over the boy, she held to him to keep him from following after Hallie Wright.

Then the next night, the young preacher with blond hair—not a strand of brown or black or gray in it, not any out of place either—delivered an even more persuasive message, in which he described hell in such detail that the sensation of heat swept over the pews. Then the preacher lowered his voice to a mere whisper and told about Jesus being able to save souls from such a fate. He gave the call, the organ struck up the melody of "Just as I Am," and a few sinners started down the aisle. Dear Frederick again looked up. "Yes," Amanda said, but even as he started out, there went Hallie once more, a second time in two nights, so Amanda held the boy back.

The third night Amanda held to her daughter, and at the call she fairly pushed Frederick into the aisle, so he could go forward alone. "You don't go three times," she told Hallie, who was clearly disappointed. "How many times do you feel you have to do it?" she whispered, feeling pangs of guilt in her own breast. Had she actually forbidden the girl to go forward? "You're only supposed to do it once in your whole lifetime," she whispered, trying to defend herself against the child's intense gaze. "It's not a daily exercise," she told her, which made Hallie whimper. Finally, thank God, the hymn was over and the young preacher counted the converted souls, nineteen for the evening, and she realized then, Amanda realized then, suddenly, that one of the nineteen was her own son, somewhere at the front of the church was her kneeling little boy, and she found herself pulled into the aisle by the desire to see him, found herself going to the front while the preacher was saying there are now twenty, and she realized she was the twentieth, and he was saying to come on now, dear woman, kneel and find Jesus, and she stopped, surprised, and heard herself tell him she had already found Jesus and wanted to find her son.

On the way home, walking up Haywood Street, Amanda told them they would not have to go forward again, that once in a lifetime, or twice in Hallie's case, was enough, that now each was a child of God's through Jesus's sacrifice.

Hallie told her she understood all that.

"I just didn't want you to think you had to keep doing it," Amanda told them. "I can't keep going through this."

"I never heard of giving children money for conversion," Amanda said.

"It just seemed natural," Pink said. He had just given Frederick five dollars.

"Well, you owe your daughter ten dollars then," Amanda reported, amused.

Each winter the water pipes froze, no matter how many rags were wrapped around them, no matter if the cold-water pipes were left dripping through the night. There would be frozen pipes, with complaining children huddled in the hallway, fussing about having to go outdoors to wash in the water in the pan on the back porch.

"Well, we have nowhere else," Amanda explained to them. She had scooped snow from the drift near the back door, had let it melt in the kitchen, but a mounded pan of snow resulted in only half an inch of water, so the whole process had to be repeated time after time, to get enough to wash faces. No water to rinse with. Hallie began complaining. "Why, there's snow all over the yard," Amanda told her. "Look at that snow waiting for you, honey."

Giggling, Hallie dug her hands into the snow there at the screen door of the back porch, plastered it on her face, while her mother laughed and instructed her, then she peeled the snow off, let it plop onto the porch floor. "Have to make do," Amanda instructed her. "Make do or do without."

There was no plumber to be had on these frozen mornings, so Pink would undertake to do repairs. Equipped with tape and wire and rags he would pry open the wooden door that secured the crawl space under the house, and with Frederick, Hallie, Amanda, and Young crouched nearby, offering rags and wire and string and advice of all sorts, he would crawl inside the dark pit.

Directly there would issue cries of pain as he cracked his head on the joists and pipes. There would be a back-and-forth discussion of the work to be done mending the pipe, he explaining that there was no way to fix it properly, the pipe must be replaced come warm weather, "but for now . . ." Always for now, maybe for a day or two, for at least long enough to get some water into the stove's hot-water tank and into kettles and to fill the pots and pans and maybe the bathtub, even that.

The woodpile was frozen now and again. Frederick used a crowbar to pry the logs loose. He would complain in a loud voice, carrying a log in each hand, dangling them, as he rushed toward the house, dropping them when they were too cold to hold any longer.

"Anybody uptown fall down in the snow, Pink?" Amanda asked.

"That fellow Finkelstein fell down in front of his shop."

"Pawn shop?" Amanda said. "Fall hard?"

"He got up, though. Went back inside to count his guns and guitars."

"I saw a number of cars stuck, couldn't get up the hill out there," she said.

"And streetcars closed down," Pink said. "Suppose their power fouled out somehow. One kept sparking. Not enough heat in our building," he added. "Gloria wore her topcoat at her desk, got ink on her sleeve."

"But your building has a furnace, a coal furnace," Amanda said.

"Goes all the time, too, but has too much space to heat." Then he winked at her. "Like me," he said.

They sat at the table in the overheated kitchen and ate what was left of the meat pie she had baked and drank mugs of hot coffee, gazing now and then through the misty window at the white yard where the chickens, just now venturing from their roosts, were pecking distractedly at the snow, as if that offered sustenance.

Once the snow melted, the yard was a mudpie. The yard planks were helpful to walk on, but the car would roll over them and splinter them, so they were pieced and interrelated like a puzzle. The yard needed new boards, but Amanda wouldn't think of spending money for boards. She kept telling Frederick to look about the sites of burnt houses, to see what boards might be had for the asking.

Then suddenly a warm drying day would lift its eyelids, would look down at their house, there in the splattered mud; the warm sun would welcome them to full life. The wood piles would thaw, the chickens would fill themselves with food, the cleaned company car would arrive from the office to whisk the family away to drive into the suburbs, or out into the sun-basking countryside.

Pink had come to be recognized as a successful businessman, but none of the other businessmen in town knew him well. As best they could tell, he had no interest in social functions, except for the presentations at the opera house and the new theatre on the square, where often he and two of his children could be seen together. He appeared to like vaudeville and plays, that sort of diversion, but he did not go to club meetings or join societies, or venture into the new country club, or even eat in the better restaurants, the ones businessmen frequented. His name would come up at most any meeting at which the mountain leaders were discussed, as would Hatch Cole's and that of J.P. Starnes, also an insurance man, and half a dozen others. The newly formed Rotary Club invited Pink to membership, never to receive a reply. Mr. Biggerstaff at the bank invited him to lunch and was told Pink had a long-standing engagement, which turned out to be dinner at home with his wife.

His insurance company now rented two entire floors of offices on the square, and was knocking doors into the brick wall of the adjoining building. His vice-president, Wallerbee, had left his job at the bank and was said to work ten hours a day at the insurance company, six days a week. The company itself was now listed by Dun & Bradstreet, but scant knowledge of it had been obtained even by that firm; assets were undeterminable, insurance in force was unknown, no stock of the company was offered for sale to the public, no bank had ever made a loan to Monarch. Apparently its funds had flowed into real-estate investments in the mountain counties, chiefly into mortgage loans to farmers, but the amounts were not ascertainable. The number of employees at the home office was given as twenty. The number of salesmen in the field was "over fifty." Obviously, it was a successful, home-grown business, yet nobody socially prominent in the community knew Pinkney Wright; most would not recognize him on the street. Occasionally, he had been known to go to dinner at the Battery Park Hotel, where he and his wife dined alone.

Among those most curious was a wealthy inventor—at least, he had invented and marketed a number of medicines and tonics—land developer and entrepreneur named Dr. C. C. Clove. He had come to believe that Asheville, which he had discovered in 1900, would become the Switzerland of America and had invested heavily in real-estate development. Dr. Clove was a forthright person who knew how to take hold of an opportunity, and this man Pinkney Wright interested him as a helper. Taking bird in hand, as he would say, one morning he climbed the flight of stairs to the Monarch offices, where he found himself in a narrow hallway, unadorned, with four office doors, not marked; now and again a young person would come out of one, close it, then hurry into another, to close that one, this scramble of bodies giving him no clue at all as to which door he ought to enter. He chose the nearest one and was repaid by a warm smile from a pretty lady who had on her desk the name Gloria Smith. He introduced himself and asked if he might see Mr. Wright. She said no, Mr. Wright was not here, that he came to the offices from time to time as suited him. Indeed, he might very well appear today, this being Monday, a day he usually was in town.

"Where does he go when he's away?" Clove asked, hoping to hear of a hunting or fishing lodge, or a resort hotel Clove frequented.

"He's usually working on the road," Miss Smith told him, her mountain accent crisp, with an old-world English twang to it.

Mr. Wallerbee received Clove, offered him the big cushion-lined rocker at the window, which he said was Mr. Wright's place whenever Mr. Wright was here, implying that should he arrive the chair would be requisitioned.

Dr. Clove waited for half an hour, looking out at the square, comparing it and its Victorian structures with his memory of the square in the city center of Brussels, which he remembered from trips abroad. He was sitting in the rocker dreaming of a restructured city when Pinkney Wright came in, shook hands, asked him how he liked Asheville, which surprised Clove since he had been residing here for many years, asked him how the climate was in Ohio, where, indeed, Clove was from, although he had not said so, asked about his mother, whom the smiling man had read about in the local newspaper, an interview printed years ago, asked about Clove's two sons, knew their names and prep schools, asked how his Clove Park development was getting on, which apparently Wright visited on Sunday afternoons when he would tromp about in the yards of the new houses and see progress of construction. Meanwhile he was motioning Clove back into the rocking chair, offering two additional pillows, which Clove placed on his lap. "You seem to know more about me than I know about you," Clove confessed. "I've come to find out more about you."

Wright brought a straight-backed chair from beside Wallerbee's desk and set it near the window, leaned back in it, and caught the shade pull in one hand. "Tell me what you want to know."

There was a sympathetic manner about him that Clove found ingratiating, courtly but at the same time friendly. He did appear to be sincerely interested in Clove, and to be ready to serve him. Encouraged, Clove found himself talking briskly, explaining portions of his own dreams for Asheville, including the possible razing of all these buildings on the square, damming the French Broad River to form a lake in the mountains to rival Lake Como in Europe, encouraging construction of new railroads, to open up the entire mountain region for passenger service and excursion cars. "Mr. Wright, don't you see, our future is in tourists, that's the secret, that's the word. Tourists. They will be the lifeblood of this region as it develops. We have at the moment a citizenry of people who do not—who are quaint, more quaint than progressive. You, of course, are an exception. I know you will agree. Facts are facts." The bright glint continued in Pink Wright's eyes; there was no counter-argument either, no protest, and this encouraged Clove to go further. "I believe in Asheville, Mr. Wright. I have such dreams for this place. You have seen what George Vanderbilt did—"

"I went out that way last Sunday with Amanda and my three children, and we were turned back at the gate. It happens every time."

"I can get you through the gate, for God's sake," Clove cried. "The gate isn't there to keep such as you out, Mr. Wright."

"Such as I?"

"You are a man of parts. That's why I have sought you out. I need you because, quite frankly, I have nobody in my developments, in my work, who is one of—these local people."

"These local people?" The courtly smile continued.

"Out there," Clove said, indicating the swarm of humanity on the square. "Those people out there."

Pink Wright laughed gently. "I see."

"Now," Clove said, placing himself on the forward rim of the chair, fixing Pinkney Wright with the steady gaze of the confident, practiced salesman, I need local people to come in with me on my next venture, one that's necessary to our city's expansion, progress. Let me explain. Asheville is now host to eleven tuberculosis sanitariums, some of them merely big houses, others sprawling institutions. They have given us a reputation as a TB center, haven't they?"

"Yes, I know," Pink told him mildly.

"Now then," Clove said, satisfied thus far with his presentation. "We can't progress with any such reputation. I want to buy them. It will be expensive. It will result in a loss of income until inns can be put in their place, but my plan is the only way."

Pink Wright pulled at the shade cord, lowered the shade a few inches, then let it go up again. "What do you want to buy them for, Dr. Clove?"

"I want to buy them all, Mr. Wright, and burn them down."

Pink Wright fiddled with the shade pull for a while longer, then released it. "Would you burn the patients as well?" he asked, the smile remaining. There was even a friendly nod of Pink's head, generous encouragement of an expected affirmative reply.

"No, I wouldn't do that, Mr. Wright," Clove said tightly.

"Well, I must say I'm relieved," Wright said in his kindly manner, complimenting him.

I have underestimated him, Clove thought on leaving. By then, his pouch belly had been warmed by a cup of tea, his mind was twirling with compliments from Wright, and from Wallerbee and Gloria Smith, and from others who Wright had insisted be brought in to meet the builder of the Clove Park Inn, the finest new hotel in Asheville. No investment was forthcoming, however, no use of Pinkney Wright's name was authorized for the announcements of the planned burnings, nothing did Clove have to show for his visit to Monarch, except courtesy.

A bedroom was built at the back of the house, opening off the children's room, but the house was still too small. There was no dining room, and the kitchen, even after enlargement, heated up during the cooking. "It's too hot, mama," Hallie complained. "Feel the heat in here. It'll burn paper."

"I've been baking. What can one expect?" Amanda asked her. "When you get to be a rich person, you can buy a house of your own with a big dining room."

Hallie unbuttoned her dress down to her belt and fanned herself with the Asheville *Gazette*. "Where is God, papa?" she asked her father. They were seated for the evening meal and grace had been said.

"Right around here," Pink told her, serving himself from the bowls and platters, serving Young, too.

"Where?" Hallie said.

"In the air," he replied, scraping butter onto his and Young's plates, waiting for the biscuits. "Present always."

"In this hot room?" Hallie said.

Pink chuckled. These days he was often finding himself caught by the girl's wit.

"I don't think that's—appropriate," Amanda told Hallie, pulling her chair close to the corner of the table where, once the food was served, she usually sat.

"Company sold fifty-four policies today," Pink announced proudly. "You consider two hundred fifty workdays, multiply that out . . ."

Hallie gave the answer at once: 13,500. Her precociousness infuriated Frederick, who kicked at her under the table.

"That's a total suitable for a millionaire," Pink added proudly, looking about.

Hallie laid her napkin across her forehead, held her head back, as if suffering heat prostration.

"We don't need any further theatrics," Amanda reprimanded her. "If my father saw you do that—"

Hallie exhaled deeply, making a noise something like a chugging train on a steep incline. "My papa thinks we need a new house," she said.

"Why, he never said that to me," Amanda told her. "He likes this house."

"Told me several times," Hallie said, wiping her forehead with the back of her hand. "Young wants his own room."

Pink continued eating, kept his head low, as if the argument were going on above him somewhere. And Young, imitating him, did as much.

As always, on Sunday afternoon, after church and dinner, rain or shine, Pink got them all in the car—and it was a carful, too—and tested his driving skills on the city streets, some thirty miles of which were now paved, new residential areas going up in every direction. In Clove Park, each lot was expensive, but each one was mortgageable even at Monarch, as Pink assured Amanda, suggesting they buy one. No, she would feel cut off from life out there, she told him, preferred smaller houses, had no desire for hired help, missed a sense of family. Even the shrubbery was of a type foreign to her. She did rather like the golf course, which at least reminded her of fields and pasture. "You don't mean they're going to use all that land for games?" she asked Pink.

Crowded in the back seat of the car, Hallie began to snicker behind her hands.

"Mama, they are for golfers," Frederick told her.

"Well, they don't need it all for games, do they?"

Hallie burst out in peals of laughter.

"It is the worst use of the land," Amanda told them, "that I have ever seen. Back home, if a King took a pasture such as that—"

"Oh, Lord," Hallie whispered.

"Don't say that," Amanda warned her.

104

"I'm sorry," she whispered.

"Back home, if a King wasted a pasture such as that, he'd be ridiculed."

A young salesman, one of Dr. Clove's colleagues, often phoned Amanda, announcing a house on the market, reminding her that her husband was a major businessman in the city, "and I wonder if the house you have is—suitable any longer." Amanda had work to do, she told him, the garden needing weeding, she was quilting for a church sale, she was baking for the birthday of one of Nettie King's sons. "Maybe tomorrow," she told him each time, shaking off the bother. The occasion did come, however, when she rose to the challenge and agreed to look at a furnished house, newly placed on the market following the death of its owner. The house occupied a wooded lot at the end of Crescent Drive and had a stone wall in front, one about four feet high, which offered a degree of privacy to the lawn but did not hide the house itself, which boldly sat on a hill looking out through trees at the expanses of green fairways. "Yes, yes, I understand," Amanda told the young salesman, moving from room to room, marveling at the moldings, at the plaster, the carnival type of plaster ceiling in the library, at the hand-done doors, the curved stairway, the two walls of walnut bookcases flanking the main fireplace, where carved statues cavorted. There were four bathrooms, one on the main floor, one over the garage, serving two servants' bedrooms, and two for the four upstairs bedrooms. There was a big square kitchen with an electric water cooler, a refrigerator built into a wall, an oven, a warmer, a sink with wide wooden drains on either side. The stove had two ovens, one big enough, she suspected, for a twenty-pound turkey. The small butler's pantry had built-in storage for the dishes, glasses, cups. By all odds, it was the finest kitchen she had ever seen, as fine as those in Hallie's and Pink's magazines.

With the salesman Amanda discussed the number of servants she would need. Judge Baker had had a staff of three, she was told, one of these for the yards and gardens and to drive him about. "Of course, around here you can hire servants for next to nothing," he said.

"Well, I like it," she admitted, allowing herself to relax into the sense of wealth the house suggested. She mulled over the matter all afternoon, entrusting the secret only to herself, until finally at supper she told her family that she had an outing planned, one she and the children must put on Sunday clothes for.

When Pink slowed their car down at the Judge Parker house gates, silence struck him and the children, all conversation stopped, awe settled. He parked in the cobblestone courtyard. Amanda noticed that even Hallie looked out fearfully at the stucco walls, the dozens of tall windows, the immense mahogany door. "It's merely something to look at, being empty," Amanda announced. She turned to Pink, trying to penetrate the smile he wore whenever he felt challenged. She had challenged him all right, she realized proudly, and the children, too; she had stunned even Hallie to speechlessness.

Young took his mother's hand. Together they approached the house, the boy and mother, step by step. They moved into the cool entrance hallway, onto the tile floor. To the right was the drawing room, or so the salesman had termed it and so Amanda called it now, with its arched ceiling, particularly beautiful this evening, with the wall sconces lighted. "I'm just not quite able to believe this," Pink told her.

Well, I'm not either, she thought.

The hallway was hollow to the children's laughter. Hallie was becoming particularly raucous, was the first to free herself of awe. Frederick and Young advanced up the stairs. "Every time you open a door," Frederick called down to his father, "there's another bathroom."

Amanda showed Pink the kitchen with its special mechanics, becoming more self-conscious about bringing the family here, afraid she had deserted her own home and upbringing.

"We need the house," Hallie told her father proudly, jubilantly. "I really do."

Amanda had been intrigued by the notion of showing the house, but now she became frightened by the prospect of living here. She retreated to the courtyard while the rest of the family circled the rooms. Pink found her finally, came to occupy the car seat beside her. Neither spoke. They listened to Young yell to Hallie, Frederick yell to Young, the children moving through the rooms, their voices made hollow by plaster and glass, their busy fingers turning on and off the lights everywhere.

"Be a sort of duke, I suppose," Pink commented.

"If you want to be." Then she said, "I want you not to be held back, Pink."

"Held back by what?" he inquired.

"By me," she said simply.

Young came bolting through the main door.

"Pink?" she asked him, prompting him, seeking assurance.

"Hush," he said.

"Some words merely come to mind," she explained.

"God knows," he said.

"I know what it's like for a man, what it's like for a man to have success."

Some time later Hallie found her parents. They were still sitting in the front seat of the car. When she went closer she saw that they were holding hands and that her mother had tears in her eyes.

That evening in her journal, Hallie wrote that she had, without speaking to them, climbed into the back seat of the car and had waited quietly, patiently as Frederick and Young ran room to room, turning off the lights in the palace. "And how scary that house did become now that it was being taken away from us, and with its pretty lights going off here and there as if its life were being taken one arm or leg at a time. Frederick was shouting to Young. Young began calling for mama. I was worrying about my father. Very strange. It made me feel cold and lonely. When the house was dark and the boys were in the car and quiet, papa left the palace's keys under the mat and answered no question about it. It was if that house had never existed at all."

Dr. Clove ran into Pink on the street and stopped to chat. "I know you went to see the Parker house," he said. "What did you think of it? Keen designed it, you know, and Sears designed the gardens. Tell you, we need some mountain natives living out there, if we can find the right ones. We are up against it, living with Floridians, Pennsylvanians, New Yorkers everywhere. We need the local flavor that you would bring to our neighborhood."

"Can you keep a cow out your way?" Pink asked at once, speaking simply.

Clove's own smile slowly faded. "Don't think so."

"Chickens be all right, I imagine. A man could cut down some of the crab apples and plant bearing fruit trees? Plow up part of the lawn for corn, beans, a few rows of cabbage. Where do you get water? Does the house have a spring?"

Clove cleared his throat uneasily. He chuckled appreciatively, tentatively.

"Now, geese are something that will give you local flavor, and local noise, as well," Pink told him.

Clove smiled grimly. At the street corner, he was still chuckling appreciatively, trying to adjust his mind to Pink's attack. The two men paused there; Pink took hold of Clove's arm. "You're a doctor, are you? Yes, I know you are." Pink's manner now was serious. "Let me ask you something. I have a change in my vision now and then. I did this morning. Every color goes brighter, and I wonder what that signifies."

"I'm not a doctor of medicine, as such," Clove said. "My spring tonic does help most ailments—"

"I was walking across Lexington Avenue," Pink continued, "and the world flashed at me. This was just a few minutes ago. I was near the rag shop. I had to stop and hold to their doorway, stood there for about a minute. Two boys were trying to come through the door. I blocked them while I gazed at that strange sight. Everything on the street was suddenly brilliant, all the colors."

"No, no," Dr. Clove said, "I have some tonics that I manufacture in Ohio, but I would advise you to see a doctor about your vision, Mr. Wright. I suggest you use Dr. Larry Lawrence." He nodded several times. "He has seen the queen. I mean by that, he actually examined her." He smiled. "Did I mention the Battery Park Hotel project to you as yet?" Clove took hold of Pink's arm now, to keep him close by. "My new project, Mr. Wright, let me mention it. I need money, a loan. I want to buy the Battery Park Hotel."

"And tear it down?" Pink asked.

"And tear it down," Clove confirmed. "Mrs. Vanderbilt thinks I'm out of my mind, and so do some others." He took from his crammed-full pocket an architect's drawing of a new building, a skyscraper about fifteen floors high. "Mrs. Vanderbilt laughed at me. She loves the Battery Park Hotel as it is, but we can't build a great city here if we have a hill in the way, now can we?" Out of his other pockets Clove brought still more papers, sorting through them. "Here," he said, unfolding a map. "Here, look at this. It's the city center that's too small." He put his forefinger on the offending hill on the map. "Tear down the old hotel, use the hill to fill in the ravine to the south, leveling all this perhaps a hundred acres, build a new hotel with a roof garden, have a dance band every night, have open terraces up there with a view of the mountain ranges. Now—" His hands were trembling, his entire body was taut; he could scarcely breathe because of his excitement. "I know it sounds strange." He was rocking now, trying to expend excess energy. He was simply filled to overflowing with ideas, plans, information about the new city he meant to build. "Here before it, below it will be a covered passageway with sixty small shops, and above them offices; fifteen stories high. Well, what about it, Wright? I can do it."

Pink rubbed an itchy spot on his neck. "Lord knows," he whispered.

"A hundred thousand dollars will help."

"A hundred thousand dollars won't impress Mrs. George Vanderbilt," Pink said.

"Yes, the idea that local capital is involved. She is diffident about outsiders taking over, but if you and your company will come in—"

"The banks are the place—"

"Oh, please don't talk to me about banks. They have no vision. I have brought five people together to start a new Citizens Bank for this very reason. We will have a bank to support exciting ideas. Just now the bankers are—dull. They are in the road, are wallowing."

"I understand," Pink said. "I knew they were in the road but didn't know what they were doing there."

"Now, I want you on the board of that new bank. But first I want you to do this hundred thousand dollar loan for me."

Pink smiled the friendly Wright smile. "No, I won't go into it."

Clove mopped his face with a silk handkerchief bearing the initials CCC. "Of course, you get the total view, don't you, Wright? Why won't you help?"

Pink smiled considerately. "I'm not one to tear down a hill, Dr. Clove. I think of this as being a town for mountain people to trade in, while I suppose you see it for tourists to use. I invest the mountain people's money and the Negroes' money—and it is their money, you understand, it's not Vanderbilt money, not Florida tourists' money. It's one of the few supplies of money the natives have in this town. You say to me, Come help me, I need local people to help with this dream of mine. Well, sir, it's a foreign dream, seems to me. I'd rather look out and see sheep grazing on the sides of a mountain than see a tunnel through it, or drag lines moving it away."

After a minute's pause Dr. Clove roused himself, shrugged, nodded to Pink briefly. He took from his pocket a bottle of Clove tonic, drank directly from the bottle. "Mrs. Vanderbilt and I love nature, too." He took another swig. "As you might know, before his death Mr. Vanderbilt started up a forestry school, to teach forest management as practiced in Europe. His wife is interested in looming—or weaving, whatever you people call it. She wants to get some of the country women in to teach others how it's done, to try to keep alive the native crafts, which the tourists like so much. We had one hundred fifty thousand visitors to Asheville last year."

"We had more than that," Pink said quietly.

"No, that counts all the hotels, the boardinghouses, the tourist homes, of which there are about two hundred."

"We had more than that sleep under wagons on Lexington Avenue," Pink repeated simply. He watched as Clove wandered on off, his exuberance bridled by the discussion.

At the square, even while he paused there, the visual aberration struck Pink once more, an eerie brightness. The square was illuminated with vibrant light, the quarry stone of the new library building sparkled, as if flecked with mica, the streetcars became a brilliant yellow, and the few tombstones displayed in front of the tombstone shop radiated, alive with hovering spirits. After a few moments, it passed on, whatever fit or spasm it had been passed on, and he felt refreshed.

Upstairs, sitting in his chair, he couldn't concentrate on the papers Wallerbee kept handing him for wondering about the attacks. He drank the tea Gloria served him, asked about her divorce proceedings, which were complex, but he scarcely heard her replies. "Wallerbee, isn't it strange that I never have taken out an insurance policy, and I own an insurance company?" he asked suddenly.

Wallerbee at once swiveled his chair, leaned across the room, and handed him a policy application. Pink read it through. Of course, he knew it by heart but had never read it before with a personal identification, with his own death in mind. He folded it, stuck it down inside the fold of his chair, where he often stashed papers. He felt well, as well as he had ever felt in his life, and he sought to calm himself with that knowledge. There had been slight dizziness during the brightness, but also sharper focus on detail. His body had lost balance, but his mind had remained clear. His memory had been intensified, he decided, had recalled a procession of images. For instance, there had been a glimpse of his father hurrying across the pasture in the snow, and that must have been decades ago. Why did his mind flash so readily, brilliantly to an early time, he wondered, and to country scenes?

Wearily, he got up from the chair. Too many thoughts. "I'll be back around," he told Wallerbee. "How's your daughter, Gloria?" he asked her.

"Well. And she likes it when I say you ask about her, Mr. Wright."

"How old is she?"

"She's ten now."

"Your mother still bedridden?"

"Yes. She's with me now, at home, Mr. Wright."

He wanted to do something for his own family; this damnable experience had made him want to draw closer to them. There was a new store in the town, a big department store, and he went there to ask for advice about a gift, but he found the store had many different counters, with each attendant representing only a limited stock. Wandering about, he saw a pair of spy glasses, which he bought for his boys, and at the jewelry counter he picked out earrings for Hallie; she had had her ears pierced this past month. At another counter he chose a pearl necklace for Amanda. It was in a blue velvet-lined case. He said he would take the case, as well, which amused the salesgirl. Pink was surprised when told how much the necklace was worth. "Well, let me see what I have with me." He kept money tucked back in his wallet and carried some money in his pants and jacket pockets. He counted out what he had, which took a while, the salesgirl watching, clearly astonished. "Seven hundred dollars," he said, pushing the money across the counter to her.

Frederick was elected secretary of his class, and the news at the dinner table, spoken in his customary ever-so-patient and considerate manner, caused instant consternation. Hallie on three or four occasions had to the family's knowledge actually announced candidacy for office at her school and had not won anything. Now Frederick was singled out. Pink was ecstatic. He never did finish his supper. How was one to account for this? Was it a high honor or was it a designation out of compromise? Was it an honest election? He could not quite believe it. Amanda, of course, floated on clouds.

Nine

F rederick began trading on Lexington Avenue, using as base the stalls of a merchant named Richardson Hice, usually called Rich even though he claimed to be at poverty's door and would in self-defense cheat a bargainer if he could, using his own starvation as excuse. The poorer the petitioners, the more assiduous Rich became in efforts to fleece them; by the same token, he was far and wide known to be a scavenger and was offered every broken hoe and sick horse. Let a mule be well enough to survive the trip into town, and it very likely would be offered first to Rich, and if whiskey had elated him for the day, he would make a deal sure as fire burns. About his stalls were to be found dyspeptic, mangy animals of all kinds, lopsided wagons, busted tools suffering from corrosion and rust. It was a sign of Frederick's honesty that he could serve Rich, take messages for him, even receive promised payment or merchandise, yet was not tarred with the same brushes that were used on Rich.

Frederick traded for a variety of items himself, among them coins and bank notes from earlier days, especially the Civil War, which northern tourists liked as souvenirs, and pearl-handled knives of all sizes and shapes, which also were souvenir items. He made a bit of money now and again and took pride in his acquisitions. Always he had in his pockets a few trinkets, for which he had paid very little, and admittedly rarely knew the true value of, but for which a buyer might be found at the Battery Park Hotel. Failing that, he could often pawn them for as much as he had paid.

From time to time, most often on a Saturday, Frederick took his brother Young to Lexington Avenue, to enjoy the excitement. The boy, only five, would sit on the curb near the water fountain, or try to work the scales at one of the shops, or listen to the banjo or fiddle playing. Sometimes one of the nice old ladies would break him off a two-inch length of peppermint candy, two inches being quite enough for him, even if he was the cutest boy ever seen.

Then came the accident, a chain of happenings, really. Rich had bought a used Ford truck, which he parked at the top of the long Lexington Avenue hill because it required coasting off to start. He had bricks placed under each wheel, to keep it from rolling. Young was sitting in the cab, waiting for Frederick, when a farmer, needing bricks, removed them. The truck teetered on the verge of rolling off, then settled into place against a curb, but a big Weaverville woman came along, sat down on the tailgate to rest, and the truck moved out and away, aimed down the three steep city blocks of the busiest trading street in this part of the world. Young looked up from his book in time to see the hood disappear under a collection of chicken crates, the view of the street reappearing on the other side, chickens now decorating the Ford. The truck delivered a glancing, splintering blow to a horse-drawn wagon, setting horse and wagon into motion, the truck careering into a stall full of used clothing, emerging from that fully draped, to rip open a stack of crates of vegetables, then to topple an awning onto half a dozen passersby. The truck rolled across the street, passing over Skip Neighbor's prostrate body, he choosing to lie down rather than chance flight. The truck threw debris into both front windows of Hiram Goodman's shop, upset a lamp post, and gathering speed once more smacked down three people who sought to stop it, knocked over two sheep, freed pigs from a pen, scatted through a booth run by the Pearson family, breaking Ball jars full of blackberries and pear preserves. Young was helpless to stop it. Seeking to turn off the key, he turned it on. The motor started, further terrifying scores of pedestrians on the sidewalk, the churning, rattling, threatening monster roaring louder than the people screaming warnings. Two mothers fled, babes in arms, truck and mothers gathering speed, a freed goat accompanying them, the truck leaving the road and ripping into a line of stalls, releasing ducks and setting hounds to howling. The truck sailed squarely toward Hugh King's store, the boy inside terrified as it entered the side wall, where it engaged rolls of fencing, hurling them about until, wire and papers in its fan, the truck's motor sputtered out, the truck stopped abruptly, and threw Young forward through the window. He landed, unconscious, on Hugh's desk.

All the way up the hill, women and children wailed, men shouted defiantly, boys waded about in seas of broken plate glass, canvas awnings strewn about, flapping. The street was awash with fowl, animals, broken eggs, busted canning jars. Far off was heard the whine of ambulances and even firetrucks. The drinking fountain began throwing a stream of water thirty feet into the air.

"Why, I was a-standing there a-minding my own business when this here trajectile come at me, a-coughing and shitting fire, a little boy's face staring out of the windows looking like Jeeter Harmon's ghost."

"Was an act of God's judgment on all this trading, on you'uns thinking too much about money, and it nothing in the world but the sweat of Satan . . ."

"Now you stop crying out so, Mary, or I'll tie your mouth shut."

"It's been prophesied that we're not ought to set on top of motors, ride on wheels. I've been telling you, we have to get shut of them vehicles."

The police cars blocked the street, unintentionally delaying one of the ambulances. Some people fled, seeking to escape any further assaults in this confused place; others arrived. Last of all to be moved was the boy lying unconscious on Hugh's desk; he was lifted onto a Civil War stretcher and carried to a waiting ambulance, Hugh and Frederick both running after, Hugh sobbing in a great voice, "Make way, make way."

At last Amanda found a chair available, and she moved it outside the boy's hospital room, set it in the wide hallway. Nurses dressed in crisp uniforms would come and go, hurrying, closing doors to rooms where the injured lay. A Seth Thomas clock hung on the wall near where Amanda sat, her hands folded, pressed against her abdomen, where this same baby boy had been once, against which he had lain so many times since.

"It's raining there now," an attendant said, rushing along, speaking to a nurse. "The streets are awash with blood, but much of it is animals'." Pink stood near the clock, his back pressed against the wall. He had waited for hours, it seemed. Dr. Patterson arrived, was directed to the operating room. Dr. Watkins arrived. He had had car trouble on the way, had commandeered a citizen's car. At the nurses' station, Watkins read the nurses' report on Young, a nurse murmuring statistics about temperature and pulse and delirium. "Doctor, I know him so well," Amanda said, interrupting.

114

"Well, yes," he said looking at her vacantly. "I know you do," he said, but he went on into the boy's room alone, closing the door firmly. He came out, wandered off to get a folding chair for Pink. He reported that the boy had broken both legs, one foot was mangled, his collarbone was broken, doubtless some ribs. Tonight would be the battle time for him. Then, staring transfixedly at the pendulum on the clock, he said he had had no experience with a mangled foot, and though young boys very likely would heal, given proper bone setting . . . "I will have the surgeon remove the foot, Pink."

"No," Pink said at once. "By God, no."

"Risky not to."

"No."

Scores of people came and went, the injured and the bereaved, doctors and attendants. The halls were sometimes crowded. Other chairs were brought from a church nearby, and finally a big urn was carried in, coffee sloshing inside. During the night Enid and Adeline King arrived, a neighbor having driven them directly to the hospital; Enid wrestled his foot locker in out of the wet. Adeline sat down in the chair Pink offered her, which was Pink's chair. The two women, mother and daughter, sat side by side, for a while. "He's in the operating room, is he still?" Adeline asked.

"You lost three, mama," Amanda reminded her.

"One to flu, one to the river, one to diphtheria."

"But you lost three, and I can't lose one."

"It's not the same. We prepared for losing some of ours. We lived with the thought—"

"How—how were you prepared?"

"By knowing it would happen, we stayed a pace removed. Today a mother can keep her children."

"Oh, I have to keep this boy, mama."

A nurse came by; Amanda asked how her son was, and the nurse expressed confidence, all the while moving along swiftly to escape. Adeline King suggested that somebody lead in a prayer, and King asked what good that would do. "Might gain God's attention," she replied.

"They're not going to cut his foot off, are they, Pink?" King asked.

"God, no," Pink said. "I won't have it."

King tried crossing his legs, then he uncrossed them, all the while staring about at the strange place, where sounds made at the far end of the building reverberated through pipes and fittings. Suddenly he spoke directly to God, using a firm voice that carried down along the hallway, alerting several people. "You'll need to do better by us," he told God outright. "When I was a boy I could count more blessings in a day that I can count now in a year's time." Adeline was staring at the far wall, at a picture of a lamb lost in snow. "You come when we call, the Bible says," King said, "But I've often counted and not found you among the numbers."

"Oh, my God," Adeline moaned anxiously, "what a terrible prayer. You ought to pray humbly," she told him.

"God damn," King told her, "God has all power, and I'm asking him as an honest preacher to help us. The boy's in there, in this cold place, being cut up. I'll make my opinion known, by God. . . ."

"Oh, my God," Adeline moaned, "listen to him. Forgive him, God."

"God will help, I know," Pink confided suddenly.

"I make no knee bends to either one of them, God or Jesus," Enid announced. "I'm tired to death of praying kneeling prayers."

"Don't pay attention to him," Adeline King requested. "He really ought to be more humble than he is."

"I'm not humble one damn bit," King declared.

"God, we humbly ask—" she began, praying.

"I ask no such damn thing," he declared adamantly, glaring at her.

"We come on bended knees, all of us—" she insisted.

"A woman is supposed to keep her mouth shut afore God," King informed her.

"God, it's my grandchild that's in there, I held him when he was first born and felt him breathe—"

"She's confusing God, that's all, confuses God and the preachers."

"And I—" she glared at her husband. "A woman is allowed to pray. Why did you say a woman is not allowed to pray?"

"Not in church," he told her.

"Well, do you think this is a church?"

"No. I know what it is."

"Well, you pray then. You lead us in a proper prayer and we'll all hush and follow." About them, up and down the hall, others were listening, tittering, whispering, watching. Something inside Enid broke in that moment, the wall of bitterness, old-world obstinacy gave way, and he raised his face and spoke out. "God, we make our way, best we can, about half lost, and ask you to mend our broken boy. . . ." Pink, staring about anxiously, began trembling. Mercifully, the prayer washed out into whispered contemplation. Walking bent over, Enid suddenly left them, seeking the men's room, banged the door loudly as he entered it. Soon he returned noisily up the hall, buttoning his pants, grimacing as he tried to get a button into the last buttonhole, ignoring the critical stares of several women.

Pink escaped, walked to the end of the hall, looked out the square window into the trees and prayed quietly there, promised God to serve him, to work in the church and do whatever else might please him, if his young son lived and was whole. The nurse brought him a fresh mug of coffee. The cup had smudges along the rim, but he welcomed it, cleaned properly or not, drank the coffee down so she could take the mug with her. At the central nurses' station, there was chatter among the nurses, and he heard Young's name mentioned several times. Later there was polite giggling. Pink heard the word "mountaineers." He supposed Enid had been put down as a simple soul, a subject for ridicule, and perhaps Pink had been, also. Mountaineers. Well, that's what we are, he thought. We are born in a home bed, we breathe common enough air, see with blue eyes as best we can, measure our height as we grow, as well as our welcomes, and can make a fire as easily as we can douse one. We laugh at our strangeness, we laugh with one another. We work, such work as needs doing, but do not pester it needlessly; a lick and a promise usually. We work with the rocky land, and with animals that are relatives of the pastures and woods, that grow from food they forage there, and they bear their young there. We harvest grains. We harvest sorghum and make syrup from it. We rob hives in old trees. We pick herbs in the woods and along the fences near the creeks and drink teas made from them. We track wild animals. We fish the streams. I have caught many a brook and rainbow trout. I have thrown many calves when they needed it. I once straddled the hog we had fattened and shot it in the back of the head, aiming to slaughter it, and it took off running with me astride, the animal losing strength as it bled, until finally it stopped and stood near a fence waiting to die, and when it fell over, I had to avoid being caught under it. We breed with our women, sometimes in beds with mattresses made of shucks on springs made of stretched rope, sometimes in flowered fields or under trees old as Indian times. We break bread with our hands. We do not say sir to anybody. We do not ask pardon. We do not offend, at least do not mean to, and should a fence be broken, we will help mend it. A mountain man does not weep. The women weep, but a man stands straight and accepts; he is the world's best accepter. He assumes what is meted out is what is due, is what Fate sends. We mountaineers sing our own songs, even of a daytime. We love our country, whatever it is, wherever it is; we know where it starts out from. We sell timber. We make whiskey and pretty good brandy and drink them—the men drink them. We bend our children in the ways they are to grow, responding to the needs and dangers. We swim in cold water pure as morning mist and often resembling it. We drink water freely flowing from the earth. We build with stone and logs we own already. We saw and notch, grub clay from banks along the creek and daub with it. We have strong, fast dogs, surprised by petting. We shoot accurately, either shotguns or rifles or pistols. We do not steal. We do not rape. We abhor mistreatment of anybody. We never forget any mistreatment of ourselves, although we tolerate it. We welcome strangers, but we do not imitate them. . . .

At dawn two doctors went inside the operating room. Pink waited amid a shower of worry. Later Dr. Watkins stepped outside, waited for Pink to come near. "We had seven to operate on. I held your boy till last, to give the surgeons time. They took off most of the right foot, what couldn't be put proper. He has part of it remaining. The boy is all right otherwise," the doctor said, and reached out his hand to Pink, which Pink did not accept.

"How much did you take?"

"Well, it's three toes and half the ball and the arch, tapering to the heel." The doctor rested the hand against the tan wall, leaned against the wall that way. "Dr. Holman did it. He's the best we have, Pink." Amanda approached, grasped Pink's arm, held to him to keep herself erect. Next day she could not remember the moment, did not recall the doctor being present. She recalled earlier her father praying and Pink walking alone to the window, standing away off down there, and why was he there? she had wondered; and then nothing. Next she knew, she was home in her own bed.

Hallie brought her toast to eat, along with apple butter and a slice of fried ham. She read poems to her, celebration of life, which Amanda listened to politely, wondering if Hallie was normal. Dear Hallie, reading in her fine, firm voice the traipsing, singing words of life and victory, while her mother chewed on the lean portions of the ham.

The relationship of all the members of the family was shaken and tested by Young's accident. If the boy had combatted a routine illness, time might have prepared them for the danger, but the surprise had confused and compromised their will. A matter of a moment, he was taken from his place in the home, and was broken and ruptured, and only after weeks was he returned in casts. He wasn't able even then to walk.

Amanda could scarcely keep her hands off him. All day she would find herself going through the rooms to give him his hugs. Well, there are his books all over the floor. Thank God. Let him remain dependent on her care forever. She noticed Pink catered to him more than ever, as well, even bought him a catcher's mitt, which the boy loved, though he could not leave his bed, and Pink assured him in time they would practice ball in the backyard, no doubt trampling her rows of beans. She didn't object to that, no jokes about the beans, though she did joke with them about base-ball itself. "Chase a white ball when you could be growing something. Swatting it, then running in a square. Nobody back home had to tell a boy where to run. If I had you up home, Young—and maybe next summer we'll visit home, when you're able to get about—I want you to fish and swim and ride ponies, chop wood, hunt and explore, do sports that boys have always done, and not hit at a ball and run in a path."

A big smile appeared as the boy considered her arguments. He was intrigued by them, by her. He liked her, she could tell. As usual his hair stood up, his blue eyes were changing hue in the shifting light, his straight, white teeth were gleaming. "Ahhh, mama," he would say, as was common whenever he was amused or impressed by her.

And the Persian kitten, consider it. "Pink, what on earth is it?" On first sight, there at the kitchen porch, she had been more than willing to take it at once into her own hands, a precious gift, a ball of blue fur with two round blue eyes, but Pink wouldn't release the kitten to her, or to Hallie, who began giggling on first stroking its fur. Nor would Pink release the kitten to Frederick. Once Pink came to Young, however, came near the wheelchair where the boy was sitting, why, Pink pushed the ball of fur into his hands. "Here, you keep it. I have no need for it." He retreated from the gasping boy, from the disappointed Amanda, from the surprised Hallie, who of course, as everybody knew, loved her father most dearly of all people on earth, retreating from his own awkwardness as Frederick clouded over, close to tears.

The boy's accident reminded Pink of his own vulnerability. The threat to his best child had resulted in his giving higher value to his own life. He reported to Wallerbee that he had decided Young was his own outstanding creation, that in the plans for his own life and work a prince was at hand, the strongest piece on the chessboard was in view. "I feel around for him," Pink confessed, "even here at the office. I make decisions with him in mind, instructing him. See what I mean? I've been thinking about him being here, taking over someday. If my arm is gone—they say if you amputate a member, you can still be pained by it."

"I don't . . . I don't know," Wallerbee said, confused by the flock of jumbled admissions, confessions, which obviously came from Pink's heart.

"Amanda thinks she's the one who loves him the most," Pink confided. Later he said confidently, "I'll have him walking soon. Running. Without a limp, too."

In the assault by the runaway truck, nobody was killed, the fact itself something of a miracle. Subsequently Rich Hice fled, so many suits were entered against him as the truck's owner; he simply passed on out of town, leaving his broken possessions for Frederick to dispose of. Pink paid the hospital bills of six of the poorer patients, without being asked.

Frederick dreamed nowadays of becoming a doctor and healing the sick, saw himself arriving most often in the nick of time, and after other doctors had failed. He was able to treat in his imagination any number of pretty ladies, and this pleased him even more than had his heroics in fighter planes over France and Germany.

• • •

When the armistice came, bells began ringing in the city at all thirty churches. A church might not have a pipe organ or even have plumbing, but it had a bell of some sort. This was a marvelous opportunity for little children to swing on the bell ropes and create a racket. Both boys and girls were worn out by 9 P.M., when adults took the ropes in hand, those who were not milling about the square clapping to string-band music, shouting greetings, and giving the rebel yell.

The poison-gassing of soldiers was over, the bloody wounding in trenches, the acts of surgery painfully performed in tent shelters in muddy fields, the sea drownings and air crashes; dancing was to start again, the boys—our boys—were to come home to be loved forever. Thousands of human beings thronged into the square, clogging Lexington Avenue and the other streets. Several cars were turned over and banged on mightily; boys frightened horses, smashed a few wagons. Train whistles sounded; so did steam whistles at the tannery, the textile mills, and other factories. "I'm deaf. I think I'm deaf," Hallie shouted excitedly. She had been cruising about the edges of the throng, she and two girlfriends, bouncing off boys who sought to hug them, avoiding at least some of the outstretched arms.

At Kenilworth Inn, converted this past year to a government hospital, the wounded soldiers helped one another onto the lawn, where they sang battle hymns till exhausted. No more casualty lists, Amanda decreed, standing that night with Pink at Hugh's store. No more restless days, wheatless days, sugarless days. No more worry about Frederick growing old enough to go off to war.

In the square a big bonfire was started out of wagon bodies. People danced about it. The fiddle, banjo, and guitar music took on a more devilish, challenging twang and thrust. Two girls passed out, victims of emotion, and Hallie, dancing with the McKinney boy—her first spate of carefree dancing ever—even felt a rising, mounting sensation ending in a spasm, which so surprised her that she hid in the crowd, then fled to the company offices. From that safe retreat, from her father's chair, she watched the remaining festivities, huddled under a quilt; between the chair's protecting arms, she watched people dance and the Kaiser burn in effigy.

PART TWO
Courtship

CHAPTER
Ten

P ink appeared not to notice Hallie's se-
clusiveness. At least, he was not critical of
it, enjoying her company himself. Amanda was the one who kept mentioning it to him. At sixteen, when other girls in the school had begun to go
with boys on occasion, to church, to movies, to chaperoned parties, Hallie
was rarely invited out. One exception was Ted McKinney, who owned a
Chevrolet with a rumble seat. Soon after the armistice, he invited her to
drive home from an evening church service, and the drive turned out to last
longer than the distance home would have required. Even though there was
another couple present, Amanda worried about the danger.

She tried to talk with Hallie about it, and about dating boys in general,
but each time she floundered. Hallie's clothing, she dressed herself even yet
in tomboy sloppiness. Her features were refined, she could be pretty if she

wanted to be—well, her ears were large, but of course she could hide them. She was well built, nobody denied that; she was ripe as a peach, all right, Amanda realized, had a beautiful body, which she disguised with sweaters and a wool dress she had bought at the rag shop. As yet Hallie didn't seem to have heard any siren calls. Amanda remembered how different she had been when young, how her longings had almost overcome her, how she had accepted every suggestion to present herself attractively. She could see in Hallie the ripeness of body but not as yet the anxiousness. Hallie had the same full breasts and narrow waist, the well-rounded hips, the long, thin legs—"You do have the prettiest legs I've about ever seen, Hallie," Brodie King himself told her, even Brodie, older, highly regarded by the local girls, this having been overheard by Frederick. Just maybe something could be arranged with Brodie, Amanda thought, a church date, something controllable, although she had heard that even older women sought after Brodie. Well, it was all too much to consider, the dangers for a girl coming of age in a city. And this dear child had yet another fault, as Amanda considered the problem; she was too brash. Even Brodie had told Frederick that she would never get boyfriends until she stopped insulting them. Somebody had mentioned Tom Wolfe as being smart enough for her, but they doubted he would like a woman who admitted she was as smart as he. These two had been in competition at the library for years. Tom had told Brodie he had read every novel on the shelves except four; he didn't read those because he found that Hallie had already checked them out twice. Not sure she wanted Hallie to go out with any of the Wolfe boys anyway. They might take more after their father than was healthy, even though they lived in their mother's house. Tom Wolfe was not a church person, either. Admittedly he had managed to steer himself between the father, with his drunken bouts, and his mother, with her mind on real estate and money; both parents had hungers that apparently they had not been able to satisfy, and this boy, in this unhappy family, had managed to make a fair figure of himself, so that his school work was outstanding and his presence in a room was noticed by everyone. Well, he was beyond Hallie, with her tied-back hair, her scruffy clothes, her critical manner, her bitten nails, her quick denial of personal interests, of any desires.

Yet she had been in the rumble seat on the ride home. "What was going on back there, Hallie, tell me that?" Amanda finally asked her.

"It was cooler back there."

"Cooler? What was cooler?" Hopelessly she considered her daughter. "Well, it wasn't hot anywhere that night, was it?"

"Mama, we went from church to a café and had a sandwich, and when we came back to the car, his friend Michael got into the driver's seat and told his girl friend to get into the passenger seat, so there was the rumble seat left."

"And McKinney felt you?"

Hallie glared at her.

"Oh, my God," Amanda said desperately. "What did he do?"

"Mama, nothing happened."

"How do you know?"

"I think he did mean to, mama," she admitted, "but there's not much room back there."

"Back where?" Amanda asked.

"In the rumble seat."

"In the car?"

"Well, yes, mama, there is not enough room for everything."

"Everything?" Amanda shouted, her hands gripping one another so that her knuckles were pure white.

"For . . . for that, mama. Oh, for goodness sake, I don't know what it is, either."

"What do you mean by 'either,'" Amanda asked.

Hallie blinked, nodded, tried to shrug. "It's always there, mama."

"It is not always there. Chaperones were invented to keep it from being always there. I mean, listen here, we have McKinneys up home. A McKinney wouldn't dare try to make me—to get me to—" Stymied, helplessly involved, confused: "Hallie, what am I to do?" she pleaded.

Hallie suddenly smiled, took her mother's hand between her hands, pressed them. "We are funny, mama," she said.

"Now what did she mean by that, Pink?" Amanda asked him lying beside him, staring at the ceiling of their bedroom.

"Appears to be easier to bring up a boy," Pink said. They were talking softly, so the children wouldn't hear them.

"I can take her home, visit the country, where no boy would dare . . . would dare get one of the Kings pregnant."

"I never did," Pink said, chuckling. "Not even Harry did—"

"I mean it's safer there, compared to here, where we don't—we don't even know them, Pink. The boys are strangers."

"Yes, well, you take her home for a week, Amanda, let her try it out up there."

"A week?" Amanda said stiffly. "A girl can't court properly in a week."

"She can make a start."

"A month."

"A month?" he said startled, sitting up in bed.

"I do think we must do this, Pink, I really do, for her sake."

"A month?"

"I'll have a girl come by every day to cook and clean for you. Frederick and Young will benefit. Yes, I'll take them as well."

"Leave Young with me."

"But he would enjoy it so."

"No, leave Young."

"For the sake of his foot, you mean?"

"Yes, for that. He's doing better but does limp, and until he's fully well—"

"Doesn't limp much."

"It's . . . enough. Boys test afflictions. Mountain boys do. I don't know why."

"What is so strange about living a month at home, Pink, when you yourself lived there for years?"

He pulled a pillow over his face.

"You don't have to stay. You drive us up there and come weekends."

"I can't spend a month going back and forth," he told her.

"Pink, you have your mother there, and your brother, and my family—"

"I know," he told her, "I know who's there."

"I wish I knew what went on in that rumble seat. I do know he must have wanted her, Pink, and that's a hopeful sign. He must have figured out what lay under all those clothes she wears. Or maybe he merely wanted to boast later about his triumph. No telling what gets into a McKinney's mind."

"Only God knows," Pink admitted.

"You know how they are, don't you? Telling what they did to Pink Wright's girl, who always had flaunted about."

"No," he said miserably. "I don't know."

"I'm going to take her home. I wish I could go now."

"Honey, it's still cold up there this time of year. Too cold."

She turned in the bed toward him. "Too cold for what?"

"Lying about on the ground."

She almost strangled on her effort to reply, then they both buried their faces in the pillows laughing.

There were several weeks of preparations, getting ready for the journey home. At first, Amanda thought surprising her parents would be appropriate, but word of the visit leaked out, and even the purpose of it. Young required special attention too, since he was being left behind, and Pink explained to him about the peculiarity of his home people, a tendency to light on any weakness or handicap to aggravate and test it. "I want you to try to get back with the neighborhood baseball team this summer, Young." He gave the boy little room for dissent, even bought new baseballs and a new bat.

Young consented after Amanda explained to him that his father needed him at home. That was reason enough, that was a world of argument to Young.

At last the time came for most of the family to leave: Amanda eager for the challenge, Hallie scared to death of it, and Frederick gleefully anticipating Hallie's courting, though anxious about his own role as a city boy in the country. Into the company car piled the troop. Red, the driver, looking askance at the pile of bags, cartons, paper sacks. Young and Pink waved to them from the front yard, called out warnings about the trip, pleas for a happy summer.

On the way out of town, Amanda sat in the back seat, Hallie beside her. Frederick was up front, where he and the driver were trying to get signals out of a new radio: the crackling noise that escaped the speaker was annoying. Within half an hour the car reached the rural roads, which had many new ruts due to a storm. In low places there were freshets crossing the road, some of them at runningboard height. There were, of course, the customary hog wallows and cave-ins to be avoided, and there were wagons, horsemen, stray calves, droves of pigs, flying and pecking chickens, and other automobiles, all of these forming a pattern dizzying to behold. Red doggedly kept his shoulders hunched, his eyes on the road, the radio sputtering static into his and Frederick's ears. Once they ascended into the higher valleys, mountains stood round them like the walls of rooms, rising for thousands of feet above them, the road finding its way around boulders, across small rivers, up steep hills. . . .

Amanda was becoming ever less secure, less confident, now that she was on the way. With Pink to talk to, she had maintained a confident attitude, contending she knew well enough how to arrange courtships. She had begun to wonder. Hallie was not a typical country girl. For one thing she had read more than people in the country, had become aware in her reading of experiences that most mountain girls would not know about. Of more consequence, Hallie knew what the real purpose of this visit was and had become embarrassed by the new clothes, the change in hairstyle, the challenge offered her. In a soft voice Amanda began to ruminate aloud to Hallie about courtship, the joys, rules, expectations. "The girl is the one in danger, of course, and I don't mean only by pregnancy, but by harshness, callousness, when the man asserts himself roughly."

Hallie was stunned to hear her mother openly discuss such matters. "Papa was rough?"

"No, your father is—if anything, he's the opposite. That's so of all his life, don't you notice?" She looked off at the flanks of the nearby mountains, deeply shaded by a wealth of green trees and rhododendrons.

"You were popular?" Hallie asked.

"I tried to be. I smiled when it was proper, laughed at the boys' stories, made slight concessions. I blushed satisfactorily." She laughed. "I thought—well, I had read about the prince kissing the sleeping maiden and she awakens and they appear to be happy together. I knew I would be awakened sometime."

"And you wanted to be?"

"Oh, yes. Oh, yes. At night it got to be a mental exercise, to want and yet not know," Amanda said, lowering her voice still further. "There's a feeling comes into a woman at adolescence, an attraction to the opposite sex. What came as a surprise to me when I was young was to find out that this desire—which you might have noticed, Hallie—"

"Oh, my," Hallie said.

"That other girls and boys have similar fascination. And what you have to do, if the pressure grows intense, is find a young man and marry him."

"Am I to marry somebody?" Hallie asked.

"It's time to marry once you begin to lose control. It's stronger in some than others."

"Could you?" Hallie turned to look at her. "Could you control it?"

Flushing, Amanda said, "Of course. It depends on the man, too, his being willing to wait."

"You're blushing, mama."

"I always was able to cope, if I do say so. But your father was considerate, did not force me into anything beyond—my depth."

At eleven o'clock the driver turned at the Vancetown Road, which at once descended the flank of the ridge toward the river valley. From prospects along the way, they could make out the church, the store, a dozen houses. Amanda explained the terrain through which courting couples might walk on their way from church to home. The journey between the church and the first bridge was the most public, and the girl and boy might hold hands, were rather expected to do so. Once beyond that, the girl would need to keep her wits about her and her hands free of encumbrances, to hold him off if need be. Entering a wood was not allowed at night. Once they reached the King yard and were within calling distance of the house, kissing might be engaged in, but the girl should keep a fence between her and the boy.

"What sort of fence?" Hallie asked.

Amanda waved aside the consideration. "You might not have all the choice in the world," she said.

"A snake fence would fall over, I'm afraid," Hallie told her.

"You don't want the boy pressing his—himself up against you, now do you?"

There was a pail of cool water on the porch of the Wrights' store, with a tin dipper in it, and Amanda drank, then let her children drink from it, wiping the lip of the dipper with the hem of her dress each time lips touched it. She went indoors and wandered about in the huge, cool room.

A few flies were buzzing about the cheese-cutting board. A young man came up to her. "You don't know me? Of course, you wouldn't," she told him. It had been fourteen years since she was last here, and the young man now was grown, was in his mid-twenties.

"Papa's gone home for noon dinner," the young fellow said.

"You must be Wurth's son Fortner," Amanda said. "Hallie, this is one of your cousins, darling." That relationship eliminated him from courting consideration, Amanda realized. A shame, too. A big boy, handsome almost to a fault, quaintly shy, and rather courtly as he greeted Hallie.

Once more in the car, they drove along the main road past the cemetery to the King family road that led into their cove, past three log houses owned by their kin, one of them her own wedding house. They reached the house of her parents, the largest in the King settlement. Here, at a recent time of flooding, the branch had risen enough to wash out the road in one place, so the car had to stop, all luggage had to be removed. "Set it under that tree," Amanda told the driver, then dismissed him, giving him a note to deliver to Pink.

Enid came into the yard to greet them. He kept patting Amanda. "Pretty woman," he kept saying to her, smiling, "pretty, pretty woman." And he greeted Frederick and finally Hallie. "So you're the one we're going to start out on courting?" he asked, beaming at her.

Hallie did a curtsy. "Best of luck," she said.

He chuckled contentedly. "I remember my courting days." Amanda shoved him playfully, and he laughed. "Oh, well," he said, "There's only widows for me now." He led the way up the hill, stopping to toss a rock at a bossy dog, shooing it away, one of several nervous hounds dancing and jumping about before them, seeking attention. They crossed a little log bridge, one without rails, so that Hallie had to stop to wonder about her balance. She moved across in three long strides. "When you're drunk, it's hard to cross. I've crawled over it many a night," her grandfather told her. Then he put an arm around Frederick's shoulders. "Going to take you coon hunting. What say?"

Frederick, surprised by the embrace, said yes without reviewing just what he was committing himself to. "Hate to kill anything, though."

"Get us a coon," his grandfather said, winking at him.

Adeline King was on the porch, wiping her hands on her apron to dry them. "Well, delivered twins last night for the Colemans," she called jubilantly, "so I've not got the house ready, it's not straightened up." Amanda joyously hurried to her. "There's no end to births around here," Adeline said, as the two women embraced, tears welling up in their eyes. "Well now," Adeline said, breaking free, unwilling to submit herself to tenderness. She motioned for Hallie to turn around so she could see the back of her, as well as the front. "She'll have no trouble, Amanda."

"Really?" Amanda said, immensely relieved. "Don't you think so?" Then she realized what a heartless-sounding confession she had made. "Well, I agree," she said emphatically. "I certainly do. She will have no trouble at all."

When Enid King took Frederick to the village, a horse was tied in the trading lot, a big black stallion, and several young men were taking turns riding it. The horse was blind in one eye, "or is might-nigh blinded," its owner admitted, "so he frightens quicker'n lightning strikes a tree." Fortner took an interest, said the owner owed the store money. He put one of the village boys, a Harmon, on the horse to test it out, and young Harmon rode him bareback at a walk around the lot. He was only seven years old but had been riding for two years. Fortner, saying that the horse needed weight and authority, managed to maneuver Frederick, the new boy, into agreeing to ride. Well, Frederick always liked to oblige. He had ridden a few horses in town and was modestly competent. Fortner helped him mount and straightened the reins just as the horse bolted forward. Frederick dug his heels into the horse's side, called out for it to stop, stop, but no, it headed toward the Wright fields, taking the top pole off the first fence, the horse bound and determined to free itself of Frederick's weight, which it managed to do near a pile of fieldstones, leaving Frederick bouncing on his buttocks across the corn rows.

Men and boys were yelling, laughing, while Enid King was roaring in rage. Frederick limped back to the lot, trying to shrug off his failure. Nobody felt he had been treated fairly, and Fortner said as much. "Nobody can ride that one," he admitted. "He's famous for it, if much weight is put on him." Fortner himself took Frederick inside the store and salved his cuts and bruises. Each became a special mark of pride, apparently a badge of acceptability. "Oh, the boy did all right," Wurth Wright said, and laid his arm on Frederick's shoulder, a rare sign of affection from Frederick's uncle, the leader of the community. "He has the same build as Pink, and that dear smile."

Pain and failure were means of acceptance here, and news that Frederick had been accepted came as an additional burden to Hallie. Next morning she took an hour to dress for church, longer than she had taken to dress in her whole life. She, her mother, and grandmother even arrived late. Hallie smiled her way through the after-service greetings from people she didn't know, who were oohing and aahing over her, exclaiming about having last seen her when she was a wee baby. A beautiful baby. There she stood now, a false smile plastered on her lips. She tried to eat the fried chicken and biscuits her grandmother and mother thrust upon her—church members ate standing at big, long tables after the morning service. "Here, taste this pie, Hallie," Adeline King said. "Now, Mrs. Crawford made this one, and it's her son who will come to call this afternoon. Their land adjoins that of both your grandfathers."

Stomach churning, fingers trembling, Hallie accidentally dropped the piece of Crawford pie on the ground, even as Mrs. Crawford approached. "Is something the matter with it, missy?" Mrs. Crawford inquired, her smile vanishing.

"Lord, no," Hallie said, then too late realized she had used the Lord's name in vain. The Crawford son who was to call that afternoon, by name Roland, was standing nearby, a boy given to confident grinning, a handsome fellow, six feet tall or near that, with the round, piggish face and puckish grin of the Crawfords. He had a heavy body and drowsy disposition and apparently would be arriving to court Hallie under duress; at least, he made no approach to her now. She thought she hated him but wasn't sure.

That afternoon, when he did arrive, he approached the house through the woods, while everybody, even Enid King, was watching the road. The same slippery grin was present. He was offered a chair in the parlor, the southeast corner room of the three King rooms, which had been swept, mopped, and dusted for the occasion. Hallie served a plate of cookies and a mug of cider. The door was closed on the two young people, who sat in silence for a while, Roland munching cookies exactly like a rabbit, Hallie decided. She mentioned two motion pictures she had recently seen, *Rebecca of Sunny Brook Farm* with Mary Pickford and *Sunshine Alley* with Mae Marsh. Roland admitted he had not seen them. Basking in native pride, he boasted that he had seen only two moving pictures in his life. He had a slingshot that would put a rock through a plank, he told her. She mentioned a few stage artists who had visited Asheville. She asked if he had as yet read Willa Cather's new novel, and the question puzzled him. She decided on pure impulse to tell him the entire story of the novel, which he tolerated distractedly while munching cookies and licking the rim of his empty cider mug. He told her he had read the Bible through. She admitted she had done that, as well. He claimed to have a clear memory of its various happenings: there was an old bearded fellow with ten commandments carved in stone by lightning, there was a whale that swallowed Jonah, who was belched up on shore. He finished the plate of cookies, licked the fingers of his left hand, and asked if there was a good spring at her house in town.

Hallie heard a rustle just beyond the wall, close by, to the left of the mantel; she thought she saw an eye appear at a small hole in the wallpaper. Her mother or grandmother was on guard. "Jesus," she whispered.

"Did you say Jesus?" Roland inquired, intrigued.

"A prayer," she assured him.

They took a walk along the creek. Boring. At the barn Hallie invited

131

Marshall, the Kings' handyman, a handsome second cousin about five years her senior, to accompany them. The three of them went tramping along toward what she was assured was the biggest local waterfall, Hallie talking mostly to Marshall, asking about hunts he had been on, horses he had ridden, trades he had made, Marshall responding factually, briefly. "He lives with his mama," Roland told her. It was Marshall she chose to walk beside, in any event, and it was to him she offered her hand for help at the dangerous places.

That evening, as on every Sunday evening, after the last hymn was sung, most of the congregation waited near the door, inside and outside the log building, exchanging comments about the weather, the crops, the babies, illness, the minister. The young people congregated at the nearby cemetery, near the tombstones of Wrights and Crawfords and Kings and others long since passed away, and waited for the sun to go down and afford them darkness for the walks home. Roland Crawford ignored Hallie until the last minute, when his mother called him and Hallie off to the side and said they could walk to the King house alone.

Other people also were walking or riding home, some of them still singing the stanzas of the last hymn of the evening, "Abide with Me." "You don't have to show me home, unless you want to," Hallie said to Roland.

"Well," he uttered, a mere breath, "I don't mind doing it." As they entered a dark stretch of the road, without a word he took her hand in his own sweaty palm, which she consented to.

"Pretty singing tonight," she commented.

Where the tree limbs hid most of the moonlight, he suddenly swung her into his arms and sought to crush her, it seemed to her, and to steal kisses. Even as he held her, she slid one foot along, scouting out the road, making some progress. Suddenly he stopped mauling her. Farther along the road at another place where she couldn't see him, or anything else, he spoke to her out of the darkness. "I think they know we're here."

A shock of fear swept through her. "Who?"

"Them owl hoots don't sound like owls." His own voice was trembling now. "Better stay close to me."

"What owls?"

"Don't mean to scare you," Roland said, once more taking her hand. "I think they're close by," he whispered to her. "Come on." He led her into the woods, she, scared to leave him or be left, consenting.

They had gone a hundred feet or so when a noise screamed toward them, a bundle struck the rock nearby, broke open releasing a number of howling cats, which awakened ghosts and terror. In the midst of cats caterwauling all over the place, Roland had grabbed her waist and was hugging her. She

132

pulled free and began running, ran into a bush. Scraping across the ground, she landed in a pile. Once more Roland had her in his arms. She kicked and crawled away, sat with her back against a tree in moody, angry silence.

Silence also for a while from Roland. Off somewhere, perhaps on the road, a couple were singing "Lindy Lou." Road's just through there, she decided. She pushed aside rhododendron limbs, began to crawl. Roland begged her to stay with him, but she crawled on. She reached a creek; the icy water burned her flesh, caused her to cry out. Roland spoke to her from the dry bank. When she reached a section of road, she paused to take stock of her muddy, torn clothes. Off somewhere behind her a few owl sounds were heard, fading away mockingly. "Did you plan that, Roland?" she asked accusingly.

"No. Why would I do that?" he asked shyly.

With him trudging behind, she walked step by weary step up the stony King drive, barely able to identify the shapes of the trees on each side. They passed her Uncle Aycock's house. No need to tell him. What would she tell him? There was no pause alongside the road for a kiss, either, no fence to stand behind. Poor Roland was now talking about how embarrassed he was. At the house, weary beyond thought, she threw the door open, stood in the doorway holding to the door. Her grandfather, sitting in his chair, looked up, and at once his voice began to gurgle in his throat. Her mother got to her feet, staring at her in astonishment. "Well, we wondered where on earth you were," Amanda exclaimed. Adeline King, entering at the far doorway, stopped in her tracks, staring at bruised, cut, bleeding Hallie, her soaked dress clinging to her body, her teeth rattling in her head, her eyes round with hurt.

"Well, now," Enid wheezed, "what sort of a raper is he?"

"Raped? Did you say raped?" Amanda said.

"I never would have thought it of Roland Crawford," Adeline King said. All this while Hallie, chattering, trembling from the wet and cold, was blocking the doorway.

Roland appeared beside her, but before he could speak Adeline rushed forward and swatted him with a flyswatter. The boy fled, calling back over his shoulder that he was sorry, sorry, sorry.

Sorry, sorry, sorry, the words went through Hallie's mind as she climbed into the loft, where she and Frederick had pallets. Little comfort in his sorry, sorry, sorry. It was my first date, she told herself despondently. I guess that boy will move to Tennessee. He's not much of a romantic.

Amanda brought her a pot of hot tea. Even her grandmother climbed the ladder into the loft. They pestered the covers, showered her with sympathy, complained about boys being boys, insisted on knowing what personal areas of her body Roland had sought to touch.

133

Her Grandfather Enid was tall, bony, angular, and he walked with his shoulders bent, his legs and arms swinging loosely. Just how old he was he didn't say. He had been born one spring, and he predicted he would die in the winter, "most any winter." Three of his four living sons had left, "deserted me, gone one place or another, flew off like a pack of crows, left only Aycock here, and him the lazy one." He had given each son a farm in the community, had supplied him with a house and barn and a few animals, and each save Aycock had sold his farm and kept the money, which Enid bitterly resented, "impoverishing me," he claimed. His face was not lined, but there were hollow contours, caught the shadows. He had a cleft in his chin. His hair was low over his brow, even at this age. His mouth had full lips, straight and firm. His head generally tilted to one side, even when he walked. In sunlight his eyes were pinched, squinting. He was imposing, a man of strength in a place and at a time when patience and endurance were of more consequence. He was not endowed with much patience. He gave Hallie the impression that he was waiting, not for slight improvement, not for minor adjustments, but for an avalanche that would set right the mighty wrongs and misjudgments already made. "You married a Wright and then you left me, too," he declared one morning after breakfast, his gaze settling on Amanda. His words were uttered like a song, a refrain, but pain swept over his face. His gaze moved on to Adeline, who was working at the wood range. "Where you going today, where you working at?" There was recurring criticism of her occupation as a midwife. Gaining no response from her, he sought out Amanda once more, tilted his head further to the side. "Married into his majesty's family and went to town." His bitter smile slowly vanished and a deeper cloud seemed to settle on him. He whispered to Amanda. "So Pink's a big success, is he?"

At the local store there was special courtesy for Enid, acknowledgment of his superior potential and deep feelings. He appreciated courtesy, calmly accepted it and always assumed it would be offered him. He was tolerant of all of them, and of human failing generally, reserving for his invective the ambitious, the successful, the superior.

At night he would sit up late, always near the fire, which burned even in summertime in the evening. "It's company," he claimed. "And it's fully as human as a person. Talks less than a woman." Sometimes, in fits of despair, he would utter the word "papa." "Ah, God no," he would moan, shaking his head. "God damn, who thought it all up, tell me," he said one night to Amanda, a cry deep from inside, "who the hell did this to me? They say God thought it up." Accusingly, he stared at her, his mouth set firmly, his eyes blazing, questioning, challenging. "You reckon anybody else would come up with anything so Goddamn crazy?"

"Is it crazy, grandpapa?" Hallie asked him, awed, humbled by his audacity.

"Your life ain't?" he asked incredulously. "Mine is."

"No, sir."

"Well, wait awhile."

Hallie said, "Maybe it's coming to be crazy here lately."

"Yes," he said after a moment. "It'll get to you." He pursed his lips, sucked at a sore gum. "When I was your age, I thought I would succeed, too." He leaned back in the rocker, focusing on her. "I didn't even know I was going to die. I was fearless then."

"Everybody's going to die," Hallie told him.

"I was reckless but now I'm careful even where I walk."

"Do all old people fear death, papa?" Amanda asked him, giving the words a casual quality, as if admitting ignorance of a matter already known about.

"No," he said at once. "Your grandma doesn't fear anything. Except me."

Tobacco. There was an acre of the big yellow leaves fanning out like palms. One of Hallie's chores was to worm them, which meant she was to deworm them, knocking the worms into a tin can she carried on a string around her neck. From time to time, Marshall, the handyman, would leave his row and walk along hers, checking her work, and if he found one worm he would make a fuss over it, claiming she would have to bite that one in two. She never did. "Well, mama would make you," he assured her.

Then too, once the cider apples came due, they had to be crushed, the juice flowing into vats to ferment, to foam up, making seething noises for a few days before being siphoned off into barrels, these having been cleaned and sulfured by King himself. "Let plenty of air in it," Enid instructed. "Don't bung the barrels yet." The barrels would rumble as the fermentation continued.

Then there was canning to do, and always there was hoeing, back-breaking, muscle-twisting hoeing. The back of Hallie's neck pained almost beyond endurance, and at night she would sink into a chair in the kitchen and wrestle with her sore muscles, keeping company with the ever-present, sniffing grandfather, half asleep in his chair. As soon as she could sneak away, she would climb the ladder to her quarters, crawl into the bed for a shivering long night of rest. One night she awoke to hear Frederick talking. He was out in the yard; she heard him laugh suddenly. Then she heard Marshall laugh and a pain went through her, a tug of desire. Maybe Marshall excited her because of his willowy tenderness, she decided, his harmlessness, aloofness. She whispered into her pillow and allowed her fingers to seek out the most sensitive part of her body. Marshall could have her at these moments of rich desire, she thought, she would take him now. She would teach him, even she, and would let him teach her, the two would discover together; she would gasp and groan with pleasure, cry out under the gentle touch of his fingers pressed into the damp, hairy wonders. She would kiss him endlessly.

"Hallie, where are you?" Her mother was calling from downstairs.

No answer. Hallie had made it a policy not to reply.

Soon Amanda was on the ladder, poking her head into the loft opening. "Oh my, in bed again. So early, Hallie. So soon."

Amanda had started out life as strong as boys her age; she had come to believe in her physical equality. As she grew older, the boys exceeded her in strength and she came to feel more vulnerable. The physical superiority she did retain had to do with giving birth. The advent of sexual contact was made richer for her because it had to do with her sphere of superiority, the process of forming, growing, delivering, nurturing babies. In sex there was no way—not that she could imagine—to use her body naturally without prospects of birth. As she lay in the parlor's feather bed, a sheet drawn over her, she felt that her own life was losing its exclusive sphere of influence, while Hallie took her place. Amanda was now to be only a housekeeper, a gardener, a maker of quilts, a canner of fruit, a baker of cakes, a stacker of pies, a drier of apples, a stringer of beans, a storer of potatoes, a gatherer of herbs, a midwife, maybe, at times a teacher, and all of them, all together did not replace the one act of life she loved the most of all, that had nourished her, fed her body, and exercised it deeply, had drawn taut her muscles, made slippery the passages through which her children had moved into their new lives, one by one.

What had she thought to find here this summer? she wondered. Another way? A course previously secret that now would lie open to her? A more perfumed air, a magic country, a new beginning, a new promise through Hallie or Frederick? "Mummy," she whispered to her bed at night, wrestling with an unseen antagonist, herself. "Mummy," she whispered into the pillow, sensing she must come of age herself, even as must Hallie.

Hallie and her grandfather sometimes went fishing. Up here both men and women are allowed to fish, he told her, "to fish and hoe are common ground." On one occasion he began talking about his farm. "Why the hell did they have to come away back up in here to live? tell me." He lashed out at the ineptness of his ancestors. "I ought to do their graves over again, you know it," he said, suddenly softening.

"You mean to dig them up?" Hallie asked.

"No. I mean the stones, the markers. They never had much to mark a grave back then, didn't have marble. You can cut names into fieldstone, of course, and they did, but the names weather out."

"Or weather in?" she suggested, looking to see if he thought that was the least bit profound. "Where does a name go when it's gone away?" she asked him.

"Into another person's body maybe. Men's into women's, women's into men's, to give them variety."

"You ever been a woman?" She was almost afraid to ask it, not wanting to rile him.

"No, I couldn't do it," he admitted at once.

One evening Hallie hooked a big trout and played it along the bank, walking upstream, giving it line enough to tire itself. Repeatedly, the fish broke water, flipped in the air; Enid cried out with excitement. She waded into the river to keep from snagging the line on bushes and ended up with water to her thighs. The fish was close at hand, and she eased it up onto a smooth rock, grabbed it with both hands, held it up for her grandfather to see. Then she yelled, she yelled loud, good feeling of success overcoming her. He was on the bank laughing and yelling, too. She stood in the water, giving what she supposed must be the rebel yell.

The trout measured twenty-two inches long. Amanda dressed it, incising a slit in its side. Through the slit she stuffed bits of apple and onion and cornbread. She rolled out a sheet of biscuit dough, laid the fish on it, then enveloped the fish in it. She and Hallie made marks on the dough, representing gills and a mouth and the fins of the fish, and she used a piece of bacon for an eye. They baked the trout until its biscuit blanket was browning, then served the fish and biscuit together.

Hallie noted that her grandfather, in naming the cats, used Shakespearean characters. There was a Prospero, a Beatrice, an Imogen, and a tabby Desdemona. A big black Othello ruled the barn loft where Marshall sometimes slept. There had been a Hamlet for two years or so, a handsome devil, but he was gone now. "I imagine he got killed in a sword fight," her grandfather told her.

Sometimes Hallie would see her grandfather standing out in the yard, staring off at the distant mountains as if listening to music, or to voices from a long way off, a look of dignity softening his features. Once she stood beside him, tilted her own head to one side, and squinted as he did, set her mouth in a firm line of determination. Enid didn't waver, not a quiver appeared, except that the nostrils of his nose would contract and expand, in rhythm, she decided, to the beating of his heart. He is in tune, she thought, to far-off voices, ones I can't hear yet, but maybe mama, who sometimes stands that same way, can hear them.

In the woods up above Charles Newton's fields was a place where bobcats had sharpened their claws on trees. Marshall offered to take Hallie there. He had a bird's wing in his jacket and on arrival at the site hung it from a bush on a string, then he dropped a pouch full of catnip onto the ground. He and Hallie crept behind another bush and waited, absolutely still and quiet, for what appeared to her to be a long time. Directly, here came a bobcat, curious to find out what was making the whirring noise, to see what sort of bird this was. This was a big male, might weigh thirty pounds, and it studied that tiny bird wing. The cat could easily jump it down, but couldn't decide what the wing was. Then the cat smelled the packet of herbs and began sniffing that, and quite simply collapsed like a housecat and began to toss it and push it with its paws, until Hallie, who had been holding herself quiet for a long while, laughed. At that sound the bobcat bounded ten feet onto a great limb and in another instant was fleeing on up the mountainside. The cat was simply gone, all in a series of flashes.

Happily, Marshall retrieved his bird wing and his bag of herbs and led the way toward home, the two young people laughing about the sights. They were almost to the topmost open field above the King house, and Marshall still had not taken her hand, Hallie realized, even to offer her help at rough crossing places. Of course, she didn't really need help, but such places afforded an excuse. She stopped just uphill of the fence, said she had a pain in her stomach. He supported her with a hand on her arm. Now and then her gaze would meet his; each time she would hold her own gaze steady until he glanced away. He is like a bird, she thought, which is about to light and in the final instant changes its mind, sweeps up or about, saving itself.

Later Hallie spent time in the barn lot watching Marshall assist a heifer deliver an oversized calf. The heifer, with the calf half born, was encountering difficulty, and Marshall took hold of the calf and worked it free. It was alive, though weak, but the heifer refused to clean it off. "Was bred to that big Gouge bull," Marshall complained to Hallie. He had often complained that the big bull ought not to be used for small heifers, he said. Now here was one result, a rejected heifer calf, soon to die, he would guess. He milked the mother and fed this first milk to the calf. He allowed Hallie to hold the milk bottle, which had a rag tied into the shape of a tit.

Hallie helped out till about nine o'clock, when she visited with the family. About nine-thirty she left the house, ostensibly going to the privy, but she returned to the barn. She managed to feed the calf some more milk. On returning to the house, she found her grandfather asleep in his big chair. She fixed a pot of tea and wrapped up the biscuits that had been left over from supper. Using one of the warmest surfaces of the stove, she warmed two pieces of country ham; all the while she was quiet as she could be. When Adeline King called out from the bedroom, asked who was there, Hallie replied at once, said she was hungry. She remained in the kitchen for a few minutes before sneaking out the door.

Marshall was just there, in the darkness, outside the barn, watching her approach. They sat on the ground, began munching, drinking, talking about his life, his home in an isolated house downriver two miles. Once he touched Hallie's hair, and she at once touched his. He began rubbing her arm to warm her, or so he told her. She touched his. On impulse she gave him a glancing kiss to his cheek. Directly he leaned close and kissed her cheek. A while later she kissed his lips lightly. He hesitated, then kissed her lips, fully kissed them this time. A pause followed, until she bent close and kissed the nipple of his breast. She felt his arms tighten around her abruptly, as if he were preparing to take possession of her, and he rolled her over and buried his face against her dress, sought through her dress to locate and kiss the nipples of her breasts. A fire of feeling swept through her, and she began to emit warning moans, to herself and him. He actually began to suck her nipple, sucking through her dress while she lay flat on her back staring at the starred sky above her, at the several stars that were the brightest. He unbuttoned her dress enough to bare the left breast and sucked her nipple while her hands moved over his head into his hair; she began to moan, and to whisper, and he began making a little-child noise, bubbling with bits of words. His hand moved up along her belly. She lay deathly still and quiet. It was as if she were spying on him as he continued to explore her body. He felt her breast, which was left exposed, he closed his forefinger and thumb around the nipple, then withdrew suddenly, but a few moments later he cupped her breast in his hand and squeezed gently on it, and she turned into his arms, admitting affection for his touch, but he, frightened, withdrew from her for a time, lay stiffly beside her. "Sorry," he said.

"It's all right. It's only the two of us."

"Sorry," he repeated, and lay stiffly, as in a trance, beside her.

He retreated to the shadow of the crib, waited as she approached the house door. Softly she pushed it fully open. It made a whining noise, as if pained. She gave Marshall one final glance before shutting the door. She was crossing the firelighted kitchen a step at a time when she noticed that her grandfather was still asleep in the big rocker, a blanket over his knees. She moved on to the loft ladder and climbed it, holding her shoes in one hand, and crawled across the loft floor to her pallet near the window; the sound of Frederick's breathing was wheezing in her ears. She listened to him breathe, trying to determine if he was merely pretending to be asleep.

Her grandfather began moving about downstairs, going into his own room. Maybe he had been awake after all. He might have known she had come in, but didn't want to intrude on her privacy. Would he care about what she had been doing, this sin of hers? she wondered. "Till tomorrow night," she whispered into her pillow, and hugged it deliciously.

Hallie found Marshall working with her grandfather in the barns next morning, hauling a tub of water on a sled, the barn spring having dried up in this dry season. Her grandfather seemed to pay little mind to her. He went on about his work, muttering, mumbling about needing horse hide for a horse harness, nothing else would hold as well. "And I have not one scrap," he confessed. "That calf died last night," he told Hallie. "I dragged it into the woods."

No, Marshall was not her boyfriend this morning, Hallie realized. He appeared to have certain other preferences, hauling water being one. She could not quite figure out his aloofness. There was a shy grin whenever he noticed her, a chagrined look in his eyes, but over all an aloofness—a withdrawal from her. Apparently he had embarrassed himself; he had tasted forbidden fruit and now didn't want to be found out.

The grandfather moved out of earshot of the two of them, complaining to himself, murmuring criticisms: "Have land, Lord knows, but I can't make a harness out of it." Hallie moved closer to Marshall. He was filling the water bucket, would dip it repeatedly into the tub on the sled. She touched his arm. Sheepishly he glanced toward Mr. King at the far side of the barn. "He can hear a long ways," he said. He filled the bucket only half full, he was so anxious to be gone, and delayed inside the third stall, stayed with the horse. Hallie swung on the stall door, watching him, considering his commonness.

When she returned to the house, she heard her mother say to Adeline, "After all the money we put into that girl's upbringing, you'd think she could find a suitor."

Her grandfather sat on a big rock, and she perched on the rock beside him and drew her knees up close to her chest, hugged them, feeling safer with him than she had ever felt with anybody, except her father. "Marshall's only a boy, even though he's twenty-four," Mr. King began, speaking with the same lilt as the creek bubbling nearby. "A girl grows up faster than a boy, but even so, he's tardy."

She stared at the water, listening, wondering how much he knew of her secret.

"His mother's strict, let me tell you. She's kept him for herself, her care, and he knows little about a woman, I would imagine."

"I—I would imagine," she agreed quietly.

"Probably doesn't know where the buttons are."

Hallie laughed out loud. "Buttons!" she sat there giggling, close beside her grandfather.

"He might learn the buttons soon enough, but will always have trouble with his feelings. His papa was a twit. It's not for me to blame the boy for that, but you never can expect much from a twit's son. His father shot a man in a disagreement about a woman. The world's full of women, and he had to have a certain one, when there's only a few hairs' difference between them. It's what's done for them and said to them that makes the difference. Left his son not much, and the boy's mother dotes on Marshall, needs him day to day. The way some women keep their sons is like slavery." He paused, gave her a chance to comment. "Pick strong men, honey, or none at all. These others can be treacherous in a pinch." He added after a few moments, "I suppose pinch is as good a word as any."

He knows something, oh yes, he was fully informed, she realized. He knew pretty well what had gone on. "Thank you, grandpa," she said, smiling briefly.

"For what?"

"For treating me like a grown person."

"Not at all," he said.

Pink arrived with Young toward the end of the visit, ostensibly to spend a few days. He drove the car himself, claimed to be surprised to find the place, described several near accidents along the way, and in general maintained his countryman's pride in not being able to drive well. He apologized for not visiting earlier. There had been a new cast of cares at the company, and business trips had taken him and Young to the south and west, not in this direction, he explained.

Dear Pink, Amanda embraced him jubilantly, pleased beyond measure to be with him again.

He planned to spend the night at the Kings' house, but he did walk down to the store that afternoon and swapped greetings and stories with his brother, saw his nephews, went on over to the family house and talked with his mother, who was withering now that her husband "has gone on over." He walked the old paths, wondering about the reason for his somberness, his inability to laugh in the comfortable manner of his youth.

He sat up late, at least late by country standards, listened to Enid denigrate the Wright family and speculate about the unfairness of insurance policies, even wondering if they ought to be outlawed. At last Pink sneaked off to the parlor, where he crawled in bed beside Amanda, who thought to try to excuse her father, saying not to mind, that he was like this with everybody. "He drinks too much of an evening."

"Did Hallie do well?" Pink asked her, speaking softly.

"Well, I don't know," Amanda said. "She's been walked home from the services three times by first one then another. She keeps her distance."

"She mentioned a time or two boys had called, and told me who had walked her home. That's all she said."

Amanda told him how the first experience had hurt her. "That Crawford boy was sleepless for several nights and got in a fight with two other boys, and his mother won't speak to the Montfords."

"Some boy will begin to court her seriously," he said.

Amanda buried her face in the cleft between his shoulder and chest. "I wish he would hurry," she whispered. "And she's turned so secretive these days, I don't know what to do."

"Before now, when we were young—that is, if we were still living up here, what would you do?"

"We'd marry her to a likable young man as soon as possible. We'd strike a bargain. Otherwise, she'll get into trouble."

A while later he said, "Is she talking about college?"

"Pink, she can't travel away off. She's not a boy, Pink. She talks about your company, that's all."

There was a coon hunt scheduled for the night after Pink arrived, one intended for Frederick's indoctrination and for Young's too, if he felt able. It was to start at nine o'clock, after full dark had set in. Pink excused Young from it. Pink was overly protective, admitted as much, but he wasn't devoted to coon hunting anyway. Young pleased him by consenting.

Charles Newton and Old Crawford were going. Each of them had a hound he wanted to try, and with Enid's two, there were four dogs, all blue ticks, and they got on well together, with plenty of snarls but no hard biting. Enid had a coonskin, which he dragged around before them, letting them sniff it until they were whining and barking to be let go. Hounds hated coons, and coons hated hounds; that was an ancient rivalry. The men led the dogs into the field, then to the edge of the woods, and it was near the biggest pear tree that one dog let out a howl and went dashing off, the pack following, their voices mellowing, celebrating.

The four men, with Frederick accompanying, made a little fire in the field and sat around it, savoring bits of pork that Adeline had fried that afternoon and sipping whiskey. The men drew in closer to the fire and contentedly waited for the coon to tree. Enid said, "Now you know this is high living."

Crawford laughed kindly. "Been missing this, ain't you, Pink, sitting on the cold ground eating poor man's rations?"

"Been wanting to go hiking up this mountain in the dark," Pink admitted.

Newton said, "Wish they'd run that coon down this a way. I'd hate to have to climb up there."

The men had a jug of whiskey, about half a gallon, and they kept that in motion. Enid used a traditional way of resting it on his crooked arm, supporting the weight of it there, with the mouth of the jug available; he taught that to Frederick. This was a new whiskey, was white lightning, which went straight to the mind taking barbs off thoughts. "Any coons live in town, Pink?" Crawford asked him.

"I don't know any," Pink said, smiling at him. "There's some bankers that might be coons."

"You been traveling much, Pink?" Newton asked him.

"Been to Raleigh. I go down there and talk to officials. There's going to be a weed patch of rules soon, if we don't mind."

"What part of the thefts do you keep?" Enid asked him, a barbed question for a friendly conversation.

"Ten percent," Pink admitted. "We make about ten percent."

"And how much your company take in, say in a year's time, Pink?" Crawford asked him.

"They won't tell me, afraid I'd stop work. Listen to those dogs," Pink said. A man could always change the subject, get away from an issue by referring to the dogs. Just now their voices were echoing off the mountain, making a far-off, bubbly sound.

"I think I hear your dog, Crawford, in the lead," Newton said. "That yours?"

"No, it's still King's dog that's leading. He must be bleeding by now."

"How long can they run?" Frederick asked, timidly intruding on the men's conversation.

"All night," Enid told him, "can run all night and all tomorrow, if needs be. A hound is tireless. Now a cat will outrun a hound for a little way, a tenth of a mile, but after that it has to tree or hide."

"Or have a fight; you ever see a bobcat fight a hound?" Newton asked. "Lie down on their backs, grab the dog with their front claws and try to rip its stomach open with their back feet. No dog I ever knew could fight a bobcat and survive it."

"Nor a coon," Crawford said.

"I've had a dog that could fight a coon," Enid said. "But there's not many dogs that can do it, to be sure."

"Come on back here and live with us," Crawford suddenly said to Pink. "You can get your land back, can't you?"

"Wurth's renting it out," Pink said.

"Well, I know that. There's a whole world waiting for you here. Must be fifty thousand acres in the Wright holding, in all."

Pink nodded. "A world of rocks," he said finally.

The hounds ran for about two hours, the men drinking and talking, warming by the fire. When the coon treed, the men scrambled to their feet, estimating how far it was to where the coon was, perhaps a mile. "Better unload here," Crawford suggested and removed the rounds from his rifle. "Boy, you unloaded?" he asked Frederick. He touched his arm finally, asked him to unload his rifle, then saw that the boy couldn't do it, didn't have coordination left, was apparently drunk, so he did it for him, put the bullets in Frederick's pocket, buttoned the pocket. The boy had been drinking too much for a hunt, and too much for a boy; probably didn't realize. The men trudged up the mountain, starting out slowly. Not much moonlight was getting through the leaves, and they kept walking into bushes and trunks of trees. Enid stopped to light a lantern. "Burn the woods down, if I don't mind," he murmured, then went on, holding the lantern out beside him. On the steep grades, the men held to one another. Now and then one would fall and might even topple the next one in line. Frederick slipped off a thirty-foot bank, but at once called up from the bottom, said not to come for him, that he was all right. He crawled back, holding to laurel roots, managed to reach the place where the men were waiting. "I'm not broke, papa," he reported to Pink.

When they reached the dogs, one of the dogs was in the tree with the coon. The coon was on a higher branch, beyond the flare of the lamp. "Must be a damn bird," Newton said. He loaded his gun, as did Enid. Frederick, weaving on his feet, suddenly launched himself at the tree, began to climb it. This maneuver was so unusual nobody knew at first what to do, but Newton knew enough about hunting to know the dog or the racoon could tear Frederick up, so he climbed after him, grabbed his feet and pulled Frederick out of the tree. The boy lay on the ground in the lantern light looking up at the men, laughing a crazy cackle, a bark. It was unnerving, really. "Why, you're drunk, boy," his grandfather told him. "He's drunk, Pink." He said to Frederick, "Now, you crawl over there to that rock and keep out of the way."

Cowed, humbly Frederick complied, sat on the rock, his head in his hands, trying to clear his thoughts. "Here's your rifle, boy." His grandfather gave him the rifle, which was still unloaded. "Crazy," Enid murmured to Pink, who was visibly shocked. Enid held his lantern high as he could. "That boy's drunk, Pink," he murmured. "Not the first time this summer."

"When did he start drinking?"

"I saw him drunk twice before, but more reasonable," Enid said, apparently unconcerned whether the boy heard what he said or not. Up in the tree the two eyes still were reflecting light. "All right, Harry, get out of the damn tree, if you mean to." Enid was talking to his hound, which was about fifteen feet up. "Oh, hell," he said, "don't want you to be shot."

"You just hold the lantern, we'll shoot them top eyes," Newton told him. Crawford and Newton both raised their rifles. Enid counted aloud to three and both fired at the coon. The reply from above came belatedly, and was gruffer, more angry than expected; the coon started down the tree and here came the dog Harry bailing out of the tree, too. The light of the lantern caught a ball of black fur following. "Good Lord, it's a bear," Enid

144

cried, handing the hot lantern to Crawford. All the men began cussing and shouting for everybody to take cover. There were two more shots as the bear struck the ground and, rolling up much like a ball, started down the mountain, moving faster than a locomotive, huffing much like one, too, seeking the dark, leaving the men and dogs.

Pink realized he had been stabbed by laurel branches, was cut across the face and chest. Crawford was standing on a rock cursing the lantern for burning his fingers. Enid was coming up the mountain a step at a time. "What the hell you hand me that damn thing for?" Crawford demanded of him. Enid sat down near Frederick, dazedly considering the hunting party, and began to sing a little ditty about joys of the hunt. Then he laughed, and all the men laughed, except Pink, who was thoughtfully watching his son. The dogs were far away on the mountainside below them and to the north, looking for the bear. They were barking but were not in chase. "Well, to hell with it," Enid murmured, uninterested in any further hunting now. "He scared me. Must have been four hundred pounds, that there coon weighed." He laughed. "Where's the jug at?" he asked, and nobody knew. They looked for it everywhere but didn't find it until they thought to look at the foot of the bank that Frederick had fallen down.

When they were approaching the field above the King house, Frederick told his grandfather that, if he would put out the lantern, the men would see a sight. His grandfather turned the lantern off. "What you say, Frederick? What is it?"

"Papa," Frederick said, looking around for him.

"I'm here," Pink said.

"He's drunk," Newton said annoyed. "That boy's drunk."

The dogs began chasing something once more, maybe a coon. "To hell with it," Enid murmured. "What does the boy want?" he asked. "Frederick, what is it?"

Pink walked in step beside Frederick down through the cornfield, trying to give Frederick his own confidence and support. The two were in the lead, and along behind came Enid King, and behind him came Newton and Crawford, delayed because of their interest in the dogs. The men moved through the wind-rustled cornfield, then through the pasture, staying just inside the droopy limbs of the cutting woods; they came into the open space above the barn almost by surprise. Frederick stopped there, Pink still beside him. The two of them stood quietly watching as below them on the bank two people disengaged themselves from an embrace. By moonlight it was difficult to see well, but two people did stand up, that was sure, did turn to look toward where the hunters were standing. Enid himself gruffly gasped, then he said, "Marshall," aloud, calling the name, and the male figure turned and ran, his naked body hurtling toward the downhill road, and the young woman grabbed up clothes and moved off, too, stumbling along, clothes trailing, moving toward the house.

Frederick groaned. He kept on groaning, a heavy snort. Of course, he was still drunk. Not a sound came out of Pink. Enid told the boy to hush for God sake, then he swiped at him with his open palm. Frederick snickered. Newton and Crawford arrived at the scene, asked what was the cause for stopping here when they could go on to the house and drink whiskey together. "No, we're done with it," Enid told them, and left them all and went at once to the house, where without a word to his wife he climbed the ladder into the loft, where he saw his darling granddaughter flopped on her pallet, crying into her blanket like a child, and he crawled to her and took her in his arms.

Soon he returned to the kitchen, brooding over his concerns, most of them about Hallie, some about Frederick's drunkenness and treachery. Once he stalked out to the barn, called up to the loft, telling Marshall to present himself. There was no reply from that place. "The bird has flown," he grumbled, returning to the fireside. "The catbird has fled." He groused about, trying to fix tea, beginning by instilling into his cup the fire of life: a few tablespoons of liquor. He talked to Adeline, whispering huskily, telling her about Hallie, telling her that natural failures are the most painful, that the soul will sacrifice the body, that the soul eats life. All the while he was rummaging about seeking tea leaves, squinting at Adeline's labels on the bags of herbs, burning his hand on the water kettle, wanting to distract himself from the barbs that snagged his nerves.

Pink and Frederick came in. The young man, whipped by doubts and guilt, crept up to the loft. Pink, without a word or nod, went to Amanda's bed. Enid steeped his tea, demanding Adeline's complete attention to his wheezing, whispering. Later he woke Pink and Amanda, presenting himself in full lantern light at the foot of their bed, announcing that they must leave Hallie with him, that he would take care of her further upbringing and education, that there was a finishing school fourteen miles away at a Mr. Parker's, a minister's, and he would take her there every Monday morning and fetch her on Friday, traveling the distance by wagon. He would buy her a piano. "No, don't interrupt," he said to the startled pair, who were looking up from their pillows, their eyes scarcely open. "I'll set it before an inside wall, and it'll be her own. I have money for it. She'll be well taken care of here. And, if there is a wood colt, a child born, I'll see to that, as well, though I won't have her married off to that certain one, you can be sure, to waste her life." Placing a forefinger against his lips, he confided in Amanda: "You don't know yet, do you? Well, it's all rumor anyway, in this life. You say your goodbye to her. You have others, I will see to this one. You know I'm a man of my word." He left them to consider the offer, retreated to the kitchen, where he piled wood onto his fire, got it to blazing enough to fill the opening, to roar into the chimney. "Yeh, clear it out," he admonished, pouring more liquor into his tea. "Jesus," he whispered devoutly, "save them boys' souls afore I kill them, Marshall and Frederick. I'll wring their Christian necks soon. They'll both be at God's feet afore nightfall. Who'd thought it of Marshall, a quiet boy, a boy to sleep till dawn. I never saw him stir in the dark one time afore tonight. Never presented himself any day different from another. Had no more gumption than a hound living in a creamery, but there by God he aroused himself, has stood tall, his cock a weapon. . . ." Seeking more reason for his anger, he moved about drunkenly, sniffing heavy warnings, blistering himself with his own fire, discarding the poker with a clang, recalled his offer to Amanda and Pink in their bed, suddenly wondering if he had awakened them and, if so, if they had stayed awake or not, and would they get up. He hoped not. He would see to this affair, himself. He could move through the world of present thoughts, which offered to scorch him at every turn. Drunkenly, poetically, half asleep, he moved about, ready to have himself brought face to face with this damning reality. His baby had been ravished, his hired hand had proved deceitful and was gone, his favorite daughter was preparing yet again to leave him here alone, where he was condemned by God to work this rocky soil, tear his own food from the rocks. His grandson had proved to be a bloody twit. "Ahhhh shit," he whispered to Adeline, who knew better than interrupt. In the lanterned room, heavy with shadows, he said, "Papa," holding his hand out to that unseen, everpresent being. "Papa."

He appeared at Amanda's bed once more, lantern held high, a fully clothed apparition, one hand free to wave in emphasis. "What say you to my offer? I know you've been in here pondering it. What say? Answer now, damn you. What say to what I told you, to leave her with me, let me bring her up properly?" No answer even yet from the startled pair. Look how wide their eyes for the middle of the night, how their eyes catch the light like a bear's. Amanda had been crying. "I'll see to her clothes. There's some clothes around here some'ers. Your own dresses, Amanda, was passed on to Florence, then she run off with that damn son of a bitch Sonny Lester and what has ever come of her, tell me, living in Arkansas, wherever in hell that is, on land flat as a tombstone, left her dresses hanging on four pegs and a roofing nail, and I said to leave them, yes, just leave them there and I'll box a cupboard over them. I have shoes around the place. I have books, them books of mine. Ahhh, she can read to me. I'm in my old age, damn you, I admit it. She can feather my nest thataway. Well—" He paused, caught at the edge of a lost thought, not sure what he was about to say. "You think it over," he told them and waded away, heavy with memories of dresses, of Florence's leaving early one morning before light, of Hallie fleeing across the yard.

He burned his hand on the lantern. He submerged the pained flesh in cold water from the free-running tap. Thoughts dense and thick, he sank into his chair and treated himself with a little song his mother had often sung while working.

Next morning Amanda moved quietly around his chair and poked kindling into the kitchen range, making not even a scratching sound, and put the kettle on the largest plate. She had not slept a wink since her father had awakened her. There he sat now, halfway in, halfway out of the big rocker, pillows poked in around him, either by his own hand or Adeline's, for she was doubtless up by now, was out milking. "Oh, God," Amanda whispered, almost overcome with anxiety, wanting to see her child, wanting to forgive her and to chastise her. Quiet, quiet, she thought, as she took a cup of tea into the bedroom, to share it with Pink, who was up. "You went back to sleep?" she said.

"I think so," he admitted, stretching, seeking a toehold on today, aware of her beside the chair, of the bedcovers trailing after him onto the floor, of the stacked boxes of unused shoemaking tools. "Where did he say he'd put the piano?" he asked, grinning at Amanda.

"Don't make me laugh," she said. "Tell me again what Hallie was doing."

He rubbed his eyes, moaned himself into life, begrudging himself the loss of drowsiness. "God only knows." He held up two fingers to remind her there had been two people out there. "I thought he was the ghost of Clarence Morrison, who died when I was seven." He tilted his head back, breathed deeply through his mouth.

Amanda took the cup out of his hand. Almost empty. She drained it herself. "Don't wake him, please."

"Had been a Moravian for years and, therefore, felt he was doomed anyway." A rain started outdoors, fine drops licking at the tin roof of the porch outside their open window.

"Mama's up, I think," she said.

"Where's Hallie?"

"In her bed, or so I hope."

"You going . . . to talk to her?" he asked.

"Tell the world I am."

"Don't tell the world," he said. "Let's not tell the world." He pulled off his nightgown, stood before her naked, yawning, before seeking to get one foot through his clean undergarments. He buttoned his shirt unevenly and she did it properly for him. He pulled on his pants, stumbled barefooted into the narrow hallway, came back for his shoes. He moved stealthily past Enid in his chair. The cold dawn mist struck Pink like a slap, washed his face, cleared his eyes, reminded him—and he needed reminding—that this was another, a new morning, not emerging out of night nor resembling the night's personality, but burst-new, born here and now, this hour arriving and wanting to be liked. The yard where he stood was mist-covered, but floods of light were bathing the fields above the house, sunlight direct, bright as new metal, drying everything. It also shafted down over there in the east field, while here about him the mist hovered thickly, flitted, being of no certain clothing, being risky, courting the farmyard fancifully and coating his face, his hands, his sockless feet, cooling him with wisps and swipes of its clean spray. "Morning, ma'am," he said aloud, speaking kindly to the unseen feathery hand, most unlike God's hand, which decorated all such mornings, apparently a female presence, shy almost to a fault. By the time he walked back along the same yard boards, the sunlight had burned through, had begun warming the ground. The female—was she a goddess of the mist?

Enid King emerged from the house, began moving about, still drunk. He and Pink carried water, sloshing it over themselves, to the penned stock, their boots slipping about in the mud. "What will I do without hired help?" Enid complained. "What on earth will I do? I have corn to be pulled and shucked and cribbed, the stalks cut for fodder, the hay cut, tobacco to cure. Marshall wasn't much help, but he did pester things."

Pink kept looking up at the hillside beyond the gate bars, recalling last night.

Enid stopped beside him. "Them women will skin that girl, if you don't take care. Nothing bothers a woman more than to see others break their rules. They'll allow a son to get away with anything, but a daughter is in bondage."

"I don't know what I'll say to her myself." Pink noticed there were scuffed places in the bank, in the grass, which he supposed were results of their wrestling.

"I knew he fancied her," Enid said, "He had one of them bird-wing stunts, such as that, kept after her."

"Bird wing?" Pink had to laugh. "Never heard of that type of courting," he said. "And I suppose she didn't have the willpower to turn him down."

Enid hung Marshall's clothes on a fence post to dry. "He must have been a sight getting home last night. Not the first naked man to cross fields around here." He had a jug of liquor in the barn, which he got out now, took a sip from it.

"Not sure what to do about Frederick, either," Pink admitted. "At least what Hallie did was natural." Quiet settled on both men for a minute or so, then they went back to carrying water.

Pink found Amanda in the kitchen sitting silent, withdrawn. He sat down next to her, fumbled for her hand. When Frederick came down from

149

the loft, the boy went directly outdoors, came back complaining of a head-ache. He sat down at the table, waited impatiently, tapping the table top with his fingers. If he was suffering remorse, he was hiding it.

Enid appeared at the doorway, beet-red of face. Even as he stood there precariously balanced, Hallie came down the ladder. Maybe she had been awaiting the arrival of her friend, protector, advocate. All eyes turned from grandfather to granddaughter and back again. Enid held out his arms to her, and she came to him and he embraced her. "It's not something ever to mention to me, honey," he told her.

Hallie sat down across from her parents, next to Frederick, who was already eating and who pretended not to notice her. There was a slight quiver to his lips, Pink noticed, perhaps a tremor in his hand, that was all.

"Well, Pink," Enid said, "tell us what you do besides shovel money from one room to another."

Pink smiled, said nothing. Young climbed down the loft ladder and went out into the yard, moving toward the privy.

Enid caught hold of the vacant chair at the head of the table, settled onto its quivering, creaking frame, belched, adjusted his fork and knife, perfectly aligning them beside his plate, then stared about, identifying each one: Pink, Hallie, the boy Frederick, Amanda, his gaze resting finally on dear Hallie at his left hand, sitting near enough to touch. Speaking in a hoarse whisper, as if for her ears alone, he said, "Marshall's gone." He beamed at her, then began chuckling, throwing sidelong glances at his wife working at the stove. "I think he's not the marrying kind," he whispered to her and winked.

"Papa . . ." Amanda reprimanded firmly.

Ignoring her, he turned his attention to breakfast, serving himself. By mishap, he got a tiny ball of grits on his plate, then by mishap he poured a torrent of gravy on top of it. Pausing to consider the results, he sought to secure a biscuit, managing to knock the top off the honey pot. Having claimed two steaming biscuits, he studied them critically, speculating as to why they were scorching his hand. He broke them into his plateful of gravy, which was coming to resemble a porridge. Onto this he dispatched several fried eggs. He paused, considered his handiwork. Finding it without appeal, he turned his attention to his granddaughter. "Your mother took fifty-two minutes one night . . ." He removed his elbow so Adeline could set a cup of coffee before him. "What was I saying?" he asked Hallie.

"Fifty-two minutes . . ."

"Uh huh," he said, not focusing on the details immediately. "It's got so busy in here," he complained, giving Adeline a steely gaze.

"Mama took fifty-two minutes to get from somewhere to somewhere maybe," Hallie suggested.

"Did she?" King asked. He got secure hold of the cream pitcher, his hand almost encircling its fat belly. He poured cream into his coffee until his cup overflowed. He set the creamer down on top of his eggs, lowered his face close to the coffee mug and sipped at its rim. "You're not leaving me," he told Hallie, looking up from the cup suddenly. "You're my daughter now."

"Sir?" she replied.

He rested against the back of the chair, stared down at his hands folded on the table. "You're all I have, all that's worth having," he murmured. Ignoring Adeline's gasp, he pounced on his eggs, chopping them into pieces and stuffing them into his mouth, eggs, grits, bits of biscuit, his jaws chewing, all eyes on him, on his adam's apple swallowing. He poured what remained of the hot coffee into this throat, tried to stand, fell over, the chair toppling with him, the big body landing on the floor heavily with a thud, Adeline crying out. He crawled to his favorite chair. "Now leave the girl alone," he shouted at the stunned family, and once sitting down, secure, placed a pillow over his face.

Hallie was making no pretense of being hungry. She served herself one piece of fried ham, which she chewed on lethargically. Her manner was watchful, her gaze now and then resting on Frederick as he continued to serve himself generously. At last she spoke, asked him if she should get him a trough to eat from.

He growled.

"Serve yourself some more grits, Frederick," she suggested. "Don't deprive yourself." The boy had piled grits over most of his plate, and now ladled a dipper of ham gravy into the center, his plate coming to resemble a giant eye staring up at him, the sediment of the gravy providing the dark red pupil.

When finally Frederick finished and Pink followed him outdoors, Amanda, now that the men were absent, thought it time to ask Hallie if she wanted to explain herself. When Hallie only stared at her, Amanda said, "We all know you didn't mean to do anything wrong." Her voice was trembling; her face was filled with anguish. "But you can't always be sure when wrong will occur."

Adeline was in course of bringing a full bowl of milk and porridge from the stove. She sat down slowly, sighing. "Well, let her tell it, Amanda. What did that man Marshall do to you, Hallie?"

Hallie shook her head.

"You don't know what he did?"

Hallie said nothing.

"Tell us what he did to you," her grandmother said kindly. "We can help you."

Hallie stammered an apology. "I am sorry."

"Did he put it inside you at all?" her grandmother asked calmly, spooning porridge into her mouth, wiping dripping milk off her chin. "Well, why do you look at me like that, Amanda? It's either he did or he didn't, that's all. Did he put it inside you, Hallie?"

"I assume he put it in her," Amanda said tightly, breathily. "What else would he do with it? Where else would he put it?"

Adeline chewed porridge and glared at her daughter. "I asked her yes or no."

"No, he never," Hallie said.

A gasp of surprise came out of both women, then a smile and a whoop came out of Adeline. She rocked back and forth, suddenly full of relief and pleasure. "Kept your legs crossed, did you? Good for you, honey."

Amanda told her mother she didn't realize Hallie knew how to protect herself so well.

"Thank the good Lord," Adeline announced to the whole room.

"Thank the Lord, indeed," Amanda acknowledged.

"I know how it can be," Adeline said, suddenly talkative, "a new boy comes along, talks bravely, compliments you, says you're the prettiest little thing he ever saw, starts making offerings, gifts . . ."

"No, he never—" Hallie began, then caught herself, decided it was wise to let her grandmother have her way.

"Some of them are good boys, some tricksters. Now Marshall is a hard worker, we all know that. I never mean to say he's not."

"Maybe I made a poor choice," Hallie said suddenly, "but it was the only choice I had."

Both women peered thoughtfully at her, weighing that.

"I mean, I had no choice," Hallie explained.

The women still stared at her.

"He's the one boy here," she said.

Amanda shook her head angrily. "We are going to have a talk about that, missy," she said. "You are not to lift your skirt for a boy, simply because he's present."

"Well, what am I up here for?" Hallie said.

"Not for that. Not for being naked. You were naked, Hallie."

Hallie turned away, sought a biscuit in the basket, broke it in her fingers. "Yes, I remember."

"Lord knows what we'll do if she ever does come down with child," Amanda said to her mother, as if Hallie were no longer present. "Marry the boy? Should she marry the boy?" Amanda asked.

"Marshall's not what I would want for her," Adeline replied. "He has nothing, except what we give him. His mother has nothing, either."

"Shameful," Amanda said, "to be naked with a hired hand. I'll not forget last night, Hallie," she suddenly said. "Your father won't either. You almost killed your father."

"No, mama," Hallie pleaded, deeply wounded.

"What Marshall's been known for around here is his singing voice," Adeline commented. "That's all I ever have heard people compliment. He's best known for a rendition of "I Come to the Garden Alone." She began to hum the tune, then sang a bit of it.

Once the sound of her voice had died out, Amanda looked over at Hallie most patiently. "Most every family has problems of this nature. They have to be dealt with, that's all, firmly dealt with," she said. "That's what a family is for."

Pink suggested to Enid that they go fishing, this only because Enid needed sobering up. They fished the creek, moving along through the underbrush, approaching the pools from downstream, assuming trout will normally be looking upstream, hoping for food to be washed down. Enid would cast his bait well ahead, let it float with the current. Pink would flip his lure out onto a big rock and let it slide down the upstream side. Sometimes a trout would strike, a rainbow seven or eight inches long. Pretty soon, half an hour after they had started, they had enough fish caught for the family's noon meal.

"Did you talk to your boy?" Enid asked Pink.

"I did, yes," Pink said. "I told him a brother is responsible for the women of the family, is a protector."

Enid put a chew of tobacco in his cheek. "He's about old enough for the army, is he? That might straighten him out."

Pink fiddled with his hook and line, fastening a bug on it. He tossed it out to float down the creek. "Oh, well," he said wearily, his thoughts heavy just now. "The boy was drunk."

Enid studied him thoughtfully. "Did you think about going off to the war, Pink?"

"I . . . had a medical examination made back then, that sort of thing." The creek was noisy and full of rasping voices, and his own voice was cushioned in among them.

"Then you decided no, you'd stay with your family?"

"I never passed," Pink told him. "Those doctors—you get different opinions, of course, but this one doctor . . ." His voice trailed off.

"Heart, lungs, or gut?" Enid asked, frowning at him.

Pink tossed his line up the creek again. He was fretful now. Apparently this subject of his health was a raw sore with him. "Heart is beating too strong." He smiled. "I'm too strong."

Enid murmured, gloomily watching him, realizing, of course, that the matter was pertinent to Pink's life. "How much too strong?"

"Now, they never told me. I feel fine," he said. "It's blood pressure."

Enid put another trout on the cord and let Pink carry them. He kept nodding to Pink as they walked back to the house, as if admitting he was thinking of him.

After the meal, soon after one o'clock, the car was loaded and the family boarded it. The mighty life weight of the departure humbled Enid. His big shoulders bent even more than customarily. He pestered the people, hugging them, touching them through the open car windows. "Don't know when I'll see you again." He took one of Hallie's hands, held it between his two, covering her fingers with wet kisses. "You come back to see me," he kept saying. The car lurched backward, responding to one of Pink's driving errors. Enid took firm hold of the open window frame of the car. "I'll not come to town just now. I know within reason you'd find me a work place if I did, find me a factory place to make the move, but I'm frankly undecided to break my roots free. I was set out here so many years ago. . . . No, I'll not make shoes for the city. I was planted away back here. I'll not move to the Goddamn city. . . . " As he talked, he backed away from the throbbing, noisy car, felt around for Adeline's hand, held her hand as the car belched and backfired its way into motion, Pink staring at him, still trying to decide how to make proper reply; the car, almost in spite of Pink, was moving, and Amanda was calling into his ear for him to pay attention. "There's a shed just there," she shouted.

He never did reply to Enid. He got the car turned around, left a few yard boards splintered, and slid down the King road, turned left into the main road, which was broad and full of holes made by wallowing hogs and home-making groundhogs; he drove past the trade lot, the church, the forge lot, and made the wide, long curve to the fording place that crossed the river.

High up the mountainside road they could see the village below, see the river with its web of creeks and springs, threads among the trees coming together from north and south, augmenting the river almost as a communal prayer is formed; the webbing was an assembly of bubbling notions, the river losing strength in the bottomlands of the Wright and Crawford fields. "Have a surprise, once we get home," Pink announced, "Young and I."

Young began to laugh, pleased with anticipation.

"Did some work on the house," Pink said. The understatement made Young laugh out loud. Neither of them mentioned making the attic into a second floor, with three small bedrooms, each with a dormer window.

Hallie sat huddled in the car, the pain inside her deeper than any she had known before, two pains really, one from a discovery that was even yet unclear, one from a disappointment that was almost despair.

The house was a masterpiece, Amanda decided. The second floor, which was not yet finished, seemed to add enough space without adding a sense of spaciousness. The stairway was quite narrow, but would do.

As soon as they had free time, the carpenters, two farmers who owed

Pink money, were to return to finish; meanwhile, the second floor had windows without glass, stud walls without paneling. Even so, as it was, Amanda gloried in it. The rooms helped relieve all their anxieties about Hallie. Apparently the child had done nothing terribly wrong, anyway, Amanda decided, nothing that would result in pregnancy. In fact, it was easy to exaggerate what Hallie had done, simply because of the dramatic surprise of its revelation. There was no obvious rejection of what sex was or ought to be. To Amanda sex was one of three beads on a chain: the woman, the sex act, and the birth of a baby, the beads inextricably linked, but for a young lady Hallie's age, beads must be examined one at a time, or so she told Pink.

Pink sat on the porch, his arm thrown across the back of the swing, watching people pass on the street, some of them waving to him. He was talking with Frederick, telling him yet again that the man must protect the women of the family, was born to that task, had been assigned to it long ago when women, handicapped by pregnancy and babies, couldn't protect themselves from marauders, whether they were Celts or Danes or Normans or Romans or Indians or beasts. "A boy who won't protect his sister . . ." Pink paused, considering the failure. "There goes Ham Harper, Frederick?"

"I think it is, papa. With his new dog."

"Is that a dachshund? I never saw one before. Read about them in the magazines. A boy who won't protect his sister—"

"Papa, I was drunk, that's the whole of it."

"Well, that's yet a second concern, getting drunk at your age. It can turn into a noose around your neck." He waved to Mr. Harper, who had recently bought a major policy. "He's an accountant," he told Frederick, "advised me to expand the company westward into the Tennessee mountains, rather than eastward to the cities, said there were many insurance companies down east, and I ought to stay in the mountains. What do you think?"

"I don't know, papa," Frederick admitted.

"I think he's right," Pink said. "I asked Hallie and she agreed." He noticed the jolt that the comment gave Frederick, the priority in the family that he had established.

Pink hired a dining room built for the house, with a fireplace. Actually, he made the kitchen into a dining room and part of the back porch into a new kitchen. The construction, which was to be completed along with the other improvements, would give the family something friendly to talk about and deal with, at this awkward time of discovery, error, healing.

CHAPTER
Eleven

Young would count the out-of-state license plates. Year by year the local children would keep totals for each state, competing with their friends. One summer Young found all forty-eight. Whenever he could, he bargained with his father to drive him to the Clove Park Inn parking lot, the wallahalla of license plate hunters. He would leap from the car like a hound freed from a pen and go dashing about, car to car, hoping against hope for a rare find. Iowa, North Dakota, Nevada. He could taste the words in his mouth. Ohio, Montana, Texas. Louisiana. Oregon. For two years running, neither of his closest friends had a single Oregon, while Young had two.

All these people come here, to my part of the world. That was what he gloried in. We don't go to theirs. This is the best place; all of them say it is the most beautiful they have found. We are living in the promised land, he decided, personalizing his understanding of the Old Testament; we are the chosen people in the promised land.

Each year he stopped counting Pennsylvania when he got to twenty-five.

During school years, Young was successful in class, and after school he was successful making trades. He appeared to have his father's interest in trading, and he possessed a marked ability to figure numbers in his head, adding and subtracting and multiplying. There was not a stall or shed about the yard that was not used to house a goat or sheep, a hunting dog or boxful of kittens, a pony, a carload of cloth from a train wreck north of town. Amanda helped take care of his things and encouraged him, and of course Pink did, both of them glorying in his successes.

Young succeeded in school, too, at least was popular, serving in various elected positions. He was not given to books, however. "Now, here," Hallie would say, ushering him along the stacks of the library on the square, "this one you'll like because it has horse racing in it. And this one is soooo beautiful at the close, when she dies . . ." They would come away with armloads of books, but weeks later they were in the main unread. Math was his specialty. He brought his new math text home and worked all the problems in two evenings, which frustrated his busy teacher. Hallie located a text on algebra, and for days he pestered its problems, even asked his favored friend, Hugh King, for advice, which amused Hugh. "You think I can do anything, don't you?" Hugh referred him to Hatch Cole at the hardware store. "He's always up to his ass in figures."

Young was awed by Hatch, that tall, bent man, a legend, feared even by adults. Once Young did linger after school near the great man's store, as if a miracle would bring them together. Finally he appealed to his father, as so often he did when he was trapped, and Pink quite happily took him along the street to Hatch's place, introduced him. Hatch peered at the boy over the top of his reading spectacles, grunts and groans issuing from somewhere inside him, his mouth screwing up as if he were tasting a lemon. "Math genius, they tell me. What's forty-nine times forty-nine?" he asked.

"Two thousand four hundred one," Young replied at once.

"No, it's not, that's wrong," Hatch said. "But it's close. What's one hundred four times—"

"Thought I had it right," Young corrected him.

"What's one hundred four multiplied by itself?"

Young thought about it. "Ten thousand eight hundred sixteen."

"Almost right," Hatch said. "What's one thousand divided by seven?"

"What does it matter?" Young said, reddening. "You're going to say it's wrong."

Hatch raised one big hand, laid it flat on top of his own head, let his fingers crawl into his hair; meanwhile, he was casting proud glances at Pink. "Wish he were mine," he murmured. He frowned at the boy. "I'm not much of a teacher, for I am jealous of people who know what I know." He scratched his head. "A good teacher is one who wants a student to equal him. A great teacher is one who wants a student to best him. I never could be a great teacher, could you, Pink?"

"My son here . . ." Pink began.

"I'd be a crooked teacher, for I have to win."

"You can win," Young told him. He smiled. "I don't mind."

"There you go, there you go," Hatch roared, slapping his palm down hard on his desk top. "Well, if you agree to that," he told the boy. "He might beat me, for a fact, Pink, and I'd not like it." He left them abruptly, walked about in his store, stirring up the dust, then turned suddenly to scrutinize the boy. "What you paying?"

"We can . . . work it out," Young replied.

"Work? You can work in here?"

"Could use a duster, I guess," Young said, smiling at him.

"You come in Saturday morning at eight and work all day, and when evening comes I'll show you how to do the first problems, show you how to do algebra for thirty minutes. You'll learn as fast as you can in thirty minutes, just sitting right here. It'll be nine hours for you and half an hour for me."

It was agreed, and in two months Young knew algebra and was moving on into geometry, and by Christmas he and Hatch both were wrestling with trigonometry. Then in the new year Hatch told him not to come back around. "There's plenty more I know," he assured the boy. "But you've cleaned up this place so clean I don't recognize it."

"One more Saturday," Young begged.

"Not worth it to me," Hatch said, waving a hand in the air, dismissing the idea and the boy, whom he loved. "Won't waste your time."

Young would climb to the top of a white pine growing at the back of Hugh King's yard, a tree so big it shaded two other lots. He and a friend, Crass Blalock, would go to the top, chuckling and joking, then they would launch themselves outward on opposite sides, sliding off boughs to the one below, sliding off that to the next one waiting. The tree boughs bucked as each boy passed. The lowest boughs deposited them on the ground, where they crawled off back of the trunk and nursed their cut hands, compared scars, pieced back together the tears in their clothes. The great tree shivered for a minute or two after each such ride. To Young it seemed to be amused inside, wherever its mind was, or enraged; anyway, it was stirred up, he and Crass agreed on that, even if they could not exactly define the emotion of a tree.

Young had other sports. He fashioned two oak runners for a sled and screwed on crosspieces for a seat; the two, father and son, would drag this contraption to the top of Missionary Hill, and Young would ride down the broom-sedged places, the sedge slick as ice. In winter, whenever there was a snow, they would make the most of that from first light of a morning. Now and then snow came at Christmastime, and that brought the union of two great joys. How warm the sheets of a Christmas Eve bed while the noise of the neighbors' little dog was muffled by the softness of big snow-flakes. Young would shine the light out the window, try to see them, marveling at them one by one, numbers overcoming, overwhelming. Sleep finally, the sleep of the downright tired-out boy who had fought sleep as long as he could.

Dawn. Chilly room. Floor cold to the feet. Don't wake mama or Hallie. Put on the blue robe that Hallie had given him last Christmas, which he saved for special occasions. Smell of pine in the hallway, coming from the Christmas tree in the parlor. Dark hallway, with a single little light. Sneak into the parlor to kneel before the tree and the gifts, piles of gifts for each member of the family from Santa Claus, or from each other—skates, a yo-yo, a cast-iron toy car. There were piles of candies, which Young knew his father had bought, this being one of his Merry Christmas indulgences; the darker and richer and more expensive the chocolates the better, as Amanda had often said.

Lying on his belly, on the rug, his head propped up on stiffened arms and hands, Young considered the gifts soon to be plundered, the aroma of Christmas filling his nostrils, pine and peppermint and herb teas, the anticipation of comforts filling his body, covering him, making him laugh.

One Christmas afternoon Hugh King came by, he and Nettie. Hallie played a few hymns on the piano, and she and Young and Frederick sang; they would have sung longer except that Hugh obviously was irritated by entertainment. Amanda served canned plum juice, which had a beautiful pink color. "The color is the best part of it," she claimed, passing out the filled glasses. On leaving, Hugh sneaked a gift into Young's pocket. "Don't you ever dare mention it," he said.

Young overheard his parents talking late at night. His father mentioned there being no medicine for his disease. Just what his disease was they didn't say. Apparently it was locked inside his body and couldn't be got out.

"Maybe it's gone on all your life," Amanda suggested to Pink.

"I have never felt bad in my life, never had a sick day."

"Well, what's a person to worry about then?" she asked.

"Watkins is going to try different medicines," Pink told her. "Last August he gave me some to try, but they don't seem to help."

"Oh, Pink," she chided him, distressed. "You must make them work. Everything depends on it."

Hugh King had a quart of new brandy to taste. He offered a sip to his son, then sent him off to watch the front of the store. He pulled up a spare chair for Pink and poured himself a whopping amount. Pink flopped into the chair, fanned himself with a church fan that had been lying on Hugh's desk, one with Jesus pictured on it as a boy teaching in the Temple.

"Is this good or not?" Hugh asked, sniffing of the brandy. "Bonny Case said it was run through twice, then aged more'n two months."

"Two months is not long, is it?" Pink asked, sniffing the brandy. He tasted it guardedly.

"Case doesn't sell it. He gives it away to me, then I give him something. He gives me two gallons of it and I give him two cured hams. Usually he takes food in trade. Once he fooled me; he came in and chose two quilts, four sheets, some pillow cases, several towels. I said, Case, are you daft? And he said he was marrying a bride from a poor family and didn't have more than her clothes and a flock of dominiquers." Hugh laughed gently at the fellow's predicaments.

"Case married the poor woman, did he?"

"Guess he had to go through with it, once he had all those sheets," Hugh said. Suddenly he was on his feet, out the door following after a farmer who owed him payment on a mortgage on his farm. Holding the fellow by a shirt sleeve, Hugh peered intently into his eyes, talking about being broke and needing cash to run his store, whispering so that nobody could overhear him. Then, as quickly as he had left, he was back again, swiveling in his chair. "A rocker goes back and forth, this'n goes side to side as well," he told Pink. The phone rang and he shouted hello into it, listened a moment, then shouted a few words, listened for half a minute before hanging up. The phone always left him disgruntled; he considered it to be yet another foreign body implanted in his store. "Well . . ." He leaned back in his chair and studied a speck on the wall. "Not for a while have we talked," he said. He turned on Pink. "How's your business doing? Somebody said you're rich as a drugmaker."

Pink laughed.

"Said you need more rooms for offices." Hugh twirled his chair halfway around, spit into a can, twirled back once more. "Why, you'll be a tycoon, Pink."

Pink beamed at him. "I tell you the truth, I was lucky when I found Wallerbee and Hatch."

"But Wallerbee can't drive it forward, as you have," Hugh said. "They tell me he can't see more'n is right there in front of him on the desk. And Hatch—I know and trust him about as far as from here to that barrel of peanuts."

"No, he's honest."

"Is he?"

"He's honest near to a fault," Pink said. "He spends all his time balancing promises. Has to be exact."

"Well, promises are never exact," Hugh said. "Words always vary." There was often some jealousy that showed through Hugh's smiles, as now. He was jealous of Hatch; he was all compliments for Pink today, but there were elements of regret there as well.

They sat together for an hour or more, exchanging stories, talking about their families in the mountains, respectfully considering themselves as offspring of them, rejectors of them, with some of the same manners and ideas and beliefs, but becoming different people, already different from them. "Maybe when I was only five years old, I was changing by then," Pink admitted. "I never did take to tending to farm animals and plowing; even the first few rows bored me."

After a while Hugh said, "I can't see yet what you invest with, Pink."

"Promises," he said quietly.

"You gamble with promises, Pink?"

"No. I gamble with real merchandise."

"What is it?" Hugh said, leaning far forward in his chair, his keen eyes piercing him.

"My family," Pink told him.

"I remember my own house as a girl," Amanda told Pink one night, sitting on the edge of the bed, staring off at the darkest corner of the room, where memory was enhanced, was better shrouded and comforted, where she could in her mind recall, could almost see her mother and father and the other children, sense the presence of gasping, breathing, choking, coughing life all about her. It was increasingly her manner these days to retreat to memory. "Was in the loft, and there was no way to close the two windows, those end windows, secure enough. Was barely able to close the gaps enough to keep squirrels out. Was up there on cold nights, and the tin roof so close to my head it swelled coldness down on my hair, matting it,

161

freezing it to crinkling, and my breath formed whiteness, almost a frozen snow on my lip. I hugged myself until the quilts were warm inside. I'd take a hot brick to bed with me every night. That was the greatest comfort; heat it on the hearth till it could not be touched except with a cloth, then carry it up the loft ladder. And every night, more often than not, it'd be stole by one brother or sister or another, and I'd have to try to figure out which one had it, then try to pry it loose. I would curl up under the quilts with the hot brick clutched to my belly, with my body bent around it, like a baby lies in its mummy's body, Pink, much the same way, like a baby lies . . . in its mummy's womb . . . and I would go to sleep with that hot pig in . . . my belly . . . Pink . . ."

"Hot pig?" he said softly.

She looked over at him thoughtfully, seeking to place the question. "That's what we called them, anything hot, whether a hot-water bottle, or the clay water bottle mama used, or the bricks, or a bag of creek sand my brother used till the cloth broke. We called them hot pigs."

Her mind kept returning to the old days, and to the country. She doted on thoughts of the country.

In February, a busy time of year for him, Pink noticed a bulge appearing on her abdomen, and he asked her if she was pregnant. She shrugged off the suggestion, but his worry persisted, and the next night he asked her again and told her bluntly that this was no time to be bearing another child.

Amanda was surprised at the acute nature of his concern, as she told him. She could have understood if he had mentioned that expenses were being increased every month as they sought to rear the three children they already had, each with special books, new clothes, tooth straightening, all the accompaniments to child rearing in the city, which every parent was doing these days. She could have understood if he had referred to the danger to her life and the possibility of leaving the family without the help she offered. Or had mentioned his own health. But he was callous, unfeeling, she decided, and in the bedroom even slapped toward her belly with an angry, instinctive movement of his hand as if he rejected completely the idea of a child.

The same night, well after midnight, she found him standing in the kitchen staring down at the tea kettle, which he had set on the wood range. He was holding his hands over the kettle, to conserve what little heat developed. She said she would build up the fire for him, but he didn't move out of the way. He seemed to her to reject even help, and she sank down at the table, frightened. "You have secrets," she said to him. "I have secrets from myself. It's the way we're living now."

"I don't have secrets."

"All that company is a secret. I don't understand it. You have rooms full of people working and have offices I've never been in."

"Do you blame the company for your pregnancy?" he asked quietly.

"I wonder what I blame the company for. I'm more lonely. I've grown lonely, Pink. I miss knowing you well."

"I'm working," he said. "In the last four years we've increased the number of applicants sixfold. Now think of that."

"I can't think of it."

"Why can't you think of it, Amanda?"

"I don't know what it means." It must be obvious to him by now that the kettle wouldn't heat on such a meager fire, but he stood there waiting, even so. "I'll fix your tea," she said. When again he didn't reply—how strange his silence, she thought—or move from the stove, she said, "You can hurt me worse than I can stand. Better if you took a piece of firewood and struck me, it might be kinder."

In the parlor, sitting on the mohair couch, she tried to think what to do. She heard the stove grate being shaken, and she supposed he was building up the fire. She hoped he was using the resinous pine; that pine would make a fire flare up at once. "The pine is in the bundle next to the sink," she called to him. It was true she might be pregnant. A week earlier she had come to that conclusion herself. She had prayed it was so, and prayed it was not so.

He appeared before her, began talking about her endangering herself, endangering these children, of her not recognizing his own ailment and the implications of his sickness, that she might soon be the one parent remaining. She fled the room, terrified of that thought. She heard him moving through the hallway, calling her name. She bit her hand to keep from answering. She heard something break in the kitchen. She climbed into bed with Hallie, hiding herself, frightened.

"What is papa doing?" Hallie asked, her voice trembling.

"I don't know," she put her arms around her. "But don't you go out there."

Hallie pulled free. Holding her torn nightgown closed, she ran toward the kitchen. She came back directly. "He's burning the kitchen chairs," she said calmly.

He left at dawn. Amanda heard the front door open and close. From a window she saw him moving off toward the street and town. She went into her own room then, welcomed the feel of the bed she had known for years. She lay there with her head buried in pillows and wept bitterly. She was comforted finally not by Hallie, but by Young, who crept into the bed with her.

She slept. She dreamed of being in fields, clods of earth breaking under her feet, the flanks of the earth spreading outward, her footprints leaving impressions. She fell to her knees, lifted dirt, and wiped it across her face, put the clean dirt on her sweating neck and arms. In the sky, far off, away up there, a hawk recovered in its fall and shot upward.

She awoke and argued with Hallie. "Do as your brother orders," she told her. "Frederick and Young are not cooks. One of us women has to cook for them."

Pink had broken two kitchen chairs. Amanda stared at the bits, dismayed. Look at those splinters, look at the frames of the chairs, broken in ever so many places. See, she told herself, see how he did. Her own father had sometimes got angry, and whenever that happened, the children had hit—anger fierce, irrational, dangerous. "Please God, what am I to do?" she murmured, and turned away from Hallie, who was approaching her, clean dish cloth in hand. "Go to school, Hallie. You don't know how to work."

Midmorning, the company driver brought her a bouquet of flowers, a note attached. She sat at the window staring at the words: All love.

Alone, Pink waited only briefly in the doctor's reception room before being called into the inner office. Dr. Watkins, who did much of the medical work for the company now, was expecting a business conversation, and the personal nature of Pink's presentation confused him and left him finally sitting in silence. He turned to look out the window at the workmen who were engaged in systematically dismantling the Battery Park Hotel. "I'm willing to perform an abortion for medical reasons, in spite of the law."

"Except for my own illness, I might risk the birth," Pink said.

"Yes. I know you can't be sure how long you'll live."

"Should anything happen to her and I be gone—"

"But I must ask for complete secrecy. You respect that."

"Yes. Will you talk to her?"

"I'll phone her at once to make an appointment."

The doctor suggested a further operation to make any other pregnancy unlikely for Amanda. "It would only take a few minutes longer."

Pink considered that silently.

"She shouldn't have another pregnancy, Pink," he said simply. "As a doctor—"

"Very well," Pink said. He went down in the elevator, walked in a trance of worry to the company car, but decided to walk home, and he started on alone, store window by store window, seeking distraction. He followed along for a block or so, lonely and morose, then walked to the

164

square, went over office notes for an hour. He phoned the doctor to say he could not bring himself to alter Amanda's body permanently. He took Gloria down the street to a new restaurant, where he had a cup of tea and ate half a sandwich and listened to her talk about Hugh King and his sons. Pink listened as he would listen to water rolling over a cascade; he was aware of her words and their meaning, he needed their companionship, the jabs they gave his own thoughts, the distractions they represented, but they were of no consequence.

He went home just after lunch and called for Amanda. She was not present, apparently. He searched room by room for her, calling her name.

Amanda heard him when he first arrived. She was sitting in the bathtub, warm water washing around her, grasping a knitting needle still warm from the fire over which she had sterilized it. He called her name as he wandered about seeking her. She inserted the needle, squirming, adjusting her hips; tears of dread and loss were rolling down her face. Even as he called her name she pushed the needle further into her body, far in, until she felt a jab of pain. As his footsteps approached the bathroom, she heaved her hips downward, accepting the needle. A cry froze on her open mouth, as Pink pushed open the bathroom door even as the blood poured from her body into the water.

CHAPTER
Twelve

In the mountain world there were rules governing all aspects of conduct. For instance, business was the man's province, the family was in most respects the woman's; man was to be the polite aggressor in matters of mating, at the same time a man was not expected to say no to the invitation of a lady.

At first it was a mere mention of sex to Brodie King, Hallie admitting disappointment in the courtship that had transpired at Vancetown, telling him she had not been courted to her satisfaction. Brodie could be a counselor to everybody; he could afford the luxury because he had developed emotional protectors; he had his father's patient, friendly manner but, unlike his father, was not yet committed to any place, any work, any persons. Hallie was a distant cousin, kissing kin by mountain terminology. "Maybe you came at courting wrong, from the wrong direction," Brodie told her sympathetically.

"I did some things crazy, Brodie," she admitted. "Or he did."

"Any trouble come from it?" he asked, his smile sparkling. He was twenty-four years old, which was enough older than seventeen for him to be a wise and confidential advisor to her.

"No, I never quite got him that far." She had to laugh at her own admission.

"Oh my," Brodie whispered, nodding. "Why do you think that's unusual?" he asked her. "Why do you laugh at yourself?" They were both quiet, were secretive for a few moments, Brodie nonchalantly leaning against the store front, she leaning back against a farmer's pickup truck, neither of them embarrassed the least bit. They could talk to one another. Hallie supposed she could talk with Brodie better than any other man on earth; she knew he cared about her as a person, would always want what was best for her, although she supposed he would never personally be committed to her.

"There are some men don't take to women," he mentioned casually.

"They don't?"

"Don't like women." He laughed gently, dismissing that simply. "And all men are frightened now and then. I was frightened first time I ever was alone with a woman, but I don't enjoy fright, so I got over it soon as I could. Don't tell papa, will you?"

"Doesn't he know?" she asked. "I thought everybody knew you were— were popular."

"He enjoys questioning me." Softly he laid his hand against her cheek. "Don't you worry about that one fellow, honey."

Whenever he saw her after that, which was over the months, he would ask if she had found a better suitor yet. No, she had not, she would admit. He might mention a few names to her, all popular boys, but they were beyond her. One day she had the audacity to mention to him that maybe he would explain to her what she ought to expect from a man, or ought to offer, should the occasion arise again in her life. He shunted the matter aside, but later in the month she brought it up again. "I want you to be honest about what—whatever it is," she said.

"Well, you're sweet," he said, looking off across the street at a farm truck loaded with pallets and blankets and chairs. "Oh my, honey, I wouldn't mind," he told her, winking playfully.

He was deep in thought about the matter, all right, she noticed. "Or maybe there's a book I can read," she suggested.

"Don't know of any books," he said. Suddenly he took her hand, pressed it. "Very well, I'll do it, Hallie."

Her heart leapt; she could not even reply for joy and embarrassment. If she would meet him here this afternoon, he was saying. She had not known Brodie could be nervous, but he did appear to be as he talked now.

"The trouble is, Hallie, it needs one of those big lights. You know what I mean?"

"A spotlight?" she asked, astonished.

"No, a fancy light, with small lights all over it."

"A chandelier?"

"It needs that," he assured her. "It ought to be discussed with style."

"I can . . . imagine a chandelier, Brodie. We can sit down in Jake's Café, and I'll imagine it."

They sat at a table near the window. He ordered a pot of tea, a single piece of pie, and two forks. They ate the pie and sipped tea, while Brodie began scribbling on a sheet of yellow paper he had with him. The two were sitting opposite one another, their legs touching. "It's the two bodies," he told her, "of the man and the woman." He showed her his best effort to do the front view of a naked man. While she watched he penciled in hair on the chest and added hair above the sex organs. It was a creditable drawing, as Hallie viewed it, simple and clear, and wasn't intended to excite her, but excited she became. Also, she noticed that Brodie was forming his words more slowly. "Now, you do a woman," he said.

She used his stub of a pencil and a second piece of paper and drew a figure of a woman, with nice breasts and thin waist, full hips, perhaps broader than average, with long legs. As directed, she put on the nipples, then smudged on pubic hair. Excitement grew inside her, in spite of her reminder to herself that this was an educational formality, that neither she nor Brodie was in any way committed personally. The two figures were about the same size and Brodie laid them side by side, both facing Hallie. "Now these two are attracted to one another, Hallie. We can imagine that. It's not something either one can take full credit for. It's natural. Let's say, Hallie, that I'm attracted to you."

Hallie's throat went dry as bread crumbs as she listened, staring at the naked figures before them.

"This instinct arouses them, Hallie, the woman and the man, and causes physical changes inside the woman and the man, and also outside." He drew an arrow from the genitals of the man and sketched in a erect penis on the margin of the paper.

"Some men are circumcised," he told her. "Their foreskin is clipped off, and I don't know just how that goes." Then he asked her to draw the female sex organ.

"Well, I don't know," Hallie said. "There's nothing much to see."

"You've poked about in it enough," he told her. "Must have."

"I don't know what it looks like."

"Estimate," he said.

"Well . . ." She began to draw a tube, about the size of the erect penis. She noticed Brodie was watching her and that the normal brightness of his eyes had intensified.

"It's damn difficult to explain the rest of it and make it effective," he told her. "Anyway, this male part hardens, fills up, and it fits into the female part, which stretches, and the parts massage one another, and there's increasing pleasure until the semen is ejected." He finished the pot of tea. "It's damn hard to explain that," he admitted to her, taking her sweaty hand in his own. Finally he looked up, emotions tugging fiercely at him. "You feel anything yourself, Hallie?"

"I feel something, yes."

"A current inside, pushing you. No reasoning to it?"

"Yes."

He folded the drawings. "Saturday afternoon, we can . . . spend more time about this, if you want to."

"All right," she said at once.

"Get dressed up, wear Sunday clothes, have more style. Could meet."

"Where are we going to meet?" she asked.

After a while he said, "The train station at Biltmore is the closest."

"Why?" she blurted. "Why a train station?"

"Eleven o'clock," he said.

On Saturday she put on a favorite dress, sneaked out of the house, and met him at Biltmore. He was already at the station, waiting, dressed in a suit. He had bought two round-trip tickets to Henry Station, the third or fourth stop east of the town, a village resting at the foot of the mountain escarpment. "Brodie, why on earth are we going on a train?" Hallie asked.

"I have no car, Hallie," he told her, as if that explained everything.

In the train's last car, she sat next to him at the window. His right hand firmly took her hand, and he began to recall the various times in his life he had met her, meetings at the store, at his parents' house, telling her how he had always liked her and had wondered what she was like. At the eastern end of the Asheville plateau was a small station, Ridgecrest, a watering point before the train started on the twelve-mile run down the mountain wall, the track clinging to the steep, eastward-facing boundary of the range.

He led her to the back door of the car, explaining that, if they stayed in their seat, on entering the tunnel they couldn't see anything except darkness, but here at the end of the car they could see the tunnel mouths being diminished by the forward rush of the train. He slipped his arm around her to steady her; indeed, the train was rocking them back and forth. He was holding her close, and she had to slip one arm around his waist. She began breathing erratically and hoped he wouldn't notice; the jiggling vibrations of the train were partially to blame for her excitement, she decided, grateful there was nobody else in this final car, except a few passengers at the far end who were looking forward in the direction the train was moving. "They say your life stops at a tunnel," he told her, "that your heart stops beating, you are given that much time, that much extra time in your life. God or somebody does it," he told her, his arm pressing her tightly. The train was swaying, jiggling, making her body alive with tinglings, and then, in the middle of a sentence, the train blacked out. All there was to see was the light at the mouth of the tunnel, which was receding, and at that moment he swung her about and kissed her. Brodie King kissed her, the first time she had ever been kissed by him, the first time she had been kissed by anybody with passion. She still was holding to him as the train, with a roar of its whistle, swept out of the Swannanoa tunnel; all the world was lighted suddenly, and as suddenly her life had taken a turn. Time had stopped in the tunnel and now began again, the afternoon opened up anew to a new person, and she could see the whole world, too, lying below her and out around her, the new world for hundreds of miles, rolling, yearning toward the old sea, disappearing in distant, smaller hills, and he was still supporting her, and he began whispering to her, into her ear: "There are six more tunnels."

Twenty-five minutes later they reached the bottom of the escarpment, Henry Station. She had, she told herself, certainly gone with Brodie King down the mountain. Outside the car, the wind slapped at her, caused her to blanch and cough with surprise. She didn't know where they were going now, or even how to inquire. Brodie was leading her along. Did one admit ignorance, or merely hold to his hand? Did it matter where he was going to take her; was there any power left to refuse to go with him?

Brodie was talking to her, saying he had noticed often how quick and smart she was, and how he had liked her sense of humor, and how he had enjoyed kissing her just now and thought she was the best lady for kissing he had found, and how pretty her dress was and the way she had fixed her hair. He chose for her a chair on one of the smaller porches of the railroad hotel and asked her to wait while he went to see about arrangements. Just what they were to be she didn't know. He returned a few minutes later with a room key. They need not walk through the lobby, he said, since there was a side door.

"Brodie, what on earth do you have in mind?"

"A bite of lunch," he said. In their room, he pulled closed one of the drapes. The mountain wall rose before them, and at the moment high on its flank a train engine was huffing and puffing its way upward.

"It's a toy," she said excitedly, and wanted to go at once onto the little porch provided for their room, but he closed the remaining drape with one hand as he embraced her. "Brodie," she whispered reprimandingly. He kissed her ear. "Wasn't this room expensive?" she asked. "Did you rent it, or borrow it? Brodie?" she said, fear welling up in her suddenly, as she felt his hands roving over her body. One hand, she realized, was unbuttoning the back row of buttons on her dress. "Brodie?" she said, wondering if indeed she did know him, after all. The tip of his tongue was in her ear, his hand was inside her dress. She was suddenly sobbing and couldn't seem to stop the sobs and gasps of excitement. His hand was on her naked back, pulling her closer to him; his other hand cupped her breast, while he explained what elation he felt and she must feel; his hand massaged her breast, and she kept saying his name. She sank with him onto the bed, he with her, talking to her about her body, kissing her body, even the soft flesh of the inside of her thighs, and then he enveloped her in his arms, entering her slowly, gently, talking about her body and his own. Elation surged in her, and helplessness, and love for him.

Just before twilight he was sitting at the window looking up along the tracks, where just now a small black bear was searching for food. Brodie was talking, explaining without emphasis that the bears would come to the railroad out of curiosity, and that on every train were passengers who would toss them cookies or pieces of bread. He said once he had seen a woman try to leap from a slow train car on seeing her first bear, and on being detained had thrown the bear her pocketbook. "He's eating a banana peel, Hallie," he told her. "Stays near the hotel, I imagine, one of several," he was saying. "Gets in the garbage cans if they don't tie the lids down."

She was in the bed, a sheet pulled over the lower half of her body, feeling luxurious.

"How do you know what they do?"

"Have a college friend who works here." He found an apple in his coat. He and Hallie shared the apple, then tossed the core off the balcony, to be found later, he hoped, by the yearling.

"They say bears lumber," she said. "I've read about lumbering bears. Bears seem to me to waddle." She was warm and had the delicious sense of being whole, complete. Later a lighted train came down the track, cautiously feeling its way. At its windows were passengers on their journey to Winston-Salem, Richmond, Washington, Philadelphia, New York, storybook places to her, which she meant to see someday. They dressed, he pausing now and then to caress her. As they made their escape down the hallway to the east door, the westbound train, which they must take, was steaming at the station.

In the diner he looked across the table at her, her hair moderately tousled, even after she'd brushed it, her eyes bright and lively, her lips red from kisses. "You want to always look like that," he told her. Then he said, "You have any money, Hallie?"

She found a few dollars, which she gave him.

They had finished dinner by the time the train swept through the last tunnel and moved onto the Asheville plateau. Stars were out, and the moon was casting a steel-cold glow on the higher mountains. "What will I ever tell mama, if she asks me where I've been?" Hallie wondered aloud. "I think I could not convince mama of anything she hasn't known herself. If I tried to tell her how beautiful it was—and I know it might not have been beautiful at all, except for you. . . ."

"It's more difficult for a woman," Brodie was saying. "A man is an external creature, a woman is touched and moved inside. A man can more easily walk away from a meeting, but a woman can't walk away. . . ."

They left the train at the Biltmore station, and with the solid feel of the earth Hallie knew the special charm of the day was over; she was not any longer the princess with her cousin prince. She had returned to the real world of headaches, of prunes and grits, of chipped bowls with green flowers. Welcome home, she thought. And Brodie was different, as well, was busy with tickets and matters of time, was anxious to board the first streetcar, to be on his way.

She took a seat and he stood beside her in the aisle. He wasn't quite close enough. Maybe, she thought, he will never be close again. She had to be on her own now, she decided. She had accepted a man, and now the tryst was ending. She had taken yet another step through the next open doorway of her life. Confidently, even if still shaking, she stood on the adult side of that doorway, looking about at a different world, and looking at people differently, too, wondering what experiences these other passengers had had, what gifts they had brought to their beds, what pleasures they had rejected, what secrets they knew, what words they used. She found herself speculating about the men on the streetcar, wondering about them and their gifts.

She did not say goodbye to Brodie. She could not. They were at the square, people were piling off the streetcar, crowding around, separating them. She allowed that. She could see that he was looking for her, but for some private reason, dear to her, she left him, hid herself among a group of people moving toward Merrimon Avenue. At the northwest corner of the square, she looked back and saw him waiting even yet, and she realized she was being rude, but she didn't want Brodie King ever to feel that she could not walk away from him.

PART THREE
Maturity

CHAPTER
Thirteen

Two years later, in 1922, a flash of colors and light disoriented Pink and sent him sprawling onto the reception-room floor of the company offices. A flight of birds had flitted through his brain, a painless passage, a few instants of disorientation, so that in reaching out for the desk he had missed the desk, the chair, had fallen to one side of them both, landing on his own side. The dizziness persisted. He was turned over by Gloria while people were crying out, one woman screaming for help, help, help Mr. Wright. Wallerbee rushed forward, white as death itself. "What is it?" he asked. To Pink, somewhere a distant voice was asking, What is it? Closer was the face of Gloria Smith, her eyes filled with tears. He could have her tears fall into his own eyes, if he would move his head a slight way, a few inches, but he could not. "What is it, Pink?" Wallerbee called to him.

Pink tried to speak and could not. He heard him well enough and knew the reassuring words he wanted to say.

Wallerbee said, "Call the doctor. Get *all of them* over here."

"No, no," Pink said. He had spoken, repeating one slurred word. He noticed Gloria's smile as she looked down at him, tenderly, lovingly. "Salty," Pink told her, tasting her tears, smiling at her, knowing he was smiling, seeing it reflected in her own face.

"Bless him," she said fondly.

"Dizzy spell," he told Wallerbee, who was on his knees, grasping one of Pink's hands. "I tell you . . ." he couldn't complete the sentence; he was locked off from knowing how to speak.

"You lie there till the doctor comes," Wallerbee told him.

Gloria nudged his face deeper into her bosom, squeezed more tightly. "I never held you before, Mr. Wright."

"Don't let it . . . be the last," he said, the words flowing automatically. A dozen others in the office laughed, and he heard the words repeated in the next room.

"God has a hammer, Mr. Wright," Gloria told him, "hit you with it, to make you slow down." She swiped tears off her face. "Didn't you know that?" she said. "You work too much, all that traveling in Tennessee. You need to relax more, and play more."

"Thinking about that . . this minute," he said, nudging her breast, and Wallerbee laughed, then they all laughed, and Gloria, who was not the least bit intimidated, held him closer.

"Don't smother him, Gloria," one of the young men said.

Pink was sleepy suddenly, was exhausted beyond any exhaustion he had ever known. Gloria began singing to him; the woman was singing to him, a lullaby in a soprano voice. He woke to see Dr. Watkins pumping up a band around his arm. Pink watched as his blood pressure was taken. "You have any pain in your chest, Pink?" Watkins asked. Watkins said for him not to try to get up. "You tired?" he asked Gloria.

"No, no," she said.

"Best pillows on earth, Pink," Watkins said.

Wallerbee was reciting what he knew about Pink's fall.

"Tell me your name, Pink," Watkins said, speaking slowly.

"Pinkney Wright," Pink told him.

"And what are you called normally?"

Pink returned his stare; the question seemed to worry him, to strain his abilities.

"What nickname have you?" Watkins asked, waiting patiently. "Are you called Pink?"

"My mother . . . says . . . Pinkney."

"Your mother?" Watkins asked. "Where are we, Pinkney?"

The eyes closed, tension showed on the face, and then the voice uttered the word "Monarch."

"Yes. Very well. What town is this, Pink?"

Again the pause, the movement of the lips as if they were seeking for speech, were preparing for it as a track man might consider the height of a difficult hurdle. "Home."

"Exactly so, Pink. Very well. Now will you rest? Please rest. Get blankets. We don't want him to catch pneumonia lying here."

Chair pillows were brought and stacked in helter-skelter patterns about him, but Gloria would not even yet relinquish him. Watkins sat down in Gloria's chair and leaned over Pink's body. "Can you hear me, Pink?"

No reply.

The office force began to disperse, as suggested by Watkins, workers lingering to take a final look at Pink, at Wallerbee, at the doctor, seeking confirmation of hopes. Their own worlds were shaken, along with Pink Wright's. Dr. Watkins took a pill from his pocket and swallowed it, asked for a cup of water. "His wife is not to know just now. She will react rather desperately. His sons—anybody know his sons?"

Hallie's name was mentioned by both Gloria and Wallerbee. "She's due to work here this afternoon," Wallerbee told him. "In about an hour she will be here to file for us. She's in business school the first of every day."

"Can one of his sons—how old are his sons?"

Wallerbee told him: "Frederick is twenty-one, Young is a boy."

"Well, can Frederick take over some of his father's duties here? His father will need to do less work, Mr. Wallerbee."

"I don't think that one can." He noticed that Gloria was listening and shaking her head. He retreated to his office, Watkins followed and they stood near the window and discussed the elder son, who had not done work for the company but was known to be less dependable than the other children. "He doesn't seem to have the knack for . . . for adapting, while his sister is into everything. And last summer he had a problem with the bottle, too. His sister and I found him in Marshall, which is a dangerous town for a drunk. You say the wrong words, and a mountaineer might straighten you out. I received a phone call from the sheriff there saying a Wright was drunk and he was afraid for his health, because he had what the sheriff said was a loud mouth. So I told Hallie, and she and I went to get him."

"How did he get to Marshall in the first place?"

"He didn't know himself. The easiest way would be the train. The west-bound train."

"His father know?"

"Not unless Hallie told him and I think she did not."

"She should have told him," Watkins said, "or you should."

"Well, be that as it may."

"In the field, in the traveling part of Pink's work, who can do it?"

"Not Frederick certainly. I can ask Hallie."

"Traveling, I say," the doctor said. "A woman can't do that."

"She works on the payroll at the moment, files, keeps track of the commissions, salaries, retirement—we have started a retirement scheme. That sort of thing. She's started in a small way. She's the clever one."

"Takes after her father?"

Wallerbee nodded hesitantly, seeking his own orientation to that idea. "I suppose so."

"I've never seen her. Is she likable?"

"Well, I like her," he said. "She doesn't seek to be liked, is reticent, but she does well. You say she is like her father, but I don't think that is quite so."

"I don't know her. I didn't mean—"

"She doesn't have his conciliatory manner, doesn't put people at ease. Pink has never met a person who didn't like him. Even such enemies as have presented themselves, he has avoided or neutralized with that gracious way he has. He can absorb most any awkwardness."

"I've noticed in my office—"

"And Hallie is not the same. I . . . I think myself, I consider her to be a friend, but . . ." He faltered.

"Do you?" Watkins said, watching him thoughtfully. "Well, it will very likely need to be her then."

"Her?" Wallerbee said. "For what, doctor?"

"To help Pink, to help do his work during his . . . this time."

"Oh my," Wallerbee said.

"Or the younger son one."

"No, no," Wallerbee said at once. "He's too young, and his father wants him to go to college. The elder son fired me. This was at Marshall. Fired his sister *as well*. Said if we forced him to come away with us, quit the tavern, we were through at Monarch, he would see to that."

"How could he see to it?"

"I know he cannot at the moment," Wallerbee said.

Pink still lay on the floor in the reception room, the door to the hallway blocked by his feet. He was covered with coats of the office staff. Although

Gloria still held him, she had allowed his weight to rest on some of the pillows.

Hallie arrived at two. She had used a back door and was detained in a clerk's office until Wallerbee told her what had happened. He gave her two pills, sedatives, which Dr. Watkins had left for her, and brought her a glass of water. She was deeply shaken. When she knelt beside her father, she took Gloria's place with him, held his head in her own lap.

Wallerbee knelt before her. "We don't want to tell your mother."

Hallie's tearful eyes stared at him.

"Dr. Watkins said not to tell her at this time."

"Yes, I think so," Hallie said.

Gloria served tea to them. She left a cup for Pink, too, should he awaken and want it.

"Will he recognize me?" Hallie asked Wallerbee.

"I think so."

When he awoke, which was fully an hour later, he did not seem to recognize her. There was perhaps a minute's delay, trying to associate her with Gloria.

"Papa," Hallie whispered to him. "Papa, I love you," she said.

Resting his head back on her lap, suddenly he smiled. "Why, I love you, too, Hallie," he said, speaking clearly.

When Watkins arrived before closing time, he listened to Pink's heartbeat, took his pulse. He asked Pink what day of the week this was. Pink smiled at him. "Ask Gloria," he said. "I never know that."

"Where are you, Pink? Tell me that."

"I'm with two pretty women."

Watkins laughed with relief to find him joking once more. "Which pretty woman has you now, Pink?"

"My daughter."

"Which daughter, Pink?"

"My only daughter," he said. "All I'll ever need."

"Very well, let's see how you look standing up, Pink."

Several office people had crowded into the doorway. Gloria and Hallie both took hold of his arms, preparing to help him rise, but Watkins said no, to leave him alone, let him do it. Pink sat up, accustomed himself to having an audience. "I always get up slowly," he told them. He took hold of the corner of Gloria's desk and stood.

"You'll be all right, Pink," Watkins told him. "Go on home and have supper."

A cheer went up, a heart-warming sound in that low-ceilinged room. A cheer went up in the next room too, and the other rooms, all the workers

began laughing, relief arriving, overcoming the miserable fears of the afternoon. Pink accepted Gloria's help in putting on his coat. Hallie put her
own scarf around his neck, asked about the company car. "Where is the
company car?"

"I want us to walk down Lexington Avenue," Pink told her. At the door
he held out his hand to the doctor, then winked at Wallerbee; finally his
gaze came to rest on Gloria, and he held out his hand to her and she came
to him at once and he kissed her.

He was pressed now even more than before. He wrote his brother
Wurth, asking if he might for reasons of health sell his land to somebody
other than a family member. Wurth wrote back, offering to buy it himself.
His offer was less than half what the land was worth. Pink wrote his
brother Harry at his last known address, in California, and his sister in
Arkansas, and reported the experience. His sister replied that she wished
she had land to sell at Vancetown, that the little bit her dowry amounted
to was spent years ago. She said to please come to see her soon, that her
children were grown and still living close enough to come together to see
their Uncle Pink.

Wurth wrote again, reminding Pink that the charge of the father had
been to keep the estate together in the family, and Pink could not sell the
land except to a family member.

Angrily Pink replied, told Wurth that the fathers had not meant to leave
power in one brother's hands to rob another brother.

Traveling together, Hallie driving, they stayed at inns in mountain
towns and crossroad villages, which at dark closed up completely, every
shop, every road, every door. Sometimes in winter they were the only
guests at an inn, the two of them constant companions, mulling over their
work in daylight, mulling over their lives of an evening, sitting in wintery
lobbies, the hearth burning wood into colors and smoke, or sitting on summer porches, tourists peering at them from big black rockers lined up along
the banisters, jobbers watching them, usually Southerners from the outlands who were flung here by adventures and could talk at boring length
about the strangeness of these highlands and their people.

"Well, it's all over now, Hallie," Pink told her one evening. The cool
breeze was just now beginning to stir the green leaves on the oak trees.
"I'm not showing any signs of ever having had a stroke."

She sat down beside him in the porch swing, nudged his shoulder with
her chin affectionately.

"I thought this afternoon, I said, Look here, Pink, you are limiting your-self, even walk slowly. Why do you act like an invalid, when there is nothing wrong with you?"

"Exactly, papa," she said brightly, but with lingering sadness in her voice.

"Your mother knows by now, I think," Pink said to her. "Knows about the stroke. She must have heard. Nettie King knows, and Nettie is as secretive as a cricket."

"You are funny, papa."

"But Amanda won't admit the stroke to me, won't dare mention it."

"She knows, I agree," Hallie said. "She has become even more critical of the company. She blames the company."

"She blames you for being in the company, too."

"For traveling with you."

"For traveling with me, while she doesn't, she can't. Your mother's world is smaller than her mother's world," he said. "Think of that."

"What say?" Hallie murmured, a breath, scarcely more, so frightened was she that she would scare away the revelation. "My Lord, papa," she whispered, awed. "Do you think so?"

"You will need to watch the fences and walls, yourself, Hallie. There are a multitude of them for women. She's fenced by babies and her fear of having them, fenced by Young needing her, everybody depending on her, fenced by my illness, almost immobilized. Now, you learn from her, best you can. I'm sorry," he said suddenly, "to be so serious. The other day I said I need to get away, to go, Hallie, to find more joy. I sense that more and more."

She turned on him. "Go?"

"I said last week to Wallerbee that I ought to go."

"Go where?"

His arm shivered under her hand. With mild bitterness, he asked, "If my life is ending, what—what have I done to test it out, show it off, find it? I'm weary of what I am, Hallie."

This was so surprising an idea she gasped. "Everybody loves you."

"I can't leave the company completely, of course. A blacksmith can't bind a man with iron more securely than I have bound myself to the com-pany. When Harry went West, he shook off all shackles. By now he has seen the country, most all of it. He wrote me, said America is eight na-tions. I recall the Pacific coast was one. The old South was one. New York City was one. An outpost of Europe, he called it. New England he had not seen, but he thought he would go there one day, and in any event that was one. Then there was the body of America, its belly and maybe its heart, which I think he divided into three countries. The Rocky Mountains were one, I recall. Chicago was capital of something, and maybe—I don't know where he put Texas, whether in the South or not."

"What about here, papa?"

"Where?"

"This place. The mountains."

"Oh, I imagine Harry forgot about them."

For the first time in his life Pink began to seek out men of the church and to read books about religion. He asked the bishop of his church diocese, a white-haired, white-bearded gentleman named Burns, if God was punishing him.

"Don't know that God is involved," Burns told him. "Why would God want to involve himself in a man's illness? He's not a sadist. Did you ask God to be involved, Pink?"

"No, I certainly did not."

"Then, why do you think he volunteered?"

Pink went away, considering that. Another occasion, he sought the bishop out. "Has he all power, does he?" Pink asked.

"Oh, no," Burns told him.

"What can't he do?"

"Cook breakfast with a snowball."

Pink said, "I understand God knows even when a sparrow falls."

"A pretty notion. Poetic. One of my favorites."

"Could God keep it from falling?"

"If God were a hawk." Burns smiled.

Pink told the minister with his entire body he hungered for relief from the life threat that was suffocating him. "It grows worse every day."

"You are in trouble, we must face that, but God will not save you, anymore than he saved John Crews last year, or the Phelps girl, or Jesus on the cross. See God in his strength. Thank God. He will embrace you in time. You will be his, Pink Wright. You will be his, but God will not be yours."

His own pastor was more comforting, less oratorical and dramatic, but he was doddery and soft-willed and too anxious to please. Pink sought out other churches. One Sunday he even crept into the back pews of the Roman Catholic church. On this first visit, he wept, moved by the poetry, the music of choir and organ embracing him, the vibrancy of the human voice penetrating into his mind. He couldn't understand the meaning, but he sensed man's greatness and, at the same time, his vulnerabilities, the agelessness of man and each man's quite temporary tenancy. Afterward, however, his meeting with one of the priests was unsatisfying. The priest was preoccupied, having just now completed mass, and the brightness and heat of the day, here on the stone steps of the cathedral—a new memorial built by rich tourists who had settled here recently—the brightness seemed to startle and annoy him. He needs a stained-glass window, Pink thought, to stand between him and the sun. The priest's accent was northern, clipped; his mouth was busy with words and breath. His dismissal of Pink was unmindful, perfunctory; Pink was another mountaineer aspiring to loftier religious services, who later would bring the usual questions about a more personal relationship with God.

The religious service that afforded him most pleasure was the Sunday-night hymn service held at the Episcopal church. He and Young would slip into a rear pew, and he would allow the music to wash over him. He would pray there unashamedly, although he never knelt or performed other rites of subservence. He sought God—as he told Young, he was awaiting the love of God, "which is what we'll all do in death, Young." So he told the boy, merely a thought that came to mind. "I don't seek it," he told him, confiding in him. "I await it." Walking home from church, he told Young one night, "It's going it alone, that is the meanest part of the scheme, don't you see? If it were not for going alone, leaving you, all of you, I could accept it more . . . rationally, for indeed it is necessary. It's being asked to do it alone . . ."

"What, papa?" Young asked him.

"Dying," he said.

By contrast, on Saturday evening, often as not he was at the movie house glowing in the shine and brusqueness of the vaudeville, usually alone, sitting in a seat near the front, marveling at the exploitation of life and love and all matters dear. Those were the two most prized ceremonies of his week: the vaudeville and the Sunday-night hymn service.

Amanda reflected on her life as it changed, just as seasons change a field or wood. *My father in winter*, she thought, the idea pleasing her. In winter the house was his skin, his place for living. Here in the city, a man had other places as important as home. Pink had. Even Hallie had, at business school and the company, and had made other retreats for herself, one at the library. Let's see, she thought, this house is mine exclusively. I am bound here. At noon the family will come visit for an hour. Today for noontime dinner I could start a joint of pork, a pone of bread, a head of cabbage, a fruit pie—might have enough to justify the family returning home, to come visiting for an hour apiece, except for Young, who is required to stay at school until three.

When the children had finally gone off on their own, what would the house be like, she wondered. What shadows would it contain, what lack of voices, what emptiness would further chide its chairs and frames? Sometimes, when she thought of this, her breath would come strange, in puffs and starts, as if anger were burning itself, and she would turn away from her tortures and soothe herself with homemade thoughts.

Sew. She began yet another dress for Hallie, another shirt for Frederick. She must stay busy. She worked on the sewing and fixed noontime dinner. The family arrived in fits and starts, Pink and Hallie and Frederick overlapping. They ate and once more left. How many times does a family leave in a lifetime? she wondered. She worked that afternoon on a quilt, something she would give to the church sale. Soon Young would be home from school; she would follow him about the house, trying to stir up a decision about when they could together spade the garden. He would be busy getting his things to go play baseball. Off he would go, laughing, pleased with himself. Never disappointing or disappointed. Like his father. Pink was always pleased with himself and everybody was pleased with Pink. At least, that had been so before the attack and his moroseness.

Young off playing ball. Hallie at the company this afternoon. Pink at the company today, then tomorrow he and Hallie would travel to another town. Poor, lonely, handsome Frederick. Did he still see the Starnes girl? The house creaked and groaned as it settled into its hours of inactivity, its screen door being its most active tongue: Not like my house was, not like my father's house was, she thought.

She put pine on the fire. Let it burn more brightly, the better to keep her company. If I had not killed the baby, she thought, he would be two years four months old.

Only into her early forties and she was already listening to what might have been, living with the dear departed, counting up the number of times the rockers of the chairs struck the wood floors. She was not old enough yet to cover her knees with a throw rug and sleep in daytime. There was bound to be something more to life than recalling it, and more than criticizing the loved ones as they passed through the house, more than wishing for the body of an unborn.

She wrote a letter to her mother: "Wondering how you are getting on these days, mama. You remember how we all worked together, grew up in one another's lives. It was later each one went out to form her own family. At home we always had the land, the stock, the nights of talking, the common calls to answer together. Well, mama, I get so lonely, lonely, lonely, here in town. . . ."

Hold on to Young. That was one hope she had. Young was conscious of it, maybe resentful. In the mountain family the youngest son traditionally belonged to the mother, as she realized, as he knew, and he was supposed to serve a career she approved. With only two sons, her claim on the youngest was fragile at best, but she did hope to exercise it. She sometimes mentioned preaching as a lifetime career for Young, from time to time engaging him in the weighty consideration, should God be willing. Of course, God being willing carried an awesome pressure on the boy. Amanda wasn't certain just what that meant, either.

Young read the Bible through twice. He tried to imagine himself standing in a pulpit leading his flock. He sought such a call, but took no joy in the search, preferring to see himself in the armor of business or war, or moving even deeper into his dear mathematics. He worried about finding a way to tell his mother, but the subject arose only obliquely, with never a challenge being given, always touched with the notion that God would reveal the decision in time.

That spring Billy Sunday's cousin moved into town, and at once he was sought after by families, invited to dinner much as if he were a famous evangelist himself, rather than a coal dealer. His opinion was sought on social issues, on all manner of squabbles and faults, and it could be said that he reaped richly, eating at different tables, interrupting his supping to deliver brief opinions. Amanda invited him to Sunday dinner three times before the busy man could accept. He arrived at her house in a Ford coupe, which he parked on her front lawn under a tree to keep it cool. He moved directly to the dining room, dispensing with amenities, giving Hallie a little pat on her rump, which surprised and confused her, left her gasping in the hallway. He sat down in what usually was Pink's chair, and he began serving his plate even while Pink was saying the blessing.

Amanda, standing in the kitchen doorway, both hands wrapped in her apron as if they were small animals seeking warmth, finally took courage, told the royal person that her own son sitting beside him was awaiting his call to the ministry. The visitor paused, his fork poised near his mouth; his little eyes sought out the boy's face and seemed, as Young testified later to Hallie, to pierce right through him like God Almighty, to study his soul. Young waited. The entire family waited for the guest to chew and swallow, and then he spoke to the mother. "I would prefer for him to be a Christian layman, as I am myself, rather than a preacher, since we have a surplus of preachers."

It was done. It was God's decision. It was all freedom for Young. He had been delivered, set free. He had been given the authority to be himself. He had been cut by this stranger from his mother's apron string. He was not required by God to preach a thousand original sermons before hundreds of thousands of people. Praise you, sweet Jesus, he thought, as he gazed before him across the new promised land of his life.

Fourteen

At twenty-one, three years overdue, Frederick left home in order to go off to Davidson College. This was pretty much Pink's doing, his effort to move him out where he could prove himself. Before he left, Hallie gloried in the promises of being without him. She would have wagered her fortune—which she figured to be about a hundred dollars—that she would enjoy having him gone, but she missed him almost as much as did Amanda, and fretted aloud at not having him nearby to scold. She even told her father she missed Frederick, and that amused him.

"Miss him, you say?" Pink asked casually, considering the matter as if it were a ripe peach in his hand. "How's that?"

"I do, I'm lonely for somebody stupid around the house."

"Hush," he said mildly. "Sisters are supposed to be considerate."

"I'll try."

"Motherly, feminine, caring."

"Like cats."

"No, that's feline. A cat has claws and scratches its mate; a feminine person is soft and embracing."

"Oh, my," Hallie said, and pretended to fan herself with an imaginary fan, as if the heat of the discussion were affecting her.

"I suppose there are women like cats, but I wouldn't care to have one."

"Mama never scratched you?" Hallie turned her rocker around to face him.

He coughed, shrugged off the question. "He is doing what he ought to be doing, going to college. What maybe you ought to do, as well."

"Sweet Briar," she said disparagingly, making a face. "With all the other finishing schoolers." They had often talked about colleges, and she had maintained the women's colleges were too precious, were suffocating with social dances and parties and riding horses in rings, too remote and artificial for her to believe they would suit her, now that she was turning into a businesswoman in spite of her mother's preferences in the matter, and for that matter, her older brother's. Frederick was intensely jealous of her working at the company, as she realized.

Only a week after he left, Frederick appeared once more at the house, set down the two suitcases he had taken with him, and announced he was home to stay. His explanations for this advent were as varied as the time of day at which he spoke. For one, he had found the other boys juvenile.

"Well, he is older," Pink conceded. "He's a year or two older than some, and that shows up on a boy. . . . "

Hallie was aghast. "Why did they kick you out?" she demanded of him.

He said they required swimming, and he found pool water made his eyes red. They put chlorine in the water, he explained. He said they assigned him to a dormitory away off, the farthest from his classes.

"You couldn't stay away from mama," Hallie told him.

Whatever the reason, there he was at the end of the Davidson College rope, once more defeated. The latest challenge had hurled him upward and forward only to smack him down. He realized he must soon shake off his tendency to fail; he must grasp confidence, somehow grasp it, wherever it was. Or whatever it was. He was handsome enough. He knew that. He wore clothes well. Women liked him. His mother loved him. He could work miracles with women. As yet, however, the magic combination had not clicked into place for his success.

Hallie made much of his new failure. She never slackened her attack. "He got drunk," she declared, speaking to her coffee cup, which she nursed in her two hands, speaking loud enough for her mother to hear her in the kitchen. "He got drunk and they threw him out." The water was turned off in the kitchen. There was a long silence, somewhat ominous, Hallie realized. "I miss you, mama," she said, mimicking him.

Amanda's shadow fell on the dining-room floor.

There was a pause, a reckoning. "Boo hoo," Hallie said, imitating a weeping boy.

Amanda sank down in the chair opposite, considered Hallie. "What did happen, Hallie?" she asked. "Was it that he was too old?"

The sincerity of the question caught Hallie off guard. "I don't know. I think he slipped about on the walks."

For four days Frederick stayed close to the house. When he did venture to the store, he was welcomed by the King brothers, but of course he had to explain why he was home so soon. "Got a job offer," he told them. "Couldn't turn it down." The job was at Clove Enterprises, he explained, and he listed some of their holdings: the Clove Park Inn, the demolition of the Battery Park Hotel, the development of the Clove Park section of the city with its golf course and the Country Club, along with several smaller inns and subdivisions.

The story took hold. It was the best story to use, he decided. One day he wrote Dr. Clove a letter, expressing interest in the writer's job that Clove was advertising. He mentioned that he had recently returned from Davidson College. His training and ambition positioned him for a writing career, he reported, something more adventuresome than his own father's insurance company. He dispatched the letter from the post office on a Monday morning, expecting an answer soon, but it was that very afternoon a car came for him. Dr. Clove's driver drove him to the Clove Park Inn for dinner with Clove himself and a young woman applying for the same assignment.

Frederick felt himself being lifted, being lifted out of himself, being carried off by the lord of local builders. And that night at dinner Clove presented him with the challenge, along with wine and broiled steak. The salary was a pittance, to Frederick's embarrassment, but the work was exciting. For instance, he and the girl were to write a romantic novel about the mountains, and were to weave into this romance descriptions of the various Clove enterprises. This novel would be published by Clove and given away to the guests at his inns and hotels, and would be mailed off to prospects for house sales and land investment. To hear Clove tell it, the story could be written in a few weeks. In a state of shock, Frederick sat on the edge of his chair, in the dining room of the fabulous hotel, alongside Henrietta Goble, blond, twenty, beautiful to distraction, she and Frederick soaking up inspiration from the great man. Clove recited from memory stories he had read in the past, any one of which he thought might do well enough for adaptation. The works of Trollope and Dickens were too heavy. "They don't float. What did you say, Henrietta? No, no," he said, "not Melville." He found the idea amusing, coughed into his white handkerchief. "No whales. No whales in Asheville. What shall we title our romance? It is a romance." He peered from Henrietta to Frederick. "What say to *The New Land of the Sky?*"

Frederick, drunk from the flow of Clove's language and his own aspirations, deferred to Henrietta. Beautiful woman, Dutch, her father an executive in the new Dutch rayon company that was locating nearby, which was to hire a thousand workers. Clove said, "What say to *Love in the Sky?* or *Love in the Land of the Sky?*"

"Is it about the hotels, or the subdivisions, or about love?" Henrietta asked him.

"We will use romance to enhance the whole," Clove told her. "Don't you love this hotel?"

Henrietta smiled, peered about at the luxurious dining room. "I don't loooooovvvvveeeeeit," she admitted, "not llloooooovvvvveeeeeit."

"Oh, I looooovvvvveeeeeit," Clove assured her. "Last year Edison sat at table number seven. Henry Ford and his wife have sat at corner table nine. Table twenty-three was given to Sarah Bernhardt when she visited for her sinuses." On he went, reciting experiences by name and table number, bubbling with enthusiasm. Then he talked about the golf courses, the swimming pool, the new tennis courts, all enchantments for the novel. "Make the hero a failure at the start, Frederick, then he meets a beautiful . . . a really beautiful girl, so coy, so untouched, so virginal, on the terrace of that old Battery Park Hotel I tore down, and she steals his heart, and causes him to straighten up his life. . . . " He spun the tale, his hands flashing the air, his diamond rings catching the candlelight, his plump body exuding perfume.

He is a puffball, Frederick decided. He might suffocate himself with smells and ideas. However, Frederick wanted to remember every Clove word. Something to do now with including a dance at the ballroom, with dinner at the Clove Park Inn, with a ride up along the jointly owned Skyland Drive.

Clove had stopped, was staring at him. Frederick blanched, his sense of self-confidence eroding. "What say, Frederick?" Clove asked bluntly.

"I'll take the job," Frederick said.

"And when will you have this first draft done—this story?"

"Oh . . . a week or two."

"And your father, will he appreciate your being employed by me?"

Frederick stared into the little man's eyes, which were suddenly sharp, intense, uncompromising. "Yes, certainly. He doesn't know anything about it yet, but I'm—"

"Will he take interest?"

Frederick cast about desperately, feeling the earth tremble. "Please say more clearly, Dr. Clove, what you mean."

"Will your father invest with us? Listen to me," Clove added, noticing reticence and hesitation, twin enemies. He reached across the table, grasped Frederick's arm with one hand, took hold of Henrietta's arm with the other. "I'm offering you two the chance of a lifetime, to move into the big world here, and I want you to bring your fathers into the big world as well. I want them to be part of what we are doing. You understand? Do you understand?"

She replied first. She said she understood. She and Clove both turned to Frederick, and Clove's hand tightened on his arm. "What say, Wright?" Clove asked him.

"I . . . I will, yes," Frederick said. "He will."

In preparation, Frederick gorged himself on romances taken from Hallie's bookcase. He sat in a hard, straight chair with a pad on the table and used a fountain pen to transcribe the words. Now and again he would write lines of his own, or add words.

Wanda lowered her gaze, her damp lashes closed over her blue eyes. Her cheeks sparkled with tears, like diamonds. "Turner, you have come from the outside world of which I know little, being a mere mountain girl; however, I have feelings much like others and a mind, and I recall your promising to come home from your travels of the world and make me the queen of your life."

"Oh, dear Wanda," he said choking, "child, the young man who said that is gone. He is pleased by your remembering and waiting, but he is not worthy of sacrifice. He has returned, but he is broken like a reed, embittered before his time. You should marry some healthy, happy person and be happy, yourself. As for me—happiness is, like the raven, nevermore."

Wanda's beautiful face became drawn; she could not look at him. The day darkened as the sun set and there were long shadows splashed across the hills.

"Come, Wanda," said Tucker, touching her hand lightly. "Let us abandon sad words and thoughts. We can be children again, have children's faith, can hope that even yet some of our dreams will come true."

As they walked away, the moon peeked out from behind a cloud.

"Perfectly lovely," Dr. Clove told him, seated in the lobby of the Clove

190

Park, the pages fluttering like living birds in his hands, his eyes darting from Frederick to Henrietta. "What's the matter with him, with this fellow?"

"He drinks," Henrietta said. "Doesn't he, Frederick?"

Dr. Clove clucked sympathetically. "Ah, yes."

"And gambles," Frederick added.

"He promised his mother not to," Henrietta said. "However—"

"Life being what it is," Frederick said.

"Ah, yes," Dr. Clove said. "So he feels unworthy, does he?" He clipped off the end of a Havana cigar, set it firmly in his mouth. "I feel the need of tobacco at times of intense creativity," he explained. A porter hurried forward, striking a match. Between puffs of cigar smoke, Clove began to grab for other of the story's tentacles. "As a young man he made promises, did he, to his girl? Do we have the scene written when he and this beautiful child first meet? I mean as children—or whatever they are. Innocents?"

"I've not written it yet," Frederick admitted.

Clove fumbled through the pages. "Do you think you can do it tonight?"

Frederick readjusted his buttocks to the hard chair. "Of course."

"You could do a draft, anyway, so we can choose. That's the trouble with . . . with being unsure, we don't know what we are unsure about. But we do see him drinking, gambling, wasting himself?"

Henrietta looked at Frederick, who looked at the ceiling of the room. "Oh, we will jot that down, as well," he said, speaking as if the life of drunkards and gamblers was a carelessly guarded secret with him.

"Have a scene by the river. You do have a river scene in mind?"

"Well . . . yes," Frederick said. "But at the moment—"

"See him deep in remorse at our new city recreation park, at the lake, with the boats. Be a way to work the boats in. Sixty-four boats."

"I thought . . ." Frederick interrupted, "thought we were working on our own holdings."

"City property belongs to all of us. The new courthouse, the new city hall. I was one who moved the city off the plate. Got it going. Parks. Playgrounds. Largest recreation park in eastern America, at least for any city this size. Lions, tigers—three tigers. Too many monkeys. An elephant. Now then, what brings the two together?"

"The monkeys?" Henrietta suggested.

"What is the pivot on which the plot turns, Frederick?"

Frederick stared at him, nonplused.

"They do get together, don't they?"

"At the recreation park?" Henrietta inquired.

"Could he not forget her? You know, there's a world of truth in that.

I've seen women I simply could not forget. Their eyes, the tilt of the nose, their pretty fannies—their shape. Do we describe Clara anywhere?"

Henrietta, blushing, shook her head.

Clove jotted notes at the upper right-hand corner of the first page: describe Clara and Turner; get a pivot for the plot; recreation park; work in dance hall in old Battery Park Hotel.

"'Love's not Time's fool, though rosy lips and cheeks' . . .What's the rest of that, Henrietta? 'Love's not Time's fool.'"

"And cheeks?" she asked.

"I think so. 'Beneath Time's—Lord knows what that line is. Another place, 'Love is not love which alters, when it alteration finds/ Or bends with the remover to remove.'" He repeated the words a number of times, until Henrietta had them written down.

"What does it mean?" she asked.

Clove told her, "It comes to mind, to this man Turner's mind. He can't forget the burning eyes, the happy cheeks, the haunting vision of that lovely face. Of Clara's face."

Frederick also was writing notes now.

"He could see her as clearly as though it were this morning at the Langren Hotel."

Frederick looked up, stung. "You own that?"

"I have money in it," Clove explained. "Describe the restaurant. Inexpensive when compared to this one, or to the Country Club for that matter. He can see her in his mind as he looks over the menu."

"The Country Club, too?" Frederick asked.

"He confesses his love. 'Love is not love which alters when it alteration finds.' He is a man of the world and she a simple mountain lass, but he can't forget her eyes, her lips pouting, her breasts—her bosom, whatever it's called. Be careful there, but do let us suggest that he is in love. 'Love's measured not by Time's brief days and weeks,/ But bears it out e'en to the edge of doom.' What's the rest of that passage, Henrietta? Did you get that down? Put it in that he can't stop this devilish infatuation with gambling and drinking, but will try if she will take him, that is, take him on, so to speak, let him have a go."

"Marry her?" Henrietta asked.

Clove hesitated. "He is to marry her, yes."

Henrietta nodded, smiled. "Because of love?" she asked.

"Yes," Clove said absently. "Must buy a lot, have a home built. Kenilworth, Biltmore Forest, Kimberly section of Clove Park. Might drive into St. Dunstan's Circle on the off chance, don't you know," he said to Frederick, "and they see those three lots I have there. And they can come upon St. Dunstan's Lodge, you see, duck in there for supper, discuss the menu.

And maybe it's Clara who recites that beautiful poem my own wife loves so much. Write it down, Henrietta. Have you lost your pencil? The poem goes: 'Oh, I'll build on a knoll by a rippling rill/ Near a copse where the wood birds trill/ Where the Judas and dogwood bend their tints'—that's tints, t . . . i . . . n . . . t . . . s, Henrietta, not t . . . e . . . n . . . t . . . s—'With the green and the rest of the hill/ In the cool twilight of the summer night/ My sense shall be at ease.' . . . And so on and so on, however it goes, Henrietta. Get it from my wife."

He called to them from the doorway of the hotel. "Grovemont, the new one, out beyond Beaucatcher tunnel, I have seventeen lots there. Got it, Henrietta?"

"Yes, yes," she called back, allowing a mere tinge of exasperation to show through.

"Roads are to be paved," he called. "Sewers are going in."

Hallie tried to discover what it was Frederick was working on. A book, somebody had told her, your brother is writing a book. Well, she knew Frederick couldn't write a book. "It's all he can do to read a book," she had confided to her co-workers. She and they had completed the Monarch salesman-by-salesman listings for the past month, and had found which salesman was first, second, third in the company, all the way down to sixty-seventh, information for the new monthly publication Hallie was putting together.

"There's a blond Dutch woman writing it with him," the informant said.

In that case it was the Dutch woman who was writing it, Hallie decided. Why didn't Frederick come to her with his problems? she asked herself. She had sometimes meant to write a book and now felt spite for him, who couldn't write a book but was writing one. When Frederick had gone to work for Clove, she had forecast he would be found out to be an empty balloon. However, he still went off to work whistling each morning, came back late at night, wore new suits and neckties, drove around in a car, now and then Dr. Clove's own Cadillac, exuded an air of prosperity. And it was also true he often was accompanied by a beautiful blonde, who was, Hallie assumed, Dr. Clove's idea of contemporary office furniture. She had read about such arrangements in *Love Story Magazine*. Some of Clove's workers were not given more work to do than stuff envelopes, or sort them in piles labeled Florida, California, Nevada. . . . "Frederick, are you writing a book?" she asked him at supper one night.

He laid his napkin down, started to reply, hesitated. He considered his father's attentiveness, glanced toward his mother at the doorway waiting for the reply. "Yes," he said.

193

"My Lord," Hallie whispered. "About what, for instance?"

"It's a . . . love story. I don't want you to read it yet, Hallie. It's not for you."

"When are you going to bring it for me to see?" Amanda asked, flushed with excitement.

"Oh—when it's finished," Frederick said.

"Perhaps we could help you," Amanda said. "Hallie has read enough books to be able to write, goodness knows—"

"No, no, no, I have help enough," Frederick said. "I am doing it at the office. Each day I give it a lick and a promise, then go on to other matters, selling lots or deciding about road rights."

"I should have known you would be a writer," Amanda said, sinking into a chair at the table. "You look like a writer, doesn't he, Pink?"

"Now, it isn't the greatest thing ever written," Frederick admitted.

"I shouldn't think so," Hallie said.

"Is it a full-sized book?" Pink asked, his brow furrowed with curiosity. "I never can keep up with what my children are up to, can you, Amanda?"

"No, I never know."

"Is it a full book?" Young asked, helping his father.

"Why, it's as much a book as anything is," Frederick assured them. "It was almost two hundred fifty pages long when I last noticed the size of it."

Hallie gasped. She began to whisper to herself, a mannerism she had developed at the office, an overflow of ideas and concerns too heated and numerous to submit to an expressible order.

Pink said, "In my house we always had two books, the Bible and Shakespeare, and then a selection of other books, that came and went. I remember we had a Byron around for a while, till Harry traded it for a shoat. Then we had four volumes of Edgar Allan Poe. That fellow will scare the pants off you. Then we had Hawthorne. Was part of a set. We had volume six. Papa bought it off of an Episcopal priest going west to save the Indians. He said he sold a volume about every forty-five miles—I think that was what he claimed, said he thought he could go farther on a Hawthorne set than any other writer." He began to laugh, and Hallie laughed.

"Had the Sears Roebuck catalogue, papa," she reminded him.

"No, not back then. I saw the first one in my life here in town. Hugh had it hid at his store. He would turn the pages, complaining about the items in it, said it was bound to destroy him. He burned it one evening when nobody else was about, took him an hour, and I asked him if he had ever burned another book, and he said that he had burned a Hubbard book he found, one about Jesus not being born of a virgin."

"Jesus wasn't born of a virgin? Who said that?" Frederick asked indignantly.

194

"Anyway Hugh burned it and the Sears catalogue."

"The Bible says she was a virgin," Frederick said.

"Whenever you have two books and there's a disagreement between them, Hugh burns one of them," Pink explained, a grin coming on his face. "He has no time for controversy."

"I thought you liked Hugh," Amanda said.

Pink's smile slowly crumpled and he nodded. He tilted his head to one side, considering her, considering the question she had raised. "More'n a peck of apples."

"Cruel," Amanda whispered, the word merely escaping from her. "Pink, that's cruel. You never said that before," she whispered. "Well . . . " She cast about helplessly, looking finally to Hallie. "He never criticizes. Pink, you never criticize anybody."

Pink shrugged, a quaint smile on his face. "What did I say?"

"Are you changing, Pink?" she asked him.

"I don't know why not," Pink said. "Everything else is." He shrugged, turned his attention to Hallie, then to Young, finally to Frederick. "You writing about mountain people, Frederick?"

"It's about Asheville," he said.

"About Lexington Avenue?"

"No, it's about the new things, papa."

"About me?" he asked, watching him.

Frederick hesitated, suddenly laughed, then helplessly looked to his mother. "Yes, Dr. Clove wants you in it. He wants the company in it, somehow." Then he added, "I'll put you in there, papa," he promised.

"Somehow. Somewhere," Pink said, watching him.

There was a long silence, while Frederick worried about his father's attitude. "I will, papa," he said.

Pink said, "Put me and a trapper in there. Put a farmer in there, while we still have some."

"A romance?" Hallie said to Frederick. "A love story?"

He coughed, embarrassed. "Yes."

"Maybe that's where our sainted virgin mother will turn up again," Pink said, rising from the table.

He moved away toward the front porch, the evening paper in hand, leaving Amanda to fret over the remark, to ask her children what on earth he had meant.

"So much he says, so much he says I don't understand," she admitted to them, "since he began to worry about his health."

Fifteen

Pink decided he didn't want to be buried in the country, near his parents. His illness had given him a sense of death impending, and he was irritated with his parents, blaming them for his place in a world turned biting and unfriendly, chiding them for the nips and bites being taken out of him, body and soul, every day.

He made an appointment to look at family plots at Riverside Cemetery, situated above the river, and less fortunately above the tannery and the livestock market and the recently begun automobile junkyard. Amanda, Hallie, and Frederick agreed to accompany him. Young, evasive from the first invitation, refused finally. The cemetery had big trees, maple and oak and hickory. There's too much shade on the ground, Pink commented to

Mr. Mosely, the lot salesman who was escorting them. Frederick had brought Henrietta; she had not met them before, and it was one of the many wonders in Pink's mind that Frederick had decided that this occasion would be appropriate.

"No, we don't want to be low on the hill," Amanda told Mr. Mosely. "I don't want people lying above me, do you, Pink?"

"Don't you now?" Mr. Mosely said with a twist of a frown. "Somebody has to."

"And I want something on the level," Amanda told him. She took Pink's hand, held to him as if he might go loping off through the trees to hide himself.

"See the sunlight fall through those oaks, mama," Hallie said, "like cathedral light. Just in there—"

"Those are the Johnson lots," Mosely told her.

"At the curve of the drive then," Hallie said, pointing to another cathedral-lighted place.

"The Walters are to go there."

"Then up above the curve of the drive?" Hallie asked.

"The Gardners, the Blalocks, Colonel Cox . . ."

"So we need to be low down here somewhere, do we?" Pink asked.

"The newer part," Mr. Mosely said. "Though, my goodness, it's all old enough."

"But we've left the big trees, Mr. Mosely," Amanda said.

"Those young roots will be inside the coffin soon enough," Pink said. Mosely drew his coat closer about himself.

"What say to that place at the rock wall, Amanda?" Pink asked her.

"It's pretty," she admitted. "It's like a calendar picture."

"The Pritchards are buried there," Mr. Mosely told them.

They walked the twisty walk together, stopping now and then where a prospect offered a view of the river or of the mountains. They paused to watch a train pass below, the cars crossing a bridge, chugging off behind riverbank trees. "I wouldn't mind being able to see the train," Pink said to Mosely.

Amanda said, "Will those little trees grow up and block the view, Mr. Mosely?"

"We try to keep them trimmed back," Mr. Mosely said.

"But is all that trimming in the perpetual-care deed?"

"No, it's current policy. We don't actually own those trees. The city owns them, but the city doesn't care about them, don't you see?"

"But in a hundred years?" Amanda said.

"Of course, I don't know," Mosely admitted. "I won't be here."

"No, but I will be here," Pink said. "I will be here, just there." He crouched down to see what view he might have from a gravesite on this certain spot. Hallie crouched beside him. They could see the river well enough, could see the train and the train bridge, could even see the new West Asheville car bridge with its burden of heavy traffic.

"But, Mr. Wright, you can move about," Mr. Mosely assured him. "You can walk about, one place to another."

"Are they—walking about?" Hallie asked, shivering, looking around.

"What?" Mosely turned. "I—I think so. On a warm day, sunny, like this one, I think so."

Hallie fastened the top buttons of her coat. "Well, mama, I don't care," she declared suddenly.

"Now, don't rush me," Amanda told her, pacing the distance along the bottom border of Pink's plot, estimating how many graves could be put side by side. "But there's no place for everybody," she said.

Mr. Mosely cleared his throat. "Perhaps a daughter or son will have his own family, Mrs. Wright."

"But if one doesn't?"

"Hallie shows no signs of marrying," Frederick interjected. "Could bury Young with his knees pulled up against his chest," he said. "Make a ball in one corner."

"I want a place big enough for all my children, and for Pink and me," Amanda told Mosely, speaking rather wistfully.

"Five places." He looked down at a card in his hand. "I don't have a plot for five."

Amanda turned away, walked to a farther plot, where she paused to consider the view, the lay of the land. "Two plots then, Mr. Mosely, for six graves."

"Six?" Pink said, speaking to her across the intervening plots.

"If a sixth should be needed," she replied.

"Is it to be needed? Do you know . . . do you have any signs?" he persisted.

"Pink," she said, "we are preparing for what might be."

He sat down on a rock wall, folded his hands, let them dangle between his legs. Hallie came to sit beside him, took one of his hands in hers, patted it. Amanda was upset, was hurt, one could see that by the way she paced off the borders of the plot, moved past Frederick and Henrietta without so much as a glance. "I don't care where I go," Hallie said to Pink.

"Except you want to be able to see the trains," he told her.

"Here my family is trooping about looking for graves."

Amanda said, "Mr. Mosely, you can try to be of more help? How much more are two lots?"

"Different prices," he said. "These two here, side by side, or those two there, top to bottom, are a hundred dollars different, in part because of that rock formation, which presents a problem for one grave to fit in."

"A hundred dollars' difference?" Amanda asked. "Very well."

"The up-and-down lots have an azalea bush. You see it? Well, not all honeysuckle bushes bloom when transplanted, but that one looks the prettiest you ever saw."

"What color is it?"

"A yellow flame. Then if you follow me . . . You see that lot up there has an extra two feet at the top. That affords more head room, that is, more room for the stones, the markers."

"The top lot might seep onto the bottom one, Mr. Mosely," Amanda cautioned.

He paused. After a while he shrugged most patiently. "A family matter. If you owned both . . ."

"Even so," Amanda said, one hand touching her face. "Pink, please be of help."

He roused himself, came stumbling along the lower walk to stand obediently near her. "Honeysuckle bushes are worth a dollar at the most," he told Mosely.

"But they don't usually bloom, Mr. Wright."

"This one can stop blooming," he reminded him.

"It's bloomed for four years in a row. That much is a certainty."

"And the stone wall, does it go with our plots?" Pink asked.

"Oh, yes. Twelve feet of wall goes with the two plots."

"Then buy those two, Amanda, and let's get out of here. Look now, Amanda, we can sit on the wall of an evening, when the rocks are warm, and let the river breeze cool us. What do you say to these two?"

She hesitated. She agreed. She said no, there were others to see. She held Pink's hand now, Hallie for a while giving him up to her, Hallie taking her place to one side.

"Did you put Riverside Cemetery in your book, young lady?" Pink asked Henrietta.

"No, sir," she said, suddenly trembling. "Dr. Clove said the best lots are all sold."

"Amanda, for God sake, decide." Pink said suddenly, then added petulantly, apologetically, "I don't know why it must be level. It will be level enough, won't it, Henrietta?"

"Yes, sir," Henrietta whispered. She was close to him now, was drawn to him by fear and wonder, as she would be drawn to a comfort long needed, never before found, a father, perhaps that only, a father more likely to please her as a father than one committed to her by blood, by law: a risky father, a capricious father, an ever-changing father, like weather in the higher mountains, sunny just now, soon to be overcast, suddenly squalling with thunder and rain, then clearing brightly. He was smiling again. She stood erect, faced him directly, delivered her assurance to herself about him, told herself he did accept her, or would. "Yes, sir," she repeated.

Hallie was sitting at the library reading *Mountain Cry*, her brother's book, now released on an unsuspecting world. The library had a cloth-back copy. Indeed, it had six such copies, all checked out, except for this one, which was assigned to the reference room. The town was saturated with the paperback edition; they were even being sold in the drugstores. Hallie was annoyed, startled, curious, perplexed. Every page was an assault on her sensitivities. The story switched from romance to salesmanship. Parts of it were outright plagiarism, as well, from books she herself owned; parts of it were taken word for word out of magazines—she could almost quote the stories herself, she had once loved them so much. Here was a compilation, the conglomerate of other people's work with inserted advertisements and her own brother's name on it as author.

"Yes, daughter," the mother said sadly, "I know all that you say, and I hope you did not ruin the happiness of two lives by your rejection."
The girl moved close enough to put her arms around her dear mother's precious neck. "Mama, I trust I will not die of a broken heart." With a smile, she held up to her mother to be kissed the sweetest mouth in all the world.

Hallie gasped. Indignantly she slapped the book closed. Astonishing, simply astonishing how brazenly her brother could maul human emotions. "Do I look like I'm dying of a broken heart?" she moaned, snorting with derision. "Sweetest little mouth in all the world." Time after time she opened the offending pages, tears of exasperation in her eyes.

Wanda was torn asunder, and her frame was shaken with spasms of anguish as she followed Felicia, the maid, into the bedroom where her mother lay dead. Time and again she hurled her own warm body upon the bed and kissed the cold lips of her mother, who had died in the night. Wanda cried: "Mama, do talk to me. Don't leave me. Oh, do speak to your daughter. Come back to me, dear little Mama. I need you, oh, my dear self, open your pretty eyes and say at least goodbye to your little girl." But death heard no appeal—it never does; no cry reached death's ear—nor ever will. Death's hunger knows no repast, and its strong will does not break, nor its silence by right of appeal turn to sound.
With heartfelt sympathy the skilled, trained embalmers of the Kaufman Undertaking Company tenderly bore the mortal remains of

Wanda's mother to their handsome parlors built in 1903 of native granite and limestone by the Charles and Marshall Construction Company.

Hallie shut the book. She stared helplessly at the reference-desk attendant, Mrs. Woodward, forty feet distant, who was watching her intently. "Oh, my Lord," she groaned. She laughed. It was too much, really; it was an incredible mixture of romanticism and commercialism, of rapture and debasement. "Oh, my father . . ." She sat on the book. She hid it from her own view. I will urinate on this book, she thought. I will steal it, all of its copies. I will devote the remainder of my life to eradicating this book. Slowly she looked up. Standing there by the table was Tom Wolfe, home from the university, a sardonic grin plastered on his face, his eyes squinting. He was a wolf in fact, there to eat her alive. "I didn't do it," she said.

Mountain Cry was the talk of the city. It was reviewed in the Asheville newspaper—most favorably, was praised as a work of genius. Beside the review, above the review, and beneath the review were advertisements for various Clove enterprises. It was praised as the first book ever written by an Asheville native.

Locally printed, paid for by Clove Enterprises and, according to a recent admission, "other businesses and industries, the story is filled with the struggle of a gallant young man, native son of the mountains, an alcoholic and gambler, seeking to overcome the sins of the flesh, in order to marry a simple mountain girl."

Hallie would arrive at the office each morning, to find other letters on her desk from people who were reveling in the glories of her brother's *Mountain Cry*. "What a beauty! How wonderful that it has been published!" She would fret over her own feelings, sensing defeat, annoyed that her brother was famous among his own people, was accepted. His horrid book was not a mere success. *Mountain Cry* was a triumph.

CHAPTER Sixteen

Young was invited by a family—father, mother, and four children—to accompany them from Asheville into Ohio, to help move the wife at the change-of-train stations, one in Knoxville and the next in Lexington. She was an invalid who had journeyed down the previous year, having heard about mineral springs in the Malvern Hills and at Hot Springs, and she had taken what cure God would allow, as she had told Young, and she had little hope of a long life. "I'll go home and die there," she told him.

Frederick received the news with an open show of jealousy, Hallie with delight, Pink with astonishment that a woman, who must be moved only twice, would need a full-time attendant and he scarcely big enough to carry her. Amanda saw certain dangers to the trip, as she confided to Pink. "You let him go away alone and you'll be responsible—"

"He's not going alone. He's with six others," Pink told her.

"He's coming back alone."

"Well, I know that."

She told Young that travel was a corroding influence on a person's character. "Where is your Uncle Harry today? What has Harry ever amounted to? And he's had the wide road all his life."

"I'll be but six days gone, mama," Young assured her.

"Sprain yourself, carrying women on and off trains."

"Mama, for goodness sake, let him enjoy the trip," Hallie said.

"Oh, Young is her dear, do you know that, Young? Hallie is going to instruct me now. She does love Young. If Frederick wanted to go to Ohio—"

"I wish he would go to Ohio," Hallie declared. "He'd be afraid of the porters."

Young said he would not go, if that was best for his own family. "They can get somebody else at the hotel," he confided to Hallie. "If it worries mama . . ."

"No, you'll not," Hallie stormed back at him.

Pink sought to escape the argument, but he did show a certain pride in Young's being chosen, and he warmed to the idea of a voyage, as he called it, all the way to Ohio, a place he had never expected to visit in his own life.

The night before Young was to leave, Pink brought him a railroad Hamilton watch, which he slipped into his pocket and advised him not to mention receiving just yet. It was a perfect watch for a long journey like this, he told him.

Young went to bed early, because he must be at the hotel at 6 A.M.; the morning train left at 7:30. He was half asleep buried under pillows, his watch in hand, by the time Amanda came in to say goodnight, and she stood near his bed, told him he went with her blessing, but he was not to poke his head out the windows, even in a station, and he was not to be rude to the porters, that a mark of a civilized man was courtesy. He was not to take tobacco—he was not old enough for tobacco, she assured him. That included snuff, chewing tobacco, cigars, and those trashy cigarettes. He was not to fall into any traps set for him by a woman of leisure, and there were such women at train stations. He was to use only the soap she was providing, and his own towel, which she had rolled up tight as she could. He was not to spend money on fancy postcards; the cheaper cards served as well. Once she had instructed him on such matters, she kissed him, then held his face against hers for a lingering moment, before easing her way out of his room.

Next morning, when he got up at six, expecting to slip out of the house without waking anybody, she was sitting at the dining-room table, coffee steaming in the cup near her hand, Young's breakfast waiting. Young sat down without complaint, said a silent grace, and ate.

Pink's memory for details, once excellent, was partially lost. Hallie noticed that; so did Wallerbee. Her father feigned competence, but his mind was subject to longings and meanderings, disinterest, forgetfulness.

"The company," he told her, "it's very dry. It has no soul to it, like even a dog has. It's merely papers, papers, papers, reports, people buying insurance, then dying."

My dear papa, she thought, you will get better soon.

"You tell me," Pink said to her, casting about for a name, a detail, staring at the splotched front office window, which was catching the midday sun on its pane. "You go on and do it, Hallie."

A human being in pain. Pinkney Wright in pain. Her father intermittently inept. Her father admitting he did not have the report finished, the figures totaled, the message expressed in his orderly way. Her father admitting defeat on his own field, the company territory. She had not really known her father before now. He had never appeared to be vulnerable.

"Your father can be cruel, Hallie," Wallerbee told her at lunch, his voice trembling.

"My father?"

"He can be as cruel as . . . as life is to him, Hallie." He frowned down at the bowl of soup before him. "He is not any longer easy to work with. He is—haven't you noticed?"

"No," she said, lying. She remembered a number of abrupt decisions he had made in the field, cutting off salesmen's complaints and even one manager's abruptly, without his customary diplomacy and sympathy.

"He is a reaper, very tough to talk to about matters he has decided. He is fighting back."

"At what?" Hallie asked, suspecting what he would say.

"Talks about a trip, trying to escape."

"I . . . we're not killing him," she said.

"No, but we are living," he said. "I am living. I am . . . not living well, admittedly. I am living for the company, but I am well."

How are you living, she wondered. Where do you live? He was a handsome man, still single, a bright man but, as he said, desk-tied, emasculated.

"He resents my not dying, although he resents me less than others because—as he told me, Hallie . . ." He halted, closed his eyes tightly, his fists clenched before him.

"Go on, please. Please."

"As he told me, Hallie, because I am already about dead."

The world stopped for her suddenly. There were for her abruptly no waitresses, no curtain on the Langren's window, no noise, no silverware needing wiping, no bowl of cooling vegetable soup before her untouched. Only him. This man. How old was he? She had never before wondered. He had been young, she knew, when her father and he had begun working together. He must be only in his thirties now, or early forties, but she had always thought of him as being dry, brittle, as being lifeless in the way that a machine is lifeless, even though it works well enough. "Pity," she whispered. "I can hear him saying that."

"Whom I . . . I love, Hallie. I love your father. I say that to you honestly. A man is not supposed to love another man. Except . . . " he smiled wryly, "except Jesus."

She said, "Do you ever hate him?"

"I never hate him. I know he is in pain. At the same time I can't— You understand when I say love him, I mean in the highest sense. I don't want to be his person. I mean by that—"

"But do you ever despise him?"

"No," he said, then nodded to her. "I have never loved a woman, Hallie," he said, with the grimness, the twitch, the crumbling pride of a man who strips himself before another person, exposes himself. He sat there shaking his head, as if denying importance to his own revelation. "I shouldn't mention that to you."

"No," she whispered.

"I live at home, my sisters and I, and my father died. He was in constant . . . needed care. He saved money by having my sisters— Oh it doesn't matter," he said irritably. "Obviously there was something not alive in me, even then."

"I forgive you," she said, and smiled. "Shall we stop talking?"

"My sisters aren't married. My family is not oriented to marriage. We live for each other."

"And you live for them?"

He considered that for a long moment. "The company," he said, "and you." He waited, gazing at her intently, holding her eyes with his own.

"Oh, my God," she whispered.

He ate in silence. She noticed the bob of his adam's apple as he drank tea. Entranced, she watched him. Slowly she reached across the table and touched his hand, merely laid her fingers on his fingers, the first time she had ever touched him in her life.

Pink mentioned traveling out West, said he would take a trip, he thought, and Amanda became upset. "It's strange, Pink. It's simply strange that at your age . . ." She had tolerated his trips to places in the mountains and of late with Hallie to Charlotte and Gastonia—trips away from home that sometimes lasted two or three nights. Her objections met with his inscrutable gaze, the one he reserved for matters he tolerated, inwardly endured. There had been many such matters recently. Of course, his illness worried him, she realized, and worried her, as well; it was a disruption, a warning from God.

Was it that Pink wanted now to walk through his life alone? She needed to know the answer to that. She had asked him about this one night, a Saturday night; she recalled the day because there had been a relaxed quality. That evening she and Pink had even taken a leisurely walk along the neighborhood streets after supper. Later he had sat on the porch in one of the big rockers, talking about his boyhood, sipping the whiskey. Hallie was inside, in the sitting room, reading and listening to the radio—she never seemed to go out with people her own age, even on a Saturday night. And where was Frederick? Away in his company car, courting his girlfriend. Amanda sat down in the swing near Pink's big chair and took a moment to set the pillows comfortably at her sides and back. "Coming to church with me tomorrow?"

"Can a baby eat while it sleeps?" Pink asked, giving the question the relaxed, casual attitude of the evening.

"He might sleep the night through, except for one feeding," she told him.

"Does he wake up for it?"

"He has to wake up for it, Pink, in order to eat."

"I think he could suck his supper while asleep. Not much work to it, is there?"

"No," she admitted.

"Saw Frederick drive by while ago. Had Clove's Cadillac. They tell me Clove sells a lot a day, or a lot option."

"I know what a lot is—"

"An option? Well, it's part of the fever. Say I buy an option to purchase four lots from Frederick, put down four hundred dollars for a month, so that within the month I can either buy the lots or sell the option—maybe to you, Amanda, for a thousand dollars, having a nice six-hundred-dollar profit. Then you sell it to Mrs. Wolfe for twelve hundred, making two hundred dollars' profit, and she sells it to a tourist for two thousand and he buys the actual lots."

"Sounds like gambling to me."

"Well, it is. Mrs. Wolfe bought six options in one month, made a profit on each, never bought any of the land. Says she has to send Thomas to Harvard. Hatch bought a six-month option on ten thousand acres, sold his option for fifty thousand dollars' profit and never even saw the land, not even a tree or shrub on it, nor knew just where it was. Sold it to Clove.

206

Frederick got a hold of part of that. There are fifty people in this town right now buying and selling bits of paper. They buy and sell on the telephone. You buy for ten thousand, sell for fifteen to a Wilson, who has in tow a New Yorker who will buy for seventeen. Men stand in the train station waiting to snag the tourists and then sell them our birthright."

"You left your birthright, Pink."

He nodded. He cleared his throat and nodded again. "I've done pretty well here, Amanda."

"Nettie says Hugh is jealous of you."

"I imagine."

"I know Frederick is selling lots, showing rich tourists around. He'll be selling tomorrow, on a Sunday, Pink, which I don't think is proper."

"No, of course not," he murmured. "God will get him if he doesn't watch out."

"Now, what say?" she asked. His frequent references to God usually bordered on the sacrilegious, but were not clear enough for her to get their meaning.

"God polices Sundays, has to keep the oxen out of the ditches," he said, the devilish grin on his face once more. "Has to see that there's milk in the mother's breasts, so the babies can wake up to feed. Has to keep the saloons closed down, stores closed. Has chores to do. Has to tend to the blossoms on your father's apple trees, or he'll be without applejack enough for his evenings; he has to fill all those fifty-five gallon kegs to quench his thirst."

"You can leave my father out of this, Pink," she said simply.

"Out of what?"

"Out of your—whatever it is. Devilment."

"Has to open the blossoms, see that they are properly dusted with male pollen. That's a full-time job, even though it's seasonal. God is a seasonal, busy fellow, a migrant worker, always has his hand into something. Has to squeeze the water out of the ground, to make the springs. Water is the blood of the ground."

"It's not blood, Pink," she said.

"Squeeze the earth, weight it down with rocks, mountains."

"They have rivers everywhere, and there are not mountains everywhere."

"You can hear them crying out sometimes," he said. "I can." Just what he meant she had no idea. It was like sitting on the porch with a stranger. Her father could be cruel at times, but at least one knew what her father was being cruel about. Pink, however, had gone to sneaking through ideas like a fox through brush, now and then stopping to listen, to look about, then to make his comment before darting on, only to stop again, turn, twist about as if looking for secrets. "I wish you wouldn't talk about God," she said, "and go to that priest, whoever he is. A Roman priest is spooky to me, always has been."

"He is remote, I think," Pink agreed. "I've not found help there."

"You're not going to be a Catholic, are you?"

"I'm going to become a duster of pollen."

A car passed and its sound faded out far down the street, sound carrying a long way tonight, just as thoughts did. He exhaled deeply, wearily. "It's a bigger room, a greater space they have, and it takes more sound to fill it. I like that. I like to sit here and listen to individual sounds, don't you?"

"Oh my, Pink, what is . . . the matter?" She had hesitated to refer to his illness directly, but there it was, her own admission of worrying about it.

"Big sounds echo. They tell me that at the seashore is where the worst of the crying is. You can hear the crying left there by emptying rivers. You think so?"

"I do not know, Pink," she said, trying to close her mind against his thoughts. She simply could not endure crumpling before his weaknesses.

"Can a man stand at the seashore and listen to the mountains moan in their bellies?"

"I wouldn't think so. Pink, I wonder if you'd care if I take in tourists this summer."

"Swishhhhhhhh, the waves go. Swishhhhh, with long pauses between. Can you hear the wind pressing on the rocks, and the rocks squeezing the blood out of the ground, so that it flows—"

"I could put 'Religious People Only' on the tourist-home sign."

"Swishhhhhhh, in pain."

"Pink, I wish you would talk about the tourists with me."

"Heavy weight on the ocean bottom, all that water. A quart of water weighs two pounds. Of course, even if it weighed but one pound, all that water—"

"Frederick wants to leave," she said, the idea still so foreign to her that she scarcely could utter it aloud. "Wants his own rooms, he told me. I told him he had a place here, that he wasn't to go off to himself until he had somebody to care for him. I don't find him in the way."

He was watching her, his face somber, eyes dull, absorbing sight rather than judging it, as if the sight later would be put with others and form a judgment about her. "Leave?"

"There's a room with its own bath and entrance two blocks north of here—"

"Why, he's . . . he's not able to care for himself. A woman has to take care of a man, Amanda."

"I do. I do and will continue, if he'll let me."

"He'll let you."

208

"A woman has the need to care for her children anyway. Except Hallie doesn't seem to have many needs as a woman, which is the reason for her strangeness, Pink."

"Maybe you can find somebody to put in her room, for her to take care of, Amanda. Some tourist. Charge him five dollars a night. Pick a little one, so she can bathe him and feed him, until he gets able to drive a car and sell lots to the Floridians and New Yorkers."

"Pink, I don't think you're being fair when you talk like that."

"Mountain people have to sell corn for ten cents a bushel, if they can find a buyer. The basket is worth that. While these tourists can light their cigars with dollar bills while they while away their nights listening to dance music in half a dozen ballrooms."

"Don't be angry, Pink."

"Buy our land, a thousand acres here, a thousand there, take the best land for fifty cents, a dollar an acre. Don't mean to use the fields for anything, or the barns or the sheds or the springs or cribs or stock. They're buying views. Now, you old people can stay in that cabin and keep your chickens and your garden, keep your cows and your pigs, because you are part of the scenery. Now, old man, can you stand next to that haystack and let me take a picture? Would you put a strand of hay in your mouth? Would you mind? Thank you. Would you, old lady, move closer to him? Could you tilt your bonnet back so the sunlight touches your face?"

"Pink, what are you talking about?"

"That's perfect, thank you. I'll send this to my friends in the North, let them see what we've bought here, and maybe they'll come visit. Do you think my son in Florida could buy the next farm?"

"Pink, are you talking to me?"

Silence, from him, quiet, except for the sound of the rockers, the creaking of the swing.

A while later she said, "It's too cool really, for porch waiting." What am I waiting for? she wondered. For him to be better, she thought, for the bitterness to pass on. "You can't stop change, Pink," she said. She wrapped a blanket close about his legs. He did nothing to assist her, said nothing about the tourist rooms. "I don't want you to make a trip, Pink. I can't be alone, you know that. I need to have somebody with me."

"I'll not be gone long, Amanda."

"It's just a dream anyway."

"What is a dream?"

"The West. I've never known it to be so."

He turned in the chair to stare at her again, impressed with her comment. His old, ingratiating smile came on his face.

"Harry caught it. He left me, and where is he? Even Harry's no longer real, is he, Pink?"

"He left you, Amanda?"

"Well, he left us all."

"He never left me."

"Oh, yes he did. Left your mother, too."

"We all did that. God knows, a man has to do that. Even Frederick."

"And he disappeared, except in memory. I remember Harry, that's all."

"Yes, I remember him, too. I thought I would try to look him up."

"Where?"

"I don't know. He wrote me once from a hotel in California."

"You might as well go looking for a tune."

"I think Wurth hears from him every Christmastime."

"Anybody can send a message at Christmastime. It doesn't mean they're real."

"What does it mean then?" he asked. "It has to mean he's out there. He has to put the stamp on the envelope."

"Somebody could do that for him."

"But he has to be there, Amanda, or why would it be sent?"

"There's strangeness to it, that's all I mean. It's not real flesh and bones, is it? I mean, you can't say Harry is alive."

"Well, I do say Harry is alive, and I want to see him."

"You won't find him," she said. The excitement of the argument fluttered in her mind, a bird seeking escape. "Please don't throw yourself away, Pink."

"All right, Amanda," he murmured.

"Not one man in four who leave for the West ever come back. It lures you, like those dark sirens on the rocks, with the ships breaking up."

"Sirens are blond-headed, Amanda."

"I don't recall. Fish bodies on the lower half, where you'd think a sailor would want a real woman to be."

He chuckled, nodded. "I agree."

"I dare say there's never been one that's complete."

"Another dream," he said. "Like the West."

"And the mountains bleeding," she added. The creaking of the swing accompanied her thoughts, which were more relaxed and kindly now that he was paying attention, and seemed even to agree. "Then you won't go, Pink?" she asked.

"No," he said. "There's nothing out there, anyway."

"Well, you can take my word for it." Contentedly she swung back and forth, back and forth. "Harry, even if he was out there, would have changed so much. Oh, I suppose somebody is there, but it's not the Harry we knew."

"And is it this other person who sends Wurth the Christmas cards, and asks him how he is, not caring, really?"

"I imagine so."

"And does Harry II send Harry I a Christmas card, or does he pick out somebody who's real to send it to?"

"Pink," she said, "you won't go out there, will you? Promise me."

"No, I won't go," he said.

She had asked him again, because she wanted to make sure, but even when he promised twice not to go she realized she wasn't certain of it. He spoke in the manner of a man who was being playful, and in that mood he said what a woman wanted to hear. Pink never had felt bound by playful promises. He spoke as if the decision were a game, that was all, as if it might change, once the weather changed. No, not that it might, but that it would, that it would surely change, was merely a sparkling piece of glass dangling from a string. Ah, Pink, please don't for God's sake go away from me, and don't, living here with me, live apart from me, Pink. "Frederick sold two lots yesterday."

"Like shooting deer in a deer park."

"I think it's grand that he's successful."

"Still works in company with that Dutchwoman, does he?"

"Inseparable, Hallie told me."

"They come out mostly in the first warm weather."

"Who?"

"Dutchwomen with the tulips. Are you hungry, Amanda?"

Hungry, she thought to herself, yes, hungry, starving. "No," she said. Help me, please, Pink, she thought.

"We might walk up the street to Clarence's," he said, and she nodded, but he didn't make a move.

She had more time on her hands than she could assign. She was one of the more active churchwomen, who made quilts and sold them for charity. Some of her friends now played bridge, and she said yes, she would get into that, and went to several bridge parties, but the cards were not important to her, were paper with royalty on them, far removed from spasms or coughing or feeding or loving of another person. Often she went by to visit Nettie, who even at her age, late forties, had recently given birth to a little boy, and Amanda was beside herself with envy. Her fingers were in pain from clenching.

One lovely evening, Pink away on the road with Hallie, Frederick gone out, Young in bed, she drank two jelly glasses full of brandy; in a haze, gaining courage enough, she pricked holes in the ends of several of Pink's rubber condom things.

Then one evening it was over. Pink left home. She had girded herself for him to leave of a morning, and each day at noon when she found out he was not gone, she relaxed for that day. He surprised her, left in the afternoon, with a note sent by one of the Perry boys.

Dear Amanda,

I will be able to ride along the river, where the railroad tracks are near the water. I can eat my dinner as I watch the sun set into the water of the river. The journey is merely a man growing older, holding out his hand; and he doesn't know what help he needs.

I'll drink a nip of liquor tonight, once the sun is down, and think loving thoughts of you, my dear self. Did you know last night when I took you in my arms that I was going away?

Pink

Hallie was invited to the emergency meeting Wallerbee called. She was told to come to the hardware store to take notes. She was seated beside the rolltop desk, that's where Hatch wanted her, where she could not even see his face unless she leaned forward in her chair. She leaned forward now, sought his expression, as dust filtered down through the light from the dirty window above his head; his glasses needed cleaning, she noticed. One finger scratched at the corner of his right eye; the fingernail needs cleaning, she thought. Maybe the eyes do, too. "Yes. Well . . . he said, his voice trailing off into the dust, vanishing brokenly. He coughed, cleared his throat, and turned toward Wallerbee. "Advance on salary," he said, "the money he took with him? Can we term it that?"

"No, I think the family will need the salary coming in."

"Salary for what labor?"

"I don't know yet," Wallerbee said, his tone insisting on reasonableness. "We don't know how long Pink is to be gone."

"A month or two, be my guess," Hatch said, continuing to ignore the girl who was tilted toward him.

"Papa took what?" she asked.

"We don't know what," Wallerbee told her. "We only know the amount. Five thousand dollars."

"A dividend, an extra dividend," Hatch said. "What say to that?"

"Five thousand dollars," she whispered. Weakly she sank back into the chair. "Why did he need so much?"

"It can be considered a dividend against future profits," Wallerbee said. "It's unusual, however. He never signed a check on the company before, except small sums for travel. He had the right to sign checks only if they were countersigned."

"The bank cashed it?" Hatch said.

"They say he came to the bank day before yesterday, about noon, and wanted the money in hundred-dollar bills. They knew him and issued it to him."

"Then they are at fault."

"If we make a claim, they will only sue him," Wallerbee said.

"It is my father you're talking about," Hallie reminded them. "He isn't well," she said.

"No, he isn't well," Wallerbee agreed. He ran his finger down along a series of tabs and brought out a two-page report. "He did this report on the recent trip to Boone. It's in poetry."

A mongrel dog, large and gangly, came up the stairs from the basement and sat down on its haunches near Hatch. Indeed, it looks like Hatch's dog ought to look, she thought, an unhurrying scavenger.

"A pity," Hatch said. "Some mind lost, I would guess, wouldn't you? It might return."

"It's playful. Devilishly clever report," Wallerbee said.

"Did he leave because of that?"

"Because of what?" Wallerbee asked. "This report? No."

"This inability to pay attention any longer to what had come to pain him?" Hatch asked.

"That might be," Wallerbee agreed.

Hatch fretted. He tapped his desk top, belched. "The bank should not have cashed the check."

"I told them that. They apologized."

"Apologies don't help," Hatch commented. "Tell them to put it back."

"But they will sue Pink."

"They can't find him. We can't find him."

"They can find his widow." Wallerbee said. "That is, his wife."

"Sue the bank," Hatch said.

"Well, it's your bank," Wallerbee reminded him.

"Yes, it is part mine."

Wallerbee nodded. "I can't do that to him, Hatch."

"Well, then, what do you propose? We have auditors; don't they arrive this month?"

"He knew they would. It's devilish, you understand."

"We can't even declare a dividend without his vote," Hatch said petulantly. "He put us in a basket and turned it over on us, didn't he?"

"He's ill," Wallerbee said, frowning at Hallie, shaking his head briefly in sudden sympathy. "I wanted you to know, Hallie, but not your mother."

"Nor Frederick," she said at once.

"No, nor Frederick."

"Nor Young, either," she said. "He idealizes papa so."

"I give Pink to reach St. Louis at the most," Hatch said. "They tell me that's the jumping-off place. Where you can turn back or decide to go on, and it's not everybody goes on. He'll find he needs clean clothes, can't figure out how to get them. How many clothes did he take?" Hatch peered around the edge of the desk at Hallie. "How many suitcases?"

"Most of his clothes are gone, except his shoes."

"How many shirts does he own in all?"

"Nine," she said.

"How do you know that?" Hatch asked, smiling suddenly.

"I've counted them," she said. "Usually I pack for his trips. He has nine perfect shirts, and he took six, wore one."

"Then he'll run out in a week, won't he? I mean, he has to have eight to go a week, won't he, Miss Wright?"

"Yes, he will, but he doesn't know that."

"No, he never thought. Takes eight to do a week, one to wear on washing day. So he'll run into problems soon enough. We could send a man after him, Wallerbee. Is that what he wants?"

"I don't know that sending a man after him would help at all. I was thinking of Hallie here. . . ."

A long while the two men sat there silently considering that. Finally Hatch said, "If he had wanted Hallie he'd a taken her, wouldn't he?" Then he said, "Might get neither back."

"I . . . I think . . ." Wallerbee sat there frowning worriedly at Hallie. "There is a punitive nature to him. He wants to punish himself. And I . . . I think he's jealous of Hallie."

Hatch grunted. He leaned forward, peered at Hallie, a quaint, friendly smile on his face. "What say to that, Miss Wright?"

"I never thought of such a thing."

Hatch lifted the Boone report off Wallerbee's knee, read it word for word, then returned it to its resting place.

"That won't do, will it? Can't use reports such as that in business. Who will do the traveling now?"

"That new man, Perkins."

"Send the girl with him."

"No," Wallerbee said at once. "No, Hallie can't travel with him."

Hatch leaned far forward, peered at her again. "You afraid of him?"

"No," Hallie said.

"I . . . it won't do," Wallerbee said at once.

"You afraid of that young man?" Hatch asked her again. He sat back in his chair, chuckling to himself. "No, she can't find her father, and even if she did he'd reject her help. And you won't let her travel with a new man. So what else do you mean to do?"

Wallerbee laid the papers aside, perched his body on the edge of his chair. "I mean to keep her in the office, give her a desk, put her in charge—make her my assistant."

"I see," Hatch said, watching him.

"Is that why she can't travel with the new man?"

"What?" Wallerbee asked.

"That you like her? That you want her in your office?"

Wallerbee stared at him. "Yes." He sat back in his chair, stared blankly at Hallie.

"Oh, yes, law yes," Hatch said at once, apparently pleased. "Travel for a woman is troublesome. Can't lie down if they get the cramps, don't have a toilet nearby. I know. My wife and I journeyed to Wrightsville Beach— Have you been there yet, Miss Wright?"

"No, sir."

"Leave your car in a shed, take a ferry over. Island, you know. Well, sir, my wife never saw a cotten field nor a tobacco field nor a shanty house nor nothing all the way down there, except for wondering when the next filling station would appear and whether it had a clean restroom."

"I understand," Wallerbee said, embarrassed, glancing at Hallie. "I thought I would put Hallie in the office."

"In your office. Yes, you said that. Next to you."

"Next to me," Wallerbee said unflinchingly. "And I'll try this new man on the road alone, and if he doesn't do, I'll fire him."

"She going to sit in her papa's big chair, is that the plan?"

"No, I'll put a desk in there."

"Pink'll object, when he sees it. He's jealous of her abilities, you tell me."

"Yes, now that she must help him, even correct him, he is."

Hallie sat there listening to them discuss her. Discuss their plans for her, the older man hid from sight. Mr. Wallerbee gamely tried to present in businesslike fashion an administrative change that the older man believed to be personal. "With Frederick a twit, maybe she's the one, all right," Hatch said suddenly. "Somebody in the family has to represent the stock. You mean to get your hand on that, I suppose, Wallerbee." A wry smile appeared. He leaned forward, gazed directly at Hallie, twitched his nose playfully. "You have charms you didn't even know about," he said.

She sank away from him, her thoughts twirling. She noticed Wallerbee redden, heard him angrily snort a reprimand. "We should be businesslike, Hatch."

"Business is what I'm thinking about," Hatch said, knitting his fingers. "Biggest business in the world."

"I am thinking of the company, and of what is possible. You cannot put the girl on the road, like a soldier."

"A woman . . ." Hatch began, then hesitated. He paused. "A son. Pink's been waiting for his younger one to come of age, has he?"

"Yes, we know about that, Hatch." He glanced uneasily at Hallie.

"He's using the daughter to fill in with."

Hallie's blood ran cold. The idea had not once occurred to her, but she recognized truth in it.

"You know that?" Hatch asked her, peering around the edge of his desk, his eagle eyes glistening at her.

Wallerbee intervened. "We all know he prefers Young to Frederick."

"Is waiting for Young to take over and has been using you to hold the place open—"

Hallie spit in Hatch's face. The dabs of spittle glistened on his forehead. Slowly he removed it, wiped it off with his sleeve. Resting back in his chair, his birdlike eyes peered briefly at Wallerbee. "Businesslike, would you agree?"

"Jesus," Wallerbee murmured. "I'm sorry, Hatch."

"Executive material there." Hatch was contented, satisfied, so he seemed to Hallie, who was stymied by her own bold rude act. She could not take hold again, even to apologize.

"Not . . . won't happen again," Wallerbee assured Hatch.

"No, of course not," Hatch said, mildly amused by the consternation showing itself. "Now, as to the five thousand dollars, Wallerbee, we can't simply sweep that under the rug, you know."

"I'll put it back myself."

"Will you?" Hatch said, surprised. He added, "Even that is not legal."

"An error, I'll say it was an error on Pink's part, and he's gone out West, no forwarding address as yet."

"You have five thousand dollars?"

"Yes, of course."

"How much money do you have, Wallerbee? Could you loan Miss Wright and me a few hundred?"

"Be serious now."

"Rich man, I imagine." He leaned forward in order to look at her. "Miss Wright, you grab onto him while you can. Why, he's a fine businessman. Without him . . . without him the company would stay in disarray."

Wallerbee, embarrassed by praise on this subject, uttered a rejection.

"He has a way with figures." That struck Hatch as being funny, and he laughed into his hands.

Wallerbee showed his warring confusion once he and Hallie had left the hardware store. He flung himself down the street, dragging her into the Woolworth's to the luncheon counter, where he ordered two cups of coffee, drank his down before even stirring it to coolness. "Damn that man. He is cold in his blood. I have no doubt it runs at something less than ice temperature. But for God sake don't spit on him again, Hallie."

Hallie laughed, illogically, mockingly escaping.

"I do care about you, want you to succeed, want you to help me and your father. But God knows, Hallie . . ."

Postcards did arrive at home from Pink, one from Denver, from the
Brown Palace Hotel there. "I never knew they named palaces after colors,"
Amanda commented to Frederick. He had come by the house to see her, as
he did every day; his tiny apartment was just down the street, about eight
houses distant, and he took his lunches with her on Saturdays and Sundays, assuming he was free from Dr. Clove. "Never a return address," she
told him, "except a hotel, some hotel he always says he's leaving tomorrow."

"No, he doesn't want to be found yet," Frederick told her.

"He can't be alone."

"Why can't he be alone, mama?" he asked her, curious about why she
had come to believe that.

"A man doesn't stay alone, Frederick."

"You . . . you think he's with a woman, mama?"

"I think so," she said, simply. "It's driving me crazy."

He shrugged. "I don't think so. I wonder if I ought to go look for him."

"Look where?"

"Well, Denver."

"Before Denver it was Arizona, Phoenix. Before that it was Missouri,
that funny-named hotel."

"Yes, the Muehlebach."

"What sort of hotel do you think that is?"

"I don't know. A proper one."

"He's not met up with Harry yet, for Harry agreed . . . your Uncle
Wurth wrote him. Did I tell you?"

"Often."

"Does it bore you, Frederick, when I repeat things to you when I'm
desperate?"

"No, of course not, mama."

"You remember Hallie at that revival meeting, Frederick? She has the
same gleam in her eyes."

"I remember her going down the aisle. Went three or four times."

"I don't think so. Went twice. She goes to work with the same glint. It's
a sin to make a religion of business."

"Yes," he said agreeably, as was his manner when faced with criticism of
Hallie.

"Mama, I asked the preacher where papa is, and he says he was going to
Portland."

"Don't believe it," she advised him, "don't believe anything Pink tells
that preacher, Frederick. They've had several arguments."

"Yes, ma'am," he whispered, watching her.

"What is your Dutch girl like? Is she a Christian?"

"She is, yes. I want you to know her better, mama."

"Oh, I don't want to know anybody else. I'm tired of knowing people. You find a nice girl from home, somebody who wants a family. And I want you to find a suitor for your sister, too. There, you have two assignments."

"Henrietta wants a family, I'm sure."

"The company is ruining Hallie's life. I told your father to separate her from the work before it's too late."

"Henrietta was made for childbearing, with those wide hips . . ."

"What wide hips?" She looked up suddenly. "What did you say, Frederick?"

"Well . . ." He stared helplessly at her. "Is there something wrong in that?"

"I suppose you are well acquainted with those hips, are you?"

He was astonished at her. "No, I don't know anybody's hips well, even my own. Hips are not—"

"I see her riding about all the time, sitting in that car."

"Well, we are a team. It's Dr. Clove's idea—"

"Going back and forth to your new room on her hips. A young woman who will visit inside a man's house—"

"She doesn't visit."

"She sits in the car?"

"No, mama, she sits on the porch."

"If I had gone into a man's room or onto his porch, I would have expected to be treated accordingly by him."

"Treated accordingly?" he asked, searching her face for meaning.

"And by everybody else as well."

"How would that be, mama?"

"Why, he would have taken me, wouldn't he? I mean, he would assume he could. It would be an open challenge to him. No need to marry me, for him or anybody to marry me. I would be common enough property, let me tell you."

"Mama, are you saying the man would be obliged to attack you?"

"To take me, wouldn't he?"

"In a storm, if you needed shelter, if you came to a house where a man lived—"

"I'm not talking about a storm."

"Mama, I don't think men need to attack women."

"No, but if this Dutch girl of yours comes prancing in with her big hips and puts them down in a rocking chair in your new room—"

He began to laugh.

"Then whatever you do— Now, what are you laughing at?"

"Mama, she's a virgin, mama."

"How do you know?"

He retreated within himself, mulling over a suitable reply.

"I prefer a girl I can understand," she said. "A girl from home. Aren't there girls from home?"

"Mama," Frederick said, feeling close to her just now, knowing how to ingratiate himself with her, "Mama, what will happen to the company with papa gone? Do you trust Mr. Wallerbee?"

She stopped the rocker, considered that; she took up her sewing and plopped it on her lap. "Your father does."

"Dr. Clove wants the company to invest in his properties. Did I tell you? Dr. Clove went to Wallerbee last week, then to Hatch Cole. You trust Hatch, mama?"

"Your father said he was honest."

"You don't trust him, do you?"

"I don't know . . . that I need to trust him. I never see him."

Frederick nodded. "Dr. Clove needs to borrow money and is willing to pay seven percent interest on it."

"Why, that's enough, I'd say. If papa could get six percent, he'd take it ever' time.

"But Wallerbee won't let him have the money," Frederick told her. He was leaning close to her now. "I work for Dr. Clove, and he doesn't like it when papa's company turns him down."

"I suppose he can go to the bank," Amanda suggested warily.

Frederick nodded. "He's borrowed already from them. They help him out. Just now he needs more than he wants to borrow from the banks, mama. He says Asheville is ready to expand again."

"Well, Hugh King says there's a big depression ahead."

"No, business is booming, especially here in Asheville. We're on a rising tide, Dr. Clove says."

"I don't see how business can prosper if farmers can't afford to live. When that happens—"

"Mama, believe me, I have nothing to do with all that. We aren't in farming. We buy land and develop it. Dr. Clove says I can come into his company, own a part."

"How big a part?" Amanda asked sharply. She was alert, well aware of the importance of this. "Frederick?"

"Five percent this year, four percent next, three more percent the third year, to make ten."

"And the Dutch girl?"

"No, no. This is between Dr. Clove and me."

"You have to get him money from your father's company?" She was scrutinizing him carefully. "Do you?"

"I don't have to. It's what he wants me to do."

"I thought you and the Dutch girl were partners."

"Only—only in some work. Not this, mama. Her father has invested in Clove Enterprises already. That is, he bought lots, and he told her to sell them for him at a profit, but Dr. Clove said to sell her father's last. My father's company has done nothing to help me."

"No. I see that," Amanda said. "When your father comes back, you must talk with him about it."

"Mama, papa might not come back this entire year. Now, do something for me yourself."

"Do? Me? I don't know what to do."

"A note to Wallerbee, saying you think it would be wise to give me support. A few words. Like this note, mama," he said, taking a typewritten note from his coat pocket and unfolding it for her.

Word for word she read it while he held it before her. Slowly she shook her head. "Not now, Frederick. No, I'm not in business," she told him. "Did you ask Hallie?"

He shouted out in frustration. "I did not ask Hallie a damn thing."

"Don't shout, Frederick."

"I am the nearest to nothing in this family, you know that? I'm not even in our own company. Not a cent do I get from it. I am a success, mama. Nobody thought Frederick would amount to anything, but I sell houses, I sell land, I design subdivisions, Dr. Clove and I are already climbing Sunset Mountain with paved roads, sewer lines, water pipes, right up the mountainside, and it takes nerve to invest that much money, takes confidence in what you're doing, and what do you say to me about it? You tell me to ask Hallie."

"Hush, please, Frederick." She put the sewing aside and went into the house.

He shouted after her from the hallway, anguished. When he left, he slammed the front door and walked stiffly to his car, furious with her. He sat there for several minutes before returning to the house and sliding the typed note under the front door.

When Wallerbee received the note, he turned it over and over in his hands, considering the typing. He knew Amanda didn't have a typewriter at home and wouldn't have expressed herself in businesslike phrases, nor thought to refer to Clove Enterprises as "our own native real-estate company." He studied the signature, decided it must be Amanda's. In any event he distrusted the entire matter, realizing perfectly well that it was manipulated by Clove. The manipulator had found a nerve; he had pierced the Achilles heel of the company.

Clove telephoned. He needed $140,000 now. He would pay seven percent interest, securing the loan with lots on Sunset Mountain, or with the golf course in Clove Park.

220

Wallerbee talked with Hatch about it. "It will be well to buy off Amanda this way, make a single loan, get that much clear."

"I thought the daughter was the one we work with," Hatch said.

"Her brother is knifing his way in. Hallie doesn't even know."

"Well, which one of them will win, the daughter or the older son?"

"Once Pink comes back . . ."

"I want to know where the power is, Wallerbee. We are talking business. Now, you like this girl, I realize, and you led me to believe she . . ."

"I'm talking business, too."

"Who has the votes, should it come to a vote?"

"Nobody has the vote just now."

Hatch waved all that aside. "I thought the girl was voting for her father, that Pink would agree to that, the family would, that she was the family representative. And here you come with the grown son and the mother. It appears nobody even asked the daughter."

"Make one terminal loan," Wallerbee said. "One loan and be done."

"Golf course." Hatch shook his head in wonder. "He's already offered that golf course as security to every bank in town."

"Make one loan. We can afford to do so," Wallerbee reminded him. "And it is seven percent."

"Make him sign it personally, as well as his company. He's desperate, is he? I wonder if Pink's grown son will sign it, too."

The idea struck Wallerbee as peculiar. "The boy has nothing, Hatch."

"His father has this company, fifty percent of it. Have the boy sign it, too."

"Don't tell Hallie," Wallerbee said. "Don't tell the girl."

"Well, she'll have to know about the loan," Hatch said, "if she's working with us."

"About her brother signing. I don't like that part of it, Hatch."

"I like that the best of all," Hatch said. "I want to put locks on that boy."

"It complicates our relationship with the auditors, in that the son of the principal owner is getting a loan."

"No, he isn't getting anything. He's only signing himself away on the line, at risk, for another man's company."

"But is it fair to have him do so?"

"Clove will advise him to sign, of course."

"But the boy has so little to gain, Hatch."

Hatch smiled briefly. "He's learning. You leave the boy to me. You have the girl, Wallerbee."

"I . . . I don't have the girl, no."

"You have the girl. Leave the boy to me. Don't give him a damn cent unless he signs, too."

Harry phoned Amanda from Portland. His voice had the same timbre and tones as when he was young, and at once she was anxious about him, wanted desperately to see him. "I've been waiting to hear how Pink is."

"He's well, Amanda. We visited for a few days, talked about mama, about papa's death, wondered if Wurth could survive his own schemes."

"Harry, where is he? Where are you?"

"Portland, Oregon. Pink was here until last night. He must have left in the night. This morning when I went by the hotel, they told me he had checked out at seven A.M. and had taken a taxi to the train station."

"Oh, my God, is he gone again?"

"He made me promise not to phone you, but I think he knew I have divided loyalties. I've never forgotten you, Amanda."

"Harry, can you find him?" Was Pink standing next to the telephone, at Harry's elbow? she wondered. "Don't lie to me, Harry. I need to talk to him. I'm desperate."

"Amanda, he's not here."

"Find him. I want to see him. Our wedding anniversary is in two weeks' time, so tell him he's to be back by then, never fail."

"I'll try to find him," Harry promised, his voice fading in and out. "Can you hear me, Amanda?"

"I can barely hear you. You find him."

"He told me he loves you," the fading voice called.

"What did you say?" she asked, having heard well enough, but wanting to hear the words once again.

"Love you," Harry said.

Harry phoned three nights later. Pink had telephoned him from San Francisco. Harry had tried to give him Amanda's message "but the cable must have been twisted, and for a while I couldn't hear him." Harry's own voice was now more static than clear. He called out his telephone number so Amanda could phone him later, but she took down only five numbers, which later Young said was not enough.

The conversations with Harry were repeated to each member of the family, even to Nettie and Hugh, and Hallie told Mr. Wallerbee and others at the company that Pink was well. She reported to her mother that the company's business continued in a steady rise, had gained six percent over performance as recently as four months ago, when Pink left, "which will please him, I know."

Mr. Wallerbee and Hatch Green decided Hallie might sit in for her father at meetings. However, privately, without her knowing, in the sixth month after Pink's leaving, they authorized a second small loan to Clove Enterprises, at Amanda's request.

CHAPTER

Seventeen

A manda dressed for dinner on her anniversary, just before the three out-of-
house guests were to arrive: Mr. Wallerbee, Frederick, and the Dutch girl,
Henrietta. She put on a silk slip, then the white wedding dress. Before
leaving the bedroom, she turned back the bed and fluffed the pillows on
her side, then on Pink's. She put his slippers in place, and his silk robe,
even though she had never known him to bother with it. Tonight he
would return. Please God, let him return.

At six precisely she turned the pieces of chicken over in the two iron
skillets, put covers on them, and pushed the skillets to the least-hot lids of
the stove. She had boiled potatoes and carrots. She had biscuits ready to

bake, so she had enough. Pink would eat mostly chicken, each piece fried crisp in its flour-and-buttermilk coat.

The front door slammed. Pink, she thought, dear Pink, and she ran into the hallway. It was Frederick. Only Frederick, sniffing the odors from the cooking. He was stopping by on his way home, that was all. "A fire in the dining room, want me to build a fire?" he said to her.

"We have enough heat in here," she told him, then reconsidered. "Yes, do a fire. Your papa loves a wood fire so."

"Mama," he said, hesitating to approach the matter, "even if he doesn't . . . come home tonight, mama . . ."

She stared at him, desperate to examine any shred of doubt. "I haven't seen him as yet," she admitted.

"We love you, in any event," he said.

Earlier in the week Pink had taken the train to Chicago, and had meant to take a train from there to St. Louis and go home the route he had traveled originally, a year or so earlier, but he had detoured to Detroit instead, having met a car manufacturer on the train. He had watched cars being manufactured in the Ford factory, then had taken the train to Washington, arriving just before dawn. As he came out of the station he saw the capitol dome nearby, the topmost ball—that only—gleaming in the dawn sun.

He checked his bags and walked along the dark streets, his heels clicking on the concrete of the sidewalk, his coat buttoned to protect him from the wetness of this unborn morning, this slippery creature trying to emerge from the dark womb. Directly, he stood beneath the domed building, its graceful arms extending to either side. He entered through a side door, found the rotunda, where Negro cleaning ladies were moving about the statues carrying buckets of water and mops and thick cloths. One woman was washing the hands of the statues. "How often do you do that?" Pink asked her.

"Oh, once in a blue moon," she said, laughing.

"Which one is he?"

"Madison," she told him. "He's my pretty one."

"What did he do, what's he best known for?" Pink asked her.

"Not another thing but being President. Ain't that enough?"

Pink said, "Does he have to stand?"

"All the time," she said.

Through the clerestory windows of the dome, high up, the dawn light was playing across the flowery designs.

When he left, about eight o'clock, the guards stared at him perplexedly, and one asked a few questions about how he had come to be inside. At the station, he sought out the next train for the deeper South, spent most of his remaining cache of money on a pullman seat. At the start he had been anxious to see it all, to absorb America, but now he was eager to be done with that, to rest from the sights and memories. He had seen enough for a while. One couldn't ever see it all.

At dusk, the train began to climb upward out of Old Fort. Home was almost within his grasp, and he began to worry about not having more gifts. He had a ruby brooch he had bought for Amanda in California, he had a Mexican comb he could give Hallie, but it had cost him so little he hesitated to consider it suitable. He had two leather belts he could give his sons. A man in Nevada had made them, and had cut and pressed into them the history of Jesus, so that Bethlehem was at the flap end of the belt and the crucifixion was at the buckle. The maker had explained carefully that he had intended the scenes to be recorded in just this way, so that the cross would be protected. He said most anybody could be born in a stable, that he had almost been born in a stable, himself. In between the birth and crucifixion he had various scenes, the selection depending on the girth of the wearer. He allowed the buyer to choose. As options he had Jesus teaching in the temple, Jesus walking on water, which the maker said was the outstanding miracle of all time, Jesus praying in the Garden of Gethsemane. . . . "It looks very much like the desert," Pink told him.

"Yes, that's it," the man told him.

So Pink had gifts, such as they were, but scarcely a showing for a long journey.

At Biltmore he took the streetcar up Biltmore Avenue to the square, sat down on a stone bench near the fountain, and renewed acquaintance with the rows of three- and four-story buildings, his own company among them. He sat on the stone bench, letting the golden streetlights soothe him. He was home. He was reborn, he had stifled his own cries of loneliness, had met friends he could leave behind, had carried on a thousand conversations he could not recall.

He picked up his two bags and made his way across the square to the company, let himself in, turned on all the lights as he went from room to room, reading reports, schedules, telephone messages, going over the monthly sales of the favorite ones of his salesmen, scanning the issues Hallie had published of the company newsletter. Harry Mawden's wife had borne twins. Claybourne Clark had sold more insurance in December than in the previous eleven months. . . . He came finally to his own office, where he considered the changes made, sat down at what appeared to be Hallie's desk, and suddenly over him came a full, overwhelming sense of belonging, so that he could not help but weep. A long way he had gone in order to come back and know he belonged here. Did he believe, had he ever thought he would be able to throw off the mantle of his company? Had he even wanted to?

He left his suitcases in the office, locked the doors, and made his way toward home, stumbling along, heady with thoughts. He cut across the top of Lexington Avenue, not having time to visit that burial place of people left behind by time and circumstance, human sacrifices on a newly fashioned social altar. He walked along Howard Street, which led him past big homes and walled yards, to his own street, to his house, which caused him to smile at its awkwardness. He noticed the cars parked in the driveway: two cars, neither of which he recognized. And from the house itself he heard singing. He sat down on the front step of the walk, there at his sidewalk, and debated just what this might mean. Had Amanda taken in roomers? Was there a party here? Was Hallie courting? Was it for Frederick? He ought to go back to the office, he decided, and spend a few more hours there. He wanted to do so, wanted to escape surprises. He had imagined himself coming home to find Amanda just as she had been, and his children always the same, but at the front lawn he had been assailed by changes.

He started up along the street, walking toward the center of the city, his coat flapping about him—

"Pink."

He stopped. Somebody had said his name, firmly, distinctly, or was his sickness playing tricks on him again? He turned. He was near the oak-darkened lawn of a neighbor. He wanted to pull the darkness back.

"Pink."

No one was there. He scanned the street. Nobody there at all. God calling, he thought, death calling, in this place. He started on, slowly now, in a rambling walk, carefully.

"Pink."

He looked back, saw her then, saw Amanda, with a wave of love and gladness overflowing.

"I kept watching," she said, approaching. "I kept watching for you from the front parlor window."

He ran to her. Holding her was holding himself. It was himself he embraced, it was his full breasts once more against his chest. His hand caressed his own wife's body, his own wife, himself, his hand felt his own waist, his hips, clutched one cheek of his own buttocks, his wife's, in the streetlight there at Madison and Starnes streets, his mind shimmering on the face of hurrying thoughts, moving creatures in currents, torrents, holding her his wife, himself, kissing her, sinking with her in his arms onto the grass of the James McAfee lawn, grappling with her, until suddenly she sat

226

up, drew back, trying to fasten the buttons of her dress, to straighten her hair, while they stared at the lights of a car that had stopped there, its headlights shining on them, blinding him. "Are you all right, ma'am?" called a man from the front seat of the car.

"I'm . . . all right," Amanda replied breathlessly.

"Is he bothering you, ma'am?"

"No, it's all right," she said. Lights went on inside the house behind her. She crawled behind the trunk of a tree, leaned against it and began laughing.

"I'm her husband," Pink called to the driver.

After a long silence, the man said, "Don't expect me to believe that, do you?" He backed up his car. "Is a proper neighborhood," he called to Pink, as the car went coasting on down the street, the driver trying to mesh its gears, scraping them, the headlights disappearing around the curve in the road.

Amanda laughing, Pink began to laugh too, softly at first. He sat on the ground and laughed, Amanda giggling, trying to get her dress straight. "You broke it," she said.

That amused him. "Which one, right or left?"

She struggled to her feet, holding to the tree. "Get up, Pink. We'll be arrested."

He crawled to the sidewalk and sat down on a step, snickering at their predicament. "I would have broke it all, Amanda," he admitted, looking up at her, then he began to laugh about that, and she had to help him to his feet.

"Broke my fountain pen and it new, in my pocket." A stranger came by, walking his dog. "He's not drunk," Amanda sought to assure him. She helped the giggling Pink along the sidewalk to the corner, where she poked his shirt in under his belt, straightened his string tie, brushed off his pants and coat. "What on earth will they say?" she whispered, as much to herself as to him.

"I missed you," he whispered to her.

"The children," she said, reminding him of them.

They helped each other up the steps to their house, he stopping once to listen to the sounds of the city. "The sounds of the machine moving," he told her.

She listened studiously. "What?"

"I hear Young talking? Listen." They held to one another as they listened to Young's voice from the dining room.

"I love to hear him."

Henrietta was first to see them. She came running forward. An apparition, Pink called her. "Angels are coming," he told Amanda. Sweat was thick on his brow, his cheeks, his chin. "Young," he called. Hallie came at once and began weeping. She wiped his face with the sleeve of her dress. "Your mother is eighteen again," he told Hallie, "been using the lawn." Young began to cry, said he couldn't help it. Even Frederick embraced him. When Pink saw Wallerbee he began to murmur apologies for his family. "It's not always like this," he assured him, then tried to embrace, so much the whole world seemed to him tonight to be embraceable.

"Did you find it, papa?" Hallie asked him, taking his hand in her own. "On the trip you took, did you find it?"

Everybody grew quiet. Standing near the hall doorway, they were watching him most seriously, each one as anxious as Hallie.

"Just a while ago," he said.

In spite of her mother's badgering her about babies and a family, Hallie did want children. Now and then, a longing for a baby of her own would creep in, and she wanted a husband of her own, wanted to belong to somebody and have somebody of her own. She had proved to herself that she could be a self-sufficient person; she had no need to prove that further. She decided there must be touching, holding, the sharing of physical and emotional experiences. When she had moved into the office, moved her desk into his office, she had taken a step toward accepting Wallerbee, a step toward loyalty to him.

That night, after the craziness with her father and mother, the rupture of logic and orderliness, and after the flow of affection as a family, Wallerbee suggested to Hallie that they go to the square for coffee. "I can make coffee for us here," she told him.

"No, no," he said, as if that suggestion were thoughtless, as if she ought to reconsider. They drove in his car to the square, found a parking place near the Plaza Theatre; it was about eight-thirty when they arrived, and the coffee place was crowded. There was not a table to be had. Anyway, he said he wanted to go by the office. When they arrived there, she noticed he locked the door from the hallway side, then led the way to their private office, closing out the light from Gloria Smith's room. The only light in their office was sifted and reflected from distant streetlamps and the lighted signs, such as the one on the theatre just across the way: Carol Dempster and W. C. Fields.

There in the office he kissed her. She pulled back from him, surprised, alerted. He had kissed her only a few times, when he had taken her home late at night, when they were on the porch. "I wasn't expecting that."

He took her hand, led her to the big chair. He pushed her back into the chair and began touching her face and hair, then her full bosom. "I'm—I must be very sensitive," she whispered, wanting to pull his hand away but being unable, unwilling, to touch it. "Oh, my God," she moaned. She whispered, "Please God." She gasped as he caressed her breast, and he kissed her, and it was all over for her, she was responding as she clutched his body with her hands, until in tatters of clothes, pieces of things, items not yet discarded, they could not deny themselves any longer, and the floor by her father's chair was the place where they met completely, her head striking her desk, her feet entangling with the chair legs, his body light on hers, fitted nicely into hers, her instincts gathering, lapping over to touch a peak, then coasting along the crest for a ways, even as he gasped; twice she erupted into sheer feeling.

A few minutes later, she lying on her side, Wallerbee on his side, two facing each other, he mentioned that a streetcar was leaving. "Hear the bells?"

"I hear bells of my own."

He nudged her with his chin, then kissed her chin. Outside another streetcar rang bells as it departed. From near the fountain, a man's voice called to somebody named Bill, at first inquiringly, then insistently. The world was continuing; the everyday facts and fancies were recurring. People were going home from the moviehouse, she and Wallerbee were lying on the rug; both were real occurrences. The two were looking up at the stars, common enough stars; the ceiling was reflecting the blinking lights of Finkelstein's Pawn Shop, and about them on the floor were company papers that had fallen off her desk.

Next afternoon, at her request, Pink went with Hallie to the café and took his customary table at the window, where he could watch Lexington Avenue. He pushed his felt hat to the back of his head and kept his raincoat on. "You say you don't know about the loans to Clove?" he asked her at once, assuming this was one reason for the trip. "Well, why didn't you know, I wonder."

"What loans?" she said.

He ordered coffee for himself, tea for her, and a few biscuits. "Just two loans worry me. How you getting on?" he asked the waitress.

"He married me while you were away, Mr. Pink," she said. "Married me to save a salary."

Pink laughed appreciatively. "Might have been a second reason," he said, winking at her.

"No, he goes on cooking in his sleep."

That tickled Pink. After he began drinking his coffee, he continued chuckling about her comment.

"Papa, please . . ." Hallie said, looking around the restaurant, seeking to restrain him. "Now, what is it worries you?"

Pink winked at Hallie. "How you coming with boyfriends?"

"I . . . I have just one," she said, blushing to the roots of her hair. "I mean to tell you about him."

"Wedding dress, all that sort of thing. Takes some time for me and your mother to get wound up for a wedding, Hallie." He sipped coffee. "Tell me all about him, Hallie."

"I couldn't stop it, papa," she whispered. "I mean there was no fence between, as mama says. That's the point."

He drank some more coffee, wiped his chin with his handkerchief. He smiled at her. "So a man got to you, did he?"

"A second man, papa."

"Oh my," he said. "How long ago was the first one?"

"I'll not say, nor who it was, either."

"You love either one of them, or is that something you wonder about?"

She hesitated. "I need—to think about it."

"Tell me about him, this man who just got to you."

"It was not so much his getting to me, papa, as I was getting to him there at the close."

He laughed softly. "Oh, well."

"Is a woman supposed to do that?"

"Don't know." Then he added, "I've not known a number of women, not so many."

"Only one, papa?"

He smiled at her, nodded briefly. "Is this one, is he the only man you're drawn to?"

"Yes."

"How long has it been?"

"That I've known him?"

"Wanted him, in the way you're talking about . . ."

"Oh . . ." She shook her head. "Where does it start, papa?"

"With the notion that maybe it would work out sometime."

"You mean whenever you go to bed alone you think about him?"

"That might be so for a start."

"I . . . less than a year ago."

Carefully he adjusted his back to the little chair he was sitting in. He took out his handkerchief again and wiped his mouth. "I ought to stop drinking coffee, Hallie. And I do now and then drink tea. Or nothing. For a month I tried hot water." He smiled at her. "The waitresses never liked that. They would serve it, then they would wonder what to charge. I'd advise them to charge the same as for tea, but they couldn't bring themselves to do it."

"How is your heart, papa?"

"Oh . . ." He smiled, but the smile crumpled. "I think my blood pressure is down, went down a tad, once I left the company."

"And your mind is clear now, isn't it, papa?"

"Oh yes," he whispered, not looking at her. "And this man of yours, this—who is it?"

"I hate to tell you."

"Do I know him?"

"I don't want to discuss it now."

He studied about that. "I know him, you say?"

"It's Mr. Wallerbee."

Yet again he wiped his mouth with his handkerchief. He finished the coffee in his cup. "You've caught me unawares, Hallie," he admitted. When she only stared like a helpless child, he said, "There's probably a world or two inside that man that can be found. And you'd have the company to talk about. You'll have children, will you?"

"Yes. Oh, yes, of course. I suppose. Oh, my God, papa, it's all so strange," she said, almost overcome, unable to speak clearly. "I want to tell you the truth."

"I'd say you have."

"He's dull, papa, I know that."

"He isn't dull in business, Hallie."

Tears blinded her eyes. "Papa, I'm crazy, I know. And he's years older than I am. Papa, should I marry him? Last night, when you returned home, I went to the office with him and I couldn't stop. Do you understand what I'm saying?"

"Yes, I understand, believe me, Hallie."

"Papa, what should I do?" she demanded passionately. "Should I marry him. I don't know what to do."

"Then no," he said. "If you aren't sure, don't do anything."

"But I'm never sure, am I? And I don't even know what other men . . . what else there is in life."

"Then no, Hallie. Don't you see, you've answered it yourself."

It seemed that everybody knew Pink was home again and wanted to talk with him to introduce a baby, to ask his advice about insurance, to obtain a loan, to refinance a farm, to borrow money from him or from Monarch, to explain why they had not been able recently to meet their payments. He encountered a flood of plain matters, most of them requiring decision. His absence had contributed to a host of problems, he admitted to himself, and new opportunities. "I was coming along College Street, on my way home," he told Amanda, "and here came the Washburn boys and said they needed money to take their Plott hounds to a show." He laughed about that. "Can you imagine a Plott hound in a show, Amanda?"

She laughed along with him, amused by his mirth.

"I can see them now, sitting there considering which of the other dogs they'll eat up."

"Oh, hush, Pink," she said, laughing. They had talked about maybe going for a ride, but they were waiting to see if Hallie came on home or not, or Frederick and the "Dutchman" as Pink referred to her. Young was off at a church young people's meeting. "Here we are, waiting for our children," Pink had said.

"I wonder if we can go back home this summer, Pink," Amanda said. "It would be so different this time."

"It always will be different," he told her, smiling at her. "You go see them if you want to. Say hello for me."

"Don't tell me you won't come with me."

"No, I'll not go up there. Stare at graves. Watch mama dying."

"Pink, I never know when you're being serious."

"I can't get a cent out of Wurth for my own land."

"And Harry, has he offered anything?"

"No, he has nothing." He began to chuckle, comforting himself with thoughts of Harry. "I went to see Harry, and I never found him, that entire year I was gone, Amanda, until near the last."

"Yes, well, he was always a difficult person to find."

That comment amused him further. "You're better than an entertainment," he told her.

"I ought to know," she admitted.

Pink had a Hershey bar in his pocket, which he unwrapped carefully, offered her part of it.

"I like the kind with the almonds," she told him, chewing on a bite of it.

"Can't have everything you want, Amanda." He bit off a big piece, savoring it. "Took this habit up on the trains. I would sit there and let these damn things melt in my mouth."

"The almond ones aren't so prone to melt."

"Can't melt an almond, no," he admitted. "Harry chose to go traveling, so I wanted to see what life had done to him, a man on his own, able to walk through any corn patch, breaking stalks at random, a man unassigned to chores of any sort, free to move on. It became a train-time passion with me, Amanda, wondering about Harry, what he was like by now."

232

"You think he was trying to hide from you, Pink?"

"I . . . I declare, I don't know. I saw people who knew him."

"But where was he finally? In Oregon?"

"Well, he's not here, they'd say. He was here just a week back, sat in the chair, brought me an armful of flowers."

"You talking to a woman or a man?"

"A woman. A man wouldn't want flowers."

"Well, I've never been out there."

"Harry was here, Harry was there, everybody knew him. And Brodie was out there."

"Brodie King?"

"Out there in Denver. Was in business, of a sort."

"Did you see him, Pink?"

"I saw him sometimes of a morning. Don't mention it to Nettie or Hugh. He's not wanting to be told to come home."

"I know Nettie would like to know he's well."

"Wish Hallie would get home, don't you? I ought to give her some of the company stock for helping so well while I was gone."

"What do you mean, give Hallie the company? There's Frederick, don't forget Young. There's too much company in Hallie now, I'd say."

"Yes, you've said so from time to time," he admitted.

"Get herself out of that company. It's time she found out what she's got, what God put on her."

Pink turned to her, a grin on his face. "What did God put on her?"

Amanda touched one of her breasts. "Not there for balance."

He settled back in his chair. "The company's not galloping forward these days like it was, but it's strong. I'm going to try to spur it on again, if Hallie will give me a year before she . . . before she takes to the bed and starts nursing somebody."

"She's not to lie there in her wedding bed and talk about the company, is she?"

"No, she's not. I only asked for a year," he added.

"Well, there's others of us have to wait that same year, Pink."

"Then you'll just have to wait," he said, "because I do need her." His eyes were set on the passing scene, each car that trundled past. He shrugged, conscious of his abruptness, annoyed by it. He pulled his jacket close over his chest. "The company is a baby, too, Amanda. It's a toddler, as well. It's my baby."

"You went off and left it."

"It's Wallerbee's baby. And I suppose it's Hallie's. Strange bedfellows all. I don't need two breasts to feed it, but it has to be fed. It's a man's baby, admittedly."

"Do you know that," Amanda said at once, "that she's not a man?"

"I realize she has to leave it sometime, yes."

"Well, how long will it be then?" Amanda asked.

"I told you," he said, "it will be a year. Then she can go home and lie down for a man. I'll find her one."

He began thinking about his arrival in San Francisco, where he had taken a room at the Mark Hopkins, choosing that hotel because he knew Harry had stayed there from time to time. He took a room facing east— back toward home—and he recalled he had sat at the window for a while considering the miracles of travel. He recalled specific places: an Indian village, its proud Indians just now engaged with fleas, a heavy-drinking lot sniveling about on their reservation while the grandeur of the Rockies rose just there, nearby. He thought of the family of ranchers who offered him a bed one evening, while to the northwest a cloud was growing, ballooning, a tumor of clouds that twirled, unmindful, uncaring of the shelterless. He thought of dusty faces awaiting springtime rains: Do wash the dust from the little girl's face and neck, from her legs. He had met a man in Houston and they talked about oil. "Just look over this paper here . . ." He had several stuffed in pockets. Two fell to the floor. He scooped them up, put them in with the others, their corners turned. "This lease has reserves of two million barrels. What is your name? You say Pink? What sort of name is that? Here, hold this one, Pink. Now, what if the price of oil goes up a cent a barrel?— You look like you could use a swig of liquor and a cigar. What kind of cigars do you smoke? Anything's all right with me, so long as it's Cubans. The workers lick them but I've stopped worrying about that. . . . Now, Pink, you still reading that paper?"

A preacher in Salt Lake City: ". . . Guarantee in the Constitution not to meddle with religion, and the government's saying a Mormon can't have but one wife, while his religion dictates otherwise. I'm talking to you, citizen. Do you understand we've busted the Constitution wide open?"

A child of five in an orange tree in California, looking down. "You won't like my little brother, mister, because he'll pull your hair."

"I planted that there field in corn, stranger, till I wore it out. I tried cotton next, till it bore only straggly bushes. Now, I'm just going to sit here and let it do what it wants to do. You can talk to a field like that'n. A long, rectangular field is the best to talk to. You can say, Well, old girl, what you want this year, what's your choice? Can I plow you now or do you want to wait till later for your tickling? Can I leave you be—I want to be left alone sometimes myself, just passed on by. I can plant your sister or brother, just let you lie here in the sun and grow the weeds, them there thistles among them, and them beggar's lice. What say, honey? You want to lie there, or be turned over one more time?"

A white-haired driver talking as they drove through the great desert, which seemed like forever, the horizon lying in sameness to greet them, in sameness disappearing out the back, the voice droning on, mostly about his daughter. "I said come live with me, I've got a big house, so she did, bringing her two children—she had just the two then—and bringing Horace, her man, who drives a truck moving furniture, brought her from . . . from . . . starts with a T. What city starts with a T, Pink?"

"Toledo, Tuskeegee, Tulego . . ."

"One of them. I don't know. Rarely saw him, always gone, anyway. He'd say, Well, I'm off to that . . . that city, whatever it is, with a T, and then about once a year my daughter would bear another baby, so there come to be five or six of the devils, then I come home one evening, and she was gone, my furniture was gone, even my washing machine. Wondered where my washing machine was. She'd taken that on the truck with her, all except the hoses."

"Trenton starts with a T."

"Does it? That's where they went, all right. I talked to Margaret on the telephone."

"What did she say?"

"Said they'd always wanted to move."

A big song, America. The faults were minor tunes. The big music was of the country as a whole, and it was voluptuous, was rousing and promising, was a shout and a happy laugh, was streams of oil and metal out of the ground, farmland in square miles yielding from its flat bellies and breasts, its groins, its forty-acre rocky toes. The desert is most beautiful at dawn, the sun rising from home country. Its rivers: "Is that real silver, papa?" Its golden chains, city lights along the boulevard. Nobody critical of America.

Tell me not in mournful numbers about America, while I sit in a hotel room in San Francisco contemplating a warm bath, anxious to be about soaping the deserts and mountains off of my skin, out of my fingernails, wondering about Amanda, feeling life in my body as desire, wondering if I might not pick up the telephone and talk to Amanda. . . .

Scare her to death.

He did so want to talk to Amanda, but he wasn't ready to escape the state of depression in which he found himself, which he reveled in.

Fellow in Mississippi talking: "Way to be sure it's a boy, not a girl, is to leave your boots on, mister."

He dried leisurely, dressed in clean clothes. On his hands he had a whiff of perfume from the soap, which annoyed him. He sneezed. Phone Amanda. Phone Young at school. Call Hallie. Yes, that would be possible.

She would survive the call all right, he knew that, or any other excitement.

He punched the elevator button for the topmost floor, took a table at the window facing west, and while drinking a glass of orange juice into which he had poured gin watched the mist roll in. The waiter told him mist rolled in most every night as the temperature changed on the bay. The mist was engulfing the Golden Gate Bridge just down there, a toy left by a child, with toy cars and trucks on it. The Golden Gate, set at the end of all the rows of corn.

A Chinese girl, or one from another Oriental country, was standing in a doorway. He was wandering about, he had come a long way, he told her. She didn't seem to understand what he said. Reluctantly he climbed the stairs, following, wondering if he was the same man as yesterday, knowing different, thinking of Amanda. The room was warm. It had a tiny fire in the fireplace. She had a pot of tea ready. "I'm not given to this sort of thing," he mentioned to her, which she didn't appear to understand. She did clearly mention money, and he was surprised when he put the bills in her hand. She began to undress, and he wondered if he would be able to perform successfully with a stranger. "My wife and I have been . . . have been true to one another." She flipped her slip off over her head and showed him her round breasts. He stood near the door, fully clothed, examining the prospects as if it were a survey of land. He was wondering about it, that was all, thinking. She came close to him, questioning; her tea breath swept across his face. She sighed sweetly, then entwined her arms around his neck, brought his head down as she stood on tiptoes. Yes, tonight, tonight, a sinner, breaker of one of God's commandments. "Amanda," he whispered, feeling about for himself in the fog of her room, of her arms.

"What's that, sir?" The waiter said, hurrying over. "Another drink, sir?"

"I was merely commenting, saying I am a sinner."

"I am, too." The waiter shrugged.

"I am a stranger to myself," Pink told him. "I've robbed my best friend tonight."

"Oh," the waiter said. "I'll only be a minute."

Sent that girl China, sent her flowers next day. He recalled that now while walking along College Street, going home, Hallie beside him, accompanying him. "Fog's deep out there," he told her. "It's a womb, like being in a mother's womb."

"How do you know?" Hallie said.

"Fog is like a soup, then," he said, laughing.

Eighteen

To Hatch and Wallerbee, Pink showed his annoyance at the loans to Clove Enterprises. "It ought to be challenged by the auditors," he decided.

"They won't, they won't," Hatch wheezed, shaking his head irritably. He smiled at Pink. "We did the best we could with a distressing situation. If you had been here—"

"We both said that," Wallerbee told him.

Pink fretted over the loan statements, read them over and over, shaking his head. "Clove Enterprises," he would murmur in misery.

Smiling contentedly, Hatch commented, "That money you took with you, we thought the auditors might question that, even though Wallerbee put it back."

"I put it back, Pink," Wallerbee assured him.

"Oh, there's things gone wrong," Hatch admitted. "Bound to, with you away, Pink."

"So it's my fault, investing in real-estate fashions, involving my son," Pink said. "My partners involving my son this way. My fault, is it my fault?"

Hatch said, "If you had been here, or if we could have contacted you, Pink, so you could have given us the final word . . ." Contentedly he was considering the problems under review.

"Amanda recommended the two loans," Wallerbee said. "Frederick too. It was a family matter, Pink."

"My good God," Pink moaned. "To this crazy schemer," he whispered. "God help you both."

Pink bought Amanda a cookbook about Chinese foods. Since it was the first cookbook she had owned, and she had been cooking for many years, she decided the gift might imply criticism. She was good-natured about that, however, and was amused by the gift's strangeness. The recipe for frying vegetables called for a one-minute frying span; she conventionally used longer, not being in any hurry, as she explained to Henrietta. She did so like the Dutch girl, who was pretty and sweet, and who did mean to marry, to start a family with Frederick. They had even looked at a rental house close by, within walking distance.

"Let's try a recipe, mama," Henrietta suggested. She had stopped by, as often she did, to spend an hour visiting.

"No, let's not." This was the situation, as Amanda explained it: she had cooked for Pink for twenty-some years, resulting in praise for her biscuits, her cornbread, her boiled grits, her fresh sausages, her roast pork, her fried cured ham, her home-cured bacon, her fried chicken, her baked duck, her roast haunch of deer, her wild-rabbit stew. "Now, that's something that no Chinaman ever made, I'll warrant you, Henrietta," she suggested. "Show me one rabbit recipe in that book."

"No," Henrietta admitted, "I don't see one in here."

"You see." Amanda took the book from her, held it at arm's length, cautious about it, making a joke of it. "Nothing about headcheese or liver puddings?"

"I don't think they have those."

"Pickled beets? Pickled beans? None of that's in here. Pork knuckles and field beans," Amanda said. "Show me a recipe for pickle relish in this book of Pink's."

Scanning the index, Henrietta admitted defeat.

"Show me a recipe for cornbread, Henrietta. On a Sunday night, sitting around the fire, hot cornbread crumbled up in cold milk is the finest dish. Pink knows that, as well as I do. Do they have that in there?"

"I'm almost certain not, mama."

Whenever Henrietta mentioned the book to him, Pink would laugh about it, admit his error. "Been better to buy her a headband," he told his daughter-in-law-to-be, and laughed.

Pink pretended indifference to the need to repay Wallerbee the $5,000. "Can't get blood out of a turnip," he told Hallie, who decided to represent Wallerbee's interests.

"Papa, he wants to fix up his part of his house, wants me to help him buy new furniture."

"Wallerbee has enough furniture, I'd imagine. His two or three sisters—"

"His two sisters are going to live on there, but he's to have his own place, and he wants it distinctive."

"If he insists on starting out housekeeping all in a single day . . ."

"He does mean to do that, papa," she told him. "Now he needs the money this week."

"It's not much furniture he needs, I imagine," he said, "just one man. You going in with him?"

"No."

"Then I'll talk with him about it. You let him and me work it out."

"Or I'll take your furniture, papa," she said firmly, her gaze set on him. "I'll take your parlor furniture."

"I . . . I need to loan the Harmons some money. You know Curtis Harmon, don't you, from Burnsville, has that big house with the three hundred acres of bottomland, has the huge sorghum press in place? He makes the best molasses—"

"And he brings you a few gallons every year."

"Yes, he does, Hallie. This is the fourteenth year—"

"And in return you take money from Wallerbee to loan him?"

He smiled briefly. "Yes."

He did that week produce a portion of the amount, enough for Wallerbee to buy a sofa and chair, and he seemed to have further repayment entered on a list of intentions. However, he loaned Phil Everete $200, once he found out Phil's sale of cattle at the market brought him scarcely enough to pay for hauling them, and he loaned the Yanceys $100. Many farmers were facing emergencies; this season their produce brought next to nothing, scarcely enough for sugar and coffee for the winter.

The economic situation was perplexing to Pink. Poverty ruled among farmers, but in town Frederick was selling lots one after another, he and Henrietta; in most towns and cities, prosperity was swinging upward, and Pink took his company to meet it. He went with Hallie to Charlotte, where he approved the hiring of three new salesmen, two black, one white. Charlotte was booming; more people every day were moving into town. The three traveled to other cities, in one month opening offices in Salisbury, Winston-Salem, Greensboro. Monarch was on the move again, and wherever Pink touched, magic was released, and success.

There were, however, signs of strain, there were warnings. Listening to the Negroes, Pink would learn much. He would listen to Lord One Eye, whose brother-in-law worked as a chauffeur, often for Dr. Clove himself. Lord knew, for instance, that Clove was opening a new subdivision on part of the Vanderbilts' estate. Also, Pink learned that Clove, Frederick assisting, was hiring even more salesmen, all of them sons of prominent citizens of the city; he judged these employees were working for commissions, and that their sales were to be made to their relatives, producing a short-lived prosperity. Then, too, he learned on Lexington Avenue that truckers now required cash from Clove Enterprises before unloading their ordered goods at the hotels. "You can send them a bill this spring, and you can be killing your hogs next winter before you see the first cent," Lord told Pink. There were many such stories on Lexington Avenue, indicating weakness.

In September, when Dr. Clove came to ask Pink for a new loan, bringing his assistant, Frederick, Pink offered them only a small loan, a pittance, provided Clove would renegotiate the two existing loans, in this way combine the three into one, and remove Frederick's name. Clove was unwilling to do so, to endanger two loans he held.

Pink had Wallerbee try to peddle the Clove loans to the local banks, to sell them even at a loss, but neither bank would buy. Pink then told Wallerbee to remove most of the company funds from these banks and put them in a Winston-Salem bank, the largest in the state, and a safer one. Of course, the transfer created consternation at the Asheville banks but pleasure in Winston-Salem, where soon Pink passed on several company loans, but even there he was unable to place the two from Clove Enterprises.

Hallie and Pink disagreed about several decisions, particularly about the Durham and Chattanooga offices, which he would not expand. Also, Hallie and Wallerbee sometimes disagreed about company policy, and each privately appealed to Pink, which left him in between, in the middle. Then, too, his traveling with her created mischief with Wallerbee, who was plainly jealous. One night at Marion, Pink and Hallie had stayed in the same room, one with two beds. "It was the last room left in town," Hallie told Wallerbee. "We went to all the places, every inn," she explained. "You know what he does in cases like that, when there are no rooms."

"No, I do not know, but it doesn't look quite right, Hallie," Wallerbee assured her.

"He sleeps in the lobby," she said. "He sits up all night, and I can't have my father sit up all night in his condition."

"No, of course not," Wallerbee admitted. "He does seem to need a lot of care, doesn't he?" And away he went, testy.

"Was there satisfaction in it, papa?" Hallie asked him one evening when they were in Barnardsville. "You make marriage sound like a handicap."

"Rich satisfaction. A lifetime of rewards."

"Yet you complain?"

"I don't know what its cost has been, Hallie, that's all. A man escapes his mother and is bound by his wife." He went on, whispering huskily, taking her hand. "I was thinking about Hatch Green and God. You know Hatch well yet? He's the ultimate in mathematically honest men."

"No, I've only met him at meetings, papa."

"Hatch is not generous. God isn't either. God is not a Christian, Hallie. Don't tell your mother. God is about as loving and charitable as a falling tree."

He knew death is for everybody inevitable, but as he told her, death as inevitable is different from death as companion. Consider that, death walking with him, he said, crossing with him to the far sidewalk, death in his chest stifling his breath. Death in among his papers. He must draw up plans for his family's housing and Young's education. He had done nothing about providing for any of it. He, an insurance-company executive, even yet owned not a single insurance policy, and his health made accepting one dishonest. He had no bonds, no stocks, except in Monarch. Even now death was entering the inn with him, the house with him.

A frantic telephone call from a salesman told Pink that Frederick was in Franklin, was in trouble, and Pink left his noon meal and prepared at once to go himself to bring him home. He would drive himself, he told Hallie, but she insisted on driving. "I'll stay out of the way," she assured him. /

"Can you?" he said. "When did you learn that?"

Young also volunteered to come along, so they agreed. The railroads didn't go to Franklin; neither did any roads meant for fast travel. Hallie pieced a way on the roads, fording streams, matching wheel width to bridge runners, scaling sides of creek gaps, some of them precipitous. The road went up the face of a rock; from tire marks of previous drivers it appeared one gathered speed on the approach and went straight ahead. At junctions the car must stop while the three adults debated which fork to take, the few road signs being abbreviated and haphazardly placed. One sign to Cherky, which Young said must be the Cherokee Indian reservation, pointed toward Heaven. Another sign said, "Hoe, Fer God Sak Sen Mony."

The town of Franklin had a population of about one hundred, but on certain nights, when the timbermen were there, it was stretched to accommodate two hundred more. Hallie waited in the sole inn's lobby while Pink and Young moved to the town's gathering place, where the heat of bodies and wood fires steamed the window panes. The crowded dives resounded to voices of timbermen freed from dangerous work, the noise raucous, challenging, fiddle and guitar and banjo music joining in, striking the window panes, splattering on the eardrums like spit on hot stoves. At a back table, Pink and Young found the Monarch salesman, who beckoned to them gratefully. Also at the table was the drunken Frederick, a happy or at least complacent drunk, shirt open down the front, a quaint smile on his face, a sense of good will about him. He greeted Pink, apologized for his condition. "I've been wondering, papa," he told him, "what day this is. Glad you're here to tell me."

"Do you care, Fred?"

The smile slowly faded, the eyes closed tightly. "Hell, no."

"Your sister's at the inn, waiting for you."

A gasp. A shrug, then a polite snicker. "Kill Hallie."

The insurance salesman came scurrying toward them, bill in hand. "He fired me, Pink," the salesman said worriedly. "I have a family."

"You'll get a bonus," Pink said.

"Thank the good Lord. I need that, too."

"Yes, I'll make it right."

"Papa makes the world right," Frederick sang softly in a wobbly voice. "My papa has two hundred men working their balls off. . . ."

"Papa has had a long trip. Come see your sister."

The smile crumpled once more. "Hallie here, you say?"

"She drove. You can drive the car going back."

"I'm . . . I'm not in driving . . . I'm not drunk, papa, but I have been drinking."

"I'll tell the world," the salesman said. "I mean it's been straight whiskey, Pink, for two days. He owes this here place ninety-two dollars, has been giving drinks away." Pink and Young positioned themselves on each

242

side of Frederick. Only a few men were watching. They were halfway to the door when Hallie appeared just inside the saloon, and once she recognized Frederick, saw his weakness, illness, his stinking, deplorable condition, she cried out, a distinctly female voice was heard in this male environment, and at once every eye turned to her, every voice was silenced. Hallie had the good sense to retreat, but Frederick, enraged, shouted after her, defying her, charging her with insult and crimes, tears rolling down his cheeks, he cried out after her.

On the sidewalk, he tried to break free. He fell over an old hitching rail, into an empty trough. Pink and Young gathered him up, bodily carried him to the inn, to their room. A moment later he threw up into a towel Pink handed him. Pink ordered Hallie out, and he and Young got Frederick undressed and washed him off with hot, wet towels. A stranger, this son, Pink thought. He toweled him dry—his naked son: broad chest, strong shoulders, firm neck, slender waist, a thin layer of fat on his abdomen. "Fred, can you sleep naked?"

"Was born naked," Frederick said.

Wurth came into town looking wan; he arrived as if fleeing and sought out the house's kitchen porch, where he stomped mud off his boots and called for Pink to come out. Failing there, he slumped down at the kitchen table and drummed the metal top with his fingernails, creating a racket. Pink came out of the bathroom and made himself ready to listen. The story Wurth told was of their mother, who had fallen and broken her arm. One of the Crawford boys had set it. He had given her a stiff dose of narcotic for the pain, had put her to sleep. "It's a fitting job of bone work," Wurth testified, "but when she was aroused from the sedative, she began talking to papa. She saw him standing there by the bed, though he's been dead for years, and she talked to two little youngins, and there were no youngins there. I said to her, What are the youngins doing? And she said they were eating porridge from a single bowl. And I said to her, Look here, mama, I'm having eye trouble, for I don't see them. And she propped herself up on one elbow and said to the youngins, Don't go upstairs until you've finished your breakfast. Now you sit back down. Then to me she said, Ohhhhh, Wurth, they've gone. They won't mind me." Wurth looked to Pink for advice, sat there sniffing and waiting. "I talked with several at the store, and they said that sometimes the old never come back."

"Was she strange before, or not?" Amanda asked, her voice tight, scared.

"Oh, she's been dreaming too much." He rubbed his eyes with the heel of one hand. "She's been sliding downhill ever since papa died years ago.

Then recently she lost her appetite, wouldn't eat much of anything. Once set the table for fourteen—had the plates near about touching. She's been talking to papa for a year now, as if he's in the room warming by the fire. But those little youngins are new."

"Does she have clear spells as well?" Amanda asked.

"She does. Now and then." He sat there for half an hour, ruminating, repeating, anxious and disturbed, then he invited Young to come with him, to trade for a while, up the street.

On Saturday Frederick drove Amanda and Pink to the farm, to see the old lady. Along the way Pink worried about his mother, fretted over papers, scarcely able to read them for complaining about too much air in the car, or too little, and about Wurth driving his mother to distraction, and about Frederick's driving, which admittedly was not professional. He got out of the car at the store, said he would go over to the house later. For an hour or so, he talked with the men sitting about in the store, then made his way across the field, lingering in the backyard of the old house, recalling moments of his childhood. He was anxious, worried about the duty just ahead. When finally he went indoors, Wurth's wife came up to him and kissed him, which was not customary. "She's been asking about you," he was told, so he went on to the parlor, where he understood his mother was. She saw him at once. "Papa," she said to him, "I've been waiting for you." He pulled a chair up close to her bed. "Papa, you make Wurth move out of my house," the old woman whispered to him at once.

Pink said kindly, "Mama, do you know papa is dead?"

She paused, considering that. A long while she lay there thinking. "Why, yes, I know, Pink," she said. "What do you think, that I'm crazy?"

"No, I don't, mama."

"Of course he's dead." Later she roused herself on her pillows, even as pain flashed through her arm, reminding her of her injury. "Papa," she said to Pink, and held out her hand to him, which he grasped. "Papa, you don't know how it is, when you start failing."

Young came into the room and sat down near his grandmother. She talked to him about his soul, calling him Pink, even after he corrected her. He came to accept whatever name she used for him; it made no difference to him. He moved closer to his father, waited there, the two looking at one another, seeking meanings for words unsaid.

It seemed most every afternoon Gloria would stop by Hugh's store on her way from work. This set anger flowing in Pink that was difficult for him to control, because of his buried jealousy of Hugh and his attraction to Gloria. Of course, an affair was not in prospect. He considered himself to be an anchored man who would not engage in such waywardness, but he had thought the same of his old partner, Hugh King, who had a wife and children. Hugh was a businessman, a conservative presence in the community, and here he was traipsing about, snatching at the skirt of Pink's receptionist, his friend, his confidante.

Pink followed her one evening along the tourist-crowded streets. She turned down Lexington Avenue, and his heart jolted inside him. His jealousy of Hugh King was a long-standing sore, minor but irritating, and here he was loping along behind Gloria—she did walk fast, her heels clicking noisily on the pavement. She bolted across the street in front of a horse-drawn wagon and disappeared into the cloth shop, where Pink felt he could not follow. Instead, he stepped inside the gun shop, looked at the used pistols Mitch Wells had on offer. One was a German Luger, a long-barreled one. Mitch disassembled it, showing it off, but when Pink saw Gloria emerge once more, he bolted from the gun shop as if a fire were after him and went hurrying down the street, leaving Mitch in the middle of a sentence, the trigger mechanism in one hand, the bolt in the other. At the edge of Hugh King's lot Pink paused, nonchalantly examined a basket of turnips. He was aware that he was making a fool of himself, but there appeared to be nothing he could do about it. He lingered so long busy Hugh noticed him, even approached good-naturedly, asking how the company was doing. "I'm left down here mired up in horse manure, and you're up high on the square, Pink."

"I see that Gloria seeks you out down here," Pink said, voicing his annoyance.

Hugh blanched. "Well, she's kin, second cousin, I think. There's several of them that are. They come by."

"Visits every day," Pink said. He was trying to put a show of good humor on his comments but was failing.

Hugh picked up an apple from the ground, broke it in two with his long fingers, tossed half of it away. Slowly he turned the other half in his hand, examining it. "You like her yourself?"

The thrust angered Pink. "That's not necessary. She's not traipsing about me."

"None of anybody's business, I'd say, speaking of myself," Hugh said, examining the apple.

"If she were here to buy vegetables . . ."

"This is your concern, is it?" Hugh asked most patiently.

"She's my employee."

"Well, I tell you, Pink, I think you're a hell of a boss," Hugh said, looking up. "Now, let me say this—"

"Her life is already tragic enough without an older man—"

"Let me say this, that I'm my own keeper, but if I ever need your help—"

"A man years older than she is—"

"I'll plow my own rows, as long as I'm able." He bit into the apple, all the while staring at Pink. "I'm about eight years older—"

"And keep your son away from my daughter, as well," Pink ordered.

Hugh grunted from surprise. "Which son?"

"Brodie."

"Why, he's gone."

"He took her to Henry Station."

"I never heard about that," Hugh said, intrigued. "He's been known to heist skirts, if the skirts are willing."

"She was too young—seventeen."

"Well, if she came after him . . . is seventeen too young?"

"You just keep him off her."

"I tell you what," Hugh said, showing plain annoyance, "when and if Brodie, bless his heart, when and if he ever comes home, I'll see to it that he meets Gloria." The threat was firmly made. The final words were said, and the friendship of many years was broken like a twig, like the discarded core of the apple Hugh discarded just now, tossed aside.

Even at Frederick and Henrietta's wedding, the culmination of weeks of planning involving the Dutch community, as he sat in the church beside his dear Amanda, Pink was thinking about the forbidden Gloria, who with her daughter was two rows behind him and across the aisle. At the reception at the Country Club, arranged by Dr. Clove, an affair used by him to place lots as well as borrow money, Pink, talking with Henrietta's family, realized he was thinking, was wondering, about Gloria.

When she came through the reception line, he shook her hand politely.

CHAPTER
Nineteen

A sense of rightness assured Pink there would be a year's time longer to get his life in order, his estate arranged, Hallie married, Young set on a career, Amanda better adjusted, the company on an even more prosperous course. He talked to Amanda about his need for a plan. "I've been thinking about the year, between now and next spring, Hallie—Amanda," he corrected himself, "to get matters in order in my life."

"You don't even know who I am," Amanda chided him. "You think I'm Hallie, do you?" Smiling she stared him down. "Can't remember my name? Well, it's Amanda. Now, what's yours?"

He had to laugh. It was so natural to confuse names. "Oh, dear God," he whispered, chuckling.

"Do you feel better, now that you know my name?" she asked.

He laughed, nodding. That was all he said to her about the plan.

Let's see, Pink and Hallie gone to Boone today, she recalled, then to Roanoke. Young at play practice till nine. Part of Mercutio. Sounds Italian. This morning Hallie spoke of Pink having a year—what did she mean by that? She had tried to joke the matter aside. He could not be allowed to announce his own death that way, and make plans leading to it, as paths lead to doorways; there was no doorway a man could designate, and then walk to it, not to death, there was no year's path in a person's life that he could move along. Was it 365 steps that he would take? Was Amanda to count the days with him? What sort of humor would a man require to walk to his death on measured ground? Or was it another bout of pessimism that had caught him, as in times past. Could Pink really believe he would in twelve months come to the door of death, and still go on about his work, his 365 dirty breakfast plates left one by one on the table? Was she to be the one to wash the plates?

She gave the telephone operator the doctor's number, and when she heard his gravelly voice, she identified herself as Pink's wife, wondering at that time if she might not better have used her own name. "But he says it will be at the end of a year. A year he says. It's as if he made a bargain about it."

The gravelly voice, deep, soothing: "Oh, the heart and mind don't count the days, Mrs. Wright. I wouldn't worry about all that. Once he has spent a year this way, he can start another year, that's all."

"Would you ask him about it?"

"A person can't live his life with the idea of the date of his death in mind. Here now, if you need something to steady your own nerves, Mrs. Wright, I'll give you a prescription. . . ."

When she was through talking with him, she dialed Nettie King and asked what she was doing that day. Nothing interesting. Then she phoned the handicraft shop on the square and asked if any of her quilts had sold. None had. Sighing, humming, she moved into the kitchen to do the dishes. "What will I do, once he's gone?" she whispered. "What you going to do, Amanda?" she asked herself, peeking into the little square mirror that hung from a nail just there, on the wall before her eyes. "Amanda?" she said, speaking more commandingly.

The front doorbell tinkled as the door opened, then she heard Wallerbee call out, ask where she was. "Law, I'm back here trying to warm my stove," she called.

He found his way and plopped a bag of groceries on the table. He sat down at the enamel-top table and beamed at her. "Thought you might get hungry while they're gone." He dug into the bag, bringing out a piece of cheddar cheese, a piece of round steak, which he thought might be enough for the two of them. He had some asparagus.

"I don't know asparagus at all," she admitted. "I don't mind cooking it for you, and tasting it."

"Well . . ." he said, content with that. "Just six spears will do for me, the rest for you."

"I'm glad you dropped by, Mr. Wallerbee," she told him honestly. "I get to wondering where my hands are."

"Your hands?"

"These two," she said, showing him her hands. She moved to the stove, brought the kettle, and filled up his tea mug, then set the kettle on the table; it was spent and silent. "You like Hallie?" she asked, dropping fresh tea leaves into the pot.

"I've loved her for years, Mrs. Wright. I mean by that, I've thought of her as being . . . as being a good worker, and possibly . . ." he tried to smile, "possibly my wife."

"I don't think a man loves anybody continuously for years, Mr. Wallerbee, except in fits and starts."

"No?" he said.

"A man loves most dearly when it's a short requirement, so he can go free."

"I see," he said, watching her thoughtfully. "Do you love Hallie?"

"Did she tell you to ask me?"

"No."

"Yes, I love her. If you'll make a wife out of her, and give her children, I'll love her more."

On Wednesday Pink came back, as planned. The company car drove up about six o'clock and Pink walked down to the chicken lot. "What on earth?" Amanda said to Hallie. "What's wrong with him?"

"We stopped by grandpa's, and he talked with Uncle Wurth, and they had an argument, that's all."

Amanda put supper on the table in the dining room, and she set Hallie a place at the table. "It gives me such a fright," she admitted, "your father walking away. We'll simply have to keep him away from Wurth." He was still standing near the chicken yard when Wallerbee arrived. "I don't know what's the matter," she said to him. She put the pork roast on the table. "There's asparagus for those who like it," she said, with a triumphant glance at Mr. Wallerbee. There was enough to eat, certainly, and she told Young to call Pink. Pink waved to him, accepting the command, and he promptly came indoors, moved to his place, but he ignored the dishes offered him, ignored the carving to be done, until there was quiet in the

room as everybody came to realize that he was sitting at the table immobilized. Nobody dared ask a question of him, because nobody dared face the
answer it might bring. Amanda, a bowl in her hand, had stopped near the
kitchen doorway. She knew, she knew everything all in a moment. Pink's
left hand rested on the table near the pronged fork. His right arm dangled
at his side. She knew that arm was useless, that his dear body was paralyzed. "Pink, don't try," she said.

"Papa," Hallie cried out.

"Pink, don't try," Amanda said. "We'll take care of you."

Awake in the parlor he could see the mantel clock's pendulum swinging.
He said "parlor" aloud and at once he heard a surprised reply from the
doorway, and Amanda came quickly forward. "Water?" she said.

"Parlor," he said.

"Yes, I'll get some," she said.

Back and forth, back and forth. Wurth Wright, Wurth Wright, that was
what the pendulum was ticking. Wurth Wright, Wurth Wright. I told him
to go to hell, that was clear enough. When was that? When I last went
home. It was a long time ago; it seems now I recall, the borders of the
fields, the walls around a garden, the thickets and hedges, that the vase in
the window was a blue quart Mason jar. The tick-tock of the mantel clock,
tick-tock of the mantel clock, tick-tock of the mantel clock . . .

"Here," she said, and supported his head with her left hand and let him
wet his lips with the water in the glass she held.

"Snuff glass," he mumbled. Wanting to speak more clearly, fully intending to do so. How did one will to speak?

"Enough?" she said, surprised.

"Doctor's on his way," a man was saying.

"Where?" he asked, although he had intended to say "Who." He had
intended to say "Who," and that he decided was a joke, a strange joke.
"Clock," he murmured.

"Yes, that's your aunt's clock," Amanda said, "the one she sent to be
repaired, and last year I sent word to her boys to come get it, if they want
it—and of course they would want something of hers and their father's,
wouldn't they?" There she stood in the middle of the parlor, watching
Pink, entertaining him with news about the clock.

"Doctor?" he asked.

"He's in the hall telephoning."

"What?" he said, meaning why.

"He says he wants a nurse. I said I'll be here to nurse you, but he said for
a few days it would help to have somebody who knows the signs."

He garbled speech, trying to say "Very well." It was terrifying to be clasped inside an unresponding body this way. Frantic fear was rising, subsiding, rising, subsiding, leaving him spent.

"Phoning Dr. Bolton, who is new here but has strokes as his specialty, but he was out in Tryon visiting a retired general."

He realized he could move his left hand. He could bend his left arm. Here and now he twitched his left toes, then moved his left foot under the covers.

She saw that, came closer to the bed. "Don't exert yourself," she said, which amused him.

Did he smile or frown, he wondered, whenever he showed amusement. "Can I get up?" he meant to say, but his words as spoken were jumbled, were in disarray; he realized they had gone venturing on their own, did not mean anything. Don't tell Young, he thought, but could not say it. He waited for proper words to enter his mind. He was confused by anxiety. Whenever she stopped talking, the fear began to increase, and he wanted her to go on and on, to distract him.

"Why, Mr. Wright, you're sweating like a pig." She wiped his face with a towel. "You were a while ago too."

"Amanda," he whispered.

"Who you want, Mr. Wright?"

This was not Amanda at all, it was some other woman. A moment ago she had been Amanda. Time also was disassembled. In what had seemed to him to be an instant, Amanda had left, this other woman had arrived. Maybe hours had passed. Frantically he looked about, to assure himself he was in the same room. He started to push himself up from the bed, using his left arm. This new woman restrained him, her hands strong on his shoulder; she knew where to take hold to stop him without hurting him, and how to push his back again onto the pillows. "Ah, you can't get up yet, but if you want anything, I'll bring it to you. Is it a bed pan you want, Mr. Wright?"

Who are you, he wondered. Amanda. What had happened to her? Had something gone awry here, in this little world, this parlor room. He spoke Amanda's name, but this time heard a word come out that sounded like daffodil. Exhausted, he allowed himself to be swept into a state of limbo. I will plan an escape soon, he thought.

Dr. Watkins sat in the rocker. Earlier he had complained of the lack of heat, so a fire had been built in the parlor fireplace. A blanket was around his legs. He was explaining that there were specialists now in strokes, and if he could only get this certain doctor on the telephone . . . Nearby sat Hallie. He had given Pink a couple of aspirin; he said he had found they calmed nerves about as well as anything else. Young knelt near the fire, his face tear-stained.

In the backyard a car arrived noisily, doors slammed; the car lights were left on, as Frederick and Henrietta hurried in, a bottle of the prescribed medicine in hand. "Your father's had a severe stroke, all right," Amanda told them.

"My God, I know he must have, mama," Frederick said. Henrietta took her in her arms, and it was then Amanda wept for the first time.

"Well, he knew it would happen," Amanda said, "but I told your brother Young this evening I never believed it. I felt we would find our way through that field, no matter how high the tassels, Frederick. I said to myself, God will take care of us. Young said he never had doubted his father's strength. I said to him we need to stay home more, not go adventuring, go to Tennessee like Pink did, then Virginia, and stop by to see Wurth, a strong-willed man, Wurth, and there's no changing him, as you'll find. There's something about any man that has muscle inside it."

"What's she saying?" Henrietta asked Frederick.

"Never be another like him, I'll tell you that," Amanda said. "Now Harry, your Uncle Harry . . ."

"No, I know, mama," Frederick patted her shoulder comfortingly. "I think the doctor doped her," he told Henrietta.

The telephone rang for the doctor. Dr. Watkins walked down the cold hallway, the blanket over his shoulder. "I didn't mean to get to you in the middle of the night," he said, then paused to listen. "Seems to be on the right side that he's afflicted. . . . Yes, he can talk, though not well. . . . Will it? . . . No, there's not been a bowel movement yet, nor kidneys. . . ." A long pause. "No," Dr. Watkins said, "I don't know if he does or not." A pause. "Is that important?" he said, frowning at the wall. "Well, yes, I'll see to it. Hold on." He put the phone against his chest and called for Amanda. "He wants to know about his bowels and kidneys and his sex organs."

"Why, I don't know," she said.

"I said I didn't know," Dr. Watkins admitted.

Amanda said, "We don't any of us know, do we?"

Watkins spoke into the telephone. Once more he put it against his chest. "He said to find out."

Amanda stared at him. "Why," she began, whispering, her breath gone from her body, "what is he going to do?"

Watkins spoke into the telephone, "Are you going to wait?" His voice became more strident. "Now, it can't all be done in a jiffy, Harold." He wrote on the wall a number, then hung up the telephone. "We'll call him back."

Amanda said, "I never had . . . any such an order."

"No. If you can merely test preliminarily . . ."

She stared helplessly at Frederick and Henrietta.

"No, now," Henrietta said to her, and took her hand and led her to the parlor door. Henrietta called the nurse outside and suggested she get tea for herself and the doctor, leave the husband and wife alone.

Amanda had uncovered him. Pink was watching her so trustingly. Such a child now. Like a boy in special need. Her boy. Her fingers coursed over the naked skin, resting finally near his testicles. She took them in her hand. "I'm supposed to do this, Pink," she said. He replied, and she wished she could understand what he said. "Well, it's not as warm as if the covers were on you, is it?" she said. She noticed his penis began to grow in size, it grew in her hand, as if it had life of its own, a creature seeking being. She watched it take on form and hardness. Pink said something else, which she couldn't understand. "I'm supposed to," she explained. She began stroking the creature, the creation. "I don't suppose it'll hurt you," she said. She stroked it, leaned forward and rested her head on his chest as she contin-ued to stroke it.

A knock on the door. She straightened as if struck by a fist, her eyes darting about. "Ahhh?" she said.

"Does it rise? That's all we want to know now, Amanda. What say?" It was the doctor's voice.

"Yes," she said breathily.

"I'm not sure we ought to go further." He opened the door, peeked inside, then came inside. Pink was lying on the bed, uncovered, his penis still hard. Pink spoke, but the words went flying off of their own accord. Watkins said, "Well, it rises, Amanda, I see that. I doubt if you ought to take him the rest of the way just now."

She drew a blanket over Pink's lower body. The doctor closed the door as he left and could be heard talking to the telephone operator. Pink mur-mured something to Amanda. "I don't know what to do, Pink," she admit-ted. She felt about under the covers and took his penis in her hand and stroked it, as she watched his face. His left hand rose to her own face, touched her face tenderly. "What you thinking, honey?" she said. His hand touched her breast, sought the nipple through her dress. "Oh, my Lord, Pink," she whispered to him. "I do love you so."

The sun almost blinded the nurse, falling, as it did, stark and bright on the Bible. She read a chapter every morning, and a chapter in the evening, and in the course of her life had gone through the Bible four times, Genesis to The Revelation. She found that the meaning was less important than the act of reading itself, the relaxation it afforded. Sometimes she read while visitors were in a patient's room. The Bible open on her knees gave visitors a guide as to attitude.

The patient spoke to her, and she carefully put a marker in the Bible and closed it. "I was reading about the begats," she told Mr. Wright, as she stationed herself beside his bed. "To think, all those people living and giving birth to one another, down through the ages, in that dry climate." She turned him on his left side and massaged his shoulder and arm, massaged his neck tenderly. She did care about her patients; they were hers, and that made them dear. "There's a woman waiting to see you, talking to your wife, name of Gloria Smith."

He grunted several words; they were indistinguishable to her even after these days of listening to him.

"Mrs. Wright has her in the dining room, she's tea-ing her, you might say, gives everybody that comes a cup of tea with the stems still in it. What sort of stems are they, Mr. Wright?"

"Spice bush," he tried to say, but said something incoherent.

"Are they? Well, there's been better ideas in the world. This Miss Smith has brought you a book of poems." Mr. Wright grunted approvingly; the nurse could tell whenever he approved of something. And he did like to be read to. "Your daughter, Hallie, was by about sixteen times. Your wife finally sent her on to work without waking you." He grunted once again. "Looking forward to surviving the begats, Mr. Wright, and hoping to get soon to the burning bush." The doorbell was ringing. "There's more people come here than comes to the train station," the nurse commented. She propped Pink up on his pillows and massaged his feet and lower legs, talking all the while. "It'll come to you one morning; you'll awaken and it'll all be over, like a bad dream, Mr. Wright. You will get out of the bed and stretch and say, What in the world has been going on these two, three weeks." He grunted. She assigned him a few words, listened to him try to say "time." Her own name was Imogene Pickett, and that name he simply couldn't say. He could say Imo, the first of it. She tried him on Amanda, and he could say Maaaa.

Amanda came into the room, reporting that Hatch Cole was here yet again, was on the porch with a bunch of flowers. Did Pink feel able to see him? Pink emitted a guttural moan, meaning no. She left and was heard outside talking to Hatch.

"I've not asked her yet if I can go on the night duty, Mr. Wright," the nurse confessed to him confidentially. "I think your wife'd do better of a daytime, and let me do the nights, once the visitors stop moving through the house like on the square." The doorbell rang. "Ah, there's what I mean. It'll be Frederick, or some farmer, or the doctor, or the specialist, or it'll be Gloria Smith again, the one your wife doesn't take to very well, though day before yesterday Gloria sat her entire lunchtime in the kitchen drinking that there stemmed tea and talking about what a great man you was, in your day."

In your day, in your day, in your day . . . the words had an echo in his mind.

Imogene smiled at him. "Wonder what stories you could tell me, if you only could and would. I know there's secrets every man has." She patted his face in a sudden fit of snuffed excitement. "If sins are counted, then I'll wilt. I'll be put in the fiery furnace, be laid among the serpents for what I've done in my day—I'm including now what I've imagined with the likes of Douglas Fairbanks. It's more'n he knowed in his whole life what I've done with him." She laughed, delighted with her remark. "And Johnny Weissmuller. How does he pronounce that, do you know? I've heard it so many ways. Here, honey, let me turn you on your bed so you can rest easy on the other side. Try to work them fingers. You'll need both hands, not one. If you could get one finger to fidget, then we could have us something to measure progress by—that's what I told your doctor, something ought to move first. Not that I mean to swing from the vines with him, you understand. I'll not have to do with apes, either. If it moves, this'n here—can you feel me pressing on it? Now if I pinch you on the wrist, what say to that? Can you still feel it? I never would have a chance with such a man, either Fairbanks or Weissmuller, they're so on the move, swinging, leaping, jumping away, flinging themselves at swords and lions and serpents. There are serpents in the Bible, two to one over other animals, did you know that, Mr. Wright? They must have had a time in the Holy Land with them. Now, if you and me was writing up a Bible for our times, we'd mention serpents, but we'd have more horses. We'd have dogs. We'd have more cats. If Jesus had died in Asheville, there'd have been schools of cats and dogs about." She wiped the sweat off his brow, smiled back at his smiling, handsome face. "Such a dear man, Mr. Wright, a sweet man. The more helpless a man is, the safer and sweeter he is. No," she said suddenly, "they've got camels, though, and we don't have those around here. You can say that for the ancients."

She entertained him royally. There was no stopping her babbling. She could talk the stobs off a halltree. She rambled around among her many interests, her words like water flowing in a cascade. Obstructions in the way were bathed in white suds. Her words were the froth of the water. Her expositions, her deviations pleasing him. He could follow all she said; he could listen to her and at the same time consider his own streams of thought. What was it the doctor had said: sometimes the blood clot is absorbed, it goes away and leaves the brain able to perform again, and the arms and legs can be taught to move, the tongue to speak. . . .

Dr. Watkins: "Here, Imogene, you step back a ways and let Dr. Bolton come up to the bed. Mrs. Wright, you step out into the hall. Hello, Mr. Wright. You hear me all right? Just nod."

Was it an affirmative nod, as he wanted it to be, Pink wondered.

"Pink, this is Dr. Bolton, who has been here before, but I'm sure you'll want to have his name again. Now then . . ."

The covers came down and the doctor asked what pain could be felt, what limbs could be moved. "It'll be necessary to massage these limbs every day, doctor," Dr. Bolton said.

"Yes, they do that. I told them you said to do that. His wife and nurse . . ."

"He's taking the medicine?"

"Yes, he is," Dr. Watkins assured him.

"Take it with a glass of milk is the best way. Now, if it is a blood clot, it might very well decrease in size. As it does so, the brain functions will return. Perhaps all. Soon we hope for him to start moving his right hand, for instance. He will have to relearn to use it. It won't be automatic."

Talking about me as if I'm not present, Pink thought, grateful to them.

"That medicine will thin his blood," Bolton said. "Makes clots less likely. We're always on the threshold of knowing, aren't we? and not knowing."

"I suppose so," Dr. Watkins said.

"Now, let me hear you speak, Mr. Wright," Dr. Bolton said. "Say hello to me. Can you say hello? It's usually one of the first words learned. Say good."

"Gooo," Pink said.

"That's close. That's like a baby does it. You must start at the first. Say mummy."

"Mum . . . mum . . ."

"That's a start, isn't it, Watkins? You say he was an insurance salesman?"

"Yes, he has his own company, a major financial institution now. This man here started the Monarch Company from absolutely nothing and has made it into—"

"Isn't that amazing," the specialist said, dismissing it, refusing to pause to consider another's miracle. "Why are tears in your eyes, Mr. Wright?" he asked him, suddenly concerned. He took a hem of the sheet of the bed and wiped his eyes. "We'll have you out of this bed in time, back at work, back at work," he said vigorously, and hastened outside. Pink could hear him explaining to Amanda about the massage, the exercise, the bathing, the efforts to speak. "It will go slow at first, but it will gain speed until one day you'll be amazed at how well he can talk. It's recommended that he try the simple words first. Tie. Toe. Bow. Say. Way. Go."

• • •

Amanda waited near the sidewalk, in case somebody was walking past that she knew and could talk with. Just last night she had lain on the bed beside Pink, rather than curl up in the big chair, and she had slept not quite as well, perhaps because of her fear of turning over onto him. A Mrs. Powell came along, pushing a baby carriage and leading a little dog, which was named Marchbanks. "Marchie's just like a big trout on a fishing line," Mrs. Powell said.

"I slept so little, worrying about turning over," Amanda said.

Mrs. Harmon considered that, then nodded briefly. "He's only six months old, and Charles said to go ahead and train him."

"Heard the clock strike every hour, except four. Our clock doesn't strike the half hours."

"You do seem sleepy, Mrs. Wright."

Amanda's stomach was churning; suddenly she was nauseated. She hurried up the walk, stumbled at the front steps, fell. Mrs. Harmon began calling for help, and that talking box, Imogene, emerged from the house, took hold even as Amanda regained her feet, hoisting her up the steps into the hall, where in the gloom, the cool, Amanda agreed to go to bed for a while. "In Pink's room," she suggested.

"No, that's where I am," Imogene informed her, propelling her into her own bedroom. "There's enough commotion goes on in there. He doesn't need more bother."

Sleep. Golden, safe sleep, the sheets cool. In her own room, sleep took her, and she was once more walking down the path at Vancetown that led from the church to her father's place, and Harry was walking beside her, his hand taking hold of her hand as they got out of sight of the church, and she began to hum the melody of the last hymn that had been sung, trying to mask her nervousness. She looked up at him, handsome lord, strong arms, as she knew, the bridge was ahead, he was holding her hand at the bridge, and when they were halfway across he paused to embrace her, to kiss her there, lifting her feet off the ground, she wriggling free again. Others would be approaching, somebody might be watching now. "Oh, Harry," she whispered, and he led her to her father's meadow, to the rail fence, and leaped the fence and turned to her, welcoming her into his arms.

She awoke, saying Harry's name, looking for him, as if she had lost him in the dark.

He was lying on the floor, his mouth open in a big O shape, his eyes round and large. Young and Imogene carried him back to the bed and covered him over. "You can't walk, Mr. Wright, didn't you know that?" she said. "You merely topple. Now close your mouth. You're not shouting. There's no sound coming out. You can close your mouth now."

Young ran a dropcord from the ceiling fixture, and placed a reading lamp on the left side of Pink's bed, where he could reach the chain with his left hand. He made a loop in the end of the chain, so Pink could put his thumb through it and pull the lamp on or off. Using this contrivance, Pink was better able to read. Both Young and Hallie spared time to rehearse him in speaking and writing.

Each evening when Hallie reached home, she would run into the house to find out how many new words her father had mastered—two, three, or even bits of words. Often as not, Amanda would be sitting in the one comfortable rocker, mentioning the visitors of the day, a pleasant, unobtrusive recitation, a monologue that kept her mind busy.

He would be found sprawled on the floor, unable to get up by himself, and Imogene would hoist him in her powerful hands. "It flops, you'll find. It won't be carried."

"Foot," he whispered, lying on the bed staring up at her.

"Yes, you have a foot attached to that floppy leg, and it's like a piece of lead. You never knowed your leg was so heavy, did you? Must weigh forty pounds."

He lay on the bed, where she had deposited him, his right arm caught under his body.

"If a man weighs a hundred eighty, his leg and foot will weigh forty, his hand and arm twenty, as a rule of thumb, so to speak." She found the analogy amusing, and stood there beaming at him, muttering "rule of thumb" over and over.

One morning, when she arrived, he was standing at the window holding on to the window's frame, staring at the birds feeding from the bushes. "More," he said to her.

"Now, look at us, would you?" she said, tossing her hat onto a wall peg. "Mr. Wright, what you thinking about now? Did your wife help you?"

He was afraid even to shake his head, afraid that might cause him to lose his balance.

"Must've," she said.

"Morn," he repeated.

"Morning to you, too, Mr. Wright," she said, and helped him across the room to the bed, but once there he kept saying "cha," which she decided might mean chair, so she set him on a straight-backed chair near the fireplace, then tied him to the chair with a sheet. "Is it a change you're after? Sit there then, till you want me to put you to bed."

Hallie read to him every evening, read poems to him.

> They were all looking for a king
>   To slay their foes and lift them high;
> Thou cam'st, a little baby thing
>   That made a woman cry.

He liked that very well, was amused by it. Most anything by Words-
worth he liked.

> The eye—it cannot choose but see;
>   We cannot bid the ear be still;
> Our bodies feel, where'er they be,
>   Against or with our will.

She would repeat certain parts, ones he appeared to appreciate particularly, and one evening he said a few lines with her.

> Love is swift of foot;
>   Love's a man of war,
>   And can shoot,
>   And can hit from far.

Young could be with him only a few minutes at a time, distress quickly
overcoming him, and he was easily annoyed by his mother's or Imogene's
companionable chatter. To him, his father's illness was a life calamity, hot
to the heart, serious as lingering pain. He went into the room first thing of
a morning, then reluctantly, tearfully would hurry to school.

After school he would make frequent short visits to his father's room,
trying not to reveal his fear, hoping always for relief, for miracles. His
mother and Hallie sought to treat the illness by comforting the ill person.
He wanted to cry out against the illness, to eradicate it. He had no sympathy for it, would never learn to endure it. He knew within his own mind
neither of them was unkind or wished his father harm, but how could a
woman make herself part and parcel of an illness?

A man could not. He could not. Talk, papa, learn the words, speak
clearly, walk, walk as well as you told me to walk when I had only part of
one foot.

One night quite late, Hallie gone to bed, Amanda came to Pink, whispering to him, saying she loved him. He was unable to reply. She undid
the bodice of her dress, sat down on the edge of his bed, and leaned toward
him, so that a nipple was close to his face. He closed his lips over the
nipple and sucked like a baby.

Sometimes at night she would lie down on the bed beside him and hold
him in her arms; sometimes she allowed herself sexual pleasures. Afterward

his fingers often entwined in her hair, his fingers pulled their way up the sheaves of hair, finally nestling close to her head, gently massaging her neck.

"My baby, my baby," she would whisper. "I love you so. Baby Pink." She did not talk with the doctor about these episodes. She never found Dr. Watkins mentioning anything of a similar nature, either. She decided these occasions were dear to Pink, were important to him, and they fed her own body. They were precious breaths they breathed together.

Pink could hear the trains rolling into the station. Or was it the sound of his own heart? he wondered. Was the sound of the train the sound of his heart beating, or some heavy-footed arrival. Harry coming home?

Amanda came in from her room to see how he was. He tried to talk to her, finding a few words he could say, could trust. She kissed him, then like a ghost fading returned to her bed, leaving him embraced by the train sound. He knew it was not a train. There was no train nearby. The heart sound would relax him. And warn him. And beckon him.

The second month of his illness, Hallie was on her way home from work when her period started. She had that morning noted the date and had made some preparations of clothing, but she had not expected it to begin for one more day. She had eaten too big a noonday meal at the Langren, paid for by Wallerbee, and that must have helped bring it on. After lunch she had felt sluggish, and the dull ache had started at four o'clock. She had thought then she had better go on home, but there were three applications from the office in Greensboro, and the manager in Hickory was urgently concerned about one of last week's rejections. It was six o'clock when she let herself out. The first cramp doubled her up. She staggered to a bench at a streetcar stop near Rachel Jewelers, sat there dazed, considering her options. She saw no one she knew. There were no taxis about. A streetcar arrived, but she wouldn't be benefited by its route. Thank God I'm not pregnant, at least I have that, she told herself. She walked home, taking one patient step after another, arriving home at seven, Amanda meeting her on the porch.

"Where on earth? Your papa's desperate."

Hallie made her way to the bathroom, where she threw up what was on her stomach, and at once the intense pain subsided, as did the dull ache and the nausea, and she was left with a craving for chocolates.

Whenever she met with her father, she would relate stories about her day's happenings, but tonight she avoided this most critical one and confined herself to talk about the company, citing from memory figures and dates. She told him about the beauty shop, too, in such a way as to convulse him with laughter; she had found a Frenchwoman to do her hair, one who spoke a capricious English Hallie could imitate, and who was given to endless confusion about what the customer wanted, whether a wash or set or permanent wave or whatever. Hallie felt better about her own appearance now, anyway. She told her father about her life as it began to untangle, with the company at the center of it, and her affair with Wallerbee, halting, advancing, almost despairing. "I don't know what the alternatives are, papa," she told him. "How does one choose from one choice?"

If propped up on pillows and given paper, Pink could write several words, most of them nouns; Hallie wanted him to learn verbs as well: go, come, bring, take, hear, speak, laugh. . . . She taught him to write "I am laughing." He had energy enough to write only a few words at a session.

Amanda was hurt, pleased, tortured by Hallie's effort. She had been brought up to choose proper soil for each crop; one did not plant wheat in new ground, for instance, nor cabbages in rocky fields. One could plant grapevines there. One did not plow ground that was so steep a rain would wash the topsoil away. "There are tricks to choosing a field, Hallie," Amanda cautioned her, "and you've chosen to plow a rocky, steep field, and it might not bear a crop. I want you not to be too disappointed." Amanda felt foolish and guilty, resenting her own attitude. She felt she ought to encourage Hallie but she could not bring herself to do so. And why didn't Hallie and Pink choose hymns, which everybody knew? Why did they have to use poems that were all ahh and ohh. She did so want Hallie to have her own home, a family for herself, instead of being in Amanda's house, taking her family.

CHAPTER
Twenty

A mean depression, cruel to its depths, had gripped the farmers all of 1928, with six-cents-a-bushel potatoes and penny-a-head cabbages, or nothing at all. "Then haul them home," grocers said. That depression touched Wall Street late in 1929 and gained the attention of the press in the big cities, even gained notice of the government. Mixed with pity, there was a certain amount of brutal satisfaction to Pink in seeing that city people were now wrestling with the beast that had driven the farmers into ever further humiliation, with families torn open, daughters exploited, sons caught in a tide of helplessness, farms abandoned, livestock slaughtered, communities disrupted. The Monarch Company tilted and slid, making loans on policies more and more reluctantly, planning delays, accepting lapses, foreclosing on mortgages, guarding its own life. Nobody had any cash except such men as Hatch Cole, and he parceled it out in order to try to save his investments.

Then in 1930 a large local bank failed. Also, the Clove empire tottered, surviving precariously. Three of the city's most progressive leaders leaped from top floors of the new City Hall, dying on the newly laid brick courtyard. As Pink saw it, the cities had now caught the ravaging illness and were releasing cries of pain; reluctantly he sensed the satisfaction of a countryman who sees a rural plague, which had been long ignored, at last receive due concern in the cities.

Families joined the soup lines that curled halfway around the square, in sight of the office windows where Hallie and Wallerbee would share the lunch Wallerbee's sisters now prepared for him each day, usually two egg-salad sandwiches—eggs could be bought at two cents a dozen—and an apple. By summer of 1930 the company had slid from two hundred salesmen to one hundred fifty. Bricks were hurled on three different occasions at Wallerbee's car, messages from despondent salesmen. He was, indeed, the lean executive, who made calculating, cold decisions concerning his own staff, his own policyholders, and anybody who owed Monarch money, and he admitted as much to Pink on occasions when he came to call on him. "And Hatch now needs money, himself, is trying to take it out of the company as dividends."

"Well . . . you stop him," Pink said, pronouncing a word at a time.

"I have to say no to everybody, Pink. It falls to me."

Amanda fixed herself a cup of tea. She sat at the kitchen table, a quarter of a piece of pound cake on the envelope that had brought her the electric bill. Have to start turning off more lights, she thought. She said aloud one of Pink and Hallie's poems, "Youth rambled on life's arid mount . . ." not knowing what it meant. She knew what arid meant, but what sort of a mount was in mind? Was it a mount like a mountain, or a mount like a horse, or was it the act of mounting a chair? A baby could say the line better than had poor Pink at first; he had often gone astray trying to locate the hard sounds, the consonants.

She took Hallie a piece of cake, mentioning that Henrietta had made it, this time a lemon cake that was not sweet enough. "She's learning," Amanda said, nodding significantly to Hallie, who couldn't cook at all well. "She has her husband, is carrying her first one. I remember that, how it was, with my first one."

"Yes, you've told me, mama," Hallie said.

"Morning sickness and wondering about what pain I would have to suffer, and if it'd die or not. Well, what you smiling at? It does pain in the worse way. I don't know that you'll ever feel it."

"I don't either, mama," Hallie said. "A pity," she added. "I do think it would be nice to have . . . to have something."

"Besides your father."

Hallie looked up startled.

"Don't know that I will ever have that same pain again, myself."

"Mama, you know you won't," Hallie said. Slowly the suggestion crept into her mind. "Mama, what did you say?"

"That pain," she said. "I don't know."

"No, you said you weren't sure. Mama, you are sure, aren't you?"

Amanda swept crumbs off her apron. "Well . . ." she said, seeking an explanation, "I'm not answering to you, Hallie, about my own life." She moved into the kitchen.

Hallie followed. "Mama, you're not doing that, are you?"

"Doing what?"

"Mama, for God's sake," Hallie shouted. "You're not endangering him that way, are you?"

"Endangering him? I'm talking about a woman's pain—"

"Doing that. Are you pregnant, mama?"

"I . . . I don't know what comes over you, Hallie. Look at you, go look at your face, the anger in your face—"

"Mama, I'll kill you, so help me God—"

"Kill me? What are you killing me for? For sleeping with my husband, are you? Are you daft? Take your hand off of me."

"Mama, I'll kill you, so help me God—"

Amanda struck her. She hit her hard in the face. She had to be free of her that very moment. Regrets, she felt regrets immediately. "Where are you going?" she asked, helplessly staring after her. "Hallie," she called. "Hallie." She heard her crying. Her sobs shook Amanda's very bones. Whenever Hallie cried it was from Hallie's belly, seemed like, it was a deep, gasping, breathless crying. "Hallie," Amanda whispered, "what did I do wrong?" She sat down on the edge of Hallie's bed. "I come to the garden alone," she sang softly, "while the dew is still on the roses. . . . Oh, my God," she whispered, "we are coming apart at the seams. Maybe I've done wrong, Hallie. I'm sorry for it and I hope you are sorry for all you've done and left undone. We have to live in the same house, Hallie, mother and daughter. So stop that crying and go give your father his words for the night, and let me fix you some supper. Hallie. Hallie." She sat there staring at her, at her daughter, the two of them being opposite sides of the same body, like opposite sides of a page in a book.

Finally the sobbing stopped. Hallie stared up at her. "Are you pregnant, mama?"

"I do hope so," Amanda said.

· · ·

264

The fall colors were beautiful every year, and every year there was discussion comparing them with last year's. If the rains had been plentiful in September, the colors in October would not attain full brightness; also, there were matters of temperature to consider, or so people claimed. The forests covering all these mountains were hardwood, and in this terrain, with its wind currents ever changing, the colors would give each mountainside a multicolored coat, and the rise and fall of mountains and mountain ranges added to the spectacle.

There were no higher mountains in the country that were hardwood covered, there was no autumn show elsewhere that compared with this October fair, painted with millions of leaves, each leaf a marvel, and each different.

Hallie and Wallerbee drove into the mountains. Car followed car that day. Also, cars parked alongside the road, picnickers relaxing. A sedan full of pretty girls caused a traffic problem as young men ran to help them change a tire. Each curve in the road revealed a wash of reds and orange and yellows and lavender.

Also, each autumn the families discussed the possible return this year of relatives, as if the call of color would be sufficient to reclaim them. Each family had a number of dear relatives who were living in the North or West, or had dipped down into the outlands to work in the textile mills or the furniture or tobacco factories. If they lived within a day's drive, they could be expected to put in an appearance, claiming a meal and hoping for a bed, during fall colors. If the driving time was greater than a day, then the family conversations would normally revolve around the railroad schedule. "Now, Brodie knows we'll meet him at the train station," Hugh King said, sitting down in Amanda's kitchen, having arrived for his first visit.

"Won't help much, if he crosses the country," Amanda said, putting a mug of coffee before him. She took the cloth off the pound cake and cut him a slice of it.

"Take . . . take about a week to get here on the train," Hugh admitted, the coffee burning its way across the roof of his mouth, giving him a moment's pause. "Take seven nights, and if he leaves the West in the middle of a day, he'll arrive here the middle of a night, which means he'd get a brother sent after him. I wouldn't go."

"You wouldn't go anyway, Hugh," Amanda said. "Pink's been sick ten months and you're here the first time this morning, and you almost didn't get to the house you were so busy seeing what was in the sheds."

"I always go around back first; my papa did."

"Well, I know," she said, remembering her own family.

"My mama's front door was used one day each spring. She'd sweep the winter out."

Amanda laughed. "Well, it's at least half true, what you say."

"How is Pink?"

"Nettie's been here, she must have told you he's every day better."

"She says he's looking better."

"He's—he's in a critical condition, it's called. He can't get out of bed for long."

"You want to sit down? I'll move my coat, if you do," Hugh said.

"Oh, you know me," she said, refusing the invitation. "He's . . . he seems to be pleased by most of what I do," she said, trying to smile. "Hallie can get him laughing."

Hugh was watching her thoughtfully, measuring her meaning through her efforts to be casual. "You know, we had a falling out, Amanda. Did you know that?"

She picked up his coat and slid onto the chair, all the while watching him. "What about?"

"Not more'n a snake's tail. It's that him and me had grown so far apart, don't you see, and I can see his world and think to myself, Hugh, you could have done it like Pink, if you'd learned to jump like Pink." His voice was low and gravelly; he was seeking ways to express his doubts, as well as his convictions, to keep company with his emotions. "And naturally I felt I was in a race with him, so to speak. And he was winning it, Amanda."

"Before he was struck down," she said.

"I'd turn down a fellow from back home for a loan, then he'd get it from Pink. Happened many times."

"You want some more cake?"

He ate the second piece of cake much as he had eaten the first, chewing with wide movements of his lower jaw, swallowing with grimaces, finally crushing the crumbs from the plate on his fingertips, eating those. "But here they've asked me to do a deposition on his—his competency."

She looked at him askance. "Why would they ask you?"

"A relative, I suppose. Hatch Cole put them on to me."

"I . . . didn't know they . . . would cast about."

He sat there staring at her, taking her measure. "You going to have to declare your husband incompetent, Amanda?"

"Life has to go on, and so does his company," she said, watching him. "Is this any of your business, Hugh?"

"Hatch sent word, asked me for a deposition on Pink, so it is my business, unless I ignore it."

She picked at the gouged cake. "Then ignore it."

"If he wants me to."

She looked into his eyes for a long moment, then turned away, crossed her arms protectively. "He's lying in there in the bed, Hugh."

Hugh finished his coffee, pushed his cup and saucer back out of the way. "I'm sorry, Manda."

"He's in there. You can judge for yourself."

He waited. "Maybe I'm making too much of it," he admitted. "Didn't mean to tell you I had come here for such a reason anyway. I've been meaning to come by, because it wasn't anything, that argument, it just wasn't anything more than a snip of string."

"He's in there in the parlor room," Amanda told him, and left him, went out into the backyard.

Hugh found his way to the parlor, where the nurse was talking to herself and the window shades, best he could judge. He spoke to Pink, and there was a groaning, not a readable response, and then the nurse interrupted. "Why, he never said no, did you, Mr. Wright?" the nurse said. "He was trying to—"

"I asked him did he see my son Brodie when he was in the West," Hugh told her. "I'm talking to him." Noticing a flash of anger in the nurse, he said, "I don't want to talk to you just now."

Imogene explained, "You have to watch his head, his eyes, his mouth, to see if he smiles, or nods, or has some other comment."

"Lady, will you let me do this."

Pink was touching a Persian cat, scratching behind its ears with his left hand, and it did seem to Hugh that he was attentive to him behind the mask he wore. "Now then, Pink, let me ask you something else. Do you have any need for me to help you in your business affairs?"

The eyes closed, as if Pink were weary beyond measure.

"His eyes close for lack of strength to hold the lids open," the nurse interjected. "Now, if you'd come here earlier—"

"Lady, will you shut up?" Hugh said. He told her to go fix tea, then closed the door after her. "That argument you and me had, Pink," Hugh said, returning to the bed, "I was mentioning to Manda that it's an empty poke. I don't know why i got upset to start with. Don't know enough about women to argue about them." He paused to reflect on that, and to notice if Pink smiled or not. No response there, except that Pink's gaze did follow him. It was hard work, Hugh decided, conversing in this room. "Pink, you've been laid up for months and a man's business interests keep getting into mischief. You have a flock of loans outstanding. Now take just that . . ."

The eyes closed.

"Take that mortgage even on your home."

There was no reply from the closed-up face, a mere reflection of a personality. Gently Pink's fingers moved against the cat's ears, nothing else.

"Suppose you resent my interfering." Hugh cleared his throat. "I'm wondering, Pink, if you've given thought to who ought to represent your business interests, whether Amanda or one of your children." That gained no response, either. "I'm thinking your daughter is the best one you've got."

For a moment, the face registered a reaction. If the face could smile, it smiled then, and the eyes did take on more vitality. "Now, I believe you agree. Pink—you can hear me?" Hugh moved closer. "I'm afraid Manda's going to favor the oldest son. It's a mother's way." Pink's eyes flashed, and there was a moment when Hugh thought maybe Pink would try to rise. "Now, Pink, your daughter and son won't work in harness, and I think that girl would make two of the boy, to be honest with you." Yes, a light was in his eyes all right, and there was a twitch of his lips as he sought speech, but there was resentment in his expression, too.

"You want me to push Amanda toward the girl?"

The eyes closed.

"Well, I know within reason you do, but you shut your eyes. Now, Pink, if you do, look at me. You can trust me, Pink."

The eyes opened.

"Pink," Hugh said, confused. "Pink, you was just now fondling that cat's ears. If you favor the girl, touch the cat for me." He waited tensely. There was no reply at all from the sick man. "Now, will you allow me to help you, Pink? I know we had a quarrel, but let that be." Amanda was in the dining room, Hugh heard her asking the nurse what had happened to the brown sugar. "Pink, if you want me to help, you scratch that cat, Pink."

Pink's hand moved across the blanket, sought out the cat with his hand, then a tiny smile worked its way onto his lips; he never, he did not scratch the cat's head. A little flicker of spit came on his lips as he looked up into Hugh's face.

Hugh moved at once to the window, which he pried open so that he could spit. He closed the window with a bang. "Not any good reason, that quarrel." He stomped back to the bed. "Pink, I'll ask you again, tickle that there cat's ears if you want me to move on your behalf." Amanda was in the hall, and he thought she might even have heard the question. She came now into the room to station herself at the foot of the bedstead.

Pink's gaze shifted from Amanda to Hugh and back again. He reached out for the cat, his fingers even sought out the hollow spots behind the cat's ears.

"Scratch its ears if you mean yes," Hugh said adamantly, doubly determined now. "Pink, I know you hear me. Now, if you want me to help you along the lines I mentioned, scratch the cat's ears."

Pink's eyes looked up into Hugh's face. The hand was motionless. It rested on the cat's head for a moment longer, then the hand withdrew as Pink's eyes closed.

CHAPTER
Twenty-one

Dear Hallie, he thought, if she had not healed him, who could heal him? She was the meaning of his life now, the legs and feet, the brain of his body, the laughter he could not express, the key to his diversions and expressions; there was no word he could not learn to say, provided she would speak it, no laugh he could not laugh if she would laugh for him, no victory he could not attain if she would help him.

After Hallie had gone to sleep, Amanda came into the room in her nightgown, her hair in a cap, which she had tied under her chin with a bow, giving her, he noticed, a little-girl look. "Hallie and Young are asleep at last, Pink." She put the cat on his bed. "You want me to stay here with you tonight, Pink?" she asked, exploring the question in her own mind even as she expressed it.

"If . . . you . . . like." He had found that sometimes when he showed enthusiasm for the idea she might decide to negate it, this being a recent expression of her will, a further exercise of control over him. He waited, watching her.

"I don't know," she said, a continuing examination of the option that was purely her own to make. "Maybe for a few minutes, Pink. I do get tired these days, there's so much weight on me. Hallie's a help, but not what she ought to be. And she has her life all planned around the company, and as you and I have decided so many times before, that's not suitable. And Imogene's more trouble . . ." Almost at random thoughts formed, evolved, dismissed each other, tails were left, heads severed. The little light bulb was hid now behind a fold of newspaper, which served as a night shade. Amanda's head bobbed against the mist of light, her head in halo. "She'll need to leave that company soon—"

"No," he said, the word as clear as he had ever said it since the stroke.

"No?" she whispered.

"No," he said again, the full reserve of pride rising inside him.

"Pink, Frederick is not to be set aside for his sister. I can't do that. Mr. Cole has come to me and begged for Frederick to work in the company—"

"No." The word was stark and naked in that clock-ticking room, shattering the air.

After a few moments, she continued. "He wants to work something out to make a success for him. He's twenty-six, has a family. Well now," she said, "I'm not in a business way, I'm not able to decide everything that's here, but you can't run the company from this bed, now can you?"

"No," he said sternly.

She was at the foot of the bed, just beyond the copper rail, studying him. "I guess you need to sleep," she said kindly. She used a chair to block the door; often she had expressed fear that the door would close in the night, and she would not hear him should he need her. "You go to sleep now, Pink," she said, her voice strained and thin. "I might have to let Imogene go, Pink. You understand about our lack of money, and she assumes more and more. Dr. Watkins told us others have had the same problem with her. She even talked with Hallie about Frederick." She touched the metal bedstead, then withdrew her hand, as if the metal stung her. "Was trying to weed out the gardens today. I've scratched my hands."

"The bay-buh," he uttered, pushing himself up on his left elbow, seeking pronunciation of an untutored word.

"Yes, the baby," she said. "Hallie told you? Well, of course she would.

You and Hallie have always been so close. Well, no, don't you worry about a baby. Chances are in the next month—"

"Bab-bee," he said.

"I only admitted that to her, Pink, because she was bedeviling me." She spoke evasively, shaking her head, covering her mouth with the fingers of one hand. "Don't you know that at my age it'd be unlikely. . . . I mean I would lose it."

He murmured, relieved by what she had told him, "Dear Manda."

"Yes, dear Amanda," she repeated with a wry acceptance of her place in his life, one subsidiary to his daughter, also to his company and to Young as well.

He heard her prop open her bedroom door across the hall. He pushed his head deeper into the pillows and stared at the dark ceiling, where reflections of moonlight lived briefly, his mind grappling with notions of the family, the company.

He stroked Young's cat with his weaker hand, which had some scant feeling returning. No longer in the night did terror come over him, the terror that he was paralyzed completely and could not even call out. His life had taken on a more positive motion, a direction toward health, and the nights were welcome as time to pace his progress for the next day's exertion, and to enjoy his mind's visits to places and ideas. This cat is free, he thought, to go out and live as she pleases. She can loll in the sun, enjoying the gifts of the earth, or she can ball up in the shade under the eaves, where only the black snake can go, or the chatting squirrels, and neither will attack her. She can copulate with Orientals, he thought, amused by that notion, without threat of self-criticism, charmingly, purringly, modestly, scratchingly, nibble at the ears of foreigners. Do cats kiss toes? Pink wondered. He had kissed the toes of the Oriental girl. The idea did not appeal to him, here alone in the bed, but it had seemed inviting at the time, though anything that delayed copulation brought moans of anxiety from her. Time was her treasure, her soul had a clock mechanism, and her anxious sighs were merely ticks and tocks and bongs of the moneychanger. She was adept at putting men in their allotments, half a dozen a night, like eggs in an egg basket, then discarding the basket. Keep few memories: one nibble, a kiss on toes, two fingers in an orifice instead of one, a tongue moving in the ear, some other such memories she might find worth clinging to for a while. China. He could say her name, but would not do so. China. Could he say that to his family? An experience paid for, mind you, and only guardedly, partially delivered. She never was fully delivered to him, to any of the men, he imagined.

Thank you, he told her to himself, speaking to the memory he regretted, and had bought and paid for.

Amanda will not bear a baby, he assured himself, and he thought he had read in her hesitancy that she would not move against his will in matters of the company.

Say what one would about her faults, she was his honest wife, a division of his life, and was incapable at her age of tearing that life apart. She was ill, too. His illness had impoverished her in all ways. He must remember that.

Hugh King was selecting apples for the new Battery Park Hotel, putting only the biggest samples in a bushel basket, when he heard Malcolm McDermit of Starnes Cove say that Harry was back. Hugh straightened, sorted in his mind all the Harrys he had known, piecing together the details of the men of that name who had remained in his memory.

"Harry Harmon?" he asked this man McDermit.

"No, no," McDermit said. "Harry Harmon is in Texas, has more land than his father and four uncles combined—"

"Well, I know that," Hugh said. "Harry Cress?"

"No, he's in Washington, D.C. Has a news shop." The man snickered. "Would you think a person could make a living out of selling magazines?"

"Harry Wright?" Hugh asked.

McDermit allowed himself a slight nod, then waited to be asked for details about health and wealth, location and dates. "Hands tremble," he commented.

"So do mine, if I only had time for it," Hugh said. "What did he come home for?"

"I thought you'd know," McDermit said. "Is he related to you?"

Hugh, weighing a bag of apples, shrugged. "Everybody is."

"Better go up and down the streets counting the women while you can find them," McDermit said.

Hugh went on toward the back of the store, laughing to himself. "Oh, Harry Wright," he said, "those men that go away, they come back charmed."

Within the hour Nettie visited Amanda, anxious to witness her expression. She walked to the house carrying her baby and told her the news face to face.

Harry, Harry, Harry. The word went through Amanda, was a delicious, tingling on her nerves, a reminder of her youth. At once she wanted to find him. Being this near Harry after all these years sent her heart racing. "Why are you looking at me so strange, Nettie?"

"You were gasping."

Nettie stayed for a cup of tea. She drank the tea, listening—both of them were listening for the telephone to ring. Amanda said there was a picture of Harry she would go find, and she went into her bedroom and shut the door. What if the telephone rang now, and Harry spoke to her after the years, the many years, the days and nights passing over her, all her youth?

The telephone rang, and she dashed toward it, but Nettie was answering it. "Why, you can stay over to my place," Nettie was saying. "No, bring your things to my house this morning—"

Amanda wrested the telephone receiver from her, spoke into the telephone itself. "You can stay here, Harry. This is Amanda King speaking. Harry, Harry—"

Nettie disconnected the call, turned to cluck her tongue critically, then began to laugh. "It was Hugh's aunt," she said.

When Nettie left, Amanda went into Pink's room. "Pink, are you listening?" She had to ask, for often he was merely looking at her, wasn't trying to understand. "You remember Harry, don't you?" She sat down on the edge of the bed. "He's in town somewhere."

A smile appeared. "Love Harry," he whispered.

"Love Harry, yes, you do," she said.

"You do," he said, and even his eyes crinkled, as if he had found her out.

"Yes," she whispered to him, "yes, I did once, Pink, before I courted with you."

His smile lingered, seemed to be evolving, fading, reappearing, as if it were independent of Pink. The telephone rang. Amanda answered it and heard his voice out of the past. "Harry," she said, trying to speak plain and clear, interrupting his asking about Pink. "Harry." She kept interrupting Harry, who was now talking about his brother Wurth writing him, advising him to come home if he hoped to see his mother alive, for she was fading, and to see Pink alive. Amanda kept saying her address to him, until finally he stopped going on about his mother and Pink and after a pause said to her in his sweet voice—very much like Pink's, actually—"Will you feed me noon dinner if I come now?"

"Oh, yes," she said.

"Well, I have a ride up home, but not till two."

"Yes," she whispered.

"Amanda, are you listening?" he said, his voice fading. It was strange the way they both were fading. "Amanda?"

"Yes, yes, I can hear you," she called.

"I've always loved you," he said.

He arrived in a taxi. Amanda watched him, waited near the sycamore tree. He was at the curb and had two big black leather suitcases, and turned to look at her across the seventy-five-foot distance, across the years, scarcely paying attention to the taxi driver, who was asking for his pay. Handsome as a lord, looking very much like Pink, he came up the walk, leaving the suitcases, and held out both arms to Amanda, and it seemed natural for her to rush to him, as in her youth, and be embraced by him.

Harry carried Pink into the dining room and propped him up in the armchair at the head of the table, then he stationed himself in the kitchen doorway, where he could talk with Amanda in the kitchen and Pink in the dining room, carrying on two conversations while devouring a bowl of green beans left over from last night, reaching out for cold biscuits from breakfast, breaking off leaves from a head of cabbage, busily occupying his mouth with food while he talked about Pink being certain to get well again. "I can tell from his coloring," he declared to the listening world. "Two brothers in Oregon had strokes and the coloring got better in one of them, and next thing you knew he had his feeling back in his legs, could learn to walk again, could speak clear as a child of seven. Was a Meredith, married to a DuPont, not one of the chemical ones, but the family that came in the gold rush in 1851, arrived through Panama with eleven sons, and they've spread out so that today one is a trucker, one is the Meredith and Sons foodstore chain, with the first store built at the corner of March and Fifth in Portland. . . ."

Apparently Harry never forgot a detail. He could go from one name and year to another, flipping through a welter of information, regaling his listeners with a swath of life evidences to support his claims that Pink would return to health once more, bringing to bear on this subject a thousand items of information having to do with jobs, ages, habits, customs, laws in Oregon and Washington State and California, the new highway along the coast, the asthma attack he had suffered at age thirty-six, the desert years, as he called them, this evidence being exact, confident, his argument sure, there being no way to answer all of it since there was no way to grasp it.

Amanda held the hot pan over the stove and banged the pan to loosen the bread. She turned the steaming loaf onto a plate and beamed at Harry as he tore his hungry gaze free and launched himself into a sequence of memories about his fiftieth birthday—not a happy one, he assured them— and before he was showing signs of abating, the meal was on the table, what parts of it Harry had not already consumed, and he was sitting at the table with Pink, complimenting Pink on his ability to use his right as well as his left hand, complimenting Amanda on the food, telling her how young she looked, insisting that she sit at the table, "and not stand about like mama, or like somebody waiting for a train." Insisting she serve her plate, too. He drank down his tea and much of Amanda's as well, ate a big chunk of cornbread, which he broke off the loaf with his hands, buttering the bread as he devoured it, gesturing with his fork to emphasize his messages of good will. "Mountain water keeps a person young-looking, Amanda, not wrinkles them like western water, which is pumped out of the ground. Spring water flows naturally. Well water is dead on arrival. See the blue blood in my veins, Amanda. Look at that vein, how blue it is. Royal blood."

Quiet, once he left. Lonely. After supper Amanda sat in her bedroom, a little fire still burning in the grate, one of her own quilts pulled about her shoulders, her body shivering, not from the cold in the room but from the chill inside her body. She listened to Young, who had massaged Pink and now was walking him there in the room.

Midnight, the children asleep, Amanda was still awake. She carried a candle into Pink's room. He was staring at the ceiling, making his big thoughts. She returned to her room and put a drop of toilet water on her nightgown at the bodice, then returned. "Pink?"

He laughed softly. "That Harry is a . . . sight."

"I suppose he is."

"You're go to . . . catch you gown . . . fire."

She set the candle down on the leather binding of his Bible. "You finished Exodus yet?"

"Yes, on the jour . . . ney. Know more about Jews than . . . Americans."

"Well, I say we all do," she said at once. "God's chosen people."

"Moses, Abraham, Dav . . . id."

"Don't know why Noah cursed his son, do you?" The candle was lathering wax onto the leather Bible, but she decided it wouldn't matter. "Says he saw him naked, so Noah cursed him and his descendants forever," she said. "I saw my father naked several times, once when he had a rash, was lathered with mama's soap, standing in the kitchen in a washtub. I came back from school—"

"Must have done . . . more than look," Pink said.

"Why, what else, Pink?"

"Play with . . . his father?"

"As in love?"

"Such as that."

"Such as what, Pink?" she asked.

He said haltingly, carefully, "David was more a singing person. He might have pushed . . . the son away and made a song. Not many songs by No . . . ah."

She patted the covers into place. "You read the Bible the strangest I ever saw." She lingered beside his bed, attracted to his presence, wanting company.

"You make peace . . . with Hal?" he asked.

"I always have been peaceful with Hallie. Why did you bring that up?"

"Hal would be hurt—"

"Hallie's all right. She's been wrung dry by that company; she's brittle, not like a woman ought to be. Now, don't get angry with me, Pink. Turn her into a man behind a man's desk, with a man's pencil in her hand."

"A man's . . . what?" he asked, pushing himself higher on the pillows.

"She's not fed properly by any pencil. A woman is not like a piece of furniture." Suddenly she said, "Goodnight then, Pink. We were having such a nice talk about the Jews, and you had to bring her into it, didn't you?"

"Manda, I want you . . . my decision—"

"The decision I have to face is to free my daughter to be a woman and my son to be a man. If you think I can do anything less, then you go on back to reading your Bible and see how the Jews would do it."

Two o'clock, loneliness and self-doubt suffocated her; new candle in hand, she returned. "I'm sorry, Pink. I can't sleep."

"No."

"What you thinking about? Getting well again?"

"Hal courting."

"Don't you bring up that summer, Pink. You know it upsets me."

"She's famous up home," he said.

"Don't you say it. Don't you say it again."

"Famous . . . in that valley, and the boy crossed the river—"

"Pink, don't you dismiss Hallie this way—"

"Walk over the water."

"So you're laughing inside, are you, at Hallie, and then you blame me for wanting the best for her."

"Saw Hal clear a fence—"

Amanda slapped Pink's leg. "Now, hush, please . . ." She slapped him on the chest. "Don't you criticize her. Why do you laugh at Hallie?"

"Scared the dogs," he said, choking on laughter.

"Feel for her," Amanda said, "can't you feel for her? Can't you feel, Pink?" she asked, tears in her eyes, rolling down her cheeks as she slapped at him.

Later, yet again she went to his room to apologize. Once more anger had dissipated, leaving a sense of blue, flabby regret. "What say to making up, Pink? What say?"

"You are clever, Manda . . . to think of it."

"Think of what? What did I do?"

"We can put Harry with Hal."

"Harry with . . . I . . . I never would trust him with Hallie."

"She ought to have a baby, I agree."

"You are tricking me, Pink. You lie there smart as a devil, and like a snake you strike." She was angry with him but unable to tear herself away from the raging emotions he was arousing in her. "God will hear you, Pink."

"He will go to her room."

"God will damn you, Pink, to suggest . . . your own brother . . ." She fled. His cruel tongue once more had driven stakes into her.

She fell asleep sitting in a chair in her room. When she awoke the dawn light was graying the world outside and drawing wavy pictures on her wall—and on my face, too, she told herself, wondering what sort of zebra patterns it was making, what type of prisoner she was, for what crime. She ladled coal on the fire and cuddled once more in the chair. She heard Hallie's door latch, heard the stairs creak, and directly there stood Hallie in a pair of Pink's pajamas, a little-girl smile on her lips. "Hallie, I want you to be more like you were years ago," she said at once. "I want all of us to be."

"Oh . . ." Hallie rubbed her face, yawned. "It's been so long, mama."

"You can try," she said simply.

Hallie consented, seemed to agree, but then paused. "What are we agreeing to, mama?"

Twenty-two

On a Monday Hatch came by. He stood on the front porch, his hat pulled down over his forehead, his scarf tightly wound around his neck, and talked to Amanda confidentially. She invited him inside and sat with him at the dining-room table, going over sheaves of papers he brought. She was intensely nervous. Her hands were clawing, seeking. "Judge Phillips is going to try to keep this out of the newspaper, by bringing it up when reporters are not present," Hatch told her.

She read all the papers, then got up from the table, embarrassed to be seated with him. "Hallie is not home. Have you talked with her about this?" she asked.

"I don't talk to anybody about matters of your family. Mr. Wallerbee would be the one, if either of us."

That was the first Monday of the new term of Superior Court. On the following Monday morning, Hatch stopped by once more, with a gift, a quilted pillowcase his wife had made, which he gave to Pink. They talked briefly, Hatch doing most of it. Later Hatch again sat with Amanda in the kitchen at the white metal table and spread the papers out before her, and she looked at them as if they were strangers. "It is not required actually to give the stock to the oldest son, to Frederick, Mrs. Wright; you merely appoint him as your agent, to vote the stock and represent it."

"Frederick agreed to give me half his company salary every month, if he could have the vote of the stock."

Hatch scratched at a bug bite on his chin. "Yes, well, that's between the two of you."

"Pink never was one for trusting to banks. He never saved money."

"No, he loaned money to others, though. Now you need money yourself."

"Young was trying to piece together the papers for all his father's loans, and it's complicated, he says, with ever so many word-of-mouth agreements." She glanced at the papers in Hatch's hands. "When he gets better, he can change all this, can't he?"

"No trouble about it. He can make his own decisions, soon as he's able." There was nothing aggressive about Hatch. He tarried on the front porch, asked when she was going home to see her folks. He was friendly and helpful.

"He even borrowed on our home, Mr. Cole," she confessed to him. "When Young found that—he borrowed on our own house, to gamble on the company," Amanda told him.

A meeting of the directors of the company was required by charter to be held once a year, and almost all the decisions at any such meeting would require Pink's approval, or his power-of-attorney's. It was expected by Hallie that her father would attend the meeting in a wheelchair and would vote his own stock on the important matters. The votes could be taken quickly, after a presentation by one of the officers, probably Wallerbee.

"Why, he won't want to go to that meeting," Amanda told her. "You see yourself the heaviness that's still over him, Hallie." She slid the pots, even the pot lids, into the sink, where soapy water was floating a bit of toast from breakfast. "It'd be better not to worry him, Hallie."

"It is his company, mama, and all he has to do is raise his left hand, doesn't have to say anything. They can even meet here, mama."

"Here?" she said, turning suddenly, dismayed. "Bring that company here?"

"If it were not for the company, I don't know what we would be living on, mama. My salary—"

"Oh." She gasped. "I don't expect you to keep giving your salary to the house, Hallie, though I thank you."

"It's not all that much, mama."

"No, I don't want them to come here. I'm not ready for them."

Hallie laughed. Here a meeting was to be held in two weeks' time, and her mother was not ready for it. Hallie knew there would be nothing to the meeting, anyway. "The company's doing well, thank you, mama," Hallie told her.

"Yes, I understand it is, but there are several matters to come up that will worry your father. He is not be worried, Hallie."

"Did Frederick tell you there were problems?"

"No, no. Mr. Cole was by to see your father."

"Hatch Cole here?"

"Oh yes. Twice, I believe it was, to see your father, as I said, Hallie."

Pink told Hallie that yes, Hatch had visited him, and a keenness came to his eyes, and a little laugh crept out of his throat, which caused him to cough. Hallie held a towel to his mouth and he spit. "Bought . . . me a . . . pill . . ."

"Mama wants me to leave the company, papa. Marry. Have babies for her to love. Make my own dresses. Get a cow."

He laughed and began to cough, so she held the towel to his mouth again.

"Might be the best trade I could make," Hallie admitted ruefully.

"No," Pink said, shaking his head. "I need you in the . . . company."

"Sometimes I think the company is my life, papa." She leaned forward and nudged his chest with her chin. "You know what I mean?"

"And what of friend Wallerbee?"

"He sees me as part of the company, I think."

His eyes closed. "I see."

"There's the annual meeting of the company coming up," she said guard-edly.

His eyes remained closed, but his breathing had changed, so she realized he had heard her. "I will tell you before the meeting what the items are. There are no money problems, not really, except we are owed still by Clove Enterprises, which has delays meeting payments." The breathing seemed almost to have stopped. "I know you don't want to be bothered, but the meeting will be brief."

The eyes opened, and she saw confidence there. He nodded.

"I won't mention it again," she promised. "I love you," she told him, and settled into a chair, situated so that the ceiling's dangling cord was near enough to light her book.

280

> Youth rambles on life's arid mount,
>   And strikes the rock, and finds the vein,
>   And brings the water from the fount,
>   The fount which shall not flow again.

Months ago, when Pink first began reciting that stanza with her, the vowels were all he could say, and his recitation was unintelligible to anyone who didn't know the verse. Hallie had repeated each line, seeking improvement, until he reached the point of exhaustion. Now he could speak it ever so clearly as they said it together.

Hallie was twenty-seven years of age and had lost most of her girlish ways. Her breasts were larger, her hips more rounded, her waist seemed thinner, and her eyes were more knowing, more cautious, were not as eager as once they had been. Responsibility—especially in these tough times—had toughened her. Gone were the easy smiles of the uninitiated. Now her lips had turned downward slightly, giving her, even in repose, a look of sadness. She was not aloof. One sensed that any touch would lead to responsiveness, that she was a person capable of offering comforts. More than aloof she was preoccupied with many worries.

Dr. Clove asked for a meeting with Pink, who consented and set aside a time. Clove came sprightly into the parlor, where Pink sat in a chair, Hallie and Young nearby. Clove was equipped with gifts of fruit and bottles of tonics, and with several maps of subdivisions. "I thought you were ill, Mr. Pink," he said, choosing a name he had not previously used. "That's what you're called now in town, you know." He talked on, even while he peeled Pink an orange and segmented it, reassembling it across the face of his folded monogrammed handkerchief, which he had centered on a little table between his and Pink's chairs. "Oranges are from Asia," he informed Pink and Hallie and Young, juice oozing from his lips. His quick tongue retrieved it, his eyes opened with wonder at the goodness. "They bring us the strength of that old continent, which knows so much about . . . about fertility." He chomped and enjoyed. "These samples are from Florida, but even so . . ."

Pink watched him with mild skepticism, as if Clove had just jumped from a magic box and was liable to jump again quite soon.

"Music is the fruit of love, and it binds people closer than anything else," Clove said.

"Poetry is—" Pink began.

"Poetry is the music of language. I've . . . always loved poetry and will . . . will publish a book of local poetry in time. I've talked with your son Frederick about that, the need for a company sponsor, such as Monarch. But I agree with John Keats: let me have music and I ask no other . . . no other food, is it?"

"No more delight," Pink said.

"Delight?" The word struck a responsive chord with Dr. Clove.

"It goes," Pink said, "Let me have music dying, and I seek no more delight."

The smile, as much a part of Clove's character as the silk necktie and the attached shirt collar, folded. "Dying?" The concept appeared to mystify him. He ate another segment of his orange, savoring the juice with critical appraisal. "Thank you," he said, dismissing the matter. "My nephew is a graduate of Princeton and has business experience in the North. He could bring a new dimension to your company, Mr. Pink, if you would hire him, since his field is mortgage loans."

"Your nephew and my Hallie," Pink said, watching Clove out the corner of his eye, "if they could marry, he would have firm claim on the job."

Hallie gasped. So did Young, for that matter. A smile came to Clove. "I would think . . . he would want to meet her for personal reasons, as well."

"She could clean his golf clubs, string his rackets," Pink said.

Clove turned to Hallie, hoping for a clue as to just what response was expected. Hallie was crimson, but was amused, so Clove managed a smile, too. "Yes, well . . . I mentioned the land already, Mr. Pink, and there is the possibility I will need a bit of money soon again."

"That comes . . . as a surprise," Pink said.

"I'm losing money on the Battery Park project—most all I own is losing. But one new property I'm planning to open up, five thousand acres, a mountainside, and the surveyors have promised to be done soon with their part in it. I have no funds to pay them."

"Jeff . . . Jeff . . . erson was a surveyor," Pink said, "and a mountaineer."

Surprised, Clove turned to stare frankly at him. "Jefferson a mountaineer?"

"One of us who came into . . . full flower." He paused, his gaze resting kindly on Clove. "You are . . . in full flower."

Clove laughed agreeably. "Thank you."

"Day lilies," Pink said. He rested his head against the back of the chair and cast a glance in Clove's direction. "Mon . . . o . . . grammed, of course."

Clove left soon after that, in a huff.

"What a pity," Pink said to the bemused Young and Hallie, who remained long enough to caution him against further jesting in business matters with a desperate man.

Twenty-three

Amanda wrote her father, asked him to accompany her on the morning of October 25th. She knew her father could not advise her about the affairs of the court or the company, but he would be a proper escort; at meetings of major consequence, a woman was expected to take her husband, her oldest son, or her father with her.

Both her parents arrived on the afternoon of the 24th, with a foot locker full of their clothes, several jars of canned fruit, and a cured ham. Also, Enid had a jar of liquor, some he had made, and a bag of cornmeal. He knew nothing about the meeting they were to attend, except that he should wear a suit, which indeed next morning he put on, and once the company car began tooting its horn out in the backyard, he roused himself from the breakfast table, accepted his wife's help in adjusting tie and coat.

She ran a comb through his mustache and beard. "How long will you be?" Adeline asked him.

"I don't know. I've not even left yet, have I?" Off he went to the meeting, daughter with proud father, the father discussing his own will and the lawyers he had used in his lifetime. "Is it a lawyer's office we're going to now?" he asked her.

"Yes, in a way," she said, lost in worry about the decisions just ahead. Depression had put its clammy spell over her, made her ill.

The county courthouse was new, another result of the abundance of local enthusiasm, and its twenty-some-floor height intimidated Enid. He rode an elevator—his first such experience—to the courtroom floor, twelve flights up, where he followed meekly through the empty courtroom to a square, well-lighted room where three bald-headed men received them. The oldest of them took Amanda aside to ask her routine questions about Pink's abilities, about the children, the ages of the three of them, about Amanda's desires in the matter under consideration. As she knew she must, she recommended that Frederick perform the duties, being a realtor, a businessman, the elder son.

Enid heard much of this but gave it little mind. He passed the time staring down from the windows at the antlike people below, which gave him an interesting hint of vertigo. Any sensation made him curious, involved him in self-adulation, even an affliction. "I'll not take the elevator down; there's no point in it," he told Amanda once her conference had ended. "It's not that I'm afraid of the damn thing, either." On the street, he noticed that Amanda was gripping her hands together fitfully, was in emotional straits. "What is it, honey?"

Abruptly, she turned, said she must go back to see the judge again.

"Not up that damn electric thing, surely," he told her.

"It's Hallie," she said.

He turned, expecting to see Hallie nearby.

"I don't think I can do this to her, papa. I do need to go back."

"I'll wait for you then," he told her, annoyed as always by delay. "I'll stand here and count the cars."

That amused her. Suddenly she smiled, took hold of his arm, firmly pressed her face against his coat, which was homespun wool that she and her mother had woven years ago. On the way to the car, he talked about maybe someday taking shop space here in town and opening a business to make shoes in the old way. "Did I tell you about Godfrey getting married again?" he asked, wanting to divert her from any worrying thoughts. "That main lawyer upstairs reminded me of Godfrey."

"He's a judge, papa, from Raleigh."

"Is he? Godfrey went to my friend Felix Jackson and asked for the hand of one of his daughters, and Felix had three daughters left, all healthy and hard-working, but none of them pretty, so he put paper pokes over their heads and showed them off to Godfrey that way." He found himself laughing alone. "I guess you don't remember him."

The driver stopped the car at Hatch Cole's hardware store. Without comment, Enid met Hatch and the company lawyer, whose name at once escaped him. Also he met a pretty woman, a secretary. Everybody stood around talking pleasantly. He noticed that a paper was changing hands, going from Amanda to the lawyer, then to Hatch, who read every word of it. Hatch said finally, "You want to read it, Wallerbee?"

Wallerbee came forward and began to scan the paper, then he bent over it, intensely studying it. When he straightened he was bloodless in the face, Enid noticed. All this commotion over a paper, he thought, over a few words; it was a lesson in life.

"But my God, Hatch," Wallerbee began, choking on his words. "She knows every nuance of the company, and Frederick knows nothing about any part, except Clove's abominable mortgage loans."

"If you please," Hatch said, speaking loud enough to silence the lawyer, "we'll go into session. Put it down that I called it to order, since Pink isn't here. Record that Mrs. Wright is present, and her father. We'll pass over the reading of the minutes of the last meeting since Mrs. Wright has asked if she can leave quickly."

People were finding chairs, all except Wallerbee. He stood as in a trance near the tall coat rack. Suddenly he said, "What have you arranged for her, Hatch, for Hallie?"

"Now, you'll want to sit down, Mr. Wallerbee," Hatch said evenly.

"Where is Pink's oldest son?" Hatch asked the lawyer. "Where did you leave him?"

"In my office," the lawyer said.

"Send for him." Hatch moved with the lawyer to the door and without haste unlocked it.

King leaned close to Amanda, whispered to her, "His clock on the wall is like the one I bought in 1910."

Wallerbee said to Hatch, "If you and I could talk privately."

Hatch paused, considered that. "Where would we go?" he asked. "You and the girl have been close, I know that, and I never questioned it, did I? Now that the boy and I—"

"Hatch, for God's sake."

"Now that the boy and I are close—"

"Hatch, she and I never had any plan to eliminate you—"

"I never said you did. I don't mean to be beholden to either one of you." The lawyer returned, Frederick with him. Hatch locked the door after them, returned to his desk, where he paused to consider the young man, who was weaving on his feet, was standing in the store's main aisle, staring at his mother, dead drunk. Hatch said to him, "You understand the trust might be temporary, depending on your father's health, Frederick."

Frederick nodded dumbly.

"Let the record show that the Superior Court has, on consultation with Mrs. Wright and her father, appointed Frederick Wright, oldest son, a realtor in Asheville for— How many years, Frederick?"

Frederick looked about. "I don't recall."

"Uh huh," Hatch said, considering that lapse solemnly. "A realtor for several years, a married man, age—how old are you Frederick?"

"I'll be twenty-seven—" He hesitated.

"He's twenty-eight," Amanda said.

Hatch said, "Let it be noted also that the company lawyer, Mr. Clarke, with an 'e,' is present. Let it be therefore noted that the company now has three directors, Mr. Wallerbee, myself, and Frederick Wright, and we will move to the election of officers."

A rattle at the door. Everybody turned. She was at the door, Hallie, at the smudged glass door, was shaking it, peering through the glass into the murky interior. Hatch stood up, key ring in hand, but once he saw who was there, he froze in place, stared bleakly ahead until the rattling stopped, then waited in silence, alert for any glance from Amanda, who sat, eyes closed tightly, next to her father, one of her hands gripping his forearm, her dry lips whispering prayers into the dusty air.

Enid King walked the chicken-yard fence, examining it. There were two chickens out but he didn't bother about them, so heavy were his thoughts of the meeting. There were tracks of a big coon in the garden, which he sought to ignore as well. "So much to watch for," he murmured. "There's robbers ever'where." When he was called to come to the house to eat, he was asked to sit in Pink's place. The table otherwise was empty. He had to insist that Amanda sit down with him. "Let your mama wait on us." She sat down, as instructed, but paid scant attention to the food, merely mixed it about as a child would. He heard the front door open, then slam, heard footsteps as somebody hurried into Pink's room at the front of the house. Amanda closed her eyes, then returned to piddling about with her food. They heard footsteps on the stairs. The footsteps soon returned to Pink's room, and there was loud talking in there, a woman's voice, Imogene's, then Hallie's, then there was quiet for a few moments. All the while Amanda sat as if lost to view and sound, mashing a potato with the back of a fork, eating now and then a bite. Enid said, "I'd need a shop eight foot wide at the least, and fifteen foot long, and then need a back room to stack leather." Words spoken by Hallie filtered in through the wall that separated the dining room from the parlor. Now and then Pink would say something. "Can repair as well as build shoes new," Enid reported to Amanda.

"Amanda, what they doing in there?" Adeline King asked from the kitchen doorway.

"I suppose she's telling him what went on at the meeting," Amanda said. "Hallie kept trying to get the hardware store's door open, and Mr. Cole never did admit her. Of course, he has the best locks."

"He had a two-key lock and a bolt," Enid reported.

"Mr. Wallerbee went to open it but didn't have the key."

"The two keys," Enid corrected.

"So he had you locked in, as well as Hallie locked out," Adeline commented.

"She was a block down the street when we did finally come out, and she saw her grandfather, must have recognized him by his size and his shoulders being bent, the way he carries them—"

"I never knew we were hurting her," Enid said. "I tell the world that."

"In the city you ought to stand up straight," Adeline told him.

"And she stood down there near Rankin Street shading her eyes with her hand, watching us," Amanda said, "but papa'll tell you there wasn't anything I could do for her."

"I wish she'd come up and live at our place," Enid said.

"A mother rarely has to decide one over another," Amanda said, "maybe once in a lifetime."

At that moment, the shuffling noise moved into the hall. The three at the table listened as the front door opened. There was more shuffling then. Amanda placed one hand on her father's arm, to detain him, and sat there listening, trying to translate the sounds into meaning. "What's she hauling out of that room?" Amanda asked, more to herself than to them. She got to her feet, hesitated.

"They're hauling something outdoors," Adeline said. "Sounds like it's heavy, a Victrola . . ."

"I'll go see about Pink," Amanda announced, and wiped her hands on her napkin. She was in the hall preparing to enter Pink's room when there was a cry from the front yard, a hollow, resonant, male shout, then Hallie's voice began to cry out shrilly. Amanda entered Pink's room, realizing even as she did so that Pink would not be there. She came back into the hallway, one hand raised to her mouth to silence her own scream. Enid was shuffling along the hallway, one shoe off, the shoe in his hand. "Papa, he's gone," Amanda said.

Adeline rushed onto the porch, Enid following, Amanda following him, and there on the lawn at the foot of the front steps was Pink, sprawled out, Imogene bending over him. Hallie was standing at the street near a company car, which she must have driven to the house. One of its rear doors was open. Amanda called out, "Now, you will need to tell me what you're planning, Pink, if you're leaving your bed. Hallie, he's not to fall, the doctor said; if he falls he might have another stroke. And he's not to have excitement. Now, are you trying to kill your father?" She moved down the wooden steps. "Pink, I don't know what to make of your being on the ground out here."

Enid went to help Pink to his feet, held him from the back with his arms around his chest. Pink was like a limp doll in his arms, his head lolling. Hallie was coming toward him on the walk, her mouth open in an unuttered ohhh; she stopped once Pink's gaze met hers. "Honey," Pink said, his voice as clear as ever in his life for that one word.

Amanda demanded, "Hallie, what do you mean to do with him? Take him back to the judge?" Anger was drowning her other emotions. "Papa, bring Pink back into the house."

"Why, I'll try, Amanda," Enid told her, straining to hold him up. "He's nigh a dead weight on me."

"Imogene, stop staring and help him," Amanda ordered. "Hallie, are you trying to kill him?" Amanda asked her. "Pink, now I never thought you would go out in the yard like this."

Hallie sought to touch him. "The stroke didn't come on you again, papa, did it?"

"No, no," he told her.

Imogene brought a rocking chair from the porch. Enid set Pink in it. "I . . . ohhh, God," Pink muttered out of exhaustion, confusion.

Amanda said, "I can't put up with his leaving his bed this way."

"You come with me, can't you, papa?" Hallie begged him.

"Leave him alone, Hallie," Amanda ordered. "Are you wanting to kill him?"

"Papa?"

He shook his head. "Can't."

"Then I'll— What can I do, papa?" Hallie asked.

"Brodie, is . . ."

"Do you know where he is, papa?"

"Denver . . . you leave here now."

"I never meant to hurt you."

"No, no. But you go."

"Where in Denver?"

"Brown . . . Palace."

"What . . . where is that?"

"Ho . . . ho . . . tel."

In a moment she was gone, racing across the lawn, starting the car with a roar, clashing its gears as she drove away, fleeing him, fleeing her mother and grandfather and home and youth.

288

PART FOUR
Death

Twenty-four

Young was on his way home from school
that day when on Lexington Avenue he
heard of the defeat of his father, his disgrace at the hands of his own
family, and Young went clammy and weak. The farmers were talking of
little else. Just yesterday preeminent among them was the insurance man,
their friend, who had begun work here—just over there—and had risen in
finance and society; he had today been leveled out by a woman, and worse
yet, his own wife. Who would have thought, one farmer asked a group near
where Young stood, the boy helpless to move away, who would have
thought there lay in any woman such fury. "No, it's his oldest son, the one
that sells land and souls to Florida," a man on the street said. The men
doing the talking today were speculative, as if this sort of affair was not

unexpected in life, but the women were spiteful, swinging angrily away even from Young, as if he were centrally involved by fact of kinship. "Oh, he's smeared by the grease, if he lives with them," he heard one say. "Where there's smoke . . ." another said.

Hugh saw the boy, took him into the store's back room, hugging him and cautioning him against listening to "them there afternoon winds. I had nothing to do with this, Young, whatever it is, something your mother has done."

This must be the most distressing afternoon of his life, Young decided, and when he reached home an aura of death pervaded each room and the eyes of the members of the family, even his kindly grandmother, who least of all of them knew what had taken place or where her loyalties ought to lie. Nor did Young know for himself; his loyalties instinctively lay with his father, but at the same time he loved his mother, had always been close to her and had no hatred inside himself. His mother had felled the giant, his father, had struck her husband, and there was no rule for family response, and no shady places for hiding. He wanted to comfort his father; also, he acknowledged the deep wound that must have been inflicted on his mother by herself.

By evening the son of Cranston Noblock, who had a way with music, was on the street trying "to get just right, if you'd only help me," a ballad about the fall of Pink Wright.

And Hallie gone. He missed Hallie. Yes, he must find her. He longed for her tough analysis, her abrupt, one-hundred-percent certainty, her chop-off-the-head solutions; he longed to have her reassure him that their dear father had not irretrievably fallen. Fallen he was just now; there he lay in the shade-drawn room, the folded newspaper tied around the dangling light cord so that the forty-watt bulb emitted only a few rays of light, lying with his eyes closed against the darkness, sweat thick on his face, a salve in which marks of his anxious fingers remained, his lips forming words too hot for prayers, his curses blasphemous. Father, what is your advice now, out of your agony? None is understandable to me. I have sat by your bed hour by hour, listening to your silence. The big nurse was nearby, breathing with steam-engine noises, talking now and then about the moving-picture shows not yet showing a wife and husband warring. "No Mary Pickford never sticks it to Douglas Fairbanks, now does she?" Oh, father, my God, will you speak to me? One word. I'm in misery. I also have hatred and fear in my throat. I feel the eyes of pity scalding me. I want to strike out in revenge against our prosecutors, but I see no adversary except those I love.

That night Young lay awake, considering what he must do to help his father. It's not my life, he repeatedly assured himself, his is not my life. Even so, the boy thought, he has been my model, my advisor, he has been my excuse for excelling over others, he was once my source of strength when I sought to correct my own affliction. Now I must be his. He vowed to go into battle, to fight Frederick and his own mother. At last he fell asleep, and, when he awoke, his mother was in the room, pestering the covers and the shades and producing a glass of apple juice, which she said his grandfather had brought from the country.

The following day, Saturday, Frederick came to the house for noon dinner. On first sight, Frederick seized Young and cuffed him playfully, asking how he felt growing up so tall. Seized by compulsion, Young grappled with him, sought to strangle him, which Frederick took to be a playful maneuver. "Oh, now, wait a minute," Frederick told him. "What the hell gets into you?" he said, going on toward the dining room, grumbling.

He didn't even pause at the closed parlor door, Young noticed. Not even a glance.

His mother called, "You come and eat with your brother, Young. You hear me? Or he'll eat it all."

Young took his place at the dining-room table, murmuring an apology for the delay, and began serving himself. Sometime during Frederick's dissertation of restaurant food, which he reported made him bilious, Young interrupted to ask brightly how Henrietta was, and later he asked how Frederick's work was going, the questions falling without rancor. Young wondered at his own ability for deception. I'm like my father, he suspected; whenever somebody on King Street had sought to cheat Pink, why, he would smile, nod, evade most pleasantly, would distract with questions about family matters. I must be kind to him, considerate of him, my dear brother, Young told himself. Has my father ever struck down an adversary? Young wondered. No, perhaps not, but has he ever been as desperate as now?

Young realized he must appear sympathetic to his mother. Each afternoon she would talk at length, explain yet again her reasons for her actions, which she could make sound most natural; she became more and more insistent on the logic of her explanation, and the boy would accept her excuses, encourage her to think well of herself, would join in criticism of her detractors.

The parlor shades were pulled down each morning when Young arrived in the room. Before the catastrophe, Pink preferred to have them left open, so the first sun would welcome him. He seemed now not to care. He was never standing at that window any longer, not these days.

"You know what you have to do, papa," Young said to him one morning. "You see what's necessary, but you find it difficult to bring yourself around."

Pink stared at him, apparently perplexed.

"You have no possibility of beating them outright, papa. You must join them, or seem to."

Pink snorted angrily, but after a minute or so a smile began to work at the corners of his mouth. He relaxed, looking at his son with new curiosity.

"How can you join them, papa?"

"How indeed," he whispered.

"A secret, papa," Young told him. "I'll help you. Now, shall we try to walk about the room? We must keep up the exercise. You must walk without even a limp, papa. You taught me, remember?"

"Another letter to Hallie, is it?" Young asked him one morning.

"Hush," Pink said, glancing at the open doorway.

"You wrote her only three days ago at Brodie's address," Young reminded him.

"A father has such fears for nis daugh . . . ter. I can't tell you. Now, you send it."

"Oh, I will."

"Have you hid it?"

"Yes." Young helped him from the bed, to begin exercise.

"Then you write your grand . . . fa . . . ther, tell him Hal's address. Oh, God," Pink cried suddenly, the pain from his body swallowing his concerns. Gasping, he moved on to the window, enduring it.

"Oh, I do understand why you had it to do, mama," Young told her. "As for those women telephoning—I think it's a matter for the police. Bothering you." He found himself agreeing with whatever she said, and by that tactic he encouraged confidences.

"She does talk too much, Pink, pries too much," Amanda said to him and Young one evening, "and with only half Frederick's salary coming— and now Hallie writes for money. I can't afford everything and must let Imogene go, seems to me."

Pink nodded. "I would . . . miss her."

294

"I have an account at Hugh's store, that saves us. Now, if papa kills us a hog, we can lay the hams and bacon out on boards in what was Hallie's room, leave the windows open enough to keep it cool in there, keep the shades down so the sun won't—"

"Yes, that's an idea, Amanda," Pink said at once.

"Put down cardboard to keep the salt from . . ." Surprised, she looked up, strained to focus on his face, there across the room. Her fingers had even stopped knitting. "What did you say, Pink?"

"Is a good idea."

"I thought you—I said in Hallie's room. I thought you would want it kept for her."

"Ought to use it. She left it."

"I did sell off her clothes, Pink. I meant to ask you."

"Had to. I can see that," Pink said, casting a single, telling glace toward Young.

"So you understand why I've had to let Imogene go?"

A long pause in that stuffy room. Pink and Young once more exchanged glances, then quietly Pink said, "Did you let Imo go?"

"This evening, when I paid her."

"This is Sat . . . ur . . . day, is it?"

Amanda kept staring at him strangely, to judge his hurt, anger, criticism.

"I don't . . . don't see how you could have kept her," he said, and smiled.

Amanda laid her knitting aside. She crossed the room, to be able to see him better. "What say?"

"Have only the family here. Better."

"I never expected you to be . . . pleased to see her go, Pink. Did you hear him, Young?"

"I'll miss her," Pink admitted. "Many times I'll miss her."

"You never cease to surprise me, Pink."

"You had to fire her, I know that. If you don't have money. If Imo is a problem, out she goes. If you have to sign legal pa . . . pers, then you must, you or Fred. Signing the pa . . . pers about me, they must have hurt you, too. I give you a score of eight, Amanda."

"Eight what?" she said feverishly, concentrating on him, soaking up the comments.

"One to ten, I give you eight bells. What say, Young?"

"Do you for a fact?" she said, flushed with excitement.

"Eight what, papa?" Young asked.

"Ten's perfect, but nobody's perfect, even though Hal used to think she was," Pink said.

"Why, listen at that," Amanda exclaimed. "Listen to him," she said, bubbling, richly pleased, turning to Young. "He's criticizing Hallie."

Frederick came to Sunday dinner, he and Henrietta, this at Young's suggestion, and at Young's suggestion Henrietta spent some time with Pink in his room. Late Sunday afternoon Young managed to get Frederick to come into the room, as well. The older brother and the father considered each other silently for a long moment, before Pink broke the silence. "Your mother suggested you drop in?"

Frederick came closer to the bed. "She said you seem to be in a better mood these days, papa."

"No complaint. No work to do. You have the worries."

Frederick admitted he did have worries. He meant to make a joke of it, but Young asked him for details. He was not accepted at the company, Frederick admitted, even yet. The clerks were surly, Wallerbee wouldn't accept his authority, so he had daily battles.

"Then they must be brought to terms," Pink interrupted, speaking sternly. "They have no right to . . . Who is on your side?"

"Nobody, not a soul," Frederick admitted.

"I think in half an hour I could find allies for you in that staff. If I were a clerk, I'd see where the power is. Why, Waller . . . bee will have to give way."

Henrietta voiced her view that it was unfair the way Frederick was being treated, that he had spent every night tossing in his bed, and his stomach had been often upset.

"What about Hatch Cole, Frederick?" Young asked his brother sympathetically.

"Hatch is using me," Frederick said, "for his own purposes, wanting loans made to this company or that, each a client of his, but he won't allow a new loan to Clove Enterprises, a loan needed to keep the company alive. Hatch brings up all manner of rules, asking for more information, different papers, blocking it."

"Is my friend Clove in trouble?" Pink asked.

"Your friend?" Young said.

"Yes, I have . . . known him for years."

"Dr. Clove admits he's in trouble," Frederick told Pink.

"You can't let him go under," Pink informed him. "He's too important to the community."

"I thought . . . I thought you didn't like his projects," Frederick said.

"I don't like those two loans Wallerbee made, but they are on the books. If all he needs is a small loan to sur . . . vive?"

"Well, I wish you would tell Hatch Cole, papa," Frederick said.

"No, I have had my day, Fred."

"I insist."

"Oh, I doubt if I can in . . . fluence him."

"Could Hallie help," Henrietta asked, "if she returned?"

"Don't be silly," Frederick said angrily, turning on her.

"No, she's well out of it," Pink said at once, his agreement surprising Frederick. "Manda for years talked about getting her out of the company, and I always wanted a few more months of her time, that's all. Ask your mother—she'll tell you. Now she's out West."

"Denver," Frederick said. "Wants money from me and mama."

"Didn't you send her that money?" Henrietta asked him.

"Not yet."

"Why not?"

"Not yet, I told you. I wish I could do everything I want to do," he said, then tried to smile, to soften his brusqueness.

Pink said, "No, Hallie is not the solution. Be one fight after another. She would fall in with Waller . . . bee again, and I can tell you about that sometime, my pains over that com . . . bin . . . ation. Tell Waller . . . bee to come by and talk to me, Fred."

"I will. I certainly will. You have to help me, papa."

"Now then, to get money for Manda, we can call in those loans I made over the years, don't you think so? Young has com . . . piled them."

"If any of the people can afford to pay—" Frederick began.

"There are forty, fifty. And I think— Where is your mother?"

Amanda joined them. The family stood around his bed, waiting direction from him. He told them debt collection required a special knack: the collector had to be persistent without being annoying, and a collector sometimes had to accept livestock or quilts or canned goods, and later dispose of them. "Young is busy in school. Frederick is working. I'm ill. But when I say the name of a man who can help us— Manda, you will want to comment, and so will you, Fred. And Young."

The family leaned forward eagerly, ready to hear the name.

"Young and I wrote up this list, and for days I've wondered who has the gift to collect the money, and who might come here and live with us, make his home here for the next few months, work on a com . . . miss . . . sion. . . ."

"Well, who is it, Pink?" Amanda asked.

"Not be a bother to the family, fit in . . ." Pink continued.

"Pink, who . . . is . . . it?" Amanda said, laughing at the suspense.

"Harry," he said.

297

Amanda sat down. Frederick retreated to the window. "Uncle Harry, Harry live here?" Henrietta asked, whispering, awed.

Breathlessly Amanda said, "I wouldn't have thought you'd say Harry."

"Only person I thought of," Pink said. "Of course, it would require some sacrifice from each one," he told them, "since Harry will need to take over a room upstairs—and be at meals, and you, Manda, with enough to do now caring for me. And he'd take . . . say, thirty percent of what he brought in, which might be several hundred dollars a month, because if he took sheep, horses, cattle in payment, or land . . . took land . . ." Pink appeared suddenly to be tired, the duty of speech overwhelming him. "Well, I leave the thought with you."

It was, Young decided, a performance worthy of any actor.

Young helped Pink write a letter to the pastor, expressing thanks for a sermon Amanda had told them about, asking him to come by sometime, "and meanwhile do defend my wife on those occasions when she is criticized for doing what she was required to do."

Together they wrote a letter to Hatch Cole, Pink saying he missed the chance to talk with him, to get his advice about the way the depression was headed. "It's a scared bull in a china shop, seems to me. I don't know a person in this town who has a better sense of economic directions and what to do with money than you do."

He wrote Hugh King, a chatty note, expressing the view that old friends are best.

He wrote Wallerbee, invited him to come commiserate with him over his problems at the company. Wallerbee did so, and the moment he arrived Pink told him the company ought to expand into Washington, D.C., that Wallerbee could send three black salesmen up there—take one from Durham, one from Raleigh, one from Winston-Salem, put them in an office in Washington near the train station, have them sell insurance, "because those government workers have money even now, don't get laid off."

"But I have nobody who can do anything like that, Pink," Wallerbee told him. "If you were back with us, Pink . . ."

"Oh, no, no," Pink said. "Fred might agree with you on my coming back, but I'd need a father-and-son a . . . gree . . . ment. Let him vote the stock, be pres . . . ident. I'd be something like chairman, a part-time job. I don't see myself going to Wash . . . ing . . . ton, but you take Stephen Russell, he could go up there and sell ten pol . . . i . . . cies a day. And maybe that Winston-Salem man—what's his name? Harold Toler? Second in the dist . . . rict last winter, and he's black. He's brown, anyway. Now, if we sent him and Lord . . ."

Wallerbee, who had arrived prepared to discuss trivial arguments, wouldn't allow Pink to stop talking, planning. It was very much like the old days, he said.

"We had Hallie then," Pink said fondly. "Could maybe hire her now to go to Washington. She could get those white government workers. She . . . might take it on."

"I . . . I wish . . . I wish you would write her, Pink," Wallerbee said, stumbling over his words because of anxiousness. "I write her, but she doesn't even reply."

"Oh, that's too bad."

"Pink, I'm going to talk to Frederick, no matter what you say. Maybe we both can persuade you to come back."

"Well, if he can think up an agree . . . ment, one that suits him, he the president and I chairman, a fath . . . erly figure, help solve dis . . . putes, open up new terr . . . i . . . tory. He'd have to get Dr. Clove to write an affi . . . da . . . vit, and maybe Hatch. You can think of a few bankers to write, too."

"Would that be necessary?"

"Oh yes. Get Dr. Watkins. You can do it."

"Oh, I can get half a dozen affidavits in three days," Wallerbee said, "if Amanda and Frederick agree—"

"Manda would have to go to court, as before, a nui . . . sance, but if Frederick wanted her to—"

"I think so."

"And my brother Harry—you know he's moving in upstairs. Harry would be fine to go to the court. You and Harry and—"

"But do we actually need to undo all that legal matter," Wallerbee asked, "unhappy as it was?"

"Oh, yes. People don t like a man who is incom . . . petent being chairman of an insurance company."

After tea, Pink asked Wallerbee to help him over to the window. The two stood together looking at the birds, now and then Pink mentioning other thoughts, the suggestions informal, casual.

Young and Pink followed up with letters. They wrote the pastor once more. Pink said his recent experiences had reminded him of the value of family, and the rewards accruing to one who is able to forgive.

Even Wurth received a friendly letter. He was entranced with it, said it was the only kind letter from a brother he had ever received. He came all the way into town to say this, and agreed to return for the courtroom session, should one be arranged. No letters needed to go to Harry, who was now present, but each day Pink had occasion to thank him for helping him, Harry and Young taking him down the back steps so he could walk as far as the sheds. Pink admitted to them both how grateful he was to have Harry here, a strong man and a loving man, who cared about Pink and who cared particularly, Pink believed, for Amanda.

Harry responded in kind, admitting to him and Young how lonely he had been the last year, since a friend of his, a lady friend, had died. He had been severely hurt by her loss. "I do wish, Pink, you could have met her, you would have loved her. She was pretty, like Amanda, grew up in France, was clever with languages, taught them to children." And he admitted to having missed home. "I do believe there is something to having roots. I do think so. I . . . I recall papa talking about water being the blood of the mountains, how it seeps out of the great bodies, forming branches, pools, feeding the trees, being the life of the trees. I was cut off from my own roots, Pink, and didn't even know it until I returned."

"I haven't long to live, Harry, I know that—well, I might go on for a while, but I have to see to my estate, make arrangements for each person. Just now Amanda denies she is . . . she is pregnant . . ."

"A tree could not move from its place, papa said. It sucked up the blood of the earth, as papa said, but could not move. Now an animal also needed to drink and eat and have nourishments—"

"She's poking out a bit, though, seems to me, but she denies she's bear . . . ing."

"I wouldn't know, Pink."

"She hasn't mentioned it to you."

"No, no."

"Well, maybe she lost it. She has lost several, she has ad . . . mitt . . . ed to me."

"The animal can move away, papa said, but it is likely to have the same sort of place. If it is accustomed to grass or meat, it has to go where that diet is. If it roosts in a certain tree, then—"

"Harry, I don't want to hear all that."

"Did I tell it to you before?"

"Papa did. I do miss papa and his flights of fancy. A mystic."

"But the point is that men can go wherever they please, can shape their habitat to suit themselves, but what I found, Pink—"

"Yes? Now we come to it."

"I found I missed the old places, the mountains, the branches, the pools, the people."

"If I can get all my affairs settled in the next little while, every person accounted for—what say, Young?"

"Well, we all have it to do, I realize that," Harry said.

"Do what, Harry?" Pink said.

"Die."

"I mean to face it the best I can, Harry."

"Now, of course a mountain lion can travel far, but it has to stay in wild country. Cattle need pasture, squirrels need nut trees, but men—"

"Fred is doing well now. Henri . . . etta says my help has meant the most she ever saw. Now I have to help Hal . . . lie, help her somehow, but don't tell Manda, for God's sake."

"You want to try to walk on down to the chicken lot or go back to the porch?" Harry asked.

"I . . . I'll settle for this much. I've done an extra bit today."

"Each day, is it? Better and better," Harry said.

"Manda's garden looks so lost. Ground needs turning, I'd say. Will kill the bug eggs if dirt's turned while the frosts— You will take care of Amanda, won't you, Harry?"

"Well . . . I . . . I don't mean to talk with you about such as that." Harry was clearly amazed.

"You and Amanda. That helps me with my plans. And Young—where is he? Young, come join us. You can go to col . . . lege. I want you to be able to hang out your shingle wherever you please. A doctor or lawyer. As for dear, sweet Hal, maybe I can think of some . . . thing for her, to give her a life."

Did Harry know he was being fooled, did any of them know, Young wondered. Did they see this plot unfold; did any one of them see it, he wondered. After a lifetime of honesty, did they see Pink conniving? He was at grips with strong adversaries, with them, with himself.

The change in Amanda, now that Pink was friendly once more, was gratifying to the family. She and Pink were not close in the earlier sense of sharing secrets; she did not seek physical affection, for instance. There was a measure of acceptance, however, and sharing.

Perhaps it was not love. Love, affection, how were they to be counted, she wondered? There were no scales made for them. They did not come in dozens. Give me a pound of love. Fill this pint jar with joy-at-being-touched. Three yards of love, please, and one skein of plain, old-fashioned, self-sacrificing devotion. Measure this affection for me; it is my feeling for my husband after twenty-some years of marriage, which have been plaid years, not solid colors. Here is the argument we had over a pregnancy; you see, this splotch of blood is dyed into the material. And this purple is for ever-so-many bright mornings lying in bed in sunlight. This is his recent sickness swatched in brown, and this is the birth of my second son; see how the light breaks through the agony of birth pain. And this is Hallie as a baby; here, her little fanny is wet, and this is her first report card from school, all A's, except in deportment, and this is— Oh, it won't measure, kind sir? Why, then give me the weight of it in ounces. No weight, indeed. You understand, these colors and shapes are memories from our lives, and I want to make them into shawls and scarves, to insure affection for the family. Just try to cut me off enough for four scarves, that's for three children with one extra to be put by for the unborn.

Foolishness. Folly. She laughed at the sweep of her imagination. Enough of that nonsense, she told herself.

Take hold of love, Amanda. Feel it in your fingers. Touch love. Squeeze—oh, do give love a little squeeze.

Giggling giddily, abandoning the traps of such thoughts, she fell into a rocker in the dining room. Idly she flicked the broom against the wood crumbs on the hearth. The broom helped return her to everyday reality. Harry, what of him? What affection did Harry feel for any of them? What did she feel for Harry now? Was it different from any affection she had known for years, say for her sons or for her husband? Did it alert her to danger, make her clutch at her own throat, seeking relief, at night? Her affection for Harry was more intense than the mellow dearness that Pink for years had occupied in her thoughts. Pink had been, even in youth, always predictable, dependable, honest, fair. Harry had been more daring, more of a question in his time, and was so still. Even now the sight of him caused danger to her mind. Harry, dear Harry, dangerous Harry. You would think by now Harry would have become weary of novelty. He claimed to be. Indeed, he had said to her this family, this house, were the solutions to his own life, he could scarcely imagine any better—what was the word he used? Anything more fortuitous. Be worth using that word, when she next saw Nettie. Be worth looking it up, when she went next to Hallie's room to turn the pork in the salt.

Last night, why had Harry lingered in the hallway downstairs? Not because of the bathroom. That door was open. Young was inside there, gathering up his clothes, but Harry didn't know that. Another thing: Pink's door was shut. Harry must have shut it. And he was standing nearby, in sight from the bathroom door, considering some speculation or other. "Why, Pink's door is shut," Amanda had exclaimed, announcing it from her own room. Once she opened it, Harry began moving on up the stairs, scurrying. Why? What had he hoped for? And down at the chicken lot the other day, as the two of them were shelling corn, tossing the kernels to the hens and to the noble rooster, Harry stood so close their bodies had touched, then his arm came around her, which caused her to stiffen and step away, and it had so shaken her emotionally that she had gone to the chopping block to sit down.

Amanda said, "Well, you can pull your lamp off whenever you want to, Pink, and you really must go to bed, Young."

"I don't want to turn the lights off yet," Pink told her. "Young is helping me make a list—"

"It's midnight, Pink."

"No, Fred has asked me to do this. I'm list . . . ing what he wants me to do. I'm getting to be trained dog act." He laughed contentedly. "But that beats doing nothing, Amanda. Did you give Harry a cup of tea?" His voice was calm, the thought seemed to be incidental, but it caused Young and Amanda to freeze in motion, stymied.

"Tea? At this hour?" she said.

"He likes a cup of hot tea at night, before he goes to sleep."

"I never heard that."

"Well, take him some."

"At this hour? He's in bed."

"I'm awake, he's awake. Young is, too."

"No, Harry sleeps like a train in the roundhouse."

He was brought up short by that analogy, considered it fondly. "Where'd you hear that?"

"Oh, I don't know. Harry maybe."

"Well, it's just a thought. If you're tired—"

"I'm never tired if there's something that needs doing."

"If you'd rath . . . er go on to bed," he said, folding the paper on which he and Young had been making notes. "I'll go to sleep now, too." He pulled the light cord; the room was left with moonlight at the windows. Young started to pull down the shades, then decided to leave them up tonight. He watched his mother prop the door open. "I'll take him some tea," she whispered.

Young was upstairs in his own room when he heard her arrive with the tea. Harry's door was open, had been open ever since he arrived in town, and he was lying on his bed reading one of Hallie's novels, filling his mind with romance, Young supposed. He heard Harry say, "What'd I do to earn this?" Then Young heard him say, "Don't go yet, Amanda." And a minute later he heard his mother walk to the top of the stairs. Harry spoke again to her and moved to her. Young couldn't see them now but imagined he stopped at the banister rail, there at the top of the stairs, and he did hear Harry say, "It's like a fence between, Amanda."

That was all there was to the incident; Young sought to draw no inferences from it pertaining to his mother or his uncle, his interest being in his father most of all, the slender body on the bed downstairs, having survived the blow his lifetime lover had landed on him at a time of weakness. Was that not a type of public adultery? Young wondered. The act had come to be known to every businessman in town and to the salespeople of his company, to Hugh King and every farmer on Lexington Avenue, most of whom considered a man whipped by his wife to have been whipped, indeed. And the assault on himself was no worse than the cutting down of Hallie. Dear Hallie—where was she tonight? Let Hallie be sad or happy—let Hallie only appear where he could talk to her, put his arm around her. Dear sweet sister of his past, a mother of his youth. Had she been preyed on by lonely months? Oh, my God, Hallie, I want to see you. Tell me what has happened to you, in the past several months in which our mother has scarcely spoken of you except in a strained voice and the past tense, as if you are dead. Oh, Hallie, why did you go? Please, sister, why did you run away, why did you turn away from our world? Do you ever pray, Hallie? I've tried that and get much comfort from it. I feel better, but the replies are capricious. Hallie, I'll whisper this to you: Our mother, now that she has got the family pants on, might be experimenting with the notion of being feminine again with our own Uncle Harry. Do you laugh, Hallie? I don't find it amusing. Did you know papa regained some more feeling in his right side the day Uncle Harry arrived?

I want to see you. I love you more than I love anybody else now, except papa. I love you as much as I loved mama when I was a boy. I'm afraid of you, also, because you do strange things, such as go away. "I am afraid of you also," he said aloud, listening to his voice, smiling proudly at the mature, masculine sound of it.

"Frederick is the one who mentioned it, maybe making your father chairman of the board, I think he named it. What do you think of that?"

"Be . . . be a wise move, mama. What a good idea," Young said.

"Your father has proved to be so helpful to Frederick."

"Yes, he loves us all, mama."

"Then . . . you don't see any reason to move . . . to move cautiously?"

"No. None at all, mama."

"I do so want everything to be better, don't you, Young? But not quite like it was."

"No, mama."

"When I had nothing."

Twenty-five

Eight months after she had fled home, Hallie arrived at Enid and Adeline King's, a somber person compared with the person who had left Asheville. At once she became Enid's pride and joy, the purpose for his life. "She is not to give up the parlor to anybody, even Amanda if she was to come visiting," he announced to his wife, Hallie present. "She came to live here, she's in that room since arrival, and in that room she'll stay, not loft-climb." Adeline clearly was astonished at such an outburst early of a morning, before even his breakfast was down his throat. "She is our guest, has been since she accepted my invitation to come here—"

"Invitation?" Adeline exclaimed, surprised.

All the while Hallie was seated at the table, patiently waiting, looking from one to another. She was wearing her blue dress, the one best designed to show off her full breasts.

"I invited Hallie to come live with us, that I did."

"And I'm sure Amanda will want to come visit us—"

"She'll need to sleep at the Wrights'."

Hallie looked from one to another, fiddling with her fork and spoon, complacent about their excitement, having grown into the walls of the house in this first week of residence, become a private witness to their arguments. She noticed that the meat was getting cold on its platter, where the two fried eggs looked like two crying mouths to her. One is me, she thought, and one is my mummy. "My mother doesn't even want to see me," she said.

"Well, I'll ask her," Adeline said.

Hallie broke a biscuit, let it breathe steam and warn her about further touching—like Brodie, she thought. "I'd like to go off somewhere, if my mother comes here," Hallie said.

"Can't flee," Adeline advised her. "Won't feel any better to flee again. Are you afraid of her?"

"Yes. Of several people."

"Which ones?" Enid asked her.

"I want to live here with you and grandma and not have anybody come here at all."

"Even Young?" Adeline said.

"No, Young's . . . all right."

Enid nodded to her, then nodded to Adeline.

"Well, I know," Adeline said, gently consenting, considering him, then Hallie, affectionately calling each name, then adding her own, so that the three names were together: Hallie, Enid, Adeline. "Our old lives are winding down," she said, "and yours is just underway, Hallie, and this house is yours."

Hallie had no reply. She never argued with them, was comfortable with them and accepted their opinions, much as she would accept the opinions of a heifer should it break through the gate, or the mule should it refuse on a certain day to leave the stall, the contrary views of others being part of the piecing together of the fabric of her life, which soon was inevitably going to be ripped again, be ruptured, denuded as she had been naked before him, body and soul, many times.

Adeline was at the stove, heating the fat to fry eggs in. "What am I to do with all these eggs, if I don't remember to cook them?"

"And where will you go, Hallie, what will you do today?" Enid asked.

Hallie turned to stare, a moan issuing from her throat. "Why, the church is nearby." Her hands were knotted together, twisting.

Her grandfather never willingly allowed her to go off by herself. Whatever work he did this week had been done in sight of the house, so he could open gates, shoo all the animals, protect her. On arrival, she had been nervous, withdrawn. She had gone to the store and to meetings at the church, but had not laughed, even occasionally; later she had become still more pensive as she came to recognize the dimensions of the life predicament into which she was crawling.

Hallie stopped near the place the creek washed around a black boulder. Marsha—was Brodie's girlfriend named Marsha? she wondered. Her name, in any case, was poetic, mysterious, exotic; all his friends seemed to have exotic names, whether original or not. Was it Margo? And Brodie—who was Brodie now? A prince of a group of people who denied having any kings.

Plump Mrs. Ford was seen coming along the valley road; she could be seen through the trees. Hallie moved to the road's edge, primly sat down on a stump, and arranged her dress. Mrs. Ford, as she approached, began to slow, and when she came within several yards she stopped, openly studying the girl's body, glancing at the folds of the dress. "Hear your Uncle Harry is living at your parents' house. Lock all the girls up, I say." She laughed briefly. "I was of his age, you know."

"Did he flount you?" Hallie asked airily.

Mrs. Ford drew closer. "What word you say?"

"It's an Elizabethan word meaning to fleece."

"Oh, dear," Mrs. Ford said, smiling awkwardly.

"You might be late," Hallie told her.

That remark caught Mrs. Ford's fancy. "Late for what, dear?"

"For somebody else," Hallie said, rising, smoothing her dress over her abdomen, then moving away.

On arrival here, Hallie had evaluated the churchgoers critically, savoring her own differences from them. These people had been imprisoned within the mountains, had never had reason to push at the walls of their lives; they clumped together with others of like mind, savoring safe companionship, each one reflecting the others. But what of you, Hallie, she wondered, are you because of recent experiences better than you were? You have exposed yourself, have pried open doors. Has it helped you?

The tea she attended, given by Mrs. Simpson to welcome her, became a cause of severe impatience to Hallie. The conversations were as predictable as strummed mountain music, one woman establishing the theme with comments about her children, relinquishing the floor to another, who then recited her children's song. For a young woman like Hallie, without a child, the hour was galling, even in the presence of pretty china cups and saucers in Mrs. Simpson's plush parlor. There was the agony of polite questions about her own plans, which were assumed to include obeisance to the idea of marriage as soon as possible and children thereafter. Her age was a factor; she stood at the dividing line and could go down either side of the hill, to marriage or to spinsterhood, the latter affording positions as teacher or nurse or family advisor. Hallie never knew how to respond in these conversations. Tell them of the cruelty in Brodie's sweet voice as he told her about the student hotel that she must move to? Did she dare tell them of falling from the pinnacle of love and desire, which she had experienced with him, into a state of loneliness, where she would torture herself on the spikes of a single bare room, bare except for a bed and dresser and washbasin? She could tell them about Arthur Pimm, whom she never had even liked, but had made love with—everybody had told her she should because he was so clever, his intelligence was over 165. I am the one who is out of step, she reminded herself bitterly; you, Hallie, are the crook, the schemer; your criticism of them is an effort to prevent yourself from revealing yourself, but you will be found out. You will most certainly be revealed, and there is no excuse you can relate about how your virtue was bartered for marriage. You will be found out, stripped bare by Mrs. Ford, by Uncle Wurth, and everybody else; you will stand naked before them all, so prepare yourself for it, but not by persecuting them now.

"It was a priest," she said aloud, rehearsing, with a smile. "I was taking up Catholicism, and he stole my virtue." Her grandfather found her strange. She knew that. He was following, she knew that, too, so she tricked him, sought loneliness, walked among the trees along the river. In that water I can lose myself, she thought; I can go into that current and allow it to drag me under. I can lie on the bottom of rocks and sand and allow the water to serve me, be the suffocating rags. The first nights she had been in Denver, Brodie had taken her into his room, had held her all night long in his arms, awakening her now and again, loving her, so that her life opened to him, and she lost her own identity. The hotel attendants knew she stayed in Brodie's room; sometimes they would call her Mrs. King, those who had not witnessed her arrival with the one suitcase, the torn topcoat, matted hair, the victim of four days and nights of sitting up on the train, sleepy, dirty, sweaty, angry; she even had an upset stomach and upset bowels, and red eyes and a bruise on her face where she had fallen in the aisle trying to get to the toilet, and her new, cheap suitcase had broken one of its two latches, so that its yawning side was showing bits of a cotton nightgown bought at Woolworth's. On a house phone, standing in the lobby, she explained to Brodie who she was, as if he might have forgotten her, and before she had finished asking for his help, she saw a tall man in a dressing robe come flying across the lobby from the elevators. Brodie. He carried her to the elevator, carried her over the room threshold, scarcely noticing heads stuck out of bedroom doors along the corridor, or whining voices saying people were trying to sleep.

Hot water in the tub. Fill it to near the brim. Stack towels around it. Sprinkle in bath salts. She had never had such suds before, and perfume, his hands massaging the soap into her skin, all over her body, into her hair, so that she began whining, thanking him, and was so excited she had to press her feet against the foot of the tub to keep from exploding.

"Hallie!"

She heard her name and looked around, and saw her brother Young standing on the bank, waving to her. Hallie realized she was in the river, halfway to the far bank, was in the water crouched down, the water covering her shoulders and washing mist into her hair.

"Hallie!"

She was wearing only her underwear; her dress was on a rock near where he was standing. She swam closer to where he stood. "Young, is it you?"

"What are you doing in swimming, Hallie?"

"Why, I don't know," she admitted. She stepped proudly onto the bank, conscious of his stares, knowing she was well formed. Brodie, himself, had told her often enough during those first weeks when he had loved her, before what's-her-name arrived and it was explained to Hallie about what's-her-name's father being president of eleven mining companies, rich, with wads of money and jewels, and her suite was just across the hall from Brodie's room. "A hotel down the street, the Prince and Princess Hotel, we can find you a room there, Hallie, for a few dollars a night," Brodie had assured her. "Here's fifty dollars . . ."

"Hallie, papa sent me," Young said.

She pulled the dress over her head and let it unroll over her wet underclothing, then she wriggled out of her wet things, wrung the water out of them. "Sometimes I like to go into the water to bathe," she explained. Brodie loved my breasts, she thought. He sucked my breasts that first night, while I bathed. Soap got in his mouth, he complained.

"Why are you standing there, looking so strange?" Young asked her.

"I'll hurry," Hallie promised. Cold shoes on her wet feet; stockingless, in her old leather shoes, she started for Enid's house. "Young, Young," she said, and returned to kiss him, then went spinning away, her wet hair flying as she turned, her shoes clomping, her hands filled with wet socks and underwear. "Oh, I'm so glad to see you," she said. She came close to him, astonished by how much older he looked. "Young, is it really you?"

He smiled. "What sort of question is that?"

"You . . . are you the same person as the boy?"

"No, but I remember him."

She laughed, delighted. "And your arms, hold out your hands."

He did so.

"Hold me for a moment."

He embraced her tightly.

"A man—you are a man all of a sudden."

"They say it happens to every boy, Hallie," he said.

Sitting in the autumn southern sun, the pile of damp underthings stuck in a tree crotch nearby, "Found me rather amusing," she was saying, "settled on me as something to laugh at in Denver."

Young had stretched out on the ground, "Give them at least something to do."

"Have a laugh at everybody who comes in out of the country."

"These were young people, were they?"

"My age. Students in college."

"And not a baker among them?"

"Baker? I don't know. One delivered Western Union messages on weekends."

"And you, what did you do?"

"I got—I got into trouble, Young." Her smile slowly vanished.

Young's left hand moved across the short stretch of ground that separated them; the fingers came to rest on her wrist. "Three months, four?" he asked.

"I don't know him very well," she said, bravely facing him.

"Does he know?"

"No."

"Why not tell him? It's not your child alone."

"It's my child, Young."

"A person has no right to run off with Brodie's baby."

"It wasn't Brodie. At least, I don't know. My . . . husband is a student with years yet to study and a future arranged for him."

"Husband? You're married, Hallie?" he whispered.

"On Saturday morning he and I needed to find something to do. We had planned a picnic, and it was raining. We got married that day."

"In one day?"

"By evening. We crossed the state line."

"Maybe it's not legal, Hallie. Let's hope not."

"Even so, I thought it was, and the baby is real enough."

"And you don't want to tell him?"

"I don't want him."

"You need a dozen brothers to make arrangements for you, Hallie. Or you need papa again. Maybe a lawyer can erase parts of it. You've been on your own eight months and have got everything topsy-turvy." A cloud rolled over the sun, encasing them in shade. A cool wind arrived to touch them. "God

310

knows what . . ." His voice trailed away into pain. ". . . What mama will think."

"I want to tell her myself. I want to plaster it on her face myself."

"Oh, no, Hallie. Since you were a child, she's talked—"

"I can't play child now. It's life and death to me."

"I wouldn't tell her, Hallie."

"I'll tell her soon as I see her. I will announce it as plain as I told you."

"No, Hallie—"

"I will strangle her with it, stuff my baby into her mouth."

"No, Hallie." He dug his head back deeply into the grass, his eyes tightly closed, his breath in puffs, wheezing. "Dr. Watkins is a friend of the family, Hallie," he reminded her.

"I've thought of that, Young. Oh, have I thought of that."

"It has to be kept quiet, but even if it's—is it too late?"

"Not for a doctor, I suppose. It's three months."

"Then I would reco . . . reco . . . would reco—"

"Mend."

"What say to that?" he asked.

She leaned close, so that her head even rested momentarily on his shoulder. She brushed his cheek with her own. "There were a few weeks with Brodie when my life took off into happiness. Then weeks when I wanted to die. I wanted to call papa but knew there was no point. And mama was not possible. Finally I telephoned Frederick and asked for a job. I telephoned him seven times."

"He . . . he never mentioned a job."

"I think I was not polite. The last five calls were collect."

"It's a wonder he didn't even tell papa or mama, except he said you needed money."

"I think maybe she knew, our Amanda. Brodie often came by my hotel room, and I could scarcely speak from hurt pride, and from despising him and wanting him."

"Dr. Watkins does so much work for the company now. . . ."

"I know I can't stop it. It's already too much a part of me."

They sat in the sun, waiting for new thoughts. He said there might be a reconciliation publicly between Pink and Frederick, some sort of title for Pink, and even a change of court record to say that he was competent. "I asked Uncle Wurth if he would attend," he told her.

"You asked him?" she exclaimed.

"An hour ago. He was at the store."

"Papa won't . . . he won't work with Frederick, surely."

"He has been helping him for months."

"Helping Frederick is a full-time job," she said angrily. "If papa thinks I'll ever come back to help Frederick . . ."

Young watched her, surprised by the degree of vehemence. "Worse and worse," he told her.

Brooding within themselves, the two young people waited for sun-down—about five o'clock at this season; by then the salesmen would be near their places for the night, the sheep in the pens, the milk cows finishing the last grain in the pails, families would be adding wood to the fireplaces and drawing in close to the cookstove. The brother and sister listened to the final noises of the working day, bells tinkling, doors closing, a mother called out the names of her brood, her words wafted on the wind, washed by the creeks. "Enid will be looking for us still," she said, hugging herself for warmth.

"Enid?"

"Your grandfather, silly."

"You call him Enid?"

"He follows me about."

Young began to laugh. A while later he said, "Mr. Wallerbee asks about you."

"About me? Does he?"

"Where you are, how you are, when he might hope to see you." He waited nearby while she put on her underclothes, now dry and warm. She hid herself only partially, which annoyed him, caused him to blush crimson, but he said nothing; there were to be no further reprimands or worries, no need to add to the day's score. They came upon Enid at the road. He was fretful, complaining even to passersby, the last fugitives of the parade home, flecks of families hurrying, Enid anxious as a hen missing chicks.

Next morning, walking toward the store where Young was hoping to find a ride into town, Hallie promised not to talk about her predicament with anyone, at least not until Young wrote her.

"Is it showing yet?" he asked.

"Can you see it?"

"No."

"My breasts are bigger. Mrs. Ford thinks she can tell," Hallie told him.

"When papa and I told Mr. Wallerbee you were back East, he became excited about that," Young said, as if entering a digit into an equation.

"Any novelty," she murmured, then laughed. "Am I a novelty, Young?"

He waited near the church, watching a cloud move from across the sun; the light on the fields shook and dissolved, then recovered. "I will see papa tonight, and maybe if I see Mr. Wallerbee tomorrow I will tell him we talked, and that you are pretty as ever."

"And he'll go back to the company papers. What will you tell mama if she finds out?"

"Lord, I don't know." They crossed the trade lot. "I will tell her, I will say Mr. Wallerbee went to find you, was out there this summer with you last . . ." Young counted the months backward . . . "last July or August . . ." He kept glancing away.

"Out where?" She did wish she could see his eyes.

"You had missed each other, and abruptly you were thrown together in a hotel, removed from restrictions. You fell into this trap, ages old."

"Worse and worse, Young, which is to say more and more."

"I'll say Mr. Wallerbee asked you to return with him."

She stared at the excited face of her brother, so like their father, and saw a smile beginning to work its way onto his lips. "And what will Mr. Wallerbee say to all this, Young?"

"I have no idea."

"Young, I . . ." She halted, spellbound by the boy, the man, the flashes of planning. "I've never heard such fancy."

"Sometimes papa hears a train, Hallie, so he tells me."

"There's no train out our way, Young."

"Which makes it all the stranger. He hears it chugging up a grade."

She bit her lip to keep from giving words to her fears.

"We must not tire him unnecessarily, Hallie. We have so little time," he said.

Hallie lay in the bed naked, her hands resting on the slight bulge on her body, thinking about Brodie far off, thinking about Wild William selecting his third major at college, who always would be going to college, she supposed, that being what he did best. Meanwhile he would trust his life to first one woman then another who would feed him, house him. It need not be luxurious quarters, either; he was not enslaved by worldly ways, as he had himself proudly claimed. What was he enslaved by? she wondered. He was as surely a slave as any person she had ever met, for all his talk about freedom. He doted on freedom, enslaved himself seeking it, serving it. Please God, I want Brodie to be the father, she thought. If she could convince herself Brodie was the father, she could bring the boy or girl up proudly. She would sleep alone with a baby Brodie in her arms. She whispered into the covers Brodie's name. "Dear Mr. Wallerbee," she whispered, that thought coming to her. Gently she massaged the unborn baby with her two hands. Of the three men with whom she had made love, which one was the most anchored, dependable for a lifetime? She thought that over, passing the three in review. "Why, Mr. Wallerbee, you astonish me," she whispered to the quilt coverings, to the child under her hands.

And what a marvel Young has become, she thought, to think he can bring about solutions to everybody's problem.

Twenty-six

T̲oday would be the first time Pink had risked himself to the outdoors since Hallie had left him, and Dr. Watkins advised him against doing so now. Pink decided if he were to be judged on his competence in a courtroom he ought to be present, so Young helped him wash and shave and dress, the two rising early, as was Pink's wont anyway. They were ready well before Amanda, and before Harry even put in his appearance downstairs. "I feel like a sheep looking over a picket fence in this new collar, Amanda," Pink told her.

She laughed, mirth and nervousness mingled, and also pride, the pride of being important in the day's activities.

Harry and Young helped him get from the car to the elevator at the courthouse. In the courthouse, Pink sat down on a back bench. Young sat with him. Amanda went forward to join Frederick and to speak to the judge, who was standing near a window looking out at his domain. Dr. Clove entered and at once approached the judge, seemed to know him well, and directly Wallerbee appeared, too, taking a seat on a front bench. The pastor arrived. He was like a bee sniffing flowers, going from Frederick to Wallerbee to Amanda to Clove, welcoming Wurth, who had been in the building since eight o'clock trying to find out where "the ceremony is to be." All were seated down front, except Pink and Young. One by one the individuals moved to the judge's desk, spoke to him in a low voice, the words being taken down by a stenographer, and the drone of the voices was all Pink heard: something about his health improving, his speech being clear enough now to be understood—that was what Dr. Clove said, who ought to know simple speech when he heard it, Pink thought, and Harry said Pink was able to get about, walk almost to the chicken yard and back. "How far is the chicken yard?" the judge asked, and Harry had to estimate. "Why, it's about as far as from here to Pink," he said.

"Pink? Where is Pink?" the judge said.

"Back there," Harry said, pointing him out.

"Why, I didn't know he was present. All right," the judge said, and proceeded to hear the testimony of Wallerbee, who said he had often gone to the home of Pink Wright for advice about the company, and believed Pink was not only well, but was the best business mind in the city. He spoke loud enough to be heard easily. Then Amanda went quite close to the judge and stated her opinions, which the judge had to lean far forward to hear, and so did the court recorder. Then Frederick spoke. Then Pink's brother Wurth said he had been in the rental business with Pink for the last twenty years and had learned to count on him. At last the judge read a few affidavits into the record, then raised his voice, spoke directly to Pink, invited him to speak if he wanted to.

Pink stepped out into the aisle. Suffering pain without flinching, he walked step by step the length of the courtroom; one wouldn't know there was pain with every step of that right foot. Everybody was watching. He stopped before the judge. The Pink Wright grin came on his face, and he said, "You use a big plow for a little field this morning, your hon . . . or."

The judge laughed. "I do know plowing," he said.

"I can tell by the roll of the sho . . . the sho . . . lder if a man has . . . plowed or not."

"Till I was sixteen, then off to college. Did you go to college, Mr. Wright?"

"No. He's going in my place." He looked about for Young, who came forward, said good morning to the judge. "They'll know he's a . . . a . . . rrived when he gets there. They might have missed me."

The judge flipped through a stack of papers, found the ones to sign; the clerk stamped them, and it was all over. At that point Dr. Watkins arrived, said he had been delayed by a patient, and the judge, who called him by his first name, said it was all right to be late so long as he thought Pink Wright was competent. "He's the only man declared competent by a court of law in the county."

The walk to the elevator. The walk to the car. No sign of pain. The walk to the bed, where he had Young close the door. Still in his Sunday-best clothes and new shirt, he collapsed and slept.

There had been so many recent conversations with his father about Hallie; Young could not number them. Yet so far as he knew his father had not written her even a note of forgiveness or advice, and he had not commented on Young's suggestions aimed at helping her. However, once the company meeting, at which he was to be made chairman, approached, he told Young to invite her to arrive that same day at the office "at pre . . . cise . . . ly four o'clock." This was the first occasion Pink had used that certain word, and Young wrote it into the note, as given. "And alone," Pink told him.

The office meeting itself was to be perfunctory. There were many items on the agenda, but the decisions were predictable. The agenda Frederick himself had prepared. He guarded it, making periodic changes, hinting at significance to his father. The meeting would take place in his office, the room Wallerbee and Pink had used for years, which now housed Frederick's new desk and massive chair, the largest available. The chair, generally referred to by the underlings as the throne, had cost more than all the other chairs in the building. Anyway, that was to be the room used, Frederick said, and those present would be Frederick as president, Wallerbee as secretary, Hatch Cole as treasurer, Pink, to be appointed chairman, and Gloria, to take notes.

"And Young, would you mind if he attended me?" Pink asked.

"No. I . . . suppose not papa, though to get more family—"

"He's off to college next September, so he won't be a bother for long," Pink hastened to assure him.

Frederick agreed, then guardedly asked if Pink had heard anything from Hallie.

"Not a word," Pink said at once, waving his hand in the air, as if dismissing the possibility. "No, no, she's . . . she's up there with Enid and Adeline, probably learning to milk."

316

The directors' meeting was to take place at two o'clock, so at noon Pink had Young help him dress. By the time they reached the office, Pink was so tired he had to sit down at Gloria's desk, rest his head forward on his hands. He waited while clerks got his old chair out of the back room. It was dusty, so Gloria vacuumed it. For half an hour he sat there watching, quipping comments, gaining strength, Young nearby, guarding him apprehensively.

When Pink walked into the front office, he found his big chair in place near a window, near Frederick's dominating masterpiece, where Frederick sat, a bowl of soup in hand. Pink was welcomed, as if he were a long-lost hero come home; Wallerbee and Gloria were particularly enthusiastic. The business of the meeting proceeded, electing him chairman of the board. That done, Wallerbee suggested Pink as chairman ought to take charge, but at once he said no, let Frederick continue with his list, since he knew the agenda.

The next item of business was for the company to hire a friend of Frederick's, the nephew of Dr. Clove previously recommended, who had gone to a fine university and owned a house in Clove Park. He could, Frederick felt, bring an air of dignity, and might well take charge of the loans of the company, which now were a big responsibility. So the presentation went, followed by questions, covering the matter of salary, additional secretary, the problem of finding an office, even the possibility of opening a separate office for mortgages. Finally a vote was called, and Pink voted against it.

At Pink's vote, Hatch's head bobbed three times, like a cork on a lake once a fish takes the bait. Wallerbee dropped the papers in his hands. Young stared with open astonishment at his father. Frederick leaned across his desk, as if being closer to Pink might reveal the error. "Papa, I thought we had an agreement," he said, his words stumbling in haste after one another.

"We do. On the big matters."

"But this—I told Dr. Clove it was assured that . . . papa, for God's sake . . ."

"Why not bring it up again next time? What else you have on the list, Fred?" Pink said kindly.

Frederick sank back in his chair, aghast. He looked to Wallerbee for help, but Wallerbee decided to retrieve his papers and put them in order. Hatch was beaming at the other men, admitting his enjoyment of the spectacle.

Following that came a second item, discussion of an emergency loan to Clove Enterprises. The loan was clearly needed to protect the interest of the Monarch Company, as Frederick proved. Wallerbee spoke in favor, after which Pink roused himself, said he felt it was in Monarch's interest to call in the outstanding loans, since Clove by not paying for several months had defaulted.

"That would throw Clove into bankruptcy," Wallerbee explained. "They are in dire straits, Pink."

"Then our company could par . . . cel out the land they own."

"And Frederick is on the loans' face. I mean . . ." Wallerbee began, unsure even yet that Pink was serious, "your son would be involved. If we sue, we are suing Frederick, don't you see?"

"But Fred doesn't have any . . . thing. A fur . . . ther loan is one more bite, and there will be other bites."

"Papa, you and I talked about this." Frederick's voice rose angrily. "We have a gentleman's agreement, papa. I explained to you at home—"

"I vote against another loan and vote to enter suit," Pink said, interrupting.

The young president sat back slowly in his chair, his mouth open, his face blanched. Hatch's grin slowly widened as he bent over his papers. Wallerbee cast worried glances at Frederick, then Pink, then at the stunned Young.

"My God," Frederick whispered.

"Enter Frederick's name in the suit?" Hatch asked perfunctorily, as if he needed an addition to his notes.

"Oh, yes," Pink said at once.

"The company—the company is to sue its president?" Wallerbee asked, gasping.

"He'll have to step down," Pink said simply.

"Papa, for God's sake," Frederick shouted, his eyes wild.

"I so vote my stock," Pink said. Whatever had been hidden was now fully revealed. Pink had spoken the few words without stress, even the mildness of his inflection had been reserved, as the father stabbed wounds into the body of the son.

People on Lexington Avenue knew the details even before Pink and Young arrived in the company car, pulling to a stop at the stand run by a farmer named Joshua Smith. Pink insisted on getting out of the car and trading for a few apples. He accepted the welcome of several people, all of whom he had known for years, each of whom had a private smile for him, acknowledging that he had come back to Lexington Avenue in style. Somebody said, "We heard about your trade, Pink."

"That little pack of apples?" Pink asked.

"No, trading for more'n apples, I heard," the man said. "Your company."

"Just tanning my boy's hide."

"Your brother came tearing through here, told me."

Others began gathering as word traveled that Pink was here. Even Hugh

King left his own store and came to his competitor's, said to Pink he needed to talk to him soon as he could, that Amanda had telephoned. Pink walked as far as the water fountain with him, holding firmly to his arm.

Hugh said, "Amanda's upset, Amanda is—Harry says you've killed her boy."

"Yes, Fred took it hard," Pink admitted.

"She said you promised one thing, then did another."

"Why, I told him the train wasn't on the track, but he should have seen the train was coming."

"She says you've crushed him," Hugh said. "That's what Harry said, too, and he said he was moving out today."

"Never know about peop . . . le, do you?" Pink took water from the fountain, swished it about in his mouth, spit it into the gutter. "Wouldn't want my other boy to go through life, think . . . ing he had a weak father." He nodded toward Young.

Young told him he hoped the assault had not been because of him, that he had been surprised by it, much as if a bolt of lightning had struck on the most sunny day imaginable.

CHAPTER
Twenty-seven

Enid King argued against Hallie's going to town. It would be ruffling dangerous pages, he told her. He was not confident of Amanda, or of Harry Wright, either one, and the situation might explode, the way dynamite in a star-drilled hole explodes walls of stone. "Stay here," he told her, "help me. Let's make peace with ways known." There were doors that led to cellars, he said, just as there were doors that led to parlor rooms. They were often of the same make. He had himself felt cold lashes of wind even while sheltered. There was dust to be encountered plowing the best field. Nothing, as he told her, was completely hospitable. There might be traps to ensnare her at her mother's house. So he talked, pestering ideas, frightening off prospects, poking words at Adeline, seeking to arouse her support, with Hallie sitting nearby full of foreboding, but persisting, insisting that she must trust her brother Young, ought to respond to his invitation to meet with her father.

"Buggy?" Adeline said, surprised. "Clean up the buggy?"

"Now, I'm doing this, Adeline, the best I can," Enid told her.

"But you can't take a buggy into that town with cars honking at you. They like to scare the horses."

"It's all I have," he told her. "It's a matter of pride that I will take Hallie to them. I wish to God I had wealth enough to make it a princess arrival, but I'll do what's possible."

He washed the buggy, then blackened its scars. He polished its enameled walls with his last wax. He washed its scarred wheels, all the while ignoring Adeline's hints that she could find time to accompany them, and on the assigned day before dawn he hitched up the two horses.

It was a slow, hard climb to the ridge crest, and chilly, with the sun still trying to get through. Mist circled, twirling, convoluting. "In storybooks, you read a good deal about princes," Hallie told him, marveling at the blanketlike closeness the breaking dawn imposed on them, and the fairy-land way of the horses' heads bobbing in the mist. "They often sleep for years and a maiden can awaken them with a kiss." She cast a glance at Enid. "You know where a prince is, grandpa?"

"Well, Hallie, I don't know, it's been so long."

"It's the charm, grandpa, a kiss will awaken him. I need somebody like that."

"If I see one, I'll let you know."

"To love me always, make me his princess."

"Choose him at once, will you? That's an old-fashioned marriage, Hallie. Used to be that way. When I was courting, my father pointed out Adeline and said to take that one."

"Did you love her?"

"Love her? Yes, I loved her all right. What do you mean, love her?"

"Did you love her as a . . . person?"

"Well, will you love this here sleeping prince you kiss in the woods?"

"I never kissed any prince in the woods. I've kissed a man in different office rooms and occasionally in a company car, and I've kissed a man in several tunnels and a hotel room because I was trying to find myself, and in Denver I lost control in two hotels."

He was astonished by her outburst and said no more about the matter.

"But you didn't even love her, didn't even know her?" Hallie asked.

"Knew her for years. She had a fine style. I'd heard her laugh many times at services. We had a preacher who was afraid of water and had changed over from Baptist to Methodist as a consequence. He enjoyed talking about that, and I heard Adeline laugh with him, just as pretty as you please."

"So you heard her laugh."

"I'd seen her around. She had the instruments, the knobs, the curves, Hallie. I could tell she was equipped."

Hallie stared at him. "Equipped with what?"

"With what attracts a man. She was well made. Back then a woman wore more clothes, but she showed the curves of her breasts and fanny, pulled her waist in tight, you know, and a woman could swing her skirts, make them into flags to attract a man, and women had welcoming smiles, those that had sound teeth, and she did. Adeline always has had sound teeth."

Hallie fretted over the matter. "Well, you didn't love her, that's what I mean."

"In that day, you married because a woman had what you needed. Later you came to like her. You did, too, for the two of you were engaged in a situation that neither of you had been in before, exploring a range of feeling a man and woman are meant to have. She and I did all of this exploring together, so you can imagine how close we became." He opened a canning jar and drank a few ounces of whiskey, then patiently, carefully screwed the lid back on.

"Was she the only woman you ever knew?" Hallie asked him. Her elbows were forward on her knees as she watched the horses' heads bob. "Grandpa, you hear me?"

"I don't recall," he said.

"You know you do. Was it the first time you knew a woman?"

"You are a nosy person, Hallie. Never in my life have I talked about any of this, even to my daughters when they were marrying, and I don't know that Adeline did, either—"

"Oh, she did. I bet she did. She and mama talked to me when I was only naked in the yard with Marshall. Grandma was very frank, I'd say."

"Well, I'm not frank. I'm scared to talk about any of it."

"You're old enough to say what you think."

"I'm not one to talk about successes or failures of a private sort. I do think this. I think a woman continues to attract a man, most any woman, because it's not the individual after all. A woman who thinks she individually attracts a man is deceiving herself. A man has an instinct for women. I tell you, a man is attracted to the prospects and curves, the smiles, the eyes, those looks he gets or wants to get, and he's not likely ever to be so taken with an individual as—"

"You are. You are, with your own wife. You said you were."

"Yes, now. But, good Lord, she was all that was ever in the house with me." They rode on. The mist was swirling, lifting.

"If a woman offered herself to you today, would you take her?"

"Unlikely prospect." Later he said, "If she could arouse me." Still later he said, "Now, don't you tell anybody else you've been with three men. A woman shouldn't tell such as that. He drove down a hill to a mossy woods. "I suppose you're angry at all three of them."

"I'm not angry."

"And at men generally."

"I am not."

"You are about to bite me."

"I never bite."

"No, you'll hide your fury inside yourself and hate us all, including that wandering fellow that liked to use the closets."

She stared aghast. "What you say?"

"You said closets to me, and I was just thinking about it."

"Closets? I said tunnels."

"Was thinking. That's all. Tunnels, was it?"

"Grandpa, you ever use a closet?"

He kept his gaze firmly trained on the road ahead. "No. I couldn't."

"Why couldn't you?"

"Because I never had one." Silence. Both of them were watching the road unfold, the proud horses' heads bobbing, the colored leaves fluttering invitingly. "You liked him, that tunnel man?" he asked.

"Yes."

"You loved them, all three, and offered yourself to them and finally got turned down," he said. "A pity. My God, it is a pity."

"I . . . never got turned down. One keeps writing me, as you might have noticed."

"To . . . meet you somewhere?"

"Wondering about me."

"Ah, well, that's nice of him."

"He has these sisters, you see."

"I don't see that that needs to matter."

"I . . . I don't know why it did."

"If that's all it is, then he'll have to do. I can't find a prince for you to kiss awake. There's so few left, Hallie."

"There are no princes left, grandpa, I know that now."

"Never were many," he said.

By noon they were on the plateau. The last ridge crossing was behind them. "Was it a woman who made you so sure of everything, grandpa?" she asked him suddenly. She took his right hand in both of hers and warmed it between her palms: leathery, coarse skin, hard muscles and sinews, veteran of bouts with plows and guns and knives and wheels, the cobbler's hand, which rarely touched a shoe. "Not the hand of a healer," she told him, rubbing it.

"Anyway, you're lonely, Hallie, men ignoring you, or hurting you, you've not known deep loneliness until you are left by your child. That's when life for me became a single stick in a field."

"Grandpa, I know loneliness."

"Years grain a child into you, then sudden as a thunder clap the child is gone, and you reach out for it, just as I'll reach out for you tomorrow."

"I'm not gone, grandpa."

"Yes, you are too," he told her, "near about. It'll be today, a few hours from now. I'll look around an' find you gone. Then what will I do? What in Goddamn life, what am I supposed to do?"

In town Enid stopped at the livery stable in order to feed his horses. The place was closed. Not only was it closed, but there were boards nailed across its wide doors, and he heard the clattering of a loose shutter upstairs, a signal of abandonment. "I used to come here as a boy," he said. "When I was helping my papa drive stock to market, we'd stop there at the inn."

"What inn?" Hallie asked, looking about at the lines of stores and market stalls.

"Oh, I don't know now," Enid admitted, aggravated, made to feel forlorn. "It'll eat us all up before it stops, whatever it is that's going on." He found one bucket of oats for sale on Lexington Avenue, only one, and fed his horses and watered them at the overflow trough from the ever-running drinking fountain. "Used to be a bold spring hereabouts," he said. "Don't recall where." They drove on to the office, arriving just before three o'clock, and he claimed he would go tie his horses at Amanda's, or visit the stockyard to look around. He would stay close, he said, but as she watched the buggy roll alongside a streetcar, then move into a line of honking cars, Enid sitting proudly on the seat ignoring the whole wide world, she supposed he was leaving her now.

Gloria appeared to be glad to see Hallie; there was loud festivity in the office; most every room vibrated with good feeling, words were called out one person to another, until after a quarter hour of celebrating she found herself in the front office. Frederick's desk had been pushed into one corner and a wastepaper basket had been set on it. Her father's old chair dominated the room, and her father was sitting in it, waiting for her, Young nearby. He had been patiently listening to the noises from the other rooms, patiently anticipating his meeting with her. "Now stand back there," he told them, after their greeting. "Let me see you. The world hasn't left a bad mark, has it?"

"Oh, it tried, papa." She backed up against the wall, as he directed. The western sun cast a golden light across her face and body.

"Young told me you're in for a change."

"I'm . . . on the start of it now, papa."

"Mr. Wallerbee," he called. "You come in and shut the door." He came in, and as he saw Hallie for the first time in months, awkwardness humbled him. Indeed, it also humbled her. The two seemed to be separated by sunlit partitions. Pink and Young watched their every flicker of expression. "Now, there she is, Wallerbee. What do you think of her?" Pink asked.

"Papa, I'm not going to stand here and be auctioned off or gawked at—"

"No, no, of course not. See, Waller . . . bee. See her. She's not obviously harmed."

"No, I'd say she has not been," Wallerbee said fondly, his voice trembling.

Hallie said, "The idea of such a statement—"

"Not a blemish on her, but she's been used. Vir . . . vir . . ."

"Virtue, papa," Young said, trying to help him.

"Vir . . . tu . . . ally new, even now. Now, Waller . . . bee, what did you do last summer?"

Wallerbee turned to him, confused. Young gasped, surprised by the frankness and speed of the bargaining.

"Honey, do stand back against the wall. Let him see what he's trad . . ing for," Pink told her.

Hallie pressed herself against the wall, her shoulders flat against it, looking askance at her father, glancing at Wallerbee to judge his reaction, and at her brother.

"Yes, you went to Wrightsville Beach, as usual, is that it?" her father was saying to Wallerbee. "Ocean Terrace Hotel, as usual? Manager is that Mrs. . . . uh . . ."

"Terrill," Wallerbee said, supplying the name, all the while hungrily staring at Hallie.

"Did we insure her? Seems like that salesman Coleman Downs sent in an application for her three years ago. Was that in August?"

"The policy?" Wallerbee said, confused, only half considering these distractions from Pink, his eyes feasting on the shy, embarrassed daughter.

"In July this year you went to Denver," Pink said. That caught him, brought Wallerbee up short and caused gasps of surprise from Hallie.

"No, in July on the 14th I arrived at the ferry at Wrightsville Sound, at the car-parking sheds," Wallerbee said, confidently recalling time and place.

"No, consider this poss . . . ibility. I prefer it. At the Brown Palace Hotel in Denver, you were there two weeks and had an affair with Hal, and the result is that she is about to show a nat . . . ural sign."

Hallie was stunned; she was lost in bright sunlight and wonder. The chances were that Wallerbee would flee, she thought; he could be outside the room quickly and be done with them.

Wallerbee thought it well to say he had sent Pink a postcard from Wrightsville in July of last year.

"And your sisters?" Pink asked, smiling suddenly. "A postcard to them?"

"I . . . don't recall."

"How are your sisters, anyway?" Pink asked, and launched into a diversion concerning them, recalling their names, wondering about the broken ankle one had suffered skating four years ago. As abruptly as he had left the subject of Hallie, he returned, speculating aloud that Mrs. Terrill, manager at Wrightsville, would doubtless confirm most any story. "I'm not trying to dot every *i* and cross every *t*, Wallerbee, for I suspect you and Hallie will want to talk about your visit to Denver privately, but I want to put on the table two cards, one pertaining to her and one to you, and admit my daughter has reason for marriage." He spoke this fluently, without slurring any word, and without giving opportunity for objection. "Now then, the dowry is an embarrassment in every discussion of marriage. All I can say is that Hal's dowry will have to be stock in this company." He had their attention now, every wink and breath; they were both waiting for the next admission. Even voices in other rooms appeared to have hushed. "I have nothing else, Wallerbee, so you must bear with me." He motioned Hallie to move a foot or two farther to the right, so that direct sunlight would continue to light her.

"Papa, this bargaining, this auction, makes me so ashamed," she admitted.

"What say to ten percent, Wallerbee?"

"Ten percent of the company, or of your holdings in it?"

Pink smiled, satisfied with the reply, pleased with his prospective son-in-law. "Not enough, is it?" Pink said. "I get your point. Very well, fifteen percent of the company, what of that?"

"My question had to do with . . ."

"Well, I can't go beyond seventeen percent and leave anything for the others. That will be one-third of what I have.

"What I was trying to say, Pink . . ." Wallerbee began.

"That seventeen won't give you and Hallie control, I realize that. Let's figure something out. With what you have, plus Hallie's seventeen percent, which I propose she own outright from today onward, you'll fall a bit short of control, so what I will do is put one-half of my remaining stock in trust for Young until he is . . . say, twenty-five, with you and Hallie as trustees. That will give you about eight, nine years of control. And I will leave the rest in trust for Amanda, for Frederick to receive when Amanda dies. Now . . ." He looked up at Wallerbee, piercing him with his gaze. "That's all. You have driven me as far as I can go. I am against the wall." To Young he said, "Now help me to the other room and let them talk privately. What say, what about twenty-five?"

"I . . . I'm . . . I'll be halfway in my grave by twenty-five, papa. Twenty-one is the—"

"Twenty-three then. I think by then you'll be able to decide how to spend your life, whether here or elsewhere. You must plant yourself carefully. Twenty-three, let that be agreed. Now, you and I will go and allow these two to discuss what a rogue I am. Words . . . escape me, to do that justice."

"Crass," Hallie suggested. "Rude, scheming, obdurate, sly . . ."

"All of that," he said, reaching for Young's arm. "More, more," he told her, as he made his way from the room.

In a back office, he sat down with the company lawyers. The strain was showing now through his resolve; his fingers were trembling like leaves now in autumn. He dictated to the lawyer his instructions, dictating last his will, leaving income from much of his stock, as well as the loans, houses, and land, to Amanda, the stock going on her death to Frederick.

"I've put it down just as you said it, Mr. Wright," the lawyer told him. "Now, is that all for the will? Anything for your brothers."

"My pocket knives," he replied, smiling. "Yes, lying there in that bed I had all the time in the world to plan what I would have to say this first day at work, and the second and third, too. I want the second day for Amanda, to take her away and buy her a present. Women like pretty things. You know that, Young?"

"Yes, sir, I've heard they do. You mean mothers?"

"Women."

"Yes, sir."

"All women are part Indian."

The lawyer began to laugh. "I'll not put that in the will, Mr. Wright," he said.

"Why don't men like pretty things as much?" Young asked him.

"Well, they have the women," he replied. "So my next few days are to be for her, and may . . . be Hugh."

"What about Frederick?" Young asked. "I was never so surprised as when you . . ."

"Hugh didn't come to the court, you noticed," Pink said.

"What about Frederick?" Young repeated.

"I don't know yet just what I'll say to Fred. I think he should go with his wife's people, if they'll have him. His wife . . . go with his strong suit, you see."

"What other differences are there between men and women, papa?" Young said, winking at the lawyer.

"Haven't you noticed any?" Pink said.

"I mean beyond what's obvious."

"Men tend to be Old Testament people, women New Testament people."

Beaming, Wallerbee came in from the front office. "We must celebrate, Pink," he said. "Surely we have some wine around."

Pink saw Hallie approaching behind him. "She has to marry you to get the stock," he told Wallerbee, "but she can divorce you later." Again to Wallerbee he said, "I'm going to set here until the trust is signed, and my will. Is the will typed yet, Mr. Clarke?"

"No, but soon now," the lawyer said.

"Who is to be the notary?"

Gloria spoke up from another room, said she would be.

"You come on in here then," Pink said. "Get ready. I begin to feel . . . so damn weary."

"First, I want to ask you questions about that unborn child," the lawyer said.

"Ask God. I don't know anything about any unborn."

"I'm told your wife alternately says she is or is not pregnant. Shall I enter a fourth child in the will? Have you decided on a name at all?"

"N.I.," Pink said at once.

The lawyer jotted that down on a note pad. "What does that stand for, Mr. Wright?"

"No inheritance," he said.

"Now," the lawyer said, "you don't want your will overturned. He is your only other child, if he exists."

"Amanda will take care of him. Bring me the papers to sign. I don't have . . . might not have . . ."

"She will feel . . ."

"Papa, come into your office to sign them, to your chair," Hallie suggested.

"No, I won't risk it." When the papers were brought to him, the stock certificates and the trust papers, he signed them across the bottom, then sat resting for a minute or so, breathing deeply, regaining his strength. Later he signed the will, then slowly he leaned his head forward on the desk, exhausted.

Gloria took the papers from under his head and notarized them.

"Papa, we'll need the car," Young said. "I'll call it."

"I don't know," Pink murmured. "If there is to be another child, Mr. Ruffin, a codicil . . ." He lapsed into silence again. "My books of English poets can go to him." He smiled, shrugged. Suddenly he pushed himself erect, energy seemed to return, he accepted Young's arm, and made his way into the front room, where he relaxed in the chair. The lawyer came scurrying along with note pad and pen, asking just what codicil he did want to add. "Mr. Wallerbee, did you tell Amanda I want to spend tomorrow with her," Pink asked.

"I . . . I didn't even know that, Pink."

"Please phone her."

"Now?"

"So she won't worry so much," Pink said. "And tell her I want to see Fred soon, another day."

"Well, I will phone her now, if you like." Wallerbee turned to Hallie.

"She worries so," Pink said. "That's another difference, Young," he said, "though not as pro . . . pro . . . nounced. They worry more. Worry, worry, worry." He seemed to be comforting himself with the easy flow of the word. "And they forgive easier. Remember that. Thank God. Ask her, Mr. Wallerbee, to forgive me."

"Forgive you for what, papa?" Hallie said, crouching down to look into his face.

"None . . . none of your business," he said. He smiled at her. "Pretty woman," he told her. "You will be a pretty woman all your life." The lights in the square were brighter, grew brighter as he watched. He was wondering about words to be chosen now. The lights approached as steadily, certainly as any other act of God; from the chair he watched the square become red and crimson, the cars exude radiance, the motion-picture marquee lights flick sparks into the air. Now even the sky was brightly flashing. One final word, something for Amanda. "Oh, I don't know," he said aloud, and felt a hand grip his and knew it must be Hallie's. He turned his head away from the flashes of light, so bright they were almost unbearable. "I would . . . think chil . . . dren are the best of it, ex . . . cept the idea is so self-de . . . feating." Hallie's face appeared golden, the look of agony on her face was flushed, spit was at the corner of her pretty mouth. "Hal, you . . . will need to get a car for me to . . ."

"What, papa?"

"Tomorrow."

"Yes, tomorrow. A car."

"To take her for a drive." The lights burned, singed his mind. He stared directly into them, waiting.

CHAPTER
Twenty-eight

Dreamlike. Hallie stumbling on the stairs. Pink breathing but unconscious, on his back on the big desk in the moviehouse-lighted, blinking room. Young sitting in Frederick's great chair; was he praying? "No answer at the doctor's office or house," Wallerbee reported.

Alive. At least Pink was breathing. Young said to take him home. Hallie concurred. Wallerbee phoned for an ambulance. "I'll go as far as the door of my mother's house, that's all," Hallie told Young. "I don't want to see her."

"You must," Young told her.

"Not tonight I won't."

"Nobody in the house at all," Wallerbee told Hallie solemnly, seeking to grasp the significance himself. Everything closed up, fires doused, the splotches of water still on the hearths, Pink's bed left rumpled, Amanda's and Harry's beds made and all Harry's clothes gone, some of Amanda's, her dresser drawers open. Must have been rushing, maybe confused.

"Where . . . where would she go?" Hallie asked.

"Oh . . . " He waited, as if the answer might mysteriously be supplied in silence. "Home to Enid, I guess."

"With Enid?" Hallie said.

The house tonight, its personality was different from anytime before; there had been many reincarnations, re-creations over the years, Hallie recalled: the cold house into which the family had moved twenty-seven years before, the house warmed and filled with baby voices, the house enlarged, enlivened by children growing up, the house of Pink's illness, the house with Frederick and Hallie gone, the house with Harry moving in upstairs, the house now empty, its fires extinguished. Not even a shutter banged against the window of the room where Pink, his face set and perplexed, lay on his bed, seeing vaguely, speaking in baby incantations.

People began to gather in the evening, coming from Lexington Avenue, parking their old cars and trucks and tethering their horses along the street, near the house—gangling farmers and their children, along with a few country women, bonneted, aproned, their long dresses flowing close to the ground. They congregated, often changing places and stance, waiting for Pink's death. They were welcomers of death, attendants. Hugh arrived, dressed in a new pair of overalls he had pulled on at the store, taking them from the long-length counter, a new black belt around his waist, a four-inch knife sheathed near his right hand, ready for whittling, paring, slicing, cutting. He brought with him a Dalmatian puppy, which he had traded for that afternoon. He patted the dog, calming it as best he could. "High-strung, are you?" he whispered to it. "So 'm I." He slipped a cord around the dog's neck, tied one end to a bush. "Don't you chew that through." He caught sight of Young and whistled. Young approached him squinting; smoke from a bonfire was interfering with his sight. "This here dog I'll name after you," Hugh said. "You want him, Young?" he asked, suddenly hitting upon the idea of giving the boy yet another gift.

Young crouched down to pat the puppy. "Mama's not home," he announced. "We don't know where she is."

"She's over to my place," Hugh said simply. "Been there since afternoon."

"Why is she there?"

"Oh, was looking for her papa, says he's in town. Phoning her mother to complain about Pink. To spend money on conversations is a complete waste."

"Is he?"

"Is he what?"

"In town?"

"I don't know. I sent a boy to the stockyard to see if he was down there. Then she's been looking for Frederick."

"Oh, well," Young said, patting the dog.

"Suppose she's heard about Pink's stroke by now. Can he see, Young, your papa? Can he recognize?"

"Yes." Young stood up. "His mind wanders, and he has visions. He saw his mama, he said, and she came to his bed and tried to choke him."

"Oh, come on, boy. His own mother?"

"Yes, he said she put a pillow over his face, was calling him ghost, ghost, and she suffocated him."

Hugh scraped his foot across a tuft of grass. He sniffed the wood smoke, peered suspiciously through the smoke at members of the gathering crowd. Somebody had begun strumming a guitar and in a nasal voice telling a story about railroads. He murmured, "I get hard of hearing, when music is played."

"He said she kept calling him by her own brother's name, that uncle I never even saw, the one that died after the war."

"Amanda telephoned Wurth, too, asked him to come and get her," Hugh said.

"She never liked Wurth."

"Not more'n a sour apple," Hugh admitted. "It was a dream you say, this here about his mother?"

"I know it must have been."

"You go in there and see how Pink is, then come and tell me," Hugh said.

Somebody had brought two ponies; they were hitched near enough to a bush to eat its leaves. "Oh, well," Young whispered, and moved through the smoke. He stopped at the porch steps, shied away from the countrywomen who were seated in the rockers, strangers all. They watched him with blue, rheumy eyes, their loose mouths working at their snuff, moans escaping from them as they rocked.

He allowed the screen door to close quietly behind him. He paused to consider the hallway. Hallie stood near the halltree, holding to one of its coat hooks. Wallerbee was sitting on the seat of the halltree, was listening to her talk, repeat: " . . . If mama's not here within a short time, she'll not see him. All her life she'll regret it. She might be at a hotel, what do you say? What do you say about her being in a hotel?"

Young said, "She's at Hugh's house." He watched as the information took hold, saw Hallie's body wilt abruptly, as if near collapse.

"Can't you go for her?" she asked, reaching out a hand to Young.

"I can soon," Young said. "After I see papa."

Wallerbee stirred briefly.

"Please," she said to Wallerbee. "You go."

Young went into his father's room, where Gloria and Imogene sat in rockers, each praying, each dazed, shocked beyond knowing. The small lightbulb was burning behind its paper shade. "Papa, she'll be here soon," Young said aloud.

"Don't bother him," Imogene told him, sitting up. Using both hands she pushed her big body upward, lurched to her feet. She took off her sweater, a man's cardigan, folded it, and laid it on a chest, alongside the cat, which moved onto the cardigan and lay down.

Young approached close to the bed. "Papa, you awake?" The eyes sought him out.

"Mama's at Hugh's. She's been talking with Wurth and trying to find Grandpa King and Frederick. Seems like she's in a rare state." He paused. "Did your mama leave you alone yet?"

Pink nodded, the barest of movement.

"A preacher's out there in the yard now."

"Oh, my . . . " Pink winked at him. "I saw . . . the old . . . himself."

"God?"

Pink frowned. "And you know . . . I was not . . . the least bit . . ." He sought the word, faltered. "I was not . . . the least bit afraid."

Imogene, from across the room, said, "Is he talking?"

"Was it God you saw?" Young asked.

"Not afraid," Pink said.

Imogene approached from the front window. "There must be a hundred people out there in that yard, Mr. Wright. How many in the backyard, Young?"

"Papa, tell me what the old man said," Young begged.

"That fire will burn the grass, I'm afraid," Imogene said.

"He saw God," Young told her, to quiet her.

"Saw him?" Imogene said, caught short by the thought. "Why, we've all saw him, Him and Jesus both."

Pink laughed, which surprised Young, and caused Gloria to rise from her chair. Imogene said, "What was he a-doing when you come upon him?"

"Resting," Pink said.

"Uh huh," Imogene said, considering that. "Had he been resting long?" The chuckle once more. "No, no."

"Was he with them commandments?" she asked.

Pink chuckled. "Your mama, where is she, Young?"

"She's been sent for," Young assured him.

"And Fred . . . ?"

"I don't know yet," Young said.

Imogene stationed herself at the foot of the bed. "What had he been doing to cause him to tire?"

Pink winked at Young. He inhaled deeply, as if inhaling strength. "Plowing," he replied.

"My God," Imogene murmured. "You tell me that?"

"Been plowing the longest field . . . I ever saw."

"Was God a-working? How you know it was God then?"

"He was using a gold plow," Pink replied.

The doctor came noisily through the hallway, coffee mug in hand—a tin cup, which was scalding him, he said. He set the cup down. "See here," he said, laying his hand on Pink's forehead. "Can you move any limb, Pink?"

"No."

"Anything at all?"

"No."

"Not a finger? Not a toe? Your tongue works though, your mouth, your breathing? Are you tired?"

"Oh, God . . ."

"Weary as in a deep sleep, are you?"

"I . . ." He paused, closed his eyes, and said nothing more, even though the doctor kept questioning him.

"He's gone off to rest for a while," the doctor said.

Much barking in the yard, then men fussing at the dogs. Young from the porch saw Enid King drive his team onto the lawn, so he could tie the horses to a porch railing. One of the women on the porch began to complain about Enid's intrusion, his interrupting their discussion of Pink's virtues, but Enid ignored her. A goat came close enough to sniff the leather of the horses' gear. "You get your ass away from here," Enid told it. "Here, who owns this 'un?"

A woman came bustling forward and tugged the rope of the goat.

"Them things caused the Sahara Desert," Enid told her. "Is Pink alive?" Enid asked the women. They ignored him. He stepped directly from the buggy onto the porch steps. "You porch women ought to be sweeping." They were staring critically at him now. Young approached, led him indoors. They moved into Pink's room, studied the sleeping face, the near-lifeless body. Soon Enid retreated to the dining room, where the doctor was holding forth about strokes being unpredictable. "Well, death is predictable, is it?" Enid asked him directly.

Young marveled at the strangeness of this certain evening. Hours sped along, disappearing without evidence, except for chatter. Even the wanderers in the yard had settled into immobile groups, somebody now and then recalling an incident that connected the storyteller with Pink. The people sought news of him; he's unconscious, he's asleep, he's lying in the parlor where the electric lights burn. Young was not sleepy, although he knew the hour was late. He noticed a woman move across the yard; she paused near the men at the first fire, moved on to the side of the house, where a horse was scraping the ground with its hoof. She was, he realized, someone he knew, although he didn't know just who she was; he followed along, but at the back of the house she was not near the fire, not among the people on watch. Very like Hallie, he thought, but Hallie had been put to sleep, he had been told; the doctor had sedated her.

Amanda watched Young until he turned the corner of the house, then went onto the kitchen porch, and from there into the back bedroom. Quietly she opened the connecting door to the front bedroom, the one she had used since Pink took ill. There were a few embers of a coal fire in the grate, so she paused to remove her bulky shawl and warm her hands. Chilly in the night, walking from Nettie and Hugh's house. She was not dressed for dead-of-the-night travel. She could have borrowed a coat but had not wanted to announce to Nettie that she was making this journey. From off somewhere in the house she heard her father speak, calling for Imogene. She waited for the footsteps of the heavy nurse to disappear toward the dining room. She was about to open the door to the hall when she heard a sigh just behind her. She swung around. Somebody was asleep on her bed. Pink, she thought, Pink was in her bed. She tip-toed closer to the sleeping person. Herself—it is myself, she thought. Younger. The age I was when I bore Frederick and Hallie. Hallie lying there, a pillow clutched to her breasts, her chin resting on it, her mouth open. Oh, my God, she thought, her animosity toward Hallie breaking suddenly, wanting more than anything to fall on the bed there, just there, and gather her up in her arms, her baby, this one more time, again, hold her and love her.

She stuffed the desire away, frightened by it. She backed off. She backed into a chair. The noise caused Hallie to stir, but only briefly. Amanda made her way to the door and opened it as quietly as she could. She noticed Mr. Wallerbee was asleep on the seat of the halltree, his legs stuck out before him, the hall light casting shadows. The door to the porch was wide open, and the crooning voices of women were clear enough, women talking, praying, reminiscing. From the yard drifted banjo and guitar music, and sad above measure was a sole fiddle, probably played by the Penland boy, who was said to have picked up his brother's fiddle at eight years of age and at once played it.

Gloria was asleep in the chair near the parlor fireplace. On seeing her, a wave of anger welled up in Amanda. She closed the parlor door without bothering to latch it. She leaned over Pink's face, seeking his life with her eyes, any sign of life. She realized he knew, even in sleep, that she was here. His breathing lessened. His breath knew her breath, so often they had joined together. "I don't know what you're thinking of, having so many people in the yard, Pink, all come to see you."

"See my ghost," he whispered.

His eyes remained closed, but there were the words, the miracle. "Can't see a ghost, can you?" she said.

"My mama can." His eyes opened and the old, same, familiar grin of human kindness was there, as in his days of health. "I was the ghost of her younger brother."

"Oh, I know the one you mean."

"She told me to leave."

"I see," she said doubtfully, not sure what he meant.

"She said to go. Ordered me out of her room. I . . . I couldn't move, Hallie."

A slap at her soul. Coldly she studied him. Hallie, indeed. A slip of the tongue, was that it? Was he confused, or had he merely called her by a loving name, a family name? "You know me?" she asked timidly, not wanting to anguish about a simple error.

"She's always been . . . afraid of ghosts."

"She's wilting in her mind, Pink. We both know that. So many do when they reach old age. It's upsetting for us all."

"Wurth put me in her room, the par . . . lor, Amanda."

"The parlor, yes." Pink did know who she was, she realized, relieved, deeply grateful.

"Wurth had put Hallie upstairs, her and Fred and Young, so there was only his bedroom left; or I could stay in the kitchen."

"Wurth always worries about details, you know that."

"He decided he might move his wife upstairs, in which case the boys could sleep in the kitchen, and I could sleep in his and his wife's bed, but he was afraid . . . his wife would get up in the night and fall down the stairs."

Softly she touched his face with her fingers. Had she hated him only this afternoon? Hate so acute it broke all restraints. Where was the hate now? Would it come rushing forward at any moment, she wondered. "So this was a dream, this about your mother, was it, Pink? You used to have dreams about being late for a ship and you got there in the nick of time, you told me, and couldn't find your ticket, had to go through your luggage, always found it as the gates closed—some sort of gates, you said, and you were the last one through. Do you recall?"

"Often I dreamed of that ship."

"Where was it going, Pink?"

"Heaven, I suppose," he said, and smiled at her. "There are some mighty big fields in Heaven, Amanda. And that fellow was out plowing with his gold plow, and had his gold belt on. He was resting, and I said to him, I like you very well, since I see that you work, and sweat . . . and have to rest. He shook his head to get the sweat out of his eyes, and he told me he had all that field to do, that he hoped to get it planted for . . . the hungry before the rains. Even then clouds were gathering. I said to him, Is gold too soft a metal for a plow? And he agreed it was. But I'm bound to use it, he said. It's an affliction, and the belt is twice as heavy as a silver one, but it's mine to wear. He stomped the mud from around his boot heels and spoke to his horses—had a fine team—and he turned his plow handles, speaking tough words to his team, and I watched him for more'n half an hour. He staggered whenever he hit a rock or root. I heard no choir, Amanda."

"Well, I know you missed the music, Pink."

"They keep talking about singing in Heaven. I would get tired of that. What I heard . . . were birds calling, the buzz of insects, a train passing to the northwest. I hear it now, Amanda."

"No train here, Pink."

"Oh, my God, I hear it."

"Pink, I'm sorry," she said suddenly, speaking aloud, tears gushing to her eyes. "I want you to know I'm sorry, not for what I've done but for having to do it."

A cry of welcome escaped him.

"It's the most difficult thing in the world to be the mother to a family, with everybody going away," she continued, hurrying the words.

Whatever apparition had seized him released him then, and he was left with a deep sweat on his face and a calm attitude once more; his mouth would not close, and his eyes were open, glassy as wet marbles. The doctor came, Imogene arrived, all in a commotion, and Amanda retreated to the hall, where she was met by Mr. Wallerbee. It was over. Broken and unfinished. Even her explanation had been pieces of a bit. She stood in the hallway weeping deeply, tears gushing from her eyes. Wallerbee put his arms around her to keep her from falling.

The women on the porch began wailing steadily, knowing without being told that the end had come. Men in the yard interrupted stories about trades and cars, leaving them unfinished. Hugh, standing near his pup, felt the chill. Out of Wales and England, from old Scotland and Ulster the wail came, out of unrecorded time the women acknowledged without pain or anger an event often occurring; they accepted death without bitterness, with wave on wave of regret, mentioning in high-pitched voices the old-beyond-measure anguish of their breed; bearers of new life, sustainers of the living, bathers of the cold, of the dead. Know the dead; they are our living. Know the dead; they are our children grown old. Know the dead; they are ourselves not yet dying. Know the dead; they are the recurring reminder. Know the dead; they are free of pain. Know that the dead bury their hatreds with them. Know the dead; they are the last remaining measure. Know the dead; they are our brothers, sisters, kin. In their dirt-covered places, they are remembered without malice. Know the dead; they were reapers of grain, gatherers of apples, sellers of hogs, cropsmen of corn and hay, stealers of wild honey. Know the dead, and lift no voice in anger; life and death are twins in league together. Know the dead, whimper not one sound, but let your voice be full and from the throat and chest, let the sound rise in unworded refrain. Know the dead and call not one word to God in anger for taking what was promised. Low, bend low in the moving chairs; old women, bend over your knees. Now rock backward as your voices rise, the volume increasing as the chair rocks backward, as your bodies rise until your faces are known to us, wrinkled, mouths slackened from loose teeth, lips formed in circles. Out of your bodies came the body; into the earth goes the body, into a hole like your mouths. Bury him sooner or later; it matters little. First must be the sound of thank God for death, thank God for death, which brings us all together at last.

Men were walking about now, incredulous of the wailing from the porch. Hugh's pup began howling. Hugh sought his company, rubbed his head behind his ears. He had traded a hundredweight of smoked hams for him, and he not weighing twenty pounds. Damn foolishness a man could get into. Fellow said he would grow to be four foot high. "Stop that noise, damn you. You're a boy dog, not an old woman. It's only old women who know."

Young stopped nearby, watching. "Know what, Uncle Hugh?"

Hugh turned to consider him: tall, straight, not a sign of tears yet. "Not for me to say," he said.

"Who . . . who says then?"

"Words don't," he said. "Them women are saying it." Across the faces of the men, across the fires, the wail drifted into the smoke; the little dog once more responded, even as Hugh touched it.

Young backed away, reluctant to accept the wail. He went off along the street to the end of the line of trucks, there burying his head in folded arms, in frustration sobbing aloud, standing beside the bed rails of a Ford, his own voice out of sorts with the wails from those women, his own voice snapping with fury. Without conscious awareness, he began beating the bed of the truck with his hands, beat it until they bled. Defiantly he shouted out through sobs, fiercely resentful of the fall of his own dear god.

PART FIVE
Birth

Twenty-nine

Go home, Amanda thought, I'll go home now, close up this house and live in the little house Pink and I started out in. Have a garden big enough for all the canning I want to do, feed my chickens and buy a flock of ducks, if I can devise a pool for them to flap their wings in. Should I have geese or not? They are loud and have been known to peck children if they won't run. Close this house. Shut its doors on life.

It was Hallie who kept her from going, the unfinished relationship with Hallie held her to the house.

"I think I know you," Amanda said one morning to her reflection in the mirror, then leaned close to it, so that her face was close to her own face. "No stranger to me, even yet."

Lonely bed. Nobody to intrude into privacy. No hand or fingers to awaken her cravings. No whispering about the children. No whispering about birthdays or what color Hallie's room should be, Hallie usually coming up with an unlikable suggestion. Orange was one. That was when she was quite young. Dark blue was one, when she was in her teens. "You can't read well in a dark-blue room," Amanda had told her, which had changed her mind. Bright yellow—was that what the child had wanted as substitute?

What had happened to the storehouse of memories? She was of an age and condition when memories were needed to comfort and enliven her. Where were they? She seemed to have so few, even of Pink. Her mind was drugged, that was one trouble with those pills Dr. Watkins had given her to take. The night of Pink's death he had given Hallie two, and she slept through her father's last hours, and on waking she had shouted angrily at the doctor about it, tears streaming down her face, and had told him she was pregnant, too, and wouldn't have taken anything at all if she had known her father would be gone.

That was a memory, but recent, from a month or two away. Where were the memories from earlier? Once she was at ease with herself again, had accepted Pink's going, would they flood into her mind?

She decided she was as smart as Harry, but not as smart as Pink. Hallie in her way was as smart as Pink. And that had made all the difference, or much of the difference, to have a child smarter than she. And smarter than Frederick, too. She had been wife and mother to a family smarter than she.

She doted on Frederick even yet. He was her favorite child, the one who still needed her; however, she spent more time with Hallie, sitting in the parlor talking. "Well, I don't know what he would have said, but I think of that second day and what it was to be. An inn, he said, Hallie? We were to stay in an inn? But that was what you and him did, I never stayed in inns with him. I was here to come home to whenever he wanted home. I suppose he decided we didn't have a home any longer, we had so near beat it to death."

"I don't know, mama, what he had in mind exactly, but he was pleased when he spoke of the second day."

"Young says he was smiling when he talked of me."

"Oh, yes."

"Young has taken it so hard. He thought so much of his father."

"I know, mama."

"What inn was it to be?"

"I don't know that."

"I keep asking you the same questions over and over."

"It doesn't matter. I simply don't know. There is the Nu Wray at Burnsville, on the corner of the square there."

"I knew some Burnses when I was a girl. They tried farming. A mountain lion killed all their cattle in a single night. Papa said that's what it was. The men waited for it to come back the next night to eat what it had killed, but it must have scented the hunters, for it never arrived."

Was it Amanda's birthday, Hallie wondered. She arrived at the house hearing laughter. What birthday would it be? Her forty-ninth perhaps. No, she was born in April. Harry must have brought her a gift, anyway. She could hear them laughing; they were out in the backyard. Her mother let out a shout: "Harry, what on earth is it?"

Hallie crept to the back window and looked at the animal Harry had brought her mother, a rope around its neck, its big moon eyes staring about innocently. "Part Guernsey and part Jersey," Harry was explaining, "and I took it as annual payment on one of Pink's loans to Michael Cummings."

Amanda stood near the porch screen door, the cow's rope in her hand. "Well, what on earth? Does it need milking, Harry?"

"I don't know," Harry said.

Amanda sat down on the bottom step and milked the cow into a pot. Harry stood nearby, beaming at her. Amanda stripped the cow and set the milk aside. "I don't know when I've had anything I liked so much," she said dully. "But you'll need to take it away."

"I thought you might decide to keep it," Harry said.

"I can't be tied down morning and evening. I . . . I wonder what you have in mind, Harry?" she said, looking up at him expecting an explanation. "If you had wanted to give me flowers, or a silver spoon . . . What does a cow mean?"

"I thought you might still have a country bone left," Harry told her. "I can trade her, Amanda, in half an hour's time, if you prefer."

For two months after Pink's death, Amanda clearly didn't know how to accept Hallie, even though they did spend afternoons together, sitting in the parlor, talking. "Well, it was a pleasure, I'll say that, to have somebody here of a daytime strong enough to lift your father about, Hallie, while he was alive, and to smile at life, as only Harry can. I realize there have been gossips, not the least of them that nurse of your father's who can't find a thing to talk about except this family, as if we've become a moving picture, and that secretary of your father's, that Gloria, who is tracking poor Harry like a tigress all along Lexington Avenue." Amanda rocked. Suddenly she turned squarely to view her daughter: wan, pretty, sad in brooding, mysterious ways. "Say what you please, I had a right to try, Hallie, to free my son, and I had to free my daughter, too. Your father had tied you up. Did you know it? No, you don't know it even yet, because you have no children, but given time you will see that a mother can't help caring about all her children. I think it is a woman's true calling, Hallie, to bear and rear her young. You have always resisted the role of a mother, yourself, you have even derided me. I have taken years of abuse from you, but a mother has that role to play, to let them cut their teeth on her. They chew her up. They chew not only her nipples, but herself. She is left in tatters by each one. Fathers come through with few marks, few strains and breaks and tears, but a mother's children chew to get their strength; then discard her once they can. I am . . . I am proud to say I am a mother, your mother, and Frederick's. . . ."

A grim smile appeared on Hallie's face.

"I am the mother of you both. Give me what blame you will, but don't attack mothers, Hallie. I'm weary of it." She appeared to be exhausted by the talking.

"I'm pregnant, mama," Hallie said.

Still as death Amanda sat in the rocking chair, mouth open to speak words that were not there.

"The telephone company billed me, says somebody phoned Denver, Colorado, Hallie. It was just before you married Ted Wallerbee. I went to the office, told them nobody here makes long-distance calls. To the Brown Palace Hotel, they told me."

"I never said I didn't phone," Hallie told her.

"To Brodie King, was it? that son Nettie talks about so much? She says she thinks you're one of the many who became fond of him." No reply. "You phoned him, did you?"

Hallie nodded.

"Had to talk with him, did you?"

"Yes, I knew he was at the hotel. He's always there at ten A.M., gets up about then."

"The telephone company said the call was made at twelve o'clock, Hallie."

"There's two hours' difference between here and Denver, mama."

"Why is that?"

"Something to do with the sun."

Amanda rocked. "Why did you phone him?"

"I couldn't forget him. I wanted to tell him I was marrying. Should I tell Wallerbee I phoned Brodie?"

"No, no," Amanda said at once. "If I were you, considering your disposition, I'd not tell my husband everything."

Hallie told her mother, "I want to name my first baby after papa."

"Not much of a name," Amanda said, "Pink for a boy."

"Boy or girl, I aim to."

"Frederick is a child of the family, too, and Henrietta is pregnant. If Henrietta beats you to the name . . . "

"She'll bear sooner," Hallie admitted, fretting. "I . . . I can't hurry it.

I'm the boat in which it's to be shipped. Mama. I feel so out of balance already, and sort of dizzy."

"Sometimes I stood in front of the mirror and looked at myself from every angle, I was so amused, and I would introduce myself to myself, as if I were not . . . not the person I had been."

"Tomorrow I'll introduce myself to myself. I'll have trouble getting to know me, I'm sure."

"I tried to find a way to sit comfortably. Never could."

"And so many different fluids. Already I keep getting wet and soggy."

"You will after it's born as well."

"It goes on and on and on, does it?"

"Oh, Hallie. I wish I had not lost Pink's last one, but at my age—I said to your Uncle Harry Sunday night when we were on the porch, I said I hope for another. . . . " Her voice trailed away. She sat quietly for a moment, considering her admission.

Hallie touched her. She reached across the intervening space and touched her hand.

One night after working late, Hallie entered the hallway, where no light was on. She stopped at the doorway to her mother's bedroom. "Mama, you in here?" she whispered.

"Why did you wait so late, Hallie?" Amanda asked. "You usually come by earlier." She was stretched out on the bed, two white pillows beneath her head, a quilt pulled over her. A somber light from the streetlight filtered in under the porch roof and through the front window.

"Where's Harry?" Hallie said.

"He's up the street trading, or at the hotel. He feels he shouldn't live in the house with his dead brother's wife. There are rules even for families, he says. So he took a room in the hotel, but then . . . then he lives here anyway."

"Do you love him, mama?"

"Oh . . . oh, Lord, I can't help it. He is something out of my youth, you know, and he reminds me of Pink. Even Frederick likes him."

"How is Frederick?"

"Frederick is as well as anybody can be. He's had the flu, or a bad cold, too much rayon gets in his lungs, working in that factory."

"Does he own the Dutch company yet?" she asked, smiling.

"He doesn't even know whether he wants to stay working there or not, so we'll have to wait a while longer. I hope you'll get to know him better, Hallie. He's a sweet boy, but disoriented."

"Papa treated him mean sometimes, I know."

"How's your baby? Is it taking shape?"

"I think so." Quiet in the room for a while, the quiet of contentment, then Hallie moved forward and pressed her legs against the bed on which Amanda lay, and took Amanda's head and placed it against her own body. "Feel its heart, mama?" she said.

ABOUT THE AUTHOR

John Ehle (pronounced EE-lee) was born in Asheville, in the mountains of western North Carolina, and grew up there. Currently, he has a house at Penland, about an hour's drive north, one built by one Henry Willis and his wife 107 years ago. He has written seven novels about the mountain people: *The Land Breakers, The Journey of August King, Time of Drums, The Road, Lion on the Hearth* (which also is set in Asheville), *The Winter People,* and this novel.

He is married to Rosemary Harris, the actress, and their daughter is Jennifer.